Pr

"*Live To The Network* is a first-class edition to the addictive Ethan Benson series. This story of kidnapping, murder, and modern-day slavery grips you from the first page and doesn't let go. Unflinching, meticulously plotted, and fast paced, this novel is a thrilling view into both a frightening underworld and into the world of media and journalism. Riveting!

Stephanie Powell Watts, Novelist and Associate Professor of Creative Writing, Lehigh University

"*Live To The Network* is a disturbing portrayal of the child sex industry in New York City. Jeffrey L. Diamond, drawing on his many years as an award-winning journalist and producer, depicts with unsparing accuracy the realities facing an investigative reporter who, defying his network bosses, commits himself to helping save the young and innocent victims abducted into a brutal world by a mysterious international conspiracy that seeks his execution. Diamond's story will leave you wondering how society can ignore an issue that is one of the most troubling of our times."

Robert Brown, Novelist and former Correspondent, ABC News 20/20

"Author Jeffrey L. Diamond once again creates a plot twisting thriller for his crime fighting character, Ethan Benson—who faces his own personal struggles with marriage, fatherhood, and a bottle—to solve unspeakable murders in New York City. Benson's skills as a seasoned news producer make him a tedious investigator for the fictional television newsmagazine, *The Weekly Reporter*, enabling him to plod through the details to slowly reveal the mystery of the deaths all while balancing his own challenging life."

Patrick Berry, former Owner, Westfield News Group

"Harsh, thrilling, and heart pounding, *Live To The Network* is an addictive, dark mystery with compelling storytelling and a pace that will leave you breathless. Ethan Benson, a TV producer at *The Weekly Reporter*, assists the police force by taking on a forgotten case of gut wrenching, seemingly related murders of several young girls to generate more public attention. He devotes himself to shedding light on the monstrous offenses, and in turn becomes obsessed with finding the killer. Danger increases as each new clue he discovers gets him closer to solving the murders, and at the same time he is battling his own demons, causing his personal life to fall apart. For fans of *Law and Order SVU and Silence of the Lambs,* this is the perfect combination of heinous crimes, sly detective work, and a difficult personal journey."

Jennifer Gans Blankfein, Blogger at Book Nation by Jen

"Jeffrey L. Diamond's insider knowledge of broadcast TV news reporting animates this thriller. His unlikely hero, the alcoholic, egotistical, but brilliant Ethan Benson shows the rough talking New York City cops how it's done, as he takes down an international pedophilia ring. Diamond's familiarity with the seamier locations of the gritty city, and his ability to bring the reader inside the frantic world of TV news, makes this a gripping novel. The crime writing is particularly vivid."

Mark Newhouse, Advance Publications

"*Live To The Network* is one of the most tautly written, deeply suspenseful, and heart- wrenching books I have read in many years. Jeffrey L. Diamond deftly weaves together the dark and complex world of international trafficking of children and the sinister world of a ruthless and demonic mob, playing a chilling game of cat and mouse with law enforcement, and a tortured but compassionate young investigative reporter for a major TV network. Jeff's years as a brilliant investigative reporter serve him well here, as this book is achingly detailed, portraying all sides with unstinting accuracy, and his own deep empathy. It is the best and worst of humanity laid out so strongly, it is truly unforgettable."

Karen Burnes, former Correspondent,
ABC News and CBS News

LIVE TO THE NETWORK

An Ethan Benson Thriller

Jeffrey L. Diamond

First Edition

PAGE PUBLISHING, INC.
New York, NY

First originally published by Page Publishing, Inc. 2019

ISBN 978-1-64544-688-0 (Paperback)
ISBN 978-1-64544-689-7 (Digital)

Printed in the United States of America

This book is a work of fiction. The characters, places, businesses, and storyline are solely a product of the author's imagination. Any resemblance to actual persons, living or dead, events, locales, or places of employment is completely unintended and purely coincidental

This novel is for Amy,
Aaron, Alex, Lindsey, Zoe, and Eli.

PROLOGUE

Pedro Juan Ignacio Rodriquez sat alone in the corner of an outdoor café drinking a *yerba mate* through a metal straw in a ceremonial red calabash gourd. The traditional Argentinean drink, infused with a layer of dried yerba leaves floating aimlessly on the surface, was bitter to the taste but loaded with caffeine that raced through every pore of his body. He took a final sip, wiped his mouth on a napkin, then leaned back comfortably in a worn wicker chair, tipping it against the outer stone wall of the café, the rickety legs creaking under his immense weight. The veranda was packed with tourists and wealthy young socialites—some alone, some in small groups of twos and threes, some working the room, trying to hook up in the moonlight on this late summer evening. Rodriquez smiled, a big propitious smile, then reached into his coat pocket and pulled out the picture of the young girl. She was exotically beautiful with silky long black hair and fine, delicate features. Her sparkling hazel eyes radiated in the glow of an overhead streetlamp, her skin the soft brown color of a chestnut, her perfectly shaped teeth as white as virgin snow. He stared at the picture, sighed deeply, and carefully tucked it back into his coat pocket. Then he looked around the bar and waved for the waiter.

"*Por favor*, a little service, my son."

"Can I get you another *mate, Padre*?" the waiter said, shifting from one foot to the next. "Maybe something stronger, perhaps an aperitif? A glass of port? A brandy? Something to warm your heart before you head to the *basilica*? What is your pleasure, *Padre?*"

Rodriquez sat quietly, his face impassive, then said in a flat, stony voice, "Just my bill, *por favor*. It's late, and God is calling. I must go."

"*Si. Si, Padre.*" The waiter carefully backed away from the table, head bowed in holy supplication, and slipped inside the crowded café.

Pedro Juan Ignacio Rodriquez was an imposing figure, one of the most powerful and well-respected clergymen in the Roman Catholic Church. A reverend deacon of the *Basilica de Salta*—the seat of the archdiocese in northwest Argentina—he was an enormous man, standing six feet five and weighing close to four hundred pounds with a corpulent belly, long brown hair that fell in ringlets to his shoulders, a heavy, unkempt beard, bushy eyebrows, and piercing black eyes. He was wearing the customary dress of an ordained minister—a simple gray shirt, white collar, and a lightweight blue jacket and trousers. Hanging from his neck was a large gold crucifix bedecked in rubies and sapphires and diamonds that he brought to his lips and kissed as he waited for his check.

Rodriquez peered at his watch.

Eleven thirty.

A half hour to his meeting.

Impatient, he dropped a hundred peso note on the table, more than enough to cover his bill, and heaved his massive bulk out of the chair, before lumbering around the tightly packed tables and into the street. Salsa music wafted out of the dozen or so cafés that lined the perimeter of the *Plaza 9 de Julio* and through the crowds of people milling about the town square. The plaza was one of the most beautiful in all of Argentina with rows of evergreen beeches, royal palms, and stately eucalyptus trees framing a series of lush flower beds of yellow daisies, white lilies, and pink carnations. Sitting in the center of the plaza was a majestic statue rising twenty feet off the ground of *General Juan Antonio Alvarez de Arenales*, a nineteenth century freedom fighter who waged a bloody revolution that freed the native population from Spanish rule.

Rodriquez smirked at the irony.

Anticipating the task he was about to perform.

He picked up his pace, breathing heavily as he passed a half-dozen ornate granite buildings, leftover from colonial times that gave the *Plaza 9 de Julio* the feel of an old European city. He crisscrossed the plaza, around crowds of boisterous revelers sitting on park benches, and approached the basilica standing like a monolith on the western edge of the plaza. It was an imposing pink and yellow structure, built in a neobaroque style, with a row of forty-foot pillars and a soaring hand-carved wooden door set back beneath a large stone portico. He stopped and gazed at the two marble bell towers flanking the front of this architectural wonder then checked his watch.

Eleven forty-five.

He didn't want to be late.

Picking up his pace, he began climbing the stone steps, one at a time, his eyes never leaving the *basilica*—his *basilica*, his home, his holy house of worship. An old woman dressed in rags knelt down and bowed her head.

"*Padre,* how are you on this blessed evening." She made the sign of the cross. "Please, holy one, say a blessing for my sweet *esposo* who's ravaged by cancer and confined to bed. He is dying and soon will leave this poor soul and our five small children all alone to beg for crumbs of food on the streets. Please, *Padre,* give absolution to my *esposo* before he is taken from me by our Holy Father in heaven."

"The Lord will take him into his arms, my child," he said, kissing his crucifix and placing it on her forehead. "Go to your *esposo.* Comfort him. Help him pass through the gates of heaven to our savior, Jesus Christ."

"Bless you, *Padre,* bless you," the old woman said, tears welling in her eyes.

Rodriquez brought the crucifix to his lips again and continued up the steps, stopping over and over to comfort one destitute person after another—their eyes downcast, seeking guidance, asking for absolution. He smiled as he ministered, bringing solace to all those who needed salvation, to hear the Word of God.

As he reached the stone portico, the church bells began ringing, thundering across the plaza, announcing the Lord's day and reminding him that in just eight short hours he'd be assisting the archbishop in Sunday Mass.

Lots to do.

Not much time.

He better hurry.

Kneeling, he made the sign of the cross one last time, bowed his head in prayer, then pulled a large iron key from his pants pocket, opened the massive wooden door, and pushed into the cathedral.

There was silence.

Dead silence.

Not a sound except the creaking of the wooden door as it closed behind him.

Making his way down the center aisle of the nave, he stared up at the stained glass windows dating back almost three hundred years, depicting scenes from the New Testament—Mary holding baby Jesus, the last supper, the ascension to heaven—all lit by a series of spotlights positioned to maximize their beauty and power. There were dozens of red and gold columns soaring fifty feet from floor to ceiling, flanking a magnificent hand-painted gold leaf dome that loomed over Renaissance masterpieces of the apostles, each positioned in the center of an arched cornice. Rodriquez stared at the priceless paintings, his eyes moving from one to the next, his heart filling with the love of Jesus as he made his way past a statue of the Virgin Mary and kneeled at the base of a ten-foot crucifix, where he cupped his hands and prayed.

"Our Father, who art in heaven, please forgive me because I have sinned, and because I'm about to sin, once again, in the holiest of all thy places."

He closed his eyes.

Crossed himself.

And hoisted his four hundred pounds off the floor, scanning the room until his eyes locked on to a small figure sitting quietly in a pew near the edge of the sanctuary steps.

"*Padre*, I no understand why you keep up foolish charade," the man said in broken English with a heavy Spanish accent. "You pretend to be holy. A man close to God. *Si?* But you really just *el criminal.* No different from me. No better than *Satanas.*"

Rodriquez's face reddened, and his body began to shake uncontrollably.

"Shut up, Carlos. You have no right to judge me," he said angrily. "You work for me, remember? You do what I say." He wrung his hands in anticipation. "So where's the girl?"

"You know where she is, *Padre,*" he said, smirking. "Where I take all your girls."

"Is she ready?"

"*Si, Padre.* I punish her. Scare her real good, like you always say. No food. No water. No clean clothes. I play with her *un poquito.* Give her beating. But not face. Just body. She not broke, and with time, she be good as new as promised." He smiled lecherously and licked his lips. "She no problem to you, *Padre.* Carlos make sure to crush her spirit on long trip from country."

"Does she speak English?"

"Speak good like you ask. Smart girl. Go to best school in village." His face suddenly hardened. "Where my money, *Padre?*"

The deacon stared at him silently, wondering if Carlos was telling him the truth, then reached into his pocket and pulled out a wad of pesos. A thousand American dollars' worth of pesos. He shuffled his bulk over to the small man, sweat pouring down the folds of fat under his chin, and handed him the money.

"Now take it and go, out the back door, and make sure nobody sees you."

"Nobody ever see Carlos. I careful, like you say. Move as silent as feather blowing in the wind." Then he pocketed the money and disappeared through a small door hidden behind the alter.

Rodriquez breathed heavily, sucking air in and out, then glanced at the crucifix of Jesus Christ and slipped into the sacristy—a small gold-leaf room tucked next to the statue of the Virgin Mary. He stopped before an old mahogany cabinet painted with images of angels fighting demons escaping from the gates of hell and searched until he found his vestments—a red silk robe with a gold cross embossed on the front—which he carefully slipped over his clerical clothes. Genuflecting, he kneeled before another statue of Christ and said solemnly, his eyes lifted toward heaven, "Please, Holy Father, grace me with your presence, because I need your love and guidance and forbearance." Then he reached for a silver paten and chalice, both covered with precious stones, opened a secret door behind a second elaborately painted wooden cabinet containing other priceless religious artifacts, and entered a different world.

Grabbing a torch propped on the floor, he lit the tightly rolled hemp dipped in wax with a large wooden match then slinked through a stone passageway, down a dank staircase, across another musty passageway, before stopping at an iron door dating back to the mid-seventeenth century when the basilica was first built.

He paused momentarily.

Checked to make sure he was alone.

And quickly unlocked the door with another key.

Then he pushed into an old dungeon. It was stale and musty, smelling of urine and feces and dead rodents. Water seeped from cracks in the ceiling, and cobwebs hung from overhead crossbeams. Along the far wall were a series of cells straight from the Dark Ages with heavy iron bars, rusted chains, and medieval weapons of torture—cattle prods, racks, iron maidens, and thumb screws. All the cells were empty except for one. Rodriquez straightened his vestments and carefully picked his way around the garbage and down to the cell, inserted a key into an ancient lock, and peered around the dark room, waving the torch from one end to the next.

Asleep on the floor, chained to the wall, was a child covered in filth. He fumbled for the photo in his coat pocket and stared at the image. It was definitely her. No doubt about it. Carlos had snatched the right girl just as instructed. After placing the photo back in his pocket, he peered at the tiny figure. She was mostly naked, her arms and legs covered in welts and abrasions, her face caked in dirt and flecked with streams of dried tears. But she was still exquisite, angelic, even more beautiful than the photo. He rolled his tongue longingly over his lips then said in a soft, kind voice, "Wake up, Maria, my child, the Lord is calling you."

The girl's eyes fluttered then opened wide, her body rigid as a statue as she climbed to her feet, covering her nakedness with her hands.

"*Padre,* I'm really, really scared. Help me," she said, sobbing uncontrollably. "That man, he stole me from my family. Did terrible things to me. He beat me. Raped me over and over, oh, so many times." She wiped away a tear and started tugging her chains. "Please, *Padre,* unlock me. I wanna go home to my mama and papa."

"Hush, my child," he said gently. "You're in the house of God, and before we talk about what he plans to do with you, you must take Holy Communion and ask our Lord Jesus Christ for forgiveness."

"But I need to get out of here right now, before that man comes back. Please, *Padre*, help me. I'm begging you," she said, wailing, more tears dripping in tiny streams down her cheeks.

"In due time, my child, in due time," Rodriquez said, his huge body looming over her. Then he reached into the pocket of his robes, pulled out the silver paten and chalice, and placed them on an old wooden table in the center of the cell, before filling the goblet with dirty water and dropping a crumb of bread on the plate. "Stop crying, Maria, my beautiful girl," he said, his eyes ablaze, his mouth watering, his countenance threatening. "It's time to drink the blood and consume the flesh of our Holy Father. It's time to be one with Jesus."

Then he advanced on her like an erupting volcano, his lips quivering, his face contorting in a mask of evil. She recoiled in terror and scooted into the corner—dragging her chains, forgetting her nakedness, her screams echoing down the empty corridors.

He punched her.

A massive blow.

And her eyes rolled into the back of her head.

Before he mounted her.

And she fell into darkness.

CHAPTER 1

The image in the monitor went blank, and Ethan Benson flipped on the lights in the editing room. Leaning forward in his chair, he finished typing a note on an iPad perched on his lap and swiveled around to face the small group of people sitting behind him. Ethan was a handsome man just shy of his forty-sixth birthday with curly black hair graying at the temples, sharp blue eyes, a strong square chin, and a smile that could light up the room. At six feet three and two hundred pounds, he was almost as imposing in stature as he was in intellect. A senior producer at *The Weekly Reporter*, the number one newsmagazine on the number one network on television, the Global Broadcasting System, he had just finished screening a rough cut of an interview with Taylor Swift that his anchorman, Peter Sampson, had shot with one of the coterie of producers on his team.

"Well, Ethan," Sampson said impatiently, "I don't have all day. It's pretty damn good, if I have to say so myself." He paused, waited for a reaction, and when he didn't get one, said, "Come on, Ethan, what do you think?"

Ethan scrolled through his notes, ruminating, then tapped a pencil he was holding on the table in front of him. He turned to the editor, Joel Zimmerman. "Go back to the top and roll it again for me."

"No problem, boss," Joel said, punching a command into his keyboard then hitting Play.

The opening scene of Taylor Swift performing her number one single *Bad Blood* at the American Airlines Arena in Miami rocked across the screen, the sound ricocheting off the walls of the editing room.

"Okay, freeze the image," Ethan said, snapping his fingers as an extreme wide shot of the stage filled the monitor—Taylor Swift a mere speck in a sea of screaming fans, surrounded by her bandmates and their equipment. The room fell silent as Ethan checked his notes again, looked up at the shot of Swift, then turned to the producer, Martin Humphrey. "The sequence is flat."

"What do you mean?" Humphrey said defensively. "It seems pretty good to me."

"I agree," Sampson said harshly. "What's wrong with it?"

"The first shot is way too wide. I wanna see the expression on her face, her emotions, what she's feeling as she's singing," Ethan said, turning back to Joel. "How many cameras did we shoot."

"Four angles."

"Do we have a tight shot?"

Joel punched a time code into the computer and replaced the wide shot with an extreme close-up of Swift, then ran the video again.

"That's better," Ethan said, rocking his body to the beat of the music. "Now I can see her face, every pore on her skin, every nuance as she belts out the lyrics." He turned to Sampson. "What do you think, Peter?"

Sampson was typing away on his cell phone, zipping off e-mails, paying no attention to the conversation.

"Earth to Peter, are you with us?" Ethan said, irritated. "I just asked you a question."

"Yes. Yes," Sampson said, waving his hand dismissively. "Do whatever you want with the story, Ethan. I'm sure you'll make it better."

Ethan locked his hands behind his head and silently counted to ten, trying to control his temper. He'd been working with Peter Sampson, the most famous anchorman on television, for over a year—since their first story about the murder of the daughter of New York City's deputy mayor. Managing his busy schedule, supervising his producers, and overseeing his plate of projects had become nothing more than a tedious routine, Ethan no longer feeling insecure or incompetent or self-conscious around him as he did when they were first paired up together. But the anchorman's cavalier attitude and his nonchalant approach to production and storytelling still made Ethan's blood boil.

"Okay, Peter, I see you've moved on to other pressing matters. I'll finish going over the rest of my tweaks with Marty and Joel. You can head off and take care of whatever is distracting you."

"A perfect plan," Sampson said, his nose still buried in his cell phone. "I have a slew of calls to return, meetings to attend, and of course, all these damn e-mails to answer. I'll retrack any changes you want after lunch. Just send me the new script and book me time in the announce booth. Shall we say three o'clock?" He stood, running a comb through his perfectly coifed silver-gray hair, and abruptly left the editing room without saying another word.

Ethan shook his head knowingly then spent the next fifteen minutes going over his suggestions, before scooting out the door, down the long corridor, and past one editing room after another—a cacophony of music, sound effects, and correspondent narrations bouncing around the second-floor editing suite. But Ethan was oblivious to the chaos around him as he pressed the button and hopped on to an elevator. He felt out of sorts—stressed, confused, agitated—worried about the direction of his career and the uncertainties in his life.

What was he missing?

He was a rainmaker on *The Weekly Reporter* with all the trappings that come with being part of management. He was mostly his own boss, only answering to Peter Sampson and to the executive producer, Paul Lang, and was paid handsomely for his role babysitting one of the most difficult stars in the business. So why was he bored supervising a staff of producers, associate producers, editors, cameramen, and broadcast associates? Why did he loathe the power and prestige? Why did he hate his job? It didn't make sense.

The elevator door slid open, and he walked into the small glass anteroom on the eleventh floor. Jennifer, the receptionist, was sitting at her desk, wearing a headset and typing away at her computer terminal. She looked up and smiled at Ethan.

"Paul just called. He wants to see you right away."

Ethan sighed and grabbed a smoke from a fresh pack of Marlboros in his shirt pocket. He slipped it between his lips and pulled a lighter from his pants pocket, clicking it on and off, watching the flame as he drew it toward the tip of his cigarette, waiting for Jennifer to react.

"You can't light that here," she said, aghast. "You know better than that."

Ethan winked. "Indeed, I do, but I like to play with it, twirl it between my fingers, hold it in my mouth, pretend that I'm smoking."

"Very funny," she said sarcastically.

He clicked the lighter three more times. "Buzz me through," he said, taking an imaginary puff. "I don't wanna keep the big man waiting. You know what happens when I'm late."

Jennifer shot him a quick smile. "You're a sly devil, Ethan Benson." Then she hit a button under her desk and went back to her typing.

Ethan pushed through the glass door and proceeded down the empty hallway. The eleventh floor had the feel of a Fortune 500 company—very formal, very staid—with thick, plush carpeting, antique furniture, leather seating, and expensive artwork hanging on the walls. All the doors were shut tight—no people, no telephones, no energy, no life, no purpose—a far cry from the insanity on the producers floor one level below where all the real work was done.

What was he doing here?

Why had he taken this job?

He was bored with being anchored to his desk, frustrated by the endless paperwork, smothered by the lack of creativity. He had to make a change before his life became meaningless.

He continued around a bend in the hallway and over to a walled-in area that separated Peter Sampson's suite of offices from the rest of the floor. A young man he didn't recognize was sitting at a desk across from Consuela Santana, the Latina assistant he shared with the anchorman.

"And who are you?" he said, perplexed.

"Your new assistant, James Lapidus," he said, standing and thrusting out his hand.

"What?" Ethan turned to Consuela. "Did you know about this?"

"Peter told me this morning."

"But I don't need my own assistant," Ethan said, turning back to James. "No offense. I'm sure you're very good, but I like our old setup just fine. Is Peter okay with this?" he said as he sat down in a chair and glared at Consuela.

"He initiated it," Consuela said, straightening papers on the corner of her desk. "You're an integral part of his team, an important person, so he felt you needed your own assistant to manage your busy schedule. Those are his words, not mine. He went to Paul and worked out a new budget line, then, *jahi esta,* James was hired."

"Why wasn't I consulted?" Ethan said, fuming on the inside.

"Because he knew you'd say no, and he no longer wants to share me with you. And besides, things were starting to fall through the cracks, and you know how Peter gets when there's something amiss in his schedule."

"Is he in his office?"

"No. He's at a meeting out of the building."

"Figures he wouldn't be around when the shit hit the fan." Ethan rolled the cigarette around in his mouth, flustered, more confused than ever.

"You can't smoke that in here."

"I know. I know. I just pulled the same stunt on Jennifer. But there's nothing more I'd like at the moment than a good smoke to settle my nerves." He placed the cigarette back in the pack then turned to James. "Sorry you had to hear all this," he said, finally shaking hands. "Welcome aboard."

James smiled back nervously then said, "I have a bunch of messages for you, Mr. Benson."

"Ethan, please, Ethan. My father is Mr. Benson. It makes me feel old when you call me that."

"Okay," he said, holding out a sheet of paper. "Do you want to go over them before you go see Mr. Lang?"

"Give me a minute to get settled then you can tell me who called, and we can chat about your responsibilities. Then I'll see Paul." He nodded half-heartedly, walked into his office, and closed the door.

After flipping on the overhead lights, he sat down at his desk, plugged in his laptop computer, and stared aimlessly out the big picture window as snowflakes began floating over the New York City skyline, the weather threatening to deteriorate into a major winter storm. *God, why can't I go with the flow?* he mused silently. *I was just given an assistant. Somebody to take care of loose ends. To make my life easier. I should be pleased, right? What's wrong with me?*

He closed his eyes and rubbed his temples. He needed to get back into the field. To direct cameras. To work sources. To experience the thrill of reporting. To produce his own stories. How long had it been? Six months? Nine months? A year? He stood and paced around the room. He'd been promised when he took this job that, along with managing Peter, he'd continue working as a journalist. Doing investigative reporting. Uncovering wrongdoing. Searching for the truth. That's what made him tick. That's what gave him purpose. But now, he was slowly moving away from what he loved. Away from who he was.

Damn, I don't care about being a senior producer.

I don't care about the big money.

I don't care about this job.

Deeply frustrated, he was about to tell James to come in when his telephone buzzed.

"Yes," he said, his voice sharp and dismissive.

"You have a call on line 1, Mr. Benson."

"Come on, James, ditch the formalities. My name is Ethan, *Ethan*, not Mr. Benson."

"Guess I forgot."

He took a deep breath. "So who's on the phone?"

"I didn't ask."

"We're getting off to a good start," he said, still unable to control the seething anger in his voice. "I'll take it from here." He rang off then hit line 1. "Ethan Benson."

"Hello, my friend, long time no see."

"Lloyd?"

"Yup, it's me."

Lloyd Howard was a private detective, a former undercover cop for the NYPD with sources at every level of law enforcement who'd helped Ethan on several high-profile stories in the past.

"So what's shaking with you?" Ethan said, happy to hear his voice.

"A little of this and a little of that. And you?"

"I'm stuck in the coal mines. Miss the good old days."

"Well, I've got a story you may want to jump on," Lloyd said, whispering into the telephone.

"What is it?" Ethan said curiously.

"Can't tell you on the phone. Too risky. Can we get together somewhere?"

"When?"

"How about right now?"

"Right now?" Ethan said, hesitating. He was supposed to see Paul. "Okay, I'll slide my schedule. Where are you?"

"Across the street at McGlades."

"That's convenient."

"I aim to please. Can you be here in ten minutes?"

Ethan checked his watch. Nine thirty. Paul was probably in a meeting anyway. "On my way."

"And, Ethan, bring Mindy. I want both of you to hear this at the same time." He clicked off the phone.

Ethan listened to a dial tone—a scratchy, humming sound. Lloyd must've called from a phone booth. Why hadn't he just used his cell phone? Puzzled, he punched in Mindy's number on his iPhone.

"Hey, it's me. What are you doing?"

"I'm booking crews for a shoot," she said distractedly. Mindy Herman was an associate producer, a close work friend of Ethan's and one of the best investigative reporters on the show. "So what's up?"

"Just got off the phone with Lloyd. He's got a story. Can you meet me in the lobby?"

"Jeez, Ethan, now?"

"Right now."

"It can't wait?"

"No."

"Guess I can finish booking crews later," she said reluctantly. "Okay. This better be good."

Ethan hung up and smiled. For the first time in months he felt like himself—excited, energized, juices flowing. An old friend was about to pitch him a story, a story that maybe he could sink his teeth into, a story that might get him back into the game. He grabbed his briefcase and opened the door.

"Gotta head out of the building for a meeting," he said as he hurried past James.

"What about your messages?"

"Later."

"And Mr. Lang?"

"Call his assistant. Her name's Monica. Tell her I'll come by as soon as I'm back."

"But she just called," James said, confusion on his face. "And she yelled at me for not sending you down right away."

"Her bark's worse than her bite," Ethan said tepidly. "Make an excuse. Tell her I'm going to see a source about a story."

Then he turned.

And abruptly disappeared down the hallway.

CHAPTER 2

McGlades was an old man's bar across the street from the broadcast center on the southeast corner of Broadway and Fifty–Seventh Street. It occupied the first floor of a hundred-year-old brownstone that hadn't been bought by a developer to make way for a supertall skyscraper to accompany the half dozen or so now rising like behemoths on one of the most expensive avenues in the world. Ethan liked to drop into McGlades for a quick glass of Scotch before heading home after work. It was part of his daily routine, a long-standing ritual, a thorn in his side like a decaying tooth. He pushed through the front door, shook the snow off his overcoat, and blew into his hands to ward off the cold. The bar was dark and musty and smelled of stale beer. There was a row of tables with plastic tablecloths in the center of the room, a half-dozen booths tucked away in the back, and lines of dirty glasses on the bar.

"Do you see him, Mindy?"

"I don't see anybody," she said, eyeballing the empty seats. "Maybe we got here first."

Mindy was short and slightly overweight with close-cropped mousy blond hair and intelligent hazel eyes. She wasn't particularly pretty, but her smile was endearing, and her outgoing personality was more than just charming.

"Should I call him on his cell phone?"

"Not yet. I just talked to him. He's gotta be here somewhere." Ethan frowned then walked up to a portly man with a meaty red face, thinning gray hair, and Coke bottle eyeglasses who was wearing a linen apron and restocking bottles of booze behind the bar. “Hey, Moe, anybody looking for me?”

The bartender didn’t turn around. “There’s a guy named Lloyd or somethin’ like that who came in a little while ago. Said you needed privacy, so I put him in the back room—even though the regulars won’t start showing up for a taste of their favorite poison for another few hours. You know where to go, Ethan.”

“First, pour me a Scotch,” he said, his eyes flashing to a half-filled bottle of Black Label.

“A bit early for that. Don’t you think?”

“Yeah. Yeah. You sound like my wife. Make it a double.”

Moe crinkled his forehead, reached for the bottle of Black Label, and filled a small glass to the brim. “Does the young lass want an eye-opener as well?”

“Hell no. It’s barely ten o’clock.” She turned to Ethan. “What’s wrong with you? You shouldn’t be drinking that shit. What if Paul smells it on your breath? He’s warned you about your drinking.”

“He won’t find out,” Ethan said, taking a long pull, the Scotch warming his insides.

“Better not, or you’ll be out on your ass.” She turned to Moe. “I’d like a coffee.”

“Got a fresh pot brewing.”

“Bring it and three mugs,” Mindy said as she followed Ethan past the empty tables and through a crooked door that needed a paint job.

Lloyd was sitting at the only booth in a tiny, windowless room no bigger than a matchbox, sipping a can of Red Bull and wearing dark wraparound sunglasses, a fringed leather jacket, a blue work shirt, black jeans, and old Dingo cowboy boots. He was tall and lanky with long, stringy brown hair, electric green eyes, and a bushy goatee that was clean but unkempt. A no-nonsense investigator, he was a player, one of the good guys, and tougher than nails. Propped on the banquette next to him was the same old, beat-up leather briefcase he'd been carrying for years. He stood as Ethan and Mindy approached.

"You back on the bottle?" he said, pointing to Ethan's Scotch. "Never would've picked this place if I thought you'd start drinking the hard stuff this early in the day. Christ, it's not even lunchtime."

"Not too early for Ethan," Mindy said frankly. "Looks like he's getting back into some serious drinking. Hope he knows what he's doing."

"Ah, Ms. Herman, a pleasure to see you. You look as lovely as ever."

"Jeez, cut the crap, Lloyd," she said, grinning from ear to ear. "How the hell are you?"

"Never better. Working around the clock, busy as a bee. I got a meeting in a little while with a rather slimy young man who's threatening to post pictures on the internet of his girlfriend in a rather compromising position unless her parents fork over a rather sizable chunk of money. Now I can't let that happen, can I?"

"I'm sure you won't," Ethan said, sitting across from him and downing the last drop of his drink. "I just ducked out on a meeting with our good friend, Paul Lang, and you know how he gets when I blow him off."

"Never pretty."

"Certainly isn't."

"What are you going to do about it?"

"I'll figure *that* out, my friend, when I get back to the office."

Moe the Bartender, walked into the room with a pot of steaming coffee, dropped the three mugs on the table, and poured a cup for Mindy.

"Another Red Bull?" he said, glancing at Lloyd.

Howard covered the can with the palm of his hand. "Already wired from the caffeine."

"Want coffee?"

"Never touch the stuff."

"Suit yourself."

Ethan banged his glass on the table. "Bring me another Scotch, Moe."

"Not on your life, Ethan," Mindy said, turning to the bartender. "Cut him off. He's not gonna drink another drop this morning." She glared at Ethan and poured him a cup of coffee. "Drink it. You need to sober up before we go back to the office."

Ethan sat quietly, trying to control his temper, then reached for the coffee as Moe slipped out of the room, closing the door behind him. "Okay, Lloyd. Why are we here?"

Lloyd picked up his briefcase, placed it on the table, and snapped open the lock. He rummaged through a stack of documents and pulled out a file folder, then pushed it across to Ethan.

"Before you take a look, let me give you some background." He finished his Red Bull, hesitated, then said, "Fuck the caffeine. I want another one." He reached back into his briefcase and pulled out a can. "Always carry an extra for emergencies." After popping the top and gulping two mouthfuls, he continued, "I've got a good friend at the Manhattan District Attorney's Office. We go way back to my days as a narc in Brooklyn. Her name's Patricia Highland, and she's an assistant district attorney who's heading up a small task force looking into a series of murders."

"Anybody behind bars?" Ethan said inquisitively.

Lloyd shook his head.

"Suspects?" Mindy said.

"Nope."

"So it's early in the investigation," Ethan said, dropping a lump of sugar into his coffee.

"Been active for a while, but it's dead in the water. No leads, no real evidence, nothin'."

"So how do we fit in?" Ethan said. "We don't do crime stories until the case has gone through the system and the killer is behind bars. Then we have a whole docket of facts to work with."

"Now take a look, and I'll explain," he said, tapping on the file folder.

Ethan grabbed the folder and pulled out three glossy color photos. He lined them up next to each other. Three girls were lying on their backs in what appeared to be the morgue. There were bruises on their faces, deep lacerations on their upper bodies, rows of slash marks on their arms, cigarette burns on their breasts, ligature marks on their wrists and ankles, and a thin red gash stretching all the way around their necks.

"What's the cause of death?" Ethan asked.

"Strangulation."

"And the physical abuse?"

"All before they were murdered."

Mindy picked up one of the photos and gasped. "My god, they look like kids."

"They are kids," Lloyd said. "The medical examiner estimates all three were no more than thirteen."

"Who are they?" Ethan said, peering at a pretty young girl with long brown hair and fixed black eyes staring into nothingness.

"Cops have no idea. Whoever killed them cut off their fingers and pulled their teeth. So we can't match fingerprints or ID them from dental records. There's also no DNA matches in CODES or NCIC or Interpol or any of the other crime databases. All dead ends."

"No parents or relatives have come forward looking for them?" Mindy said, studying the three photos sitting in front of her.

"Nope."

"Do we know where they're from?"

"Cops are still searching."

"Runaways?"

"Your guess is as good as mine."

"So they're Jane Does," Ethan said, fingering the photos.

"So far," Lloyd said, finishing his Red Bull and neatly lining up the can next to the first one.

Ethan scanned from one picture to the next, then turned to Lloyd and pointed, "What happened here?"

There was a perfect square of skin, two inches on a side that was carefully sliced and removed about three inches above the ligature marks on each girl's left ankle, leaving an ugly, raw hole in their legs.

"Cops haven't figured that out yet," Lloyd said. "Lots of theories. Maybe weird trophies the killer took? Maybe some sadistic ritual the guy gets off on before he kills them? But no definitive explanation, not yet." He waited for a reaction from Ethan, but didn't get one. "There's one more thing. Each of the girls had sex shortly before they were murdered. The medical examiner found semen in their vaginas during the autopsies."

"The killer's?" Ethan said.

"Cops don't know. The girls had sex with different guys. Many different guys. But the medical examiner couldn't find a DNA match on the vaginal swabs of any of the girls. The lab tests are inconclusive."

"Were they hookers?" Mindy asked.

"Don't know. No arrest records."

"And there are no leads?"

"Nope."

"And no idea who killed them?" Ethan said, cocking his head.

"A big fat zero."

Ethan picked up a photo and stared at the dead girl.

"So what *do* we know about the killer? The pictures indicate the same MO for each murder, and that whoever killed them may have sexually abused and brutally tortured them, before strangling each victim possibly with a lightweight rope or maybe an electrical cord," he said, his analytical mind spinning. "Could there be more than one maniac out there?"

"That's one theory on the table, but the cops are working under the premise that the same guy is doing all the killing," Lloyd said, staring into Ethan's eyes.

"So it's a serial murderer?"

"Didn't say that, Ethan. The cops don't know. Not enough evidence. The case is wide open at the moment."

Ethan stared long and hard at the three dead girls. "Okay, Lloyd, why are you sharing this with us?"

Lloyd leaned over the table. "Because we're talking about kids, little kids, and Patricia Highland is unhappy with the progress she's making with her investigation. Her task force is small, and she can't get more resources to beef up her manpower. She knows you and I have worked together in the past, and she asked me to feel you out."

"About what?"

"About coming on board."

"She wants to bring me into the investigation?" Ethan said, beginning to see interesting possibilities for a good story. "Why me?"

"Because she watches *The Weekly Reporter* and knows your reputation. How you nailed the deputy mayor in the Pavel Feodor case and single-handedly discovered that Dr. Rufus Wellington was a serial killer who murdered more than thirty prostitutes."

"That's flattering, but doesn't mean I can catch this killer."

"She knows that and has been getting flack from members of her task force who think bringing you on board is a bad idea, but there's something else you'd add to the investigation that, so far, she's been unable to get."

"What's that?"

"Publicity."

"Come again?" Mindy said. "I don't understand."

"Run a computer check when you get back to the office. There's been little reporting on the three murders. Each one got a day or two of coverage, mostly on the inside pages of the tabloids. Then the stories dried up."

"Why's that?" Mindy said.

"Murders are a dime a dozen in this city."

"But these are kids. Raped, tortured, then murdered," Ethan said, aghast. "And the papers didn't care?"

"Nope."

"And didn't link the killings?"

"Nope. That's why Patricia is reaching out to you, Ethan. She wants you to cover the story, get it on television, make it a front-page headline, so she can get the powers that be to give her more money to catch the guy before he does it again."

"And what do I get in return?" Ethan said, knowing that Paul Lang would never program a story without concrete evidence and a suspect sitting in a jail cell.

"She wants to tell you that herself."

"When?"

"As soon as you can take a meeting," Lloyd said, stroking his beard.

Ethan stared at the three dead girls one last time then placed the pictures back into the folder. "We go way back, Lloyd, and I trust you. So if you think there's a story here, then call the ADA and set something up."

"I knew you'd be interested," Lloyd said, reaching into his briefcase and pulling out a pile of documents. "These are some of the police reports. Patricia Highland thought a little background would help you prep for a meeting." He handed Ethan the documents. "When's a good time?"

"No day's better than the next," he said, thinking about the wall-to-wall meetings he had scheduled with Sampson and his producers. "Let me know what works for the ADA, and I'll be there."

*****

Ethan hurried down the long red hallway with its gallery of the rich and famous—Paul Lang standing beside Presidents Trump and Obama, Hilary Clinton, Derek Jeter, Barbara Streisand, Tom Cruise, and countless other masters of the universe—all smiling, glad-handing, posing with happy faces. Ethan chuckled to himself at Paul's raging ego, at his need to surround himself with high-profile celebrities to feel important. Maybe that's why he yelled and screamed all the time. Maybe that's why he belittled his staff. Because he only felt worthy hob-nobbing with superstars.

"Why am I here?" Mindy said, tugging at Ethan's sports coat.

"Because if I sell Paul the story, I want you working with me," Ethan said, adjusting his tie. "You've got sources all through law enforcement, here and in Washington, that you can tap into if and when we need answers to questions that Patricia Highland can't or won't give us."

"Can't Lloyd do that?"

"He doesn't work for us."

"But why do you need me to pitch the idea to Paul?"

"Let's just say you're my insurance policy. Paul's not gonna want me working up a story from ground zero. He's gonna think it'll take too much of my time, that he's gonna have to pick up the slack with Peter. And he certainly won't like that. That's what he pays me to do. So if I can get you assigned from the get-go and tell him you'll do most of the legwork, then presto chango, I can pressure him into giving me a research budget."

"But you'll be all over the story."

"Of course. But he won't know that, will he?"

They stopped in front of Monica's desk and waited while she finished a telephone call. Then Ethan said, "Is he free?"

"Well, the prodigal son finally makes his appearance." She glanced at her wristwatch. "Only two hours late."

"Is he alone?" Ethan asked, unfazed.

"All alone and on pins and needles waiting for you." Monica glanced at Mindy. "She's not on the schedule. Is she going in with you?"

Ethan nodded yes.

"Good luck. You know how Paul loves surprises."

Ethan buttoned his sports coat, pushed open the door, and walked into the executive producer's office. Paul was sitting at his big Florence Knoll glass desk, scribbling notes on a yellow pad, his jacket draped over the back of his chair. He was wearing an expensive handmade blue pin-striped suit, a starched white shirt with solid gold, Harry Winston cufflinks, and an Hermes silk tie. His long blond hair was pulled back in a ponytail that fell halfway down his back, and his John Lennon wire-rim glasses were perched on the tip of his prominent nose.

"Where the hell you been, Ethan?" he said, peering at his brand-new Patek Philippe—twelve sparkling diamonds instead of numbers on the face of the watch.

"Discussing a story with a source."

"Why is Mindy here?"

"She was at the meeting." Mindy stood silently next to Ethan.

"Care to sit down?" Paul said, still writing on the yellow pad, but not making eye contact. They both dropped into richly appointed Eames swivel chairs made with the finest leather money can buy. "Before we get into your story, have you read these ideas Peter just pitched us?" He waved half-a-dozen green sheets in the air. "They're preposterous. An interview with a Tibetan monk, a story on fish farming in Alaska, a profile of Adolfo Cambiaso—"

"Who?"

"My sentiments exactly," Paul roared. "He's the number one polo player in the world. Who the hell cares? Not our audience," he said, not missing a beat. "I'm not doing any of these, and it's your job to make them go away. When are you planning to talk to him?"

Ethan slumped in his chair. It would take him all day to convince Peter these stories weren't right for the show. He could picture the endless hours of bickering, the yelling and screaming, the name-calling, the frustration.

"I'll meet with him as soon as we finish up here."

"Good." He leaned back in his chair. "So brief me on your story before I tell you why I wanted to see you first thing this morning." His eyes bored into Ethan. "I'm sure it's terribly important. It always is with you."

"A crime story. Maybe a good one," Ethan said, not backing down.

Paul began doodling on a fresh page of paper, a nervous habit that always irritated Ethan.

"I thought you'd gotten producing out of your system." Silence. "Don't you like being Peter's senior producer? I'm paying you a lot of money to do it."

"It's been a long time, and I miss producing."

"But you're an important part of my team," Paul said, shooting daggers across the table. "I'm not sure I can afford letting you work up a story. It'll take up too much of your time. Who will manage Peter? Who will work with his producers? Who will talk him out of his ridiculous story ideas?" He waved the green sheets. "That's your job, not mine."

"Nothing will change with Peter."

"Does he know you're here pitching me an idea?"

"Not yet."

"He's not going to like it."

"True. But he knew when I took this job I was going to produce my own stories. And you knew that too, Paul."

"Yes. Yes," he said, waving his hand dismissively. "So what's the story?"

"I don't know yet."

"That's not an answer," he said, pausing midstroke, before putting down his pen. "Does Mindy know? Is that why she's here, to give me specifics?"

Mindy began to mumble, but Ethan interrupted. "She doesn't know either, but I need her to help me nail down the facts."

"We're talking in circles, Ethan," Paul said tersely. "What do you have?"

"An inside look at a murder investigation." Ethan spent the next ten minutes carefully explaining what he'd learned at the meeting with Lloyd Howard—about the autopsy photos, the unsolved murders, and the search for suspects.

"So what's the story? Who are the victims? Who's the damn killer? Why'd he do it?" Paul said sarcastically. "Sounds like you're wasting your time. You've got nothing, Ethan, nothing. This is a run-of-the mill murder story without characters or an ending—like a million other unsolved murders out there. I don't want it for my show."

"But the victims are little kids—Jane Does—brutally tortured and murdered. Don't you care?"

"I didn't say that."

"Don't you want to find out who butchered them?"

"I didn't say that either."

"Well—"

"You don't give up, do you?" Paul said icily. "Who's the ADA?"

"Patricia Highland."

"And what's her pitch?"

Ethan hesitated, knowing this was the make-or-break point. "She's going to give us complete access to her investigation."

"What does that mean?" Paul said, curiosity creeping into his voice.

"Won't know until I meet with her."

"Is that why you need Mindy? To set up a meeting?"

"And to do some of the heavy lifting while I work with Peter."

Paul placed his pen on the desk and looked from Mindy to Ethan. "So you'll know more about this story after your meeting. Is that what you're telling me?"

Ethan shook his head.

"And you want me to give you time to see if there's anything there?"

Ethan shook his head again.

"Well, you've rarely disappointed me in the past," Paul said, leaning across his desk, "and against my better judgment, you've got my attention. One week. Not one day more to figure out if this is, indeed, a story I should spend my money on. I don't want you wasting any more time than that." He turned to Mindy. "Can you add this to your workload?"

"I'll juggle," she said.

"Good. Brief Peter on your story after you kill *his* story ideas. I don't want him left out of the loop."

Ethan stood, made his way across the room, then stopped at the door. "By the way, Paul, what did you want to talk to me about?"

"James."

"What about James?"

"Have you briefed him on his responsibilities?"

"Not yet. I just met him."

"When will you sit down with him?"

"Guess, when I get back to my office. What's the big deal?"

"He's my nephew, the son of my wife's sister. We're very close."

Ethan felt cold sweat suddenly soak the back of his shirt. "I'm sure he's a bright young man, and I'm looking forward to working with him."

"I'm counting on that," Paul said, brow furrowed. "He wants to learn the business, and I'm sure you'll teach him everything he needs to know from the bottom up."

"Will do my best."

Paul dismissed him with a wave of his hand, Ethan hurrying out the door, past Monica still talking on the telephone, and then down the long red hallway.

"Shit. That's all I need. A spy in my office."

"What are you talking about, Ethan?" Mindy said, vexed. "Who the hell is James?"

"My new assistant."

"You have an assistant?"

"You just heard it from the horse's mouth. He's a plant from Paul to keep tabs on me."

"That's crazy. You're being paranoid. Paul loves you. So does Peter."

Ethan stopped dead in his tracks and swiveled around to face her.

"Am I? You're that sure I'm just dreaming this up? Well, Paul doesn't trust me. He never has. Not since I was a producer, and certainly not since I started working as Peter's senior producer. He always gives me a hard time about everything I do."

"Jeez, Ethan," Mindy said heatedly, "he just gave you a week to look into a story without any facts. Based on your reputation as a producer and your ability to work with Peter Sampson who's one of the most difficult people in all of television. What's eating at you, Ethan? Something's wrong. I can see it in your eyes. Is that why you're hitting the bottle again?"

Ethan stared at her blankly.

Then turned and briskly walked away.

Without saying another word.

CHAPTER 3

It was seven o'clock when Ethan pushed open the door and walked into McGlades. The temperature had dropped into the low teens, and the snowstorm had turned into a blizzard, already shutting down much of the city. A shiver ran up his spine as he pulled off his gloves and overcoat and settled in at the bar between an old man nursing a warm beer and a pretty young woman hustling for a date. Ethan knew he should be heading home on the bus, that Sarah and his seven-year-old son, Luke, were waiting, that dinner would soon be on the table. But he'd been fighting all afternoon with Sampson about the story ideas neither he nor Paul wanted to put into production and couldn't shake off the fear that his career was spiraling down the wrong path. He needed a drink to take off the edge.

"Moe, pour me a Black Label. Make it a double."

The bartender stared at him pensively. "Sure you want to do that, young lad? Been a while since you came in here twice in the same day."

Ethan tapped his finger on the bar.

"Have it your way."

He wiped the inside of a shot glass with a clean dish towel, dropped it in front of Ethan, and poured him a generous portion of Scotch. Ethan was an alcoholic, a full-blown alcoholic, who'd been in therapy trying to control his out-of-control drinking for over a year. Every week, sometimes twice, he trudged across town from his apartment on the Upper East Side to see his psychiatrist, Dr. Fred Schwartz, a specialist in drug and alcohol abuse. At times it seemed to be working, and Ethan could resist the tug of alcohol, going several days, even weeks, without touching a drop. But whenever he felt pressure, especially from his job, he would hit the bottle with renewed urgency and drown his sorrows in Scotch.

He downed his drink and banged the glass on the table. "Another one, Moe. Another double."

Moe refilled his glass, and he drank it all at once.

"Take it easy, Ethan," he said. "You're hitting it too hard. You know what'll happen." Ethan stared back at him, then looked down at his shot glass, his eyes glazing over. "Haven't seen you like this in a long time. What's eatin' at you?"

"Don't wanna talk. Pour me another."

"Not gonna do that. Not until you tell me what's goin' on."

The room was beginning to spin.

"Tough day at the office?" Moe said as he poured a draft of beer for the old man sitting next to Ethan. "Is the big boss, or that guy, Peter Sampson, givin' you a hard time?"

"Not gonna talk about it, Moe," Ethan said obstinately, banging his glass on the counter again, everybody in the bar turning and staring. "One more for the road," he said insistently, a slur edging into his voice.

"Not happenin', Ethan. Not tonight," he said, staring deeply into his eyes. "I knew somethin' was wrong this mornin' when you ordered a Scotch after you and that pretty young lass came in to meet that fella in my back room. Go home to your family. They're waitin' on you. I ain't gonna serve you another drop."

*****

Ethan climbed off the bus on the corner of Ninety-Second and Madison Avenue. The wind was howling, the snow blowing sideways. Traffic was at a standstill, cars and trucks stacked up as far as the eye could see, honking their horns, clogging the streets. Ethan staggered down to Ninety-First Street, nearly slipping on a patch of ice, then turned toward Fifth Avenue and headed to his condo in the middle of the block. He'd been living in the same apartment in the same building since he was a child, and the neighborhood felt safe and familiar as he pushed through the front door and walked into the lobby. He pulled off his wool cap and shook off clumps of wet snow that spilled to the floor.

"Evenin', Winston," Ethan said as he passed the front desk.

"Evenin', Mr. Benson," the doorman said, tipping his hat. "Ain't fit for a dog out there tonight."

"I'm sure Holly won't be happy when I walk her. She hates the cold and the snow."

"Everything all right, Mr. Benson?" he said, tilting his head to the side. "You seem a bit shaky."

"Just fine, Winston."

"Well, stay warm and say hi to the missus."

Ethan didn't respond, embarrassed the doorman could see he was drunk, as he wobbled across the lobby to the elevators, stumbled through the first door that opened, and rode up to the ninth floor, propped against the back wall for support. When the elevator stopped, he made his way down the hall, fumbling with his keys until he found the lock, then pushed into the foyer, where he pulled off his overcoat and dropped his briefcase on the floor. His Labrador retriever scampered into the room, smiling, her claws clicking the marble floor as she danced at his feet like a puppy. He bent over and scratched her head, still dizzy, his stomach sour.

"Good girl, good sweet girl, you never give Daddy a hard time."

Then he began looking for Sarah—Holly scampering along behind him—poking into the bedroom and the living room, before heading to the kitchen. Sarah was sitting at the table moving food around on her plate, quiet, sullen, worried.

"Where's Luke?" he said.

She didn't look up at him.

"Something wrong?"

"We waited as long as we could, Ethan, then he ate his dinner, and I put him to bed."

"Was he upset?"

"What do you think?" There was a tinge of sarcasm in her voice. "You come home late every night. You're always preoccupied. You hide in your office. You never spend time with him."

"What time is it now?" Ethan stared at his watch, not tracking the conversation.

"Nine thirty," she said, giving up. "Your dinner's in the oven."

He crossed the room tentatively and pulled out his plate, eased back to the table, and sat down across from her. Sarah was a beautiful woman, a couple of years younger than Ethan. They'd been married for over a decade. She had long, flowing blond hair, blue eyes that sparkled like stars in the night, small delicate hands and feet, and creamy, fair skin. They still loved each other deeply, but his drinking had put a strain on their marriage, a deep chasm that was testing their relationship. She stared at Ethan, probing, searching, then whispered, "I got a call from Moe."

"He called you?"

"He always calls me when there's something wrong. You know that. He told me about today. That you came in this morning and ordered a drink, then showed up after work and started belting down one Scotch after another. He said he asked you to leave because you were royally smashed. He's worried, Ethan, and so am I." She stood, pulled her chair around the table next to him, then sat and held his hand. "I know you've been drinking every night. Your breath always reeks of Scotch. What going on with you?"

Ethan slumped in his chair.

All the energy draining from his body.

"It's been simmering for a while, babe," he said, looking down at his plate of cold food, before pushing it across the table.

"No appetite?"

"Upset stomach."

"From the alcohol?"

He didn't answer.

"So what happened, Ethan?" she said, growing more irritated. "Maybe if you talk, it'll help."

He took a deep breath and peered into her eyes. He saw sorrow and anger.

"I feel lost, overwhelmed, because I hate my job. I spend all day going from one meeting to the next, listening to producers complain, fixing their problems, sucking up to Paul, kowtowing to Peter. It's an endless merry-go-round with nothing in it for me, like I'm sinking in quicksand with no way to get out." He reached for a cigarette. "I don't know, babe, I can't do it anymore."

"So how do we fix it?"

"I don't know," he said, eyes downcast.

"Ethan, you're scaring me," she said, withdrawing her hand. "You sound just like you did after the baby."

"I know. I know. That hurts too. Always."

Ethan rocked back in his chair, lost in the harsh memories of the past, remembering that terrible night when he and Sarah had lost a newborn baby girl shortly after they'd been married. She had given birth all alone in their living room, Ethan working late in an edit room, ignoring her phone calls for help. When he'd finally gotten home in the middle of the night, he'd found her covered in blood, rocking back and forth on the floor, cradling the dead baby in her arms. He'd never forgiven himself for not being there when she needed him, for killing their baby. That's when the drinking had started—to ease the pain, to get through the day. A nightcap before he went to bed, then two, then at lunch, at dinner, then all day long. He'd been battling the bottle ever since.

Sarah stood and began pacing. "I can't take another of your downward spirals, Ethan. We've been through too many of them. What triggered the drinking today? You've been complaining about Peter since you took the job. So what the fuck happened? You've been under control for such a long time."

Ethan took a deep drag on his cigarette.

"I told you," he said icily, "I hate my job."

"It's gotta be more than that," she said quietly. "Tell me what happened."

He sighed deeply then said, "When I got to the office this morning, I was already feeling the itch, that pull for a taste of Scotch. Then I found this kid sitting outside of my door."

"What kid?"

"My new assistant."

"You have an assistant? What happened to Consuela?"

"She's back to only working for Peter," Ethan said dejectedly. "And you wanna hear the topper? This guy, my new assistant, James Lapidus, is Paul's nephew."

"So?"

"Paul put him there to spy on me," he said, now agitated. "Can't you see that? He still doesn't trust me after all I've done for him and Peter and the show since I took this damn fucking job."

"Keep your voice down. You'll wake up Luke," she said, exasperated. "You sound irrational, Ethan. Get over it. This new kid was hired to make your life easier. You're a senior producer with a ton of responsibilities. What's wrong with you? You wanna throw away your career because your boss gave you an assistant? That's crazy, Ethan, crazy. Let's call Dr. Schwartz. Maybe he can talk some sense into you."

"No."

"You won't talk to Dr. Schwartz?"

"No."

"You want to keep talking to me?"

"No."

"What about dinner? You gonna eat?"

"No."

"You gonna keep drinking?"

He glared at her but remained silent.

"So that's it? You got nothing else to say?"

He pushed the chair away from the table and stood angrily, still glaring.

"Don't you walk away from me, Ethan Benson. If you keep drinking and go down that sinkhole again, I'm not going to stick around. You're on your own."

He waved his hand dismissively. "I'm going to my study. Got work to catch up on."

"Sit down. I'm not finished."

"We're finished," he said as he stormed out of the kitchen.

*****

Ethan's study was at the end of the center hallway, tucked away in the back of his apartment. He pushed open the door, a stream of light flowing into the darkness, walked over to his desk, and flipped on the lamp. The room was cluttered with stacks of papers haphazardly strewn over every surface and big ashtrays overflowing with dead cigarettes. He sat in an old chair, the red leather worn and cracking, and lit another Marlboro, inhaling the nicotine, before blowing a long stream of smoke out his nose that wafted up to the ceiling. Closing his eyes, he thought about his new assistant and his meeting with Paul and his afternoon of arguing with Peter and wondered why it had upset him so much.

Maybe Sarah was right.

Maybe he was being paranoid for no reason.

He thought about going back out and apologizing, but then he heard her stomping down the hallway and slamming the bedroom door. Better wait. Give her time to cool off. Then he'd make it right before they went to sleep.

He glanced around the room, taking in the wall of bookshelves, the photos of Sarah and Luke sitting on almost every counter, and all the awards he'd won during his career. Then he reached down, opened his briefcase, and pulled out the folder Lloyd Howard had given him that morning. It was labeled with the official stamp of the Manhattan District Attorney's Office and filled with color photos and detailed police reports from all three crime scenes. Ethan carefully separated the photos into neat rows, then looked at the police reports. They were affixed with the seal of the Sex Crimes Division of New York City's Special Victims Unit.

He licked his lips.

He needed a chaser to clear his head.

Standing, he picked his way around the furniture and made a beeline to the wet bar, grabbing a bottle of Black Label and pouring a finger of the gold liquid into a clean glass. He sipped slowly, savoring the warmth as it spilled through his body.

Better.

Much better.

Maybe now he could concentrate.

And forget about his argument with Sarah.

He walked back to his desk, placed the police reports on top of a pile of random documents, and picked up the first stack of crime scene photos. Jane Doe number one. They were labeled with the letter A, numbered one through ten, and dated October 5, 2017. He googled the murder and found a story on page 7 of the *New York Post*. There were no follow-ups. Then he checked the television coverage. The story led the eleven o'clock news for a day then disappeared—just like Lloyd had said. Funny. He thought a crime of this nature should've garnered much more press coverage. Then he scrolled through the other headlines from that week. Bingo. The Harvey Weinstein sex scandal on the front page of every newspaper every day—follow-up stories filling the inside of all the tabloids. So that's what had killed the press coverage of the first Jane Doe murder. A more sensational story.

Then he went back to the crime scene photos. Number A-1 was a medium shot of a dead girl—completely naked except for a pair of sandals—propped in a folding chair, her arms crossed pushing up her breasts, her legs spread revealing her shaved and bruised vagina. She was covered in blood from head to toe, her eyes staring hauntingly, her long black hair matted, hanging in clumps to her shoulders, and coated with filth as if she'd been dragged unceremoniously through the gutter before being posed in the chair. Her skin was blotchy and dotted with deep abrasions and what appeared to be dozens of new and old cigarette burns. There was dried blood crusting her chin and hanging from the ends of her missing fingertips, and her arms and legs were riddled with old scars and what appeared to be fresh wounds from a sharp instrument. Prominently displayed in the photo was the girl's left leg, the neat square of skin above her ankle surgically removed. Ethan closed his eyes, sickened by the ghastly image, and inhaled the rest of his Scotch. The girl had been physically abused, maybe for months, then sadistically murdered.

The killer was a psycho.

A maniac.

Ethan put the empty Scotch glass on his desk and rifled through the rest of the pictures. They were a series of tight shots, all showing close-up details of the horrific wounds covering the dead girl's body. Ethan lit another cigarette then looked at the last picture in the series, number A-10. It was a wide shot of the murder scene—Lower Manhattan and the new World Trade Center in the distance, a handful of cars on the West

Side Highway, and a single person on a bicycle. The girl's body, propped in the folding chair, her face grotesquely frozen in a death mask, was sitting in what appeared to be the wooden bow of a Boston Whaler extending over the Hudson River in a children's playground.

Ethan spread the ten photos on his desk.

And poured another Scotch.

Then glanced at the pictures of Jane Does numbers two and three.

His eyes floated back and forth across the images—slowly, meticulously—studying the details. And like the first victim, the tableaus were identical—the victims posed in the same exact way in the same kind of chairs, with the same patterns of cuts and abrasions, the same mosaic of cigarette burns, the same missing patch of skin, the same ghostly expressions on their faces.

Curious.

He carefully studied each grouping of pictures one more time until he reached the wide shots. They, too, were identical—the victims propped on what appeared to be the bow of a boat, in a children's playground, with the skyline in the background, and the Hudson River flowing aimlessly toward the harbor at the southern tip of Manhattan. The killer had murdered each girl, playing the same ritualistic game with their bodies, taunting the authorities.

But why?

Ethan sat quietly, thinking, speculating, wondering what access to the investigation Patricia Highland would give him in return for generating more publicity about the killings. Still surprised by the lack of press coverage, he checked the dates of the second and third murders on the back of the photos. November 6, 2018 and March 24, 2019. Hmm. There was over a year between the first and second killings and a little over four months between the second and third. Was that important? Maybe. He googled both dates and found only a handful of stories buried in the middle of the *New York Post* and the *Daily News.* And just like the first murder, they were knocked off the front page by other, more pressing headlines—the Democrats taking control of the House and the Mueller Report purportedly absolving Donald Trump from colluding with the Russians before the 2016 presidential election.

So the three murders had become old news.

Cold cases.

Forgotten.

Ethan collected the photos and shoved them back into the folder, then headed to the wet bar to top off his drink. How many did that make today? Five? Six? More? Sarah was right. He had to get control of his drinking. But not tonight. Maybe tomorrow. Or the next day. As he reached for the bottle of Black Label, Luke pushed open the door and padded into the room, Holly on his heels, wagging her tail.

"What are you doing awake, Lukie?" he said, looking at his watch. "It's well after midnight."

"I had a nightmare, Daddy."

"And you couldn't find Mommy?"

"She's in bed. Asleep." He rubbed his eyes. "I'm scared. I need a story."

Ethan locked the crime scene photos in his desk, hiding them so Luke wouldn't find them, then glanced at the police reports. They'd have to wait until tomorrow.

"Okay, a bedtime story it is." Then he swept him off the floor and planted a kiss on his nose.

"You gonna bring your Scotch, Daddy?"

Ethan was taken aback. Even Luke knew he was drinking, that something was wrong. Then he reached for his tumbler of Scotch, hesitated, and left it on his desk, before carrying his little boy back to his bedroom.

CHAPTER 4

Maria lay in darkness on a damp, cold floor curled in a ball. She was hungry. Her throat was parched. And she was scared. Real scared. Her naked body was covered in black and blue marks from all the beatings, and her nipples and loins ached from the horrible things all the men had done to her since they'd snatched her from her small village in the mountains. How long had it been? Three days? Four days? A week? She had no idea. She yanked on the chain and tried to stand, but the room began spinning, and she collapsed into the corner of her cell, exhausted. Then she heard the incessant scratching. Bugs. Big bugs. She couldn't see them, but she knew they were everywhere—on the walls, hiding in the links of her chains, crawling on her skin. She swatted one away hysterically, tearing at her arm until it bled, then listened; rats were scurrying across the stone floor. Leaning over, she retched, but nothing came up, because there was nothing in her stomach. Then she searched, looking for a crumb of bread she might have missed after the *Padre* brought her last meal. But the bugs and rats had scavenged everything.

She pulled her hair in frustration.

Then started to scream.

Terrified.

And when nobody came, she started to sob.

"Why? Why me?" she wailed, tears flowing down her cheeks. "I was a good girl. Oh, such a good girl. I went to church. Prayed to Jesus. Why would he let those men do this to me? Why? Why?" She curled back into a ball and fell into a state of semiconsciousness.

Maria Fuente was fourteen. She had a little brother, Julio, and an older sister, Juanita, and lived with her parents in a modest adobe dwelling in *Humahuaca*, a small village tucked away high in the *Misione* mountains of northeast Argentina. Her father was an accountant and her mother a waitress who worked in a roadside café catering to tourists who flocked to the town square each day to listen to the bells in the *Cabildo* clock tower as they chimed twelve times at noon, and then gazed at the hand-painted wooden statue of *Saint Francis Solanus* as it emerged through a bronze door in a seventeenth-century church, making the sign of the cross to bless them. Maria stopped at that church every day on her way to school, kneeling amongst the tourists, spellbound, praying for *Saint Francis* to forgive her sins.

But it was at that special moment on that warm February afternoon.

When her life was shattered.

Maybe forever.

As she'd left the town square and walked down the pretty cobblestone street to the little schoolhouse where she studied English, she was attacked by three burly men, dragged into a vacant building, and beaten unconscious. The next thing she remembered was waking up disoriented in the trunk of a car as it bumped along a rutted dirt road, her hands and feet bound by thick rope, a coarse burlap bag over her head, and a gag in her mouth. She had tried to scream, kicked at the hood of the trunk, struggled to wrestle free until the car suddenly pulled into an isolated glen. The three men had taken her out of the trunk and dragged her behind a stand of trees—where they slapped her until she couldn't climb to her knees, and then raped her over and over until she passed out.

The next thing she remembered was opening her eyes.

Alone.

In total darkness.

Chained to the wall.

Maria blinked, trying to get her bearings, as a rat ran across her foot. She screamed—a long, haunting scream that reverberated around the stone walls and echoed down the long stone corridor. Her chest heaved up and down as she tried to calm herself, tried to be brave. Then the door at the top of the steps creaked open on its rusty old hinges.

He was coming.

The *Padre.*

And she started to wail again.

*****

Pedro Juan Ignacio Rodriquez started down the old stone steps, dressed in his ceremonial vestments, his hands tucked into oversized sleeves gently resting on his fat belly, the foot of his robe sweeping ominously across the dirty floor. He had just left the cardinal in his bedchamber after saying evening prayer and was making his way through a warren of winding passageways and into the sanctuary, where he checked to make sure he wasn't being followed, before hurrying out the side door where two men were waiting in a beat-up white panel truck. They greeted each other, whispered a few words, then headed back into the *basilica* through a rarely used door in the back of the building.

"You have the girl?" the first man said.

"Yes, my son."

"She pretty?" the second man said.

"All girls are pretty in the eyes of our Savior," Rodriquez said, kissing his crucifix. "Come, follow me."

They weaved single file into the sanctuary, through the sacristy, opening the secret door, and then descending the stone steps into the catacombs, where they lit torches that flickered in the darkness, throwing eerie shadows up against the walls. The first man behind the *Padre*, Julio Sanchez, was short and squat, standing no more than five feet four. He was a *mestizo*, with dark, droopy eyes and long black hair that hung as straight as an arrow halfway down his back. He was covered from head to toe in tattoos—the illustrated man—with deep scars of fire-breathing dragons carved into his heavily muscled forearms. He was carrying a rope and a large cloth sack and was sweating profusely.

The second man, Manuel Rivera, was much larger, nearly six feet one and two hundred pounds, with huge hands and feet, long arms and bowed legs, and a chicken-like neck. He was a full-blood Inca Indian, with a barrel chest and small waist, and a sixth finger on each hand. He was dragging heavy iron chains, which rattled in the near silence as he swung them back and forth along the ground.

"My turn fuck girl, *si*, *Padre?*" he said in broken English.

"All in good time, my son," Rodriquez said as he unbolted a door and pushed down another dingy passageway. "You know where to take her?"

"*Si*, *Padre*. Not first time for Manuel and Julio. We help *Padre* disappear many girls. I want fuck girl first."

"Patience, Manuel, patience. Not much longer and then you can have a go at her."

They proceeded down another narrow corridor and a series of stone steps, Julio lighting torches on the walls, scaring the hungry rats hiding in the shadows, as Manuel deftly swatted them with the chains, smashing them against the walls.

"I hate rats," he said with veracity. "They vermin. Unholy. Kill them all."

"They're God's creatures, too, my son. Be patient. Soon you'll have the girl, and you'll be gone from this unholy place."

They continued walking another five minutes, unlocking more doors, lighting more torches, until they reached a heavy iron door, where the *Padre* reached into his vestments, pulled out his key ring, and opened the ancient lock.

"Now time to fuck girl?" Julio said anxiously, his tongue running over his lower lip.

"Soon," Rodriquez said, "very soon."

Then they pushed into the dungeon.

*****

Maria listened to the footsteps approaching, shuddering uncontrollably in the darkness, as she heard the key and the door slowly open.

"Someone's coming. Someone's coming," she shrieked to herself, making the sign of the cross. "Please, Lord Jesus, help me. Help me. HELP ME!" Then she saw the torches and shadows of three figures growing closer.

The *Padre.*

The monster.

And two other men.

"Protect me, Holy Father," she cried, furiously yanking on her chains as they stopped outside her cell, waving their torches, leering at her naked body. She covered herself with her hands, before her mind began to shut down, drawing deeper into itself, as the *Padre* placed the key in the lock. Whimpering, she backed into the corner, as the small man with the tattoos waved the rope and the burlap sack in front of her face, and the Indian slammed the set of handcuffs and leg irons on the floor.

*****

Pedro Juan Ignacio Rodriquez peered down at the small girl, at her dazzling black eyes, her perfectly shaped ass, and her firm breasts. He remembered what he'd done to her, wanting to take her again, wanting to keep her for himself. But that wasn't the plan. Not today. Not ever. He was working for a powerful man who'd paid him handsomely, and who wouldn't hesitate to kill him if he double-crossed him, not for a split second. He pulled the chalice and the paten from his vestments, then placed his massive right hand over her head as she tried to wriggle away.

"Hush, my child, don't be afraid. Partake in the body of our Lord, and drink of his blood so you can be one with Jesus Christ."

Then he grabbed her by the chin, his long fingernails digging into her flesh, forced open her jaw, and poured rancid water into her mouth.

Maria gagged.

Swallowed.

Then spat a wad of phlegm in his face.

"I hate you," she said, still choking. "Let me go."

"Now. Now, my child. That's never going to happen. You work for the Church. For Jesus Christ, the Almighty. And if you don't listen to what he says, he'll cast you out through the gates of hell." Then he forced a piece of moldy bread in her mouth, nodded to the two men, and said, "Remove her chains."

Maria screamed, then spit out the bread, and the *Padre* slapped her across the face, whipping her head back and forth.

"Listen to me, you little whore," he said, looming over her. "You do exactly what I say, or I'll go back to your stinking village, and I'll kill your brother, your precious sister, and then your mother and father. I'll slit their throats and hang them from the rafters of your home like butchered pigs ready for market." He waited, watching horror spread across her face, then said, his voice now softer, "Do you understand me, Maria?" She nodded. "Do exactly as I say, and I won't murder your family, and I won't tell them it was you who signed their death warrants."

"Don't hurt them. Please, *Padre*."

"Ah, now we have an understanding." He turned to Manuel. "Take her."

The Inca pounced instantly, grabbing her by the throat and squeezing, her eyes bulging as she struggled to breathe. Then

Julio unlocked her chains, and they beat her savagely—yanking her by the hair, kicking her groin, twisting her nipples—until she lay prostate on the stone floor, no resistance left in her. They stepped back and waited for the *Padre's* signal. Then Manuel rolled her on her stomach, tied her hands behind her back and bound them tightly to her feet.

Then they both pawed her body like animals.

"Not yet," Rodriquez bellowed viciously.

"When? When can we fuck little bitch," the Inca said, glaring up at the *Padre*.

"After you get her in the truck, and you're back on the road. Then both of you can fuck her brains out. Just make sure you drug her when you're done and seal her tightly in the wooden crate before you pass her off to Hector tomorrow."

"And our money?" Julio said greedily.

"It's waiting on the other end. Now get her out of here before the cardinal figures out what we're doing."

Julio grabbed the sack and trussed it over the girl.

Manuel bound her in chains and heaved her over his shoulder.

Then they followed the *Padre* through the dungeon, along the passageways of the catacombs, and out of the *basilica,* tossing her recklessly into the back of the white panel truck, before driving off into the night.

CHAPTER 5

Ethan blinked and opened his eyes. Early morning sunshine was streaming through the venetian blinds, throwing a kaleidoscope of patterns over the walls and furniture in his bedroom. He slowly sat up and rubbed his temples, his head pounding, his mouth parched like a cotton ball. He peered at his alarm clock. Six thirty. Damn. He'd only managed four hours of sleep. He glanced at Sarah lying next to him naked, the covers hiked down to her waist, her silky blond hair spilling down her back. He kissed the nape of her neck, careful not to wake her, not wanting to spark another argument about his drinking, then slipped out of bed and walked to the window. It was still partly overcast, puffy gray clouds drifting across the sky, but the storm was over, blanketing the ground with a foot of snow. Madison Avenue was deserted, impassable, a handful of cars stranded in snowbanks. But he could hear snowplows in the distance clearing the streets, getting the city ready for rush hour.

He rubbed his eyes, then pinched the bridge of his nose.

A hangover.

A big one.

After climbing into his bathrobe, he grabbed his iPhone and cigarettes from the dresser and made his way to the kitchen. Holly padded out of Luke's bedroom, stretched, and fell in behind him, nuzzling, hoping for breakfast.

"Too early, sweet girl, not until after I walk you."

She sat at attention, tail wagging, staring at him, smiling. He patted her head, then inhaled the rich aroma of fresh coffee sitting in the automatic coffeemaker. After pouring a cup, he opened the cabinet over the dishwasher, reached for the bottle of Motrin, and chewed three tablets, the bitter taste exploding in his mouth. Then he headed to his study, Holly trailing behind him, still hoping for a bowl of kibble. The shades were fully drawn, the room dark and foreboding. Shaking a Marlboro from the near-empty pack, he stumbled around the furniture, bumping into a coffee table, before flipping on the desk lamp and sitting heavily in his chair. His head still pounding, he booted up his laptop and clicked on his e-mail. Quickly scrolling the list, he found the message from Mindy, the one he was waiting for. It had landed in his mailbox just before midnight. Shit. Why hadn't he checked before going to bed? Stupid. Careless. That's what happens when you drink too much. He took a long drag on his cigarette and leaned it in an ashtray, then sipped his coffee and began to read:

> *Just got off the phone with Patricia Highland, the ADA in the Manhattan District Attorney's Office. We talked a long time about the murders. She's outgoing, intelligent, and eager to meet you. She has time tomorrow and suggested we get together at noon. Can you make it? Can you square it away with Peter? Let me know. Mindy.*

Ethan immediately fired a response, saying he'd be there, then looked for the e-mail from James with his schedule. There was a full morning of meetings with Sampson, beginning with a pre–shoot at nine with Leslie Cohen, a producer working on a gun-control story, a screening at ten with Martin Humphrey to fine-tune his changes in the Taylor Swift profile, and a pre–shoot at eleven with Elena Podoritz, who was taking Peter on the road for a segment on the latest diet craze. Then he was free until one thirty, when he was booked in the executive producer's office to go over new story ideas for the show. That gave him roughly an hour and a half of free time. Could he get down to the District Attorney's Office in Lower Manhattan and then back to Paul? Close, but yeah, if everything went off like clockwork, he could do the meeting with Highland.

He made a mental note to tell Peter about the new child-murders story when he got to the office—something he'd neglected to do the day before—then reached for the police reports still sitting on the corner of his desk, lit another cigarette, and separated the documents into three piles—Jane Doe 1, 2, and 3. He checked the time. Seven o'clock. Ninety minutes before he had to head off to work. Holly rustled under his desk, and Ethan rubbed her with his foot as he scanned one stack of documents to the next. The lead detective working each case was the same woman, Gloria Alvarez, out of the Manhattan Special Victims Unit. He opened a fresh page of notes in his iPad, jotted down her name, then ran a Google search.

She popped up immediately.

Gloria Alvarez was a decorated homicide detective with twenty years of service in the New York City Police Department. She'd started as a beat cop in Greenwich Village, did a stint in vice where she was given the Medal of Valor for bringing down a prostitution ring operating out of an NYU dormitory that catered to wealthy businessmen, then got her gold shield before being transferred to SVU in Harlem. She was forty–three, a first-generation Mexican immigrant, and the divorced mother of two little girls. Ethan made a mental note to ask Mindy to run a Lexus-Nexus search, then punched several key words into Google, and double-checked for any newspaper or magazine stories he might have missed on the police investigation into the murders.

But there was nothing.

Then he began skimming the police reports. They, too, were sketchy with many paragraphs redacted. Had they been sanitized by the District Attorney's Office? Maybe. He wrote a note in his iPad to find out. Then he read vague descriptions of the crime scenes containing some of the names of the cops, crime scene investigators, lab technicians, and coroners—along with sketchy diagrams, evidence lists, DNA tests, and fingerprint reports. But there was little else on the fruits of the investigation. No leads. No witnesses. No suspects.

The police were at a dead end.

Just as Lloyd had said.

Ethan reached for another cigarette, but didn't light it. This case was different from other crime stories he'd produced. Beyond the preliminary police reports, there were no attorney motions, depositions, expert witnesses, bereaved families—and no one behind bars accused and convicted of the three murders. Christ, how was he going to build a story? Who was he going to interview? What was he going to shoot? And how was he going to convince Paul to commit time and manpower to a project that might never get off the ground especially in this era of budget cuts?

Was he wasting his time?

Should he take a pass on the story?

But what about the little girls?

They weren't much older than Luke.

He leaned back in his chair and sipped his coffee. It was cold and bitter, much like his mood. Then he scrolled through the notes in his iPad, made a list of the pros and cons of the story, and decided what to do.

*****

Traffic on the West Side Highway was surprisingly light as Ethan made his way in a yellow cab from the broadcast center to the District Attorney's Office at One Hogan Place in Lower Manhattan. Except for a broken-down car blocking traffic in the right lane before the exit to Forty-Second Street, it had been relatively smooth sailing. The storm had ushered in a warm front, and the temperature had climbed over freezing, the deep snow melting furiously, creating lakes of water on the highway and surrounding side streets. Ethan was staring aimlessly at the new office towers rising like mountain peaks at the old Penn Central Railroad Yards, trying to make sense out of what he'd learned—or hadn't learned—about the murders, when his iPhone suddenly buzzed. He reached into his pocket and peered at the LCD screen. Mindy.

"Hey, what did you find out?"

"Not much more than we already know," she said earnestly. "I did a Lexus-Nexus search on Gloria Alvarez—she's definitely a first-rate detective—then checked a bunch of free criminal databases: National Criminal Search, the New York State Department of Correctional Services, the Sex Offenders Registry. What else? What else?" Ethan could hear her shuffling papers. "Oh, yeah, and the Nationwide Arrest Warrant Database."

"And?"

"No record of suspects. No record of the investigation."

"What about your sources in Washington."

"Nothing there, either—at the FBI, Justice, Quantico, any of them."

"So all we know is what Lloyd told us and what the ADA agreed to share," Ethan said reflectively.

"That about sums it up, Ethan. So why do we care about this story? We got nothing to work with."

"You may be right. We may be on a wild goose chase. But the victims are kids. Little kids. Isn't that enough to ignite our journalistic curiosity? Plus, I trust Lloyd and wanna hear what Patricia Highland has to say. I told Paul I'd update him when I got back, and unless Highland has some blockbuster proposal for us, I won't waste any more time on this."

"We're already wasting time, Ethan. Are you so desperate to get back into the field that you'll pursue anything that falls in your lap? That the real reason we're taking this meeting? So you can get away from the office? Away from Peter Sampson?"

He sighed and stared out the window, frustrated. Maybe Mindy was right. Maybe he was grasping at straws. Maybe he was more screwed up than he thought. He changed the subject.

"Is Lloyd joining us?"

"Meeting us in front of the DA's Office."

"And where are you?"

"In a cab two blocks away."

"Good. Be there in a few."

*****

Ten minutes later, Ethan pulled to the curb at One Hogan Place, paid the driver, and hopped out of the back of the taxi. The District Attorney's Office was located in a fourteen-story nondescript building, sandwiched between the federal courthouse and the Manhattan Detention Center, an outdated, overcrowded city lockup more commonly known as the *Tombs,* where suspects are detained prior to their court hearings. He stepped ankle-deep in cold, slushy water, soaking his shoes. He cursed out loud then picked his way through the unshoveled snow on the sidewalk, spotting Mindy and Lloyd standing at the top of a broad stone staircase leading up to the front door of the building.

"I see you did battle with the elements," Lloyd said jovially.

"Funny. Funny. Funny," Ethan said. He shook Lloyd's hand. "So what gives? I went through the documents. Mindy did some digging, but there doesn't seem to be a story beyond the murders."

"Have I ever steered you wrong, my friend?"

"Not yet."

"Well, don't jump the gun. Hear out Patricia, and then tell me what you think. Come. One of her assistants is meeting us at the elevator bank."

They pushed through the revolving door and arrived at a lobby security checkpoint where they were met by a young, slightly overweight police sergeant dressed head to foot in NYPD blue.

"What's your business here today?" he said sternly.

"A twelve o'clock meeting with Patricia Highland in the DA's office," Lloyd said. "She's expecting us."

The officer quickly searched a database in his computer.

"And you're Ms. Herman and Mr. Benson?" he said, staring at the two of them.

"From the Global Broadcasting System," Ethan said, nodding.

The guard picked up the phone, asked for Hilda, the receptionist, then listened as she confirmed the appointment.

"Sorry about that," he said. "Can't be too careful. Homeland Security just bumped us to an orange alert with all those terrorist bombings in Europe. Ms. Highland's up on the tenth floor. One of her assistants, a Mr. Newton, is waiting for you at the elevator bank."

They emptied their pockets and walked through an x-ray machine, then collected their things and proceeded into a crowded lobby where they were warmly greeted by an impeccably dressed man in his late twenties.

"ADA Randall Newton. I'm assisting Patricia Highland on the Child Sex Murders."

"Is that what you're calling this case?" Ethan said, shaking his hand.

"The girls were all raped before they were garroted and butchered and displayed like mannequins. The official cause of death, according to the medical examiner, is strangulation as I'm sure Lloyd told you, but the cops started using the *child sex* moniker after the third murder, and it kinda stuck." He motioned toward the elevators. "Highland's waiting for you."

They went up the elevator in silence, exiting on the tenth floor and walking down a long marble-floored hallway leading to a door stenciled in gold letters edged in matte black *Manhattan District Attorney's Office: Homicide Division.* Ethan followed Newton into a noisy bullpen with dozens of people sitting in long rows of cubicles, leafing through documents, talking on the telephone, and typing on computer keyboards.

"Looks busier than the last time I was here, when I was working the Pavel Feodor story," he said, watching a young paralegal carrying a heavy box of files into an empty conference room.

"Lots of murders in Manhattan," Newton said wryly. "Benson. Benson. I thought I recognized your name. Your wife works in white-collar crime. Down on the eighth floor. I met her last year when I was prosecuting a mob killing involving an investment banker who was laundering Columbian drug money. Pretty. Very smart. You as smart as your wife? You gonna solve this case for us? I highly doubt that, but I know you're gonna give it a try." He pointed down another long hallway stretching the length of the building and said sharply, "We're set up in the big conference room."

They continued at a brisk pace, Ethan leaning over and whispering into Lloyd's ear, "What's with that guy? He have a bug up his ass?"

"He's frustrated like everybody else on this case," Lloyd said, cupping his mouth with his hand, "and pissed that Highland has to reach out to you because she can't get the publicity or the money she needs to beef up her task force. Give him some time to get to know you. He'll come around. We all want the same thing. To catch this guy who's killing little girls."

Many of the attorneys stared as they made their way past a rarely used law library and into a huge wood-paneled room with thick carpeting and a long mahogany table covered with computers, printers, yellow pads, pencils, and stacks of file folders. Ethan felt the same chilly reception from the half-dozen people sitting around the table that he experienced parading through the bullpen—except from a distinguished-looking African American woman in her early forties with wise jet-black eyes, a short well-styled Afro speckled with streaks of gray, and creamy brown skin with no trace of wrinkles. She stood, straightened her blue Ferragamo suit, and walked straight over to Ethan, her slightly crooked body no more than five feet tall.

"You must be Ethan Benson," she said briskly, "and you Mindy Herman. I'm Patricia Highland. Welcome to the war room." She pulled out a chair for Ethan and motioned to Mindy, then introduced everybody in the room. "My staff at the DA's Office, and of course, Randall here, who I've asked to be your point person if we decide to work together."

She sat down at the head of the table—Ethan pulling his iPad out of his briefcase to take notes—and wasted no time getting to the point.

"We have three murders. Grizzly. No need to describe them. You've seen pictures of the girls. Questions?" She paused briefly and continued before Ethan could say a word. "We set up a task force after the second murder, a very small task force, indeed, with a handful of detectives from Special Victims and the Sixth Precinct in Manhattan where the bodies were found. The police commissioner tosses us a little extra money and manpower after each new killing—then cuts the resources when we don't come up with useful evidence or any significant leads. At the moment, we're dead in the water. That's where you come in, Mr. Benson." She stood and paced the room. "I need your help."

Ethan stopped typing and placed his iPad on the table. "Don't take this the wrong way. I'm disgusted by child killers as much as the next guy, but I'm a journalist. A producer. Not an investigator. I report on crimes that've gone through the system. I don't solve them."

"I think you're being modest," she said, leaning over the table, her tiny body looming larger than life. "Can I call you Ethan?"

He nodded silently.

"Okay. Let me explain. I've been watching your career ever since you and your anchorman, Peter Sampson, brought down the deputy mayor and my colleague, Nancy McGregor. You are his senior producer, right? Yes, you are," she continued, like a run-on sentence. "And then the two of you worked together last year on that serial killer case, if I know my facts, and I do know my facts." She paused briefly to catch her breath. "And *you*, Ethan, are the only reason the deputy mayor is in jail, and that the police found all those bodies Rufus Wellington buried on the grounds of his estate." Ethan began to respond, but she held up her hand. "Now I want you to help me, and generate all that publicity that surrounds every one of your stories."

"So you want me to help convince the police commissioner to give you more resources," Ethan said laconically.

She nodded.

"And more manpower."

She nodded again.

"So you can build a bigger task force."

"I knew you were a bright young man," she said, glancing at Randall Newton who was sitting quietly in the corner. "I need more people busting their asses, working the case. It's the only way we're gonna catch this guy, before he butchers another little girl. So what do you think?"

Ethan glanced at Mindy, who shook her head no, then traced a circle on the table with his finger, still indecisive, trying to frame a response.

"Well?"

"There's nothing more I'd like than to help you catch this guy," he said, "but I need a story, before I can commit and give you airtime. I need facts, evidence, suspects," Ethan said pointedly. "And at the moment, none of that exists. So I have nothing to pitch to Peter Sampson. And nothing to convince my boss, Paul Lang, that this story is worth pursuing. What can you give me, Ms. Highland? That I can use to convince them to commission a segment for *The Weekly Reporter.*"

"Total access to my investigation."

"What does that mean?"

"Just what it implies."

"I need specifics."

Patricia Highland stood and walked over to a coffee machine sitting on a side table. "Drink this stuff all day. It gives me the shakes but keeps me alert. Want a cup?"

Ethan and Mindy both nodded no.

"So where were we?" she said, sitting back down.

"Specifics," Mindy said.

"Right. Right. I'll give you access to everything the police are doing as they unravel the case. And I do mean everything—all the meetings, strategy sessions, undercover stings and operations, stakeouts, and even the busts, if and when we solve the case. Then I'll give you all the documents and let you bring your cameras into the court as I prosecute the killer and toss his sorry ass in jail."

"And we'll have an exclusive?" Ethan said.

"That's what I'm saying. No other news organization will be given *any* part of the inside investigation."

"And we can bring in our cameras from soup to nuts?"

"Each step of the way, as long as my detectives agree that you and your equipment don't pose a danger to my people or to my investigation or to you and your team."

"But that gives you an out, a way to bar us from anything you want if someone decides we're getting in the way," Mindy said, still skeptical.

"No, Ms. Herman. That won't happen. The lead detective, Gloria Alvarez, has already agreed to my terms and discussed it with her team. They're all on board, understand the risks, and want your help."

"But right now your investigation is at a dead end, right?" Mindy said. "And all you're offering is access to your investigation as you try to solve this case." She turned to Ethan. "Won't be enough to convince Paul to give us the green light. No way he's gonna commission this story."

"I wouldn't be so negative, young lady," Highland said, turning to Randall Newton. "Where are we on the murder book?"

"What's a murder book?" Ethan asked questioningly.

"It's the bible of the investigation," Lloyd said, interrupting. "Every document, every fact, every morsel of information the detectives amass on a case. It's a living and breathing catalogue that changes from day to day. It lays out the clues, the leads, the sources, the suspects, the experts. Everything the detectives do as they work to solve a crime. It's never given to the press."

"And you'll give me a copy?" Ethan said, intrigued.

"That's what I'm proposing."

"And there's something in that murder book that's gonna help you catch the killer?" he asked.

Patricia Highland folded her arms and peered across the table. "You're a tough customer, Mr. Benson. Read the book and tell me what you think. We may be lacking manpower, but there are many working theories—good ones—on who may have killed those girls. If you're as good an investigative reporter as I think you are, you'll see what I'm talking about."

"And there'll be no redactions in the book? Like in the police reports you gave me?"

"Some of the material in those police reports is sensitive, and since we hadn't yet talked about whether you'd be comin' on board, I thought it prudent to withhold that information from you. But now that I've met you, there'll be no redactions in the murder book, not a one."

Ethan tapped his fingers on the table. "When can I see it?"

"Randall, set up a meeting for Ethan with Gloria. Somewhere private. Away from the Special Victims Unit. And bring Ethan one of the books."

"There's more than one?" Ethan said.

"Many more," she said. "I'm gonna ask Detective Alvarez to give you an annotated copy with the most up-to-date information, some of the hard data, and status summaries at the beginning of each section, so you'll know exactly where we stand, or don't, in catching the killer."

"I thought you were giving us everything?"

"I will. Once you commit."

Highland turned to Lloyd Howard. "Can you join them and make the introductions?"

"I'll make time."

"Randall, you be there, too, to represent the DA's Office." She peered at Ethan through steely eyes. "What works for you?"

"I can do it tonight. Then I won't have to change my schedule with Peter Sampson or tell him I'm doing legwork on this project before I get my boss, Paul Lang, to commit to the story."

"I'll make it happen," Highland said. "Anything else you need before we adjourn?"

"Something concrete to tell Paul would be nice. So he gives me the money to do the research."

"Read the murder book, Mr. Benson, it's all in there," she said, pushing away from the table. "So I can count on you to produce a piece about my investigation and help me catch the killer?"

Ethan smiled. He liked the ADA and her no-nonsense style. "Can't answer that question quite yet."

"Didn't think you would, but don't take too much time. I want to work with you, but I need help from someone in the press I trust, and there are other producers at other networks who'll jump at getting the inside scoop on something like this." She stood and picked up a stack of documents. "You've got two days. No more. Then I pull the offer off the table."

CHAPTER 6

It was well after two o'clock when Ethan walked into Paul's conference room, all the senior management packed around the big oak table—the two other senior producers, Lenny Franklin and Joyce Cox, the editorial producer, Dirk Fulton, and Paul's assistant, Monica, standing in front of a large board, moving stories around in the schedule and adding new projects approved by the brain trust. Peter Sampson was sitting at one end of the table, Consuela taking notes on an iPad just behind him, Paul across the table doodling incessantly on a yellow pad.

"You're late," Paul said, not looking up from his scribblings. "What's your excuse this time?"

"Couldn't be helped. Just got back from a meeting at the District Attorney's Office."

"I thought Mindy was doing all the initial digging on your story. That's what we agreed to."

"She is, but I had to be there too."

Paul glared, exasperated. "Christ. Pull up a chair and sit down."

Ethan nodded contritely, signaling for James to come into the room. "I hope it's all right, Paul. I thought it might be helpful for James to see how the show makes programming decisions." The executive producer shrugged, and Ethan introduced his new assistant to everybody in the room, not mentioning that he was Paul's nephew. "What have I missed?"

"Catch up on your own time. I've got fifteen minutes before there's another damn budget meeting with the head of the network on the twenty-fifth floor. More cost cutting. The suits upstairs think we make widgets, not television. Soon there'll be nothing left to program the show, and I mean nothing. We'll have to get out the news on Twitter—like our illustrious president, Mr. Trump."

Ethan ignored his sarcasm and turned to Peter. "Have you updated Paul on your plate of stories?"

"He knows the status of everything we talked about, no thanks to you," he quipped abruptly. Peter Sampson, the lead anchor of *The Weekly Reporter,* was demanding, autocratic, and sometimes downright rude, playing the role of the anchor monster to perfection. He frowned and said, spitting bullets at Ethan, "And what the hell were you doing down at the District Attorney's Office? That was nowhere on my schedule, or was it, Consuela?"

"No, Mr. Sampson. Ethan never told me he'd be out of the office before the planning meeting."

"James? Why didn't you tell me Ethan was going to be late?"

James, in a panic, looked to Ethan for help.

"I didn't tell him either," Ethan said calmly. "After we finished blocking out your diet story with Elena, I had an hour and a half of free time before the meeting. I slipped out to see an assistant district attorney about the murder story I'm researching."

Peter swung around to Paul. "What murder story? I don't know anything about a murder story."

"Just came up, Peter. It's a low-priority item that Ethan and I talked about the other day." He stopped doodling and looked toward Ethan. "I thought you briefed Peter?"

"I needed something to brief him with. That's why I didn't tell him about the story. And the ADA handling the case insisted on seeing me. That's why I was out of the office," Ethan said firmly, hoping to ease the growing tension in the room.

"Who's the ADA?" Dirk Fulton interrupted. Fulton was the elder statesman on *The Weekly Reporter*, responsible for overseeing the editorial development of all stories produced for the broadcast.

"Patricia Highland," Ethan said.

"And what's the story about?"

"Haven't nailed down specifics yet."

"What does that mean?" Peter said furiously.

"Let me explain," Ethan said, keeping his cool. He then spent the next ten minutes filling in Peter and the rest of the senior management about the three dead girls, the task force, the status of the investigation, and what the ADA was proposing. "There's a psycho out there killing kids. Little kids," he said icily. "Nobody knows who they are. Where they came from. Or why they were tortured and brutally murdered." Ethan scanned the room. He had their full attention. "And the story's flying totally under the radar. There's been little to no press coverage—just a handful of stories in the papers and on television. And the ADA wants us to help her make this into front-page news—the case everybody and his damn brother is talking about."

"And how do we do that?" Paul said, doodling again on his yellow pad.

"ADA Highland will give us total and complete access to everything, and I mean everything the cops do to build their case. An exclusive. We'll have an inside look on just how the cops catch a killer."

"So we're talking a process piece," Fulton said. "That's been done before—maybe not on the scale the ADA is proposing. But how do we know they'll catch this guy?"

"We don't," Ethan said, not backing down. "But I think the story's worth pursuing."

"And why's that?" Paul said, growing more impatient.

"Because I've seen the crime scene photos," Ethan said, staring from Paul to Peter. "These are ritual killings—the girls are sexually abused, tortured the same way each time, before they're sadistically murdered, then displayed like grotesque artwork in a little kid's playground on the Hudson River. That alone makes this story worth doing."

"Okay, so there's a monster out there. But this story could take a lot of time and money with no payoff," said Joyce Cox, the senior producer responsible for getting the show on the air each week. "Months of work and the cops may never catch the killer. Than what do we have?"

Ethan ran his fingers through his hair and then said calmly, "A story that could be very big for the show. Access to a *major* police investigation—that means strategy sessions, ride-alongs as they look for evidence and pursue the killer, and ultimately arrest the guy. Nobody's ever shot anything like this before. You don't think our audience will be interested?"

"No," Peter said emphatically.

"I agree," said Lenny Franklin, the senior producer in charge of segment production. "If the cops don't catch the killer, we got nothing."

"What if I were to tell you the task force is calling the case the Child Sex Murders," Ethan said, seeing his story slipping away. "Think of the promotion possibilities."

"Makes no difference what they call it," Peter said. "We should not waste any more time on this. Paul?"

"What do you think, Dirk?"

"Peter's right. There's no story here."

"Lenny? Joyce?"

"Agreed," they both said at the same time.

Paul wheeled around to Monica, who was still standing at the storyboard. "Don't add it to Peter's list of projects, and Ethan, call the ADA, thank her, then move on."

"We're making a mistake," Ethan said, not ready to give up. "Patricia Highland's gonna give it to another network. It'll end up on *20/20* or *Dateline NBC* or *60 Minutes*."

"Don't care," Paul said firmly. "I'm killing the story and don't want you spending any more time working on it. And that's final, Ethan." He looked around the table. "Now unless there's any business that can't wait, I gotta head upstairs. Monica, get my budget proposal, and let's go see if we can wring enough money from the pencil pushers to keep our show afloat."

*****

Ethan slipped into his office, angry, disappointed, despondent, and stared at the Emmy Award he'd won for a story about political corruption in Washington, then plopped down in the brown leather chair behind his desk. *They're making a mistake, a big mistake. They wouldn't know a good story if it bit them on the ass,* he thought, wondering when he could sneak out to McGlades for a quick pop of Scotch. He checked the time—*too early, gotta wait a few more hours*—then buzzed James on the telephone.

"Call Mindy and tell her to come up."

"Right away."

Swinging around to his computer, he began typing a list of tasks to launch the story. Ten minutes later, Mindy walked through the door holding a cardboard tray and handed Ethan a black coffee.

Christ. That's not gonna do it. I need something stronger. Much stronger.

"So what happened with Paul?" she said, cutting to the chase.

"No go," Ethan said, turning back to the computer and typing another note.

"I told you he wouldn't buy the story. Should I call Patricia Highland and tell her we're passing?" Mindy said, sitting in a swivel chair in front of Ethan's desk.

"No. I don't care what Paul thinks. These are kids. Jane Does. Snuffed out. And at the moment, nobody but a handful of cops and a couple of prosecutors wanna find out who murdered them."

"But Paul doesn't want to do the story?"

"But I do—on my own time. I need to know who's butchering these kids."

"Jeez, Ethan, you have a death wish?" Mindy said sternly. "What about Peter? Your workload here at the office? When will you have time?"

"At night. After I leave the office," Ethan said, not missing a beat.

"But Sarah? Luke?"

"I'm not giving up this story. Not till we know more about it."

Mindy started to protest again, but Ethan held up his hand, then stood and walked over to the door. "James, come in for a minute." He waited for his assistant to sit in a chair next to Mindy then closed the door. "Can I trust you, James?" Ethan said, locking eyes.

James squirmed uneasily. "Not sure what you mean, Mr. Benson?"

"It's Ethan. Not Mr. Benson."

"Sorry. I keep forgetting."

"Don't." Ethan tried to calm down. He could taste a Scotch. "Look, I don't mean to jump down your throat. I wasn't expecting your uncle, Paul, our boss, to react the way he did to my story. So let me ask you bluntly. Can you be discreet about my comings and goings during the day."

"If that's what you want."

"And you won't tell your uncle if I ask you to keep something quiet?"

He shook his head.

"Or Peter?"

"I guess I won't tell him either."

"Good," Ethan said, relieved. "But let me warn you, if I find out you're going behind my back to either one of them, you'll be out of here faster than you can blink. Understood?"

"Okay," James said quietly.

Ethan leaned back in his chair. "Call the ADA, Mindy, and set up the meeting with the lead detective, Gloria Alvarez, just as we planned. Let's say ten o'clock tonight. Tell her we'll meet anywhere Alvarez wants. And make sure she brings the murder book. I need to read it."

"This isn't smart, Ethan."

"Just do it. And make sure Lloyd knows when and where."

"But—"

"Set up the meeting and then back off," Ethan said, suddenly exhausted. "I don't want you working on this until after I iron out the loose ends and get Paul and Peter to agree the story's worth pursuing." He shifted his gaze to James. "So you want to learn the business from the bottom up?"

"Yes, Mr. Benson—*Ethan*."

"Excellent. I want you to come with me tonight. I may need your help the next couple of days until I can square things with Paul. And, Mindy, go make the call right now. Lemme know Alvarez is good to go."

*****

It was a few minutes before ten when Ethan and James descended the stone staircase into the underground food court at Grand Central Station. Restored to its original grandeur in the 1990s, the beautiful marble floors were beginning to crack and were covered with a thick layer of grime. The elaborately domed ceiling was peeling and rust-stained, and an army of buckets were strategically placed to capture torrents of melting snow leaking through the cracks in the walls.

"What happened to this place?" James said. "I thought it was landmarked by the city."

"It was, but there's not enough money for maintenance. Like there's not enough money to catch our killer."

"Where we meeting?" he said, peering at a homeless man spreading cardboard on the floor and staking out territory to curl up for the night.

"Across the concourse. At *Juniors*."

"What's that?"

"Not from New York?"

"Des Moines, Iowa."

"Serves the best cheesecake in the city. It's an experience."

They weaved across the floor, past a handful of commuters waiting for trains, and were stopped by a panhandler dressed in layers of filthy clothing who was shilling for a handout. Ethan gave him a dollar and waved him away. Then he hit on James, before giving up to work someone else. Most of the restaurants were empty and getting ready to close, and when they reached *Juniors* and didn't see Lloyd—or anyone else for that matter—Ethan made a beeline to a bar that was still serving and ordered a Scotch.

"Want one," he said, downing the shot.

"Don't drink."

"You know, Winston Churchill once said, 'The water was not fit to drink and to make it palatable we had to add whiskey. By diligent effort, I learned to like it.' And that, young man, is exactly my philosophy," he said jokingly. "Sure you don't want a taste?"

"Not tonight, Ethan."

"Suit yourself," he said, ordering a second.

He hoisted the Scotch and wiped his mouth on the back of his hand. "Much better. Now I can think." Then he spotted Lloyd descending the stone staircase with Randall Newton and a small, stocky woman dragging a heavy briefcase.

"Come, they're here." He paid for the drinks and walked over to *Juniors.* "Evenin', Lloyd. This is my new assistant, James Lapidus."

Lloyd nodded and shook James's hand then said to Ethan, "This is Gloria Alvarez, lead detective on the Child Sex Murders case, and you already know Randall from the District Attorney's Office."

"He ain't supposed to be here, *no*?" Alvarez said curtly, pointing to James. "I thought it was just you tonight, Benson?"

"Got a lot of ground to cover," Ethan said, looking directly at the detective. "And a short deadline with Patricia Highland. I need James to help me make the decision on whether we should commit to the story."

"Well, I hope you take a pass. I ain't buyin' in to the ADA's plan to make you a *honorary* member of the team. No way that works for me. No way."

"Come on, Gloria, chill out," Randall said forcefully. "Patricia is committed to the idea. So if Ethan agrees, we work with him."

"Still not buyin' it."

A tall, heavyset man with a pencil-thin mustache and bushy sideburns walked over and pecked a quick kiss on the detective's cheek. "All set for you guys in the back."

"*Mi amigo especial*, Fernando, is manager here, *si?* He got special room where we talk in private."

They followed him through the restaurant, across a small kitchen where three men in dirty white uniforms were standing and smoking cigarettes, and into a storage room stacked with paper products and industrial cleaners. A round table covered with trays of silverware was sitting in the middle of the floor with four folding chairs neatly spaced around it. A single exposed lightbulb dangled from a wire cord suspended from the ceiling.

"*Por favor,* Ferdie, bring us pot of coffee," Alvarez said, setting the briefcase on the floor next to her chair.

"And maybe a strawberry cheesecake for my assistant, the out-of-towner, who's never had the pleasure of tasting what's a true New York City delicacy," Ethan said, winking at James.

"*Vamoose, moo cha cha,* I gotta work with these guys." Then she bored in on Ethan. "So, Benson, what do you wanna know about my investigation?"

Ethan tried to get a reading on the detective. She wasn't at all what he'd expected. She was tough on the outside—confident, aggressive, forceful—but then, gentle and feminine with her boyfriend. Sitting ramrod straight, she had a gold shield clipped to her belt and a Sig Sauer P226 handgun shoulder holstered under a wrinkled blue polyester suit jacket. Everything about her said cop.

"Let's start with manpower," Ethan said, turning to James. "Take notes so we can put together a production memo."

"Got maybe a dozen people working full-time, *sí*? *A* couple of patrol units, a handful of undercover *policia* walking the neighborhood around James and West Streets where we find bodies, and a big-time profiler from *FBI*. So this is a kinda *multijurisdictional* investigation," she said, emphasizing each word in her singsong Spanish accent. "Plus we got computer guys, lab guys, and a couple of CSIs who come and go with each murder. Not enough to catch this *asesino*. That's why you here, Mr. *Journalist-Investigator*. To help me do my job, *sí*?"

Ethan leaned back in his chair, ignoring her sarcasm, as Fernando walked back into the room and placed a tray on the table with the cheesecake and coffee. "Help yourself," he said, before heading to the door. "Let me know if you need anything else, Gloria."

"Thanks, *guapo*," she said, turning to Ethan, her mood tough again. "What else you wanna know, Benson?"

"Describe the crime scene for me."

"The victims were found on Pier 51 along Hudson River Park. It's a small playground for children. Swings, slides, sprinklers in the summertime. That kinda shit. It closes at dark and is blocked from passing cars on West Street by a row of big trees and a small maintenance building. The perfect place to dump body at night, *no*? 'Cause nobody can see what you're doin'."

"And the pier falls under the jurisdiction of the Sixth Precinct?"

"You've done your homework, Benson," Alvarez said briskly.

"So why are you running the investigation. You're out of Special Victims. That's way up in Harlem, right?"

Alvarez poured herself a cup of coffee. "Because I am senior detective out of SVU and these are worst kind of killings. *La muchacha.* Abused. Raped. How you say it. *Violated.* After third murder like first two, we had *epidemic*. So the district attorney pull investigation from the Sixth and give it to me to catch killer. SVU handles all murders of *little kids*. So now I in charge, *si?*"

Ethan leaned back in his chair, knowing he was walking a tightrope with the detective. Choosing his words carefully, he said, "And you don't know who the kids are?"

She shook her head. "No way. No *physical evidence*. No *eyewitnesses*. No way to trace them. But they all Latina. Maybe that means somethin'. Maybe not."

"You getting all this?" Ethan said, turning to James.

James nodded and continued scribbling.

"Who's the lead detective out of the Sixth Precinct?"

"A guy named Henry Dinkus."

"And he reports to you?"

"They all report to me."

"And you report to Patricia," Randall Newton said testily.

"That's the chain of command," Alvarez said, glaring at ADA Newton.

A little tension between the two of them? Ethan thought. *What's that all about?* Then he said, "And when can I meet Dinkus?"

Alvarez cracked a half smile. "One step at time, Benson." She pulled the murder book from her briefcase and handed it to Ethan. It was at least four inches thick. Her faced hardened again. "This is special book Ms. Highland told me to give you. Took me all day to collect evidence and get ready. Waste of time."

"Cut the crap, Gloria. This is important," Newton said aggressively, turning to Ethan. "As soon as you go through the book and give us a decision, we'll see about setting something up with Dinkus. Of course, if you don't do the story, then there's no reason for a meet and greet."

Ethan thumbed through the murder book. "Looks like heavy reading. How many more of these are there?"

"Four and we working on fifth—all data from investigation," Alvarez said obstinately.

"I was told there wasn't much evidence?" Ethan said, surprised.

"Lots of evidence," she said, "just no leads, no suspect, *si*? That's why I stuck babysitting you."

"Enough. Work with Benson, Gloria," Newton said. "Those are your marching orders."

Ethan hefted the book. "It's gonna take time to go through this."

"You've got forty-eight hours," Newton said. "Check that. You've already used up ten. So that gives you thirty-eight more to decide. Then we take back the book and give the story to *60 Minutes*. They're next up on the hit parade."

Ethan nodded and tucked the murder book into his briefcase, stood, and headed for the door, just as James dug his fork into the cheesecake.

"No more time for that, James, let's go."

*****

Ethan walked into McGlades and headed straight to the bar, Lloyd and James pulling up stools on either side of him. It was after midnight, and only a handful of regulars were still drinking and watching *SportsCenter* on a big plasma TV hanging over the rows of liquor bottles.

"Back again, Ethan?" Moe said, wiping the counter with a dish towel. "Didn't expect to see you after the other night. The missus sounded pretty pissed when I told her, how should I put this, that you were totally shit-faced."

Ethan ignored him. "Pour me a Black Label, and give my friends whatever they want."

"Just one, no more," the bartender said, glancing at Lloyd. "Your pleasure?"

"Draft of Bud."

"And I'll have a bottle of Becks," James said.

"You legal?"

"He's my assistant. I'll vouch for him."

Moe nodded. Then he turned to get their drinks.

"So what do you think, Lloyd?" Ethan said, plunking the murder book on the bar. "Should I do the story?"

"Bet your ass you should do it."

"I don't know. Alvarez wasn't all too happy she was giving me her evidence. And Newton made that crack this morning before our meeting." He gulped his drink. "Man, I'm going around Paul just doing the digging. Maybe I should see the handwriting on the wall. Maybe I should just let it go."

"That doesn't sound like you, Ethan."

"I know. I know. I know."

"Read the murder book and then make a decision."

Ethan belted down the rest of his Scotch and flipped open the book. "There's gotta be something concrete in here I can use to convince Paul and Peter. Otherwise, I may never change their minds about the story."

"Give me a piece of the book," Lloyd said. "I know what to look for, and I won't charge you unless we move forward."

"I wanna help too," James said.

"Think you're ready?"

"I, I, I—"

"You're ready." Ethan pulled out the first section—a short introductory letter, personnel bios, and a table of contents with a list of primary documents—and handed it to James. Then he gave Lloyd the section from the Special Victims Unit and took the materials from the Sixth Precinct for himself.

"My first meeting with Peter isn't until nine thirty tomorrow, so let's regroup here at eight. The daytime bartender serves eggs and coffee. So we'll do breakfast. That gives us seven hours to find something in all this stuff to sink our teeth into." He dropped the murder book into his briefcase and wondered if Sarah would be awake when he got home—worried they'd argue again about his drinking—then dismissed his fears as ludicrous. *She'll be asleep. Won't have any idea I've been drinking.* Then he waved to the bartender. "One more Scotch to top off the night. A double."

"You gotta lay off that stuff, Ethan," Lloyd said, putting his hand on Ethan's shoulder. "You're gonna kill yourself."

"Just this last one."

"Do you wanna do this story or not? Because if you don't stop drinking, you ain't gonna have a choice. You smelled like a brewery tonight, and everybody knew you were loaded. There's no way Patricia Highland is gonna hand you the story if she thinks you're a drunk. Ain't gonna happen."

CHAPTER 7

It was 2:00 a.m., and he was waiting for a phone call in the back of an ancient yellow Ford Econoline Van. From the outside it looked like any old van—the front end dented and in dire need of a paint job, the antenna bent and rusted, the passenger window cracked. The roof was covered in six inches of snow and the sides caked with blotches of sand and salt from the partially cleared streets. But on the inside, well, that was a different story. It was shiny and clean and custom built as a torture chamber—with polished stainless steel, no side or rear windows, the floor, ceiling, and walls all lined with a thick layer of the best soundproofing money could buy. There was a high-end surgical table anchored to the support beams under the carriage, an RLM examination light on the ceiling, and boxes of anesthetics, syringes, and bandages neatly tucked into each corner. He was perched in a small chair, scooting back and forth across the floor on rubber rollers as he examined his tools of death sheathed in a long leather case lined with red felt—*Karl Storz* surgical knives, *Balfour* abdominal retractors, a half-dozen *V. Mueller* surgery scissors, *Weck* clamps and curettes, *Pilling* flexible graspers, and a *Satterlee* six-inch bone saw with a set of newly purchased blades.

He ran his hand over each instrument.

Lovingly.

Then gently arranged them in their proper place.

Closed the case.

And locked it in a custom-built cabinet under the surgical table.

He stood and checked the time, then slipped to the front of the van and sat in the passenger seat, opening the glove compartment and grabbing a worn leather notebook filled with pictures of young adolescent girls—his girls, his victims, his conquests. Slowly, he thumbed through each photo in anticipation—his mouth watering, beads of sweat forming on his brow, his loins aching.

His name was Quay Chaoxiang—but everybody called him the Butcher. Chinese by birth, he was slight in stature, five feet four and maybe a hundred and fifty pounds, with jet-black hair set in a long braid, a wispy goatee, and plucked eyebrows. He had piercings above both eyes, a diamond stud in his left nostril, and an earring in the shape of a cross hanging from his left ear. He was covered in tattoos, but it was his eyes that were truly frightening—two pools of hate, two beacons of a cold-blooded killer, a nightmare waiting to happen.

Glancing at the pictures one last time, he carefully closed the notebook and placed it back in the glove compartment. Then he lit a joint the size of a cigar and slowly inhaled, blowing the smoke out his nose, feeling the power, the euphoria of the high.

He checked his watch.

Two fifteen.

Not too much longer.

He closed his eyes, took another hit on his joint, and waited.

Five minutes later, his cell phone buzzed, and he answered the burner immediately.

"You set?" a man said, his tone hesitant on the other end of the phone.

"Always ready for you, my friend," the Butcher said, his voice smooth and melodic with a hint of a Mandarin accent.

"You high?"

"Of course. The weed gives me power, strength, and stealth."

"Can you take the package?" the man said urgently.

"Have I ever let you down?" His voice was now cold and hard.

"Must be done right away."

The Butcher smiled, but didn't answer.

"Where are you?"

He looked out the window and watched a lone police car, lights flashing but no siren, as it cruised west on Houston Street. "Might be better if you didn't know." He took another drag on his joint. "Where's the pickup?"

"The usual place," the man said, sounding stressed.

The Butcher took one last hit and tossed the joint out the window. "Why the rush?"

"Just talked to my contact in Argentina. A new shipment is on the way. Should be here by the end of the week. So I need to get rid of this one. No use to me anymore, a wilted flower. No more sweet scent of jasmine."

"Name?" The Butcher always liked to know who he was terminating.

"Lotus."

"Chinese, not South American?"

"My clients have varied tastes."

"When can you drop it off?"

"Maybe forty-five minutes," the man said. "Lots of snow and ice. My associate needs to be careful. Many cops roaming the roads."

"Does he have my money?"

"All twenty thousand in small bills, like always, Mr. Quay."

The Butcher smiled and hung up, then opened the door and climbed out of the van. *Time for a new cell phone,* he thought. *Don't wanna give some dumbass cop an easy target to nail me.* He dropped the burner on the icy pavement and crushed it with the heel of his combat boot, picked up the pieces, and tossed them into a dumpster. He glanced up and down the street, deserted, except for a stray dog gnawing on a bag of garbage, and climbed back into his van, turned on the engine, lit another joint, and slowly eased away from the curb.

He headed north on Avenue A, past East Sixth, East Seventh, and East Eighth Street, the roadway narrow, treacherous, barely drivable through the unplowed snow and angled cars buried in snowbanks. He passed a young couple making out in a doorway, a junkie—arms wrapped around his tattered overcoat trying to stay warm—and a hooker working a corner looking for a trick.

"Not tonight," he said, laughing out loud. "Too cold to fuck an ugly, old bitch like you."

He hung a right on East Fourteenth, still driving under the speed limit, and rolled by Avenue B and Avenue C, the tenements older, more decrepit. There was a small gang of Latino tough guys braving the cold, mist pouring out of their mouths, eyeing his van with contempt as he slowly cruised by. He rolled down the window and shot them the finger then sneered malevolently. Something about him was threatening, sinister, evil, and they scattered in every direction all at once.

He continued driving, stopping at a red light on Avenue D. Snowflakes began floating onto his windshield, so he put on the wipers and turned up the heat. Checking again for a cop car, he waited for the light to turn green and made a right, cruising slowly down the lifeless street, through mounds of snow and ice the snowplows had missed. When he got to PS 34, the Franklin Delano Roosevelt School on Twelfth Street, he pulled over and stopped next to a fire hydrant. He peered out the window. No cars cruising. Nobody hanging on the street corners. No lights illuminating the adjacent tenements. He smiled broadly to himself. The neighborhood was desolate. A ghost town. Perfect for his plan.

He pulled away from the curb and drove one more block, cutting his lights and coasting into an alley between Avenue D and Szold Place, a cobblestone passageway separating the elementary school from the Dry Dock Playground. The street lights were all smashed, except for one casting an ominous shadow through the trees lining the park. Icicles as big as stalactites hung like sharp teeth from the swings, the slides, and the merry-go-round—the playground looking more like a house of horrors than a wonderland for small kids and their parents.

The Butcher killed the engine, flicked the joint out the window, and waited.

It didn't take long.

Ten minutes and a car pulled into the alley from Szold Street and stopped, flashing its headlights three quick times. He fired up the engine, checked the rearview mirror, then pulled forward without his lights until he was ten feet from the car—a black Cadillac Escalade. He turned off the engine and sat another five minutes in the shadows. When he was sure they were alone, he slipped out of his van and walked over to the Escalade. The driver's door swung open, and a giant of a man, six feet eight and three hundred pounds, slowly climbed out. His name was Bingwen Ho, and his face was covered in scar tissue, his left eye covered with a black patch, his yellow skin mottled a pasty shade of gray.

"Ah, so we meet again, my ugly friend," the Butcher said icily. "Nice ride. Looks like a pimpmobile."

Bingwen shifted from one foot to the next, but didn't answer.

"Cat got your tongue," he said tauntingly. "You scared? Couldn't possibly be scared of little old me."

"Shut the fuck up, Chaoxiang. Just get the package, but stay away from me."

For kicks, the Butcher made a feint in his direction, and the big man stumbled back.

"Damn right, I'm scared. I know what you do to these girls."

The Butcher laughed. "Go get our sweet little pussy yourself, and put her into the back of my van. Quick! I need to finish before the sun comes up."

He stared at Bingwen.

And waited silently.

The big man circled the front of his SUV, staying as far away from the Butcher as possible, clicked open the hatchback with his key fob, and grabbed a small burlap bag that seemed to weigh almost nothing. He hoisted the package over his massive shoulder and quickly headed to the Butcher's van, once again, taking a wide berth around him.

"Tiny little thing," the Butcher said, his eyes beaming in anticipation.

"A waif. No tits. Only eleven."

"Ah, very, very young, a mere child. Should be loads of fun. Hee. Hee. Loads of fun. Can't wait to get started," he said, his face dark and foreboding.

"Crazy motherfucker," Bingwen said, never taking his eyes off the Butcher as he opened the back door and stared in horror at all the gleaming medical equipment. "This where you do it?"

"Yes, indeed, my chamber of horrors, and all the little girls love it."

"Don't start until I'm gone," Bingwen said, tossing the sack into the van, bouncing the girl off the surgical table and onto the floor. "All yours, asshole. Call the boss and let him know when it's done." Then he got in his car, fired up the engine, and stomped on the gas, his wheels spinning in the snow as he sped down the alley, turned left on Szold Place, and tore off toward Houston Street.

The Butcher watched until he disappeared, then walked to the back of his van and pawed the young girl—still hidden in the burlap bag. She tried to wiggle away as his fingers probed her body, caressing the nipples on her flat chest, moving down to her stomach, and then between her legs. He instantly grew hard.

"Ah, my pretty, sweet Lotus. Time to play with your master."

Then he pulled off the burlap bag, the girl's naked body shivering in the cold, strapped her to the surgical table, and clamped down on her throat with his coarse hands. She tried to scream, gasping for air as he climbed on top of her and thrust a six-inch surgical knife into her stomach.

Her blood sprayed the inside of the van.

And the Butcher shrieked like a banshee.

His madness echoing through the silence of the night.

CHAPTER 8

Kicking the snow off his shoes, Ethan opened the door to his apartment and quietly eased into the foyer. It was 1:00 a.m., and he was just getting home from McGlades where he'd continued drinking long after his meeting with Lloyd and James had ended. Making his way to the kitchen, he brewed a pot of coffee and tiptoed down the center hallway, hoping he wouldn't wake Sarah, hoping to avoid a scene. He peeked into Luke's bedroom, his son fast asleep, the covers pulled to his chin, Holly on the floor next to the bed. Quietly, he made his way to his study, pushed open the door, and flipped on the overhead lights. Sarah was sitting at his desk, her eyes moist, her face streaked with dry tears.

"I waited up for you, Ethan. Where were you?" Her voice was cold, distant, accusatory.

He stammered, but didn't answer.

"McGlades?"

He remained silent, his eyes avoiding her acid stare.

"Tell me."

He stared at the floor.

"Christ, Ethan, what's wrong with you? You're damn stinking *drunk*."

"Lemme explain."

"Too late."

"But, Sarah—"

"Don't Sarah me. You're a mess. A total *mess*. And look at this place. It's a pigsty. A *fucking* pigsty. Cigarette butts in the ashtrays, dirty glasses, empty bottles of Scotch on the floor. Don't you care at all? I won't let Luke come in here anymore. I won't. I don't want him to see how you're falling apart." She swept her hand across his desk, knocking all his documents to the floor. "How much did you drink tonight?"

"Well—"

"How much?" she said, raising her voice. "I wanna know."

"Babe, what can I say? I just had a few—"

"Liar. You *fucking* liar. You're hopeless, Ethan, hopeless. You won't even admit it to yourself."

"But, babe—"

"No more. You goddamn *fucking* drunk." She stood, furious, and headed to the door, Ethan reaching out, trying to stop her. "Don't you dare touch me," she said coldly. "You disgust me. *Disgust me.* Just keep hiding from yourself in your damn Scotch and forget about me and Luke."

"Sarah, please—"

But she dismissed him with a wave of her hand and stormed out of the room.

Ethan sunk to the floor, surrounded by documents, and began slowly sweeping them into piles. *What should I do? What should I do? What should I do? I'm losing her.* Then he stood, dismayed by his own insensitivity, and slowly made his way down to their bedroom. Sarah was under the covers, crying softly, the room in utter darkness, a thin sliver of light streaming in from the hallway.

"Sarah," he said softly, "let me explain."

He waited, but she only sobbed into her pillow.

"Sarah, listen to me—"

"It's too late, Ethan. Go back to your story. I don't want to talk to you anymore. I already know what I'm gonna do."

"What does that mean?"

"Go away. And leave me alone."

Crestfallen, Ethan turned and headed back to his study, locking on to an unopened bottle of Black Label sitting on the corner of his desk. He grabbed a dirty glass, wiped it on his shirt, then sighed deeply, thought about Sarah, and walked the glass and the bottle back to the wet bar. *I gotta stop. Right now. Before it's too late.* Shaking uncontrollably, he plopped down at his desk and grabbed the annotated murder book from his briefcase. *Bury yourself in your story, Ethan. Then climb into bed and hold Sarah. She'll understand. She's got to.* He poured a cup of black coffee and stripped the book, carefully organizing the documents by topics, clipping the stacks of paperwork with butterfly clamps, and cataloguing each entry on his laptop.

As he worked, Sarah slowly receded into the back of his mind.

There was a lengthy summary, a complete set of crime scene photos, dozens of police reports without redactions, and all the evidence collected by detectives working under Henry Dinkus at the Sixth Precinct. How was he ever going to get through all five books of documents if they were packed with materials like this one? Christ, he'd need an army of helpers. He sipped his coffee and eyeballed each pile—twenty in all—and picked up the one labeled *Property Reports*, the thirty-six pages stamped with the logo of the New York City Police Department.

He placed the packet in front of him. It contained a list of items found at Pier 51 around the bodies of the murdered girls, each page labeled with the name of the victim—Jane Doe 1, 2, and 3—dated, and signed by the different detectives who'd worked on the document. Ethan scanned through the pages, roughly an equal number for all three victims—every piece of physical evidence collected and analyzed by crime scene investigators. There were candy wrappers, cigarette butts, discarded paper cups, soda bottles, even a torn suitcase stuffed in a garbage can. Then he spent an hour carefully studying each line item—searching for any shred of evidence he could use to convince Paul the story was worth pursuing. But in the end, there was nothing, except for one item found at the third murder and listed on page 33—a brand-new Karl Storz No. 6 surgical knife. Grabbing a cigarette, he highlighted his discovery with a yellow sharpie and marked the page with a Post-it, then searched through the rest of the documents on his desk until he found Henry Dinkus's *Overview* and read the ten pages until he got to his summary:

> *The CSI concentrated on the fifty feet around the bodies searching for evidence left by the killer. No DNA, fibers, hairs, fingerprints, saliva, blood, semen, or other materials were found linking the girls to a suspect. The killer was meticulous, obsessive, and possibly trained in the art of forensics.*

So the killer had removed every trace that could lead to his identity or link him to the murders. He was smart, cunning, and knew exactly what he was doing—a sadistic hit man who took pleasure torturing his victims before killing them. After underlining the passage, he took a long drag on his cigarette and scanned the rest of the summary, looking for any mention of the surgical knife. But there was nothing. Hmm. Weren't there fresh lacerations on the victims? He rummaged through his briefcase and found the autopsy photos he'd been given by the ADA. He spread the photos on his desk until he found a close-up of Jane Doe number three's left arm. It clearly showed a row of fresh slash marks each about an inch long. Then he grabbed the police report written by Detective Dinkus and scanned through it. No mention of the surgical knife in there either. An omission? Maybe. But maybe not. He peered at the hundreds of documents neatly stacked on his desk. Shit. Another police report mentioning the Karl Storz surgical knife could be sitting in any one of the piles. It would take days to find it. Time he didn't have. Maybe the story was just too big to investigate while he carried out his other responsibilities as Peter Sampson's senior producer.

He rubbed his eyes and stared at the bottle of Black Label.

A taste would calm him.

Motivate him.

No.

No more tonight.

He'd promised himself he'd stay clean for Sarah.

He rubbed his temples, his body wasted by drink, and decided to call it a night, see if Sarah was still awake so he could bare his soul, plead for forgiveness, try to make it right. He was about to head to the bedroom when his iPhone pinged. What now? He peered down at his watch. Four o'clock. Then at the LCD screen. The DA's Office.

"Ethan, it's me, Randall Newton. Did I wake you?"

"No. I was going over the case documents from the murder book. What's goin' on?"

"There's been another murder."

Ethan sat down and lit a cigarette. "When?"

"A little while ago. A patrol car just found the body."

"Same place? Pier 51?"

"A different location."

"You're kidding. Where?"

"Can't tell you at the moment. You haven't committed to the story."

"Sure it's the same killer?"

"Same staging. Same mutilation of the body. Same killer," he said, harried. "Look, Patricia Highland's on her way to the crime scene, and she'd like to pick you up at your apartment if you want to go. Ever been to a crime scene?"

"Only after the fact."

"Game?"

"Sure."

"Ten minutes in front of your building. All hell's breaking loose. Need to put a lid on the chaos."

Ethan clicked off the phone and opened the top drawer of his desk, shuffling through discarded documents, until he found his Canon VIXIA HF G20 digital camera. Shoving it into his briefcase, he headed to the bedroom to tell Sarah he was leaving, that there'd been another murder, but she was facing the window, her back to the door. *Is she awake?* He stood motionless for a long moment and decided to say nothing, to wait until he got home when there'd be more time, then silently walked into the foyer, grabbed his overcoat from the closet, and left the apartment.

*****

You could hear a pin drop, the silence so profound, as Ethan made his way through the empty lobby and onto the street. The temperature had fallen into the midtwenties, leaving a thin layer of ice crusting the snowpack, and fresh icicles hanging from the awning in front of his building. Ethan pulled a woolen cap over his ears and hurried to the nondescript blue Crown Victoria idling at the curb. Patricia Highland was sitting quietly, typing on a laptop computer, a cell phone resting in the crook of her neck. Her face was drawn, sullen, unreadable.

"Keep them a couple of blocks away from the crime scene," she said. "And post cops along the barricades so they don't try to sneak in. I don't want them trudging over the crime scene. I'll do a press conference later today and release whatever information about the murder we decide will help the investigation. Do you understand?" There was a short pause. "That's my plan. Until then, we need to keep this under wraps." She clicked off the phone and turned to Ethan, who had slipped into the back seat next to her.

"That was Randall Newton. Word leaked out that a little kid's been murdered and left naked in a city park. Every news organization including your affiliate, WGBS, has set up shop at the crime scene. It's an absolute cluster-fuck." She flashed Ethan a quick smile. "My case is about to get a lot of press coverage. Maybe I won't need you after all."

"Then why am I here?"

She turned dead serious. "Because I'll get a day or two than nothing. I need you to keep the story alive. So it doesn't fade from the headline and become old news—like the other three murders. Here, this is for you." She handed him a Styrofoam cup filled with black coffee. "Have you gone through the murder book?"

Ethan took a sip. It warmed his insides. "Only got it a few hours ago," he said, staring out the window at the near-deserted streets, the Crown Victoria making a right onto Ninety-Sixth Street—lights flashing, sirens blaring, running traffic lights as it made its way to the entrance ramp of the FDR Drive.

"Interesting?"

"Not sure," he said. "I need to keep reading, before I take another crack at convincing my boss to put the story into production. Maybe things will change after I see the new crime scene."

"That's my plan. To keep sucking you in," Highland said, the Crown Victoria pulling onto the highway heading south and crossing into the left lane—the driver, a plainclothes detective, pushing the car to ninety as he dodged a handful of yellow cabs and avoided patches of black ice. "How much longer," she continued, checking her watch. "Sun's comin' up soon. Need to process the murder and get the body to the morgue before rush hour."

"Fifteen minutes," the detective said, cranking the unmarked car to a hundred.

"Where we going?" Ethan said. "Randall Newton wouldn't tell me."

"I told him I'd tell you when you were in the car. The Dry Dock Playground. Just off Tenth Street and Avenue D."

"That's where the killer left the body? Another playground?"

"Right out in the open. Sitting in another fucking chair. In front of the swings, for all the world to see."

"And you're positive it's the same killer?"

"No question. Only difference from the other Child Sex Murders is where the bastard left the body."

The Crown Victoria slowed, exited the highway at Houston Street, and started weaving through back roads on the Lower East Side. When they got to Avenue D, they hung a sharp right and headed north, passing liquor stores, pawnshops, and one bodega after another. An occasional junker blocked their way, slowing progress, until they maneuvered around it. As they approached Eighth Street, the Crown Victoria decelerated then stopped at a police checkpoint, two patrol cars angled on either side of a blue barricade forcing traffic to detour around the crime scene. A uniformed cop wearing thick gloves and earmuffs walked over, recognized the ADA sitting in the back seat, and waved them through. They cruised another two blocks to Tenth Street, passing a half-dozen patrol cars and dozens of cops, before making a left into a narrow alley with two sets of tire tracks embedded in the snow.

"That's it?" he said, pointing. "The Dry Dock Playground?"

Highland nodded and rolled down her window as Randall Newton approached the car. "Anybody been in there yet?"

"Just the patrolman who noticed the tracks and found the body. Been waiting for you before sending a team in to process the murder scene."

"Where's the girl?"

"Blocked by the trees and the merry-go-round."

"Was the playground locked?"

"He cut the padlock like at Pier 51."

"Guy's taunting us," she said as she put on snow boots before getting out of the car. "And where'd you set up the press?"

"We've got the newspapers and a whole line of TV remote trucks a quarter of a mile away, up at Fourteenth and Avenue D. All the streets leading up to the playground are blocked. No way anyone can get to the crime scene."

"What about the tire tracks?" she said.

"Two sets. The CSI will make molds," Newton said, "then we'll figure out what kind of cars were here."

"And what are you doing about the people hanging out of the windows and shooting video on their smartphones?" Ethan said, pointing to a low-income housing project across the street.

"Nothing we can do about that," Newton said curtly.

"Are you canvassing for eyewitnesses?" Ethan said. "Maybe somebody saw the killer, and you can catch a break in the case."

"Got plainclothes checking every building, knocking on every door, questioning every tenant," Newton said, ignoring Ethan and turning to ADA Highland. "You'll have the videos and any written statements on your desk as soon as I get them, but I'm not expecting much. They all hate us down here."

The ADA frowned. "Pull the security cameras. Maybe we'll get lucky, and there'll be an image of the killer." She gestured to Ethan. "Give him a visitor's pass so he can roam around the crime scene freely without anybody questioning what he's doing."

Newton rummaged through a briefcase, pulled out a plastic sleeve dangling from a chain, and handed it to Ethan. It said "Official Police Business" in big black letters superimposed over the logo of the New York City Police Department—and it was signed by the commissioner, Jordan Langley.

Ethan draped the pass around his neck. "I'd like to record this."

Highland looked at his camera, then up to Ethan. "No problem, as long as you don't broadcast anything you shoot tonight. I want publicity, but I don't want to show the body and start a panic in the city. I have your word?"

Ethan nodded then tossed his briefcase into the back seat of the Crown Victoria and peered through the viewfinder—panning the camera back and forth, checking the settings.

"You ready, Benson?" Newton said impatiently.

He nodded again.

"Send them in," Highland said before motioning to Ethan. "Shoot anything you want. Maybe it'll help convince your boss."

A line of flood lamps positioned around the perimeter of the playground were punched on, and Ethan focused his camera on a team of crime scene investigators dressed head to toe in white protective gear as they exited a mobile forensic lab housed in a blue-and-white panel truck marked with the police department logo. He fell in behind them and followed as they approached the gate, removed the chain and broken padlock, and entered the playground. The floodlights illuminated an area one hundred feet square around the body of a tiny, little girl propped in a folding chair.

Ethan stopped, planted his feet firmly in the snow, and made a medium shot—panning from the CSIs to a dozen cops now entering the playground then over to the body. The girl was Asian—younger than the three Latina victims—no more than ten or maybe eleven years old with narrow hips, small hands and feet, and long black hair, caked with snow and dirt and dried blood. Her breasts were undeveloped, her hips narrow, her body void of pubic hair. Ethan lowered the camera, numbed by the brutality. She was covered in welts and bruises and cigarette burns. Her fingertips were missing and all her teeth had been pulled, blood dripping out of her mouth and freezing on her chin. Ethan tried to visualize the other three girls then looked back at the latest victim. She, too, had a square patch of skin removed from just above her left ankle and precise one-inch slash marks running up and down her arms.

Ethan lowered the camera.

Could the incisions have been made by a surgical knife?

A Karl Storz No. 6 surgical knife?

Like the one in the murder book?

Ethan made a mental note to ask and resumed shooting. The girl was posed in the same position as the other victims—

her arms tied behind her back, her legs spread, her head lolling on her chest, eyes open, terror on her face. He circled the body, making a three hundred sixty degree tracking shot, always staying clear of the CSI combing for evidence and the police photographers and videographers documenting the crime scene.

He captured every angle and every detail.

The scene surreal.

He shot the police dogs tethered on short leashes patrolling the perimeter of the park, then swish-panned to Patricia Highland and a crime scene investigator holding a case of equipment.

"Make a mold of the footprints and the tire tracks before they melt," Highland said. "Might give us evidence we can use to tie a suspect to the crime scene if we ever catch the son of a bitch."

Ethan zoomed in as the ADA barked more orders then followed her as she walked over to the body and stared at the young girl, shaking her head in disgust. Then he panned back to the CSI and kneeled to steady his shot as the investigator poured a plastic-like substance into a footprint, waited a moment or two for it to solidify, and pulled a perfect impression from the snow.

"We're lucky it's so friggin' cold tonight," he said. "The mold of the guy's shoe is perfect."

"What will you do with it?" Ethan said, still rolling.

"We'll compare it to footprints we picked up at the other crime scenes."

"What will that tell us?" Ethan said.

"Whether it came from the same person," the CSI said. "Got a gut feeling it's going to match." Then he stood, hurried the footprint over to the forensic truck, and began pouring a mold of one of the tire tracks.

Gloria Alvarez walked up to Ethan and said curtly, "Ah, you've come to poke around my crime scene, *amigo, si*? You capture everything on your camera, *no*?"

"The pictures are gruesome."

"Makes me want to puke. *La mierda.*"

"Find anything?" Highland said, directing her question to the detective as she joined them.

"*Nada,* just more crap like Pier 51," Alvarez said. "Lotsa junk layin' around in snow. Nothin' connected to the murder. The killer's one smart motherfucker."

Then there was shouting on the far side of the playground.

The CSI had found something.

Ethan made a tracking shot to a small group of investigators who were carefully clearing the snow from around an object.

"What is it?"

"Fuck, man, looks like a knife, *no*?" Gloria Alvarez said as she leaned between two CSIs to get a better view.

Ethan panned from Alvarez to Highland then zoomed into the object now fully exposed as a CSI wearing Latex gloves carefully lifted a surgical blade and placed it on a sheet of plastic. It was covered in fresh blood. Ethan zoomed into an extreme tight shot, focusing the lens on the name of the manufacturer etched near the bottom of the handle: Karl Storz Surgical Equipment.

"That's the same brand of knife you found at the third crime scene. Is it significant?"

"Won't know, Benson, until we test it at lab, *sí*?" Gloria Alvarez said, motioning to the CSI to drop the knife into an evidence bag.

"But it's more proof linking this murder to Pier 51," Ethan said, panning from the detective to the ADA.

"Could be a lead?" Highland said. "But don't jump the gun. Got a long way to go before we link the two blades."

Ethan nodded and lowered his camera. "Sun's up, and from the look of things, the cat's out of the bag," he said, gesturing to the huge crowds hovering on the far side of the police barricades.

"Gonna be a bigger public outcry than the other Child Sex Murders. And I'm gonna run with it, bet your damn ass I am.

Maybe get a few more days of coverage, before the press moves on to something else," the ADA said, closing the top button of her Ferragamo overcoat as the wind picked up, making it feel colder than it already was. "And you won't be able to hide your involvement in my case, Ethan. Your comrades will figure out pretty damn quickly that somebody was taking pictures at the crime scene, and that *that* somebody was Ethan Benson from *The Weekly Reporter.* They're gonna be screaming to know why you got access and they didn't."

"So you're gonna tell them?" Ethan said.

"Later this morning. At my press conference," she said dryly. "So make a decision. Either you're in or you're out."

"I'll get you a decision," he said, raising his camera to make one last shot of the coroner zipping the little girl into a body bag and preparing to load the corpse into the back of a blue-and-white van from the Medical Examiner's Office.

"Why don't I accompany you back to your office?" Highland said. "Maybe with a push from me, we can convince your bosses to move forward with our story."

CHAPTER 9

It was almost ten thirty when Ethan led Patricia Highland through the glass door of the waiting room and down the long corridor on the management floor of the broadcast center. He'd been awake for almost thirty hours and was weary from lack of sleep and all the Scotch he'd consumed during his marathon day. He hadn't showered, shaved, or changed clothes, and all he wanted was to climb into bed and pull the covers over his head. When he reached his office, he stopped and introduced the ADA to his assistant, James Lapidus.

"Where's Consuela," he said, looking at the empty desk.

"Going over the schedule with Peter. He's been looking for you all morning. He's plenty pissed."

"You'll get used to Peter," Ethan said cynically. He turned to Patricia Highland. "Would you like coffee?"

"Never turn down a cup."

Ethan nodded to James. "Make us a pot, please. Then call Mindy and Paul and tell them to come to my office."

"What about Peter?"

"No need. Won't take him long to figure out I'm here."

"Sure thing, Ethan," James said, heading to the kitchen.

Ethan unlocked his door, turned on the lights, and motioned to the ADA to take a seat on the leather couch with matching leather armchairs near the heavy mahogany table he used for meetings like this one. Then he sat down at his desk and loaded the video he'd shot at the crime scene into the hard drive of his state-of-the-art Dell Precision 5810 desktop computer. As he was finishing, Peter Sampson stormed into his office like a bull in a china shop.

"Where have you been?" he said, snorting. "You missed a story meeting and a pre-edit and a pre-shoot, and damn, you know how I hate that—"

He stopped midsentence, flustered, when he noticed the distinguished-looking woman sitting quietly on the couch.

"I'm Patricia Highland from the District Attorney's Office," she said, thrusting out her hand. "And you must be Peter Sampson. I'm a big fan. Been watching you anchor *The Weekly Reporter* for years."

Peter smiled and turned on the charm as he sat across from her. "Pleasure to meet you. Are you the prosecutor handling that murder investigation Ethan's been telling me about?"

"The Child Sex Murders. I'm in charge of the task force."

"Here's the coffee you wanted," James said entering the room, followed close behind by Mindy Herman.

"Ms. Herman," Highland said, smiling broadly. "So sorry you didn't join us this morning."

"What happened this morning?" Mindy said, shooting a quick glance at Ethan.

"Let's wait for Paul," Ethan said, pivoting to James. "Is he on his way?"

"I'm here, Ethan," he said coldly. "Why are you late?"

"Afraid that's my fault," Patricia Highland said, standing and introducing herself. "I just took Ethan on a field trip to see the crime scene of the latest murder."

"What murder?" Lang said, his tone softer.

"Sit, Paul. Let me walk you through it." Ethan spent the next fifteen minutes describing the task force investigation at the latest murder, Patricia Highland jumping in and adding context every now and then.

"You shoot video?" Lang said as soon as Ethan finished.

"He did, indeed," Highland said. "In all my years as a prosecutor, I've never let any member of the press document a crime scene during an active investigation. This was a first for the Manhattan District Attorney's Office.

"I want to screen it," Paul said, barking at Ethan.

"Already cued up."

"Play it," Peter said in his most authoritative voice.

They all gathered around Ethan's computer, sipping coffee, and screened the video from beginning to end, Ethan providing commentary and a strong warning the images of the dead girl were difficult to watch.

"What in God's name did he do to her?" Sampson said, repulsed.

"He tortured her—maybe for quite some time—before he strangled her to death. Used some kind of garrote. See the deep gash running around her neck," Highland said, pointing. "Just like he did to his other three victims."

"She looks like a kid," Paul said, stone-faced.

"She is," Highland said warily. "They were all kids—barely in their teens."

"And you have no idea who they are?"

"No."

"And nobody's come forward reporting them missing?"

"We have no leads on their identities."

"Any theories on why he killed them?" Peter asked.

"Nothing concrete," Highland said, finishing her coffee.

"She looks posed in that chair. Like somebody took a lot of time staging the body," Peter said. "This is a ritual killing, right?"

"Looks that way."

"But why?" Paul asked.

"That's the million-dollar question, and that's why I need your help."

There was a moment of silence. Then Paul said, "I don't understand, Ms. Highland. I know Ethan wants to do this story, but I'm not sure it's right for my show. I told him that. So how can we help you?"

She turned to Ethan. "Run the video down to the clue you focused in on this morning." He fast-forwarded to a tight shot of the Karl Storz surgical knife. "Ethan knew right away the significance of that knife."

"Why's it important?" Paul said, puzzled.

"Because the same kind of knife—it's actually a scalpel—was found at one of the other crime scenes," Highland said. "It may be the only piece of physical evidence, beyond the staging of the bodies and maybe some footprints, that links at least two of the murders."

"How'd you figure that out?" Paul said, turning to Ethan.

"I spent half the night reading an annotated copy of the murder book Ms. Highland's office gave me."

"What's a murder book," Peter said with an inquisitive eyebrow.

The ADA stood, walked over to the mahogany table, and poured herself another cup of black coffee. "Drink too much of this damn stuff." Then she sat back down across from Sampson and gave him a detailed answer. "It's the blueprint of our investigation. We already have five large notebooks and counting. We gave Ethan a sample of the raw data. That's also a first for my office. Nobody ever gets access to the evidence in the murder book until a suspect is convicted and the killer's behind bars—especially someone from the press."

"Let me get this straight," Paul said. "The murder book contains everything—the evidence, clues, theories, experts—that you and your team are working with to catch this guy."

"In a nutshell, yes."

"And how big is the task force working the case?"

"It's small. Two detectives full-time, one crime scene investigator, four lab technicians, three coroners, one profiler on loan from the FBI, a second ADA named Randall Newton, plus Ms. Highland," James said from the corner of the room.

"How'd you know that?" Paul said, staring at his nephew.

"I took James to a meeting last night with Randall Newton and the lead detective on the case, Gloria Alvarez," Ethan said. "Then I gave him part of the murder book. Looks like he did his homework."

"Very good, Ethan. You've got James immersed in research. I knew you'd take good care of him." He turned to Patricia Highland. "So what's the bottom line for us?"

She stared from Paul to Peter then back to Paul. "You know the deal, Mr. Lang. I'm offering you a bird's-eye view of my investigation. I'll give Ethan and *The Weekly Reporter* full access to everything my task force is doing, because I need him to help me catch the killer."

"How will he do that?"

"He's got good instincts. He's proved that in the past. And my task force needs more full-time manpower and more resources. After each murder—as you saw in the video Ethan shot—the crime scene is flooded with people looking for clues. But when we don't catch the killer and the press coverage dies down, most of my team is pulled to work other crimes. Then we're left with the small staff James just told you about. Not enough to conduct my investigation."

"Okay," Paul said, "so you think we can get you more publicity and help you build a bigger task force."

"And that's the reason I'm offering *The Weekly Reporter* this deal."

"And this would be an exclusive?" Paul said, the wheels in his head churning.

Patricia Highland nodded.

"Nobody else would be given any of the evidence?"

"Nobody," Highland said, "and as Ethan can tell you, the press was out in full force this morning, but kept far away from the actual investigation."

"But how can you ensure us the story, or parts of the story, won't leak?" Peter said skeptically.

"Because I plan to hold a series of press conferences, the first one later today, where I'll tell everybody else exactly what I want them to know. Nothing more. Ethan will be the only producer to get behind the scenes. He'll know everything we know as soon as we know it. I guarantee that."

Paul's secretary, Monica, knocked on the door and walked into the room. "You've got a call from Georgina Wannager, the news director at WGBS. I told her you were in a meeting, but she said it was urgent."

"What does she want?"

"One of her reporters, Winston Peabody, was there," Ethan said, "doing a live insert in their morning show. I saw him as we left the crime scene. He must've found out I got through the police line with Ms. Highland. Guess he wants the video I shot."

"You can't give it to him, Mr. Lang," the ADA said forcefully. "No other news organization, including your affiliate, can have access to the footage. That's my only ground rule. I don't want the killer to know what we're doing and what leads we're pursuing. If you let Ethan produce this story, you can shoot whatever you want as long as you don't air it until the killer is behind bars."

"And if you don't arrest the killer?"

"We'll get him, and when we do, you'll have a story for *The Weekly Reporter* that every other news organization in the country will covet. You'll be able to show just how we caught the Child Sex Murderer, and that, Mr. Lang, will be a very big story."

Paul stroked his chin. "Monica, tell Ms. Wannager I'll call her back in fifteen minutes." He whipped around to the ADA. "I'm gonna roll the dice and put the story into production."

"But what about Ethan's other responsibilities?" Peter said, almost whining. "He's my senior producer."

"You still want to do the story, Ethan?"

"You know I do. I saw what this guy is capable of doing. He kills little kids. So if I can help the task force catch him, I have a moral responsibility to do whatever I can."

"Peter?" Paul said, addressing his anchorman. "You agree?"

"I'll go along with whatever you want, Paul," Peter said, grumbling.

"Done," Paul said, turning to Patricia Highland. "This story is a big risk for my broadcast, but I have faith in Ethan. I think he can juggle his role as Peter's senior producer and produce this story at the same time. So I'm gonna let him work with you. Let's see what happens. This could be a real blockbuster if you catch the killer or a real bust if you don't."

*****

Ethan spent the rest of the day placating Peter, who was furious he'd agreed to a story he cared little about. They were in and out of Paul's office debating the merits of the project versus the hardships Peter envisioned if Ethan split his time on the Child Sex Murders while carrying out his other responsibilities managing the anchorman's busy schedule. At one point, Peter actually insisted that Paul pull the assignment and give it to another producer. But Ethan didn't back down, arguing that Patricia Highland specifically asked for him, and that if another producer was arbitrarily assigned, she'd give the story to a different network. After much screaming, Paul finally put his foot down.

The story was Ethan's.

But the stress of fighting all day with Peter took its toll, and Ethan felt drained, disconsolate, and thirsty for the sweet warmth of a shot of Scotch. So he locked the door of his office and left the broadcast center. It was seven o'clock, and he headed to McGlades where he'd scheduled a production meeting with the small staff he'd wrangled from the executive producer—Mindy, James, and a crack researcher, David Livingston, who Ethan had worked with on previous stories. Trudging through the melting snow, the traffic on Fifty-Seventh Street still paralyzed by the storm, he crossed the street and walked into the bar. The room was packed full of people watching the Knicks play the Celtics on ESPN and listening to Aerosmith belt out *Back in the Saddle* on a jukebox. Ethan sidled up to the bar, apologizing as he pushed past a young couple holding hands, then waved to Moe the Bartender.

"Scotch on the rocks."

Moe grabbed a bottle of Black Label and poured a hefty shot over a bed of ice. Ethan drank it all at once, then banged on the table for another. Moe refilled his glass then said, "Mindy and a couple of fellas are in the back room." He stared at Ethan. "You look like shit. Don't hit that stuff too hard tonight."

Ethan thought about Sarah, knowing she'd be pissed he was drinking, but pushed it to the back of his mind.

"I can handle it, Moe. Put the drinks in the back room on my tab." Then he picked up his Scotch and weaved through the crowd, already feeling a buzz. *Just what I need,* he thought. *A little taste to straighten my head and keep me goin' a few more hours.*

Mindy immediately stood when he walked into the room. "Jeez, Ethan, you've been up for two days. Why the hell you drinking that stuff? You're gonna get wasted. Have you eaten anything today?"

Ethan shrugged and sipped his Scotch, the alcohol hitting him harder than he first thought. "Ate with Peter while we were arguing about our story. I'm fine, Mindy. We'll do a short production meeting, and then I'll go home." He finished his second glass and waved to Moe to bring another. "What are you guys drinking?"

David Livingston lifted a mug. "Coffee."

"Me too," James said.

"Can't entice you guys to join me with something a little stronger?" Ethan said, slurring his words. "Hate to drink by myself if I don't have to. Where's Lloyd?"

"I called," Mindy said. "He's working another case tonight."

"Shit," Ethan said loudly. "I wanted him here for this meeting."

Mindy shot David a knowing glance as Moe walked into the room and placed a fresh glass of Scotch in front of Ethan. "You're in no shape to be drinking. This is the last one." Then he walked out of the room, shutting the door behind him.

Ethan stared at the Scotch, his vision double. What the hell was wrong with him? He was falling into a deep hole, jeopardizing everything. Soon everybody in the office would know he was hitting the bottle. How would Paul react? Peter? And Sarah? He was testing their marriage, something he'd sworn he would never do again. But the rich, golden liquid was calling to him. Beckoning him. So he picked up the glass, tipped it back, and drank—the alcohol slipping down his throat, soothing, inviting, comforting.

"Ethan," Mindy said, getting no response. "You need to go home and get some sleep." She turned to James. "Schedule a production meeting tomorrow morning in Ethan's office."

He pulled up Ethan's schedule on his iPad. "He's all jammed up. Got a nine thirty with Peter, a ten o'clock with Bob Wilcox to discuss a possible interview with the Speaker of the House, and then a screening to lock the Taylor Swift profile in Joel Zimmerman's editing room. That's at ten thirty. Then he's got to go to the studio to tape Peter's bridges for this week's show. The day is booked solid."

"Make it for eight thirty," Mindy said. "I'll make sure Lloyd joins us." She turned back to Ethan. "I'm taking you home."

Ethan didn't respond, his mind too clouded by the alcohol.

She rummaged through her purse for her cell phone, pulled up her Uber app, and ordered a car. "Be here in seven minutes," she said to Ethan, disquieted. "Can you make it to the door?" He nodded, but still didn't answer.

"David, help me get him out of here," she said as she punched another number into her phone. "Hey, Sarah. It's Mindy Herman. Look, Ethan's had a little too much to drink.

I'm bringing him home. Should be there in about twenty minutes." Then she whipped around to David and James. "Not a word about this to anyone."

*****

Sarah was waiting at the front door, visibly upset, when Mindy got off the elevator, an arm tucked around Ethan's waist, and helped him navigate the fifty feet down the corridor to his apartment. Sarah hurried to his side, lifting his free arm and draping it over her shoulder, the two guiding Ethan into the foyer, down the center hallway, and into the bedroom, Luke watching from his doorway, his little face torn with anguish.

"Help me get his shoes off," Sarah said after they laid him on the bed, Ethan mumbling incoherently as he rolled over on his side. "Stay there, Ethan, I'll be back in a minute to get you undressed." Then she took Mindy's elbow and whispered, "Let's go to the kitchen. I need to know what happened tonight."

She quietly closed the bedroom door and walked straight over to Luke, still standing in the doorway, clutching his teddy bear.

"Is Daddy gonna be okay, Mom?"

"He's gonna be fine, Lukie," she said, kneeling down in front of him. "He was up all night working on a story. Ms. Herman brought him home to get some sleep. You remember Ms. Herman, don't you?"

Luke nodded. "But Daddy's drunk, isn't he?"

"Yes, Luke. He had too much to drink."

"He's getting drunk every day."

"I know, Luke, but Daddy made a big mistake tonight."

"He's not supposed to," Luke said, whining.

"Mommy's gonna talk to him about it when he wakes up. Don't you worry. Now go wash up and brush your teeth. Then you can watch TV until I come and tuck you in. I need to talk to Ms. Herman for a little while."

Luke turned and sulked into his room, swinging his teddy bear.

Sarah led Mindy to the kitchen and poured two cups of coffee. "What happened?"

"I'm not really sure, Sarah," Mindy said, sighing. "He seemed okay when we met with Paul this morning. Tired from being up all night, maybe a little tense, but other than that, I didn't see anything wrong. The rest of the day he was in meetings with Peter. That was probably stressful. Peter doesn't want to do this story, and I'm sure he was all over Ethan. Then when we got to McGlades for a production meeting, he started drinking, one Scotch after another. Has he been doing this at home?"

"He's been drunk every night, but not like this."

"James said he was drinking last night at Grand Central Station, before meeting the lead investigator on our story."

"He had a couple more in his study when he got home, but he was mostly drinking coffee as he read the case documents. He was gone to the crime scene when I got up this morning. So I guess he could've had a bottle. I wouldn't put it past him." She slumped in her chair. "Christ, Mindy, I can't take it anymore," she said pensively. "Does Peter know?"

"I don't think so."

"What about Paul?"

"Not yet."

Sarah stood and began pacing. "Paul found out about his drinking after the Rufus Wellington story and put him on notice. Said he'd have to take a leave of absence and go to rehab if he didn't stop. We took a long vacation so Ethan could dry out, then started seeing our therapist twice a week."

"Are you still going?"

"Got a session Wednesday."

"Don't let him cancel it. He needs help."

"Damn straight he's going. He doesn't have a choice."

"Look, Sarah, the Child Sex Murders story is a minefield for Ethan," Mindy said delicately. "Peter's pissed it's taking

Ethan away from his senior producer responsibilities, and Paul's gonna blame him if the story doesn't pan out."

"Is that a possibility?" Sarah said anxiously.

"Ethan doesn't think so, but if the cops don't catch the killer, and in my opinion, there's a strong chance they ain't gonna find him, Paul's not gonna run the story, and Ethan will have wasted a lot of time and money chasing a ghost. So he needs to be careful that Paul doesn't decide his drinking was the real reason the story failed. It'll be the end of him if he does." Mindy checked the time. "You need to put Luke to bed and take care of Ethan." She pushed away from the table. "One last thing. The entire production team was at McGlades tonight—me, David Livingston, and James Lapidus."

"Is Lapidus a good guy?"

"I sure hope so. We agreed to keep tonight's incident quiet, but James is Paul's nephew, and I'm not sure we can trust him not to tell his uncle. I'll try to keep him in line," Mindy said frankly, "but you gotta get Ethan to stop drinking, or he's gonna be out on his ass."

CHAPTER 10

Maria blinked and opened her eyes. Where was she? She was hungry, her mouth parched, the rotting stink around her unbearable. How long had she slept? A day? Two days? She peered into the darkness, confused, and the memory returned of her terrible ride in the back of the panel truck with those two horrible men. They'd put her in a cage, taken all her clothes, mocking her, then took turns raping her. Her body ached and was covered in sores, and she hadn't bathed since the morning she'd been abducted from her village. How long ago was that? A week? Two weeks?

Where am I?

Where am I going?

I want my momma and papa.

She screamed and shook the bars, then remembered what happened when she'd asked the big man driving the panel truck, the Indian, Manuel—at least that's what the other man called him—if they could stop so she could use the bathroom and get some clean clothes. He'd laughed and made her hold her bladder until she thought she'd burst, before ordering Julio, the man with the tattoos, the really scary man, to stop the van so she could relieve herself.

But that's when they beat her.

And put their things inside her.

I wanna go home.

I want my mamma and papa.

So where was she now? She was still moving, rocking back and forth, tilting up and down, like a bumper car ride. She closed her eyes tightly, listening to the new sounds all around her—the traffic, people laughing, screaming, angry, all at the same time. And the horrible smells—exhaust fumes, pollution, rotting fish, mixed together in a nauseating fugue. Then she heard seagulls and ship horns, and the truck suddenly stopped moving—the back door swinging open, light streaming in, and she caught a glimpse of the longshoreman and the boats and the river.

A port.

The port of Buenos Aires.

She'd been there before with her family.

Terrified, she didn't move, seemingly paralyzed, as a tarp was thrown over her cage, and the two men dragged it out of the panel truck and began walking for what seemed an eternity. Another ship horn blasted in the distance, and the smell of rotting fish and polluted water filled her nostrils, making her gag. She listened to small children playing and workmen sawing and hammering and building something. But what? Then her cage was hoisted into some kind of container, the tarp pulled off, the door unlocked, and she was yanked out by her hair and viciously tossed up against the back wall of her new prison.

A wooden crate.

Small.

Claustrophobic.

Manual laughed like a hyena, his face cold and hard as he said, spittle flying from his mouth, "Last time you see me, bitch. Last time you see your home, your little village, your sweet Argentina. Now start new life in new place, and you no forget what fat *Padre* tell you at *basilica,* that if you no listen to new masters, he hunt down your family like animals, torture them, make them suffer, then kill them. *Entender pajarito?*" He tossed her a dirty dress and beat her one final time—slapping her face, punching her stomach, and kicking her between her legs until blood flowed like a river.

That was the last thing she remembered.

The last thing.

Before she blacked out.

*****

Maria's eyes fluttered, and she began to wake. More voices. More darkness. More swaying. Different from before—now smoother, more gentle. Tears began pouring down her cheeks as she felt between her legs, her privates tender and encrusted in dry blood, but the bleeding had stopped. She patted around the floor and found a wooden bowl with some kind of gruel and a plastic cup filled with warm water. Then she stood, no longer chained, and began exploring—running her hands across the wooden walls, crying out when she caught a splinter in her thumb, but continuing to search, probing, looking for a way out. After touching every square inch, tripping over the bowl and spilling the water in her cup, a small voice called out to her, whimpering, "Please, don't beat me. I'll be good. Promise. Just leave me alone."

Maria listened as the girl dragged herself into a corner.

"Don't be afraid. I won't hurt you," she said softly, trying to calm her.

"Who are you?" the girl said, now hysterical.

"Maria Fuente from *Humahuaca.* What's your name?"

"Juanita.

"Juanita what?"

"Juanita Bianca," she said, gasping as she talked.

Maria slowly crossed the wooden crate, approaching the girl cautiously. "How old are you, Juanita?"

"I just turned nine."

"I'm fourteen."

"You're a big girl. Much bigger than me."

Maria smiled. "Where are you from? Can you tell me?"

"La Plata."

"That's south of Buenos Aires. A little village. Mostly farmland? Right?"

"My daddy raises cattle and sells milk to the shopkeepers."

"You speak very good English, Juanita," she said, trying to keep the girl talking.

"My mommy is from America. She teaches English part-time in our school. I've been speaking English since I was little."

Maria sat and draped her arm over the girl's shoulder. She was tiny, a waif, all skin and bones. "How did you get here, Juanita?"

She began to cry, huge tears rolling down her cheeks. "I was helping my daddy feed our cattle, and he told me to go home for lunch. He said to tell mommy we should start without him. That he'd get there as soon as he finished herding the cattle into the meadow. So I started skipping down the path through the woods, and before I got to the clearing, this big man jumped on top of me and punched me in my tummy. Oh, it hurt so bad. I couldn't breathe. Then he threw me over his shoulder and started running through the forest. Very fast. And I kicked my feet, trying to get away, and screamed." She paused to catch her breath. "But I was far away from my house, and Mommy didn't hear me. Then the big man got mad and threw me on the ground and hurt my arm and hit me all over for a long time. Then he put a cloth on my face, and it smelled so sweet like flowers, and I fell asleep. That's all I remember. I didn't wake up until I heard you."

"Are you in pain?" Maria said, straining to see the little girl in the darkness.

"Everywhere, especially my arm."

"Which one?"

"This one. My left arm."

"Can I touch it?"

"No. I told you it hurts, a lot."

"I'll be gentle, Juanita. We're friends, right? I just want to make sure you're okay."

Juanita recoiled from her touch, then sat quietly as Maria ran her fingers over her tiny arm, beginning at the shoulder and gently making her way down to her elbow, her forearm, and then to her wrist. Juanita pulled away.

"*Oh dios mio,*" Maria said, alarmed. "Your arm is broken. I can feel the bone sticking through the skin. I can feel puss. It's infected."

Juanita started screaming.

"Hush, hush. I know that hurt—a lot," Maria said soothingly. "I'll tear a strip of cloth from my dress and make you a sling. Maybe then it'll feel better."

She grabbed the hem and stripped off the bottom, then heard Juanita gasp, then wail, "They're coming."

Maria listened as footsteps approached, the wooden prison pitching back and forth a little faster as bigger waves hit the bow of the boat. She huddled close to Juanita, the little girl terrified as a key was thrust into a lock, throwing a dead bolt, and the door slowly opened, casting bright light across the floor and into the crate. Maria was temporarily blinded, until her eyes adjusted from the darkness as two men lumbered into the room. She smelled them before she saw them, their bodies reeking of sweat and filth.

"What do you want," she said firmly.

"Isn't that sweet," the first man said, walking across the room, towering over them. "The big girl is taking care of the little one."

"A real mother hen," the second man said, laughing. "She's taking care of her broken wing."

Americans, Maria thought silently, *is that where they're taking us?* Juanita shriveled into her arms. "Who are you?"

"Shut the fuck up," the first man said, sneering. "Brought you a fresh slop bucket. Stinks like piss and shit in here. How do you stand it?"

"I brought food and water," the second man said. "Don't smell much better than what's in the can." The two men laughed. "Gotta keep you looking pretty until we get to New York and we offload you to the big boss. Hey, just made a joke. We offload the sweet girls like dry goods at the market."

They continued laughing even louder.

What's gonna happen to us in New York? Maria thought, trying to tap down her fear as she pulled Juanita closer.

"What about her? You didn't bring her food or water? Can't you see she's starving?"

The first man bent over, his face six inches from Maria—his teeth rotting, his breath stale, fetid. "She don't need none of that stuff. She ain't goin' all the way to New York."

Juanita shuddered, Maria stroking her back, trying to comfort her. "What do you mean?"

"The asshole who snatched her damaged the merchandise," the second man said, leering. "The big boss won't want her."

"But she just needs a doctor. Then she'll be better. Really."

"Shut up. It's time to get rid of her," the first man said, grabbing the little girl by the throat, tearing her away from Maria. "But not before we have some fun with her."

Juanita screamed, trying to break free from his viselike grip, Maria standing and striking him with her fists, until the second man smacked her across the face and dragged her into the corner. As the first man held Juanita tightly, Maria watched helplessly, all the energy draining from her body, as he pulled off her torn shift and tossed her on the ground, the little girl clutching her shattered arm, writhing in pain, trying to crawl away. Then he unbuckled his belt, lowered his pants, and climbed on top of her, wrapping his big hands around her tiny neck and squeezing as he entered her.

"Get off of her," Maria said helplessly. "Why in God's name are you doing this? She's only a little kid, you fucking monster."

But the man paid no attention.

He continued pumping in and out.

Squeezing her tiny neck until he finished and her little body went limp.

Maria slid to the floor, tears flowing down her cheeks. "You killed her for no reason. Why? Why? Why?"

"Shut the fuck up," the first man said, hiking up his pants. "Or you'll end up dead just like your friend."

The second man let go of Maria, laughed, then pulled a large plastic bag from his overcoat and swished it back and forth until it opened.

"Stuff the sweet little thing in here," he said callously. "It's the middle of the night. Nobody will notice when we toss the trash overboard."

"What a pity," the first man said coldly. "She was so young, so delicate. They would have paid a pretty penny for her in New York. Now she's just junk food for the sharks."

Maria slid across the floor as far away as possible, the two men lifting Juanita, folding back her arms and legs and stuffing her into the plastic bag.

"Eat your food before we come back," the first man said. "We need you lookin' pretty. The big boss ain't gonna pay us a fucking dime if you look like a piece of shit."

Then they left.

Dragging the plastic bag.

And locked the door behind them.

Maria screaming silently in the darkness.

CHAPTER 11

Sarah walked into the bedroom with a cup of black coffee, placed it on the side table next to Ethan, and opened the curtains, streams of sunlight spilling into the room and across the bed. Ethan rolled away, covered his eyes with a pillow, and groaned.

"What're you doing, babe? The light is blinding."

"Get up and take a shower," she said, seething. "You need to sober up."

Ethan sat up, his head pounding, his vision blurred, his mouth dry and foul tasting, then fell back on the bed.

"Jesus, I'm still dressed."

"Thought about taking off your clothes when you got home, but I couldn't bear to touch you. Ended up sleeping on the couch in the living room."

"What happened?"

"You got smashed at McGlades. Like you do every night, but this time, Mindy had to bring you home. Just made it, before you passed out."

Ethan closed his eyes, trying to remember, but much of the past forty-eight hours was nothing but a blur. He searched his mind frantically. There were sketchy memories of going to the crime scene with Patricia Highland and shooting visuals of the murder. But that happened the night before. Didn't it? And meeting with Paul in his office about the story later in the morning, then fighting with Peter all afternoon and leaving the broadcast center and walking to the bar.

Then there was nothing.

Shit.

A blackout.

That had never happened before.

"Are you angry, babe?" he said meekly, already knowing the answer.

Sarah sighed deeply, her eyes furious. "You're damn fucking straight I'm angry. You work all night, don't bother to call me, then get so stinking drunk that Mindy had to dump you off like garbage. Get out of your clothes and into the shower. Then maybe I can stand being in the same room with you."

He peered at the alarm clock. Nine o'clock. He was going to be late for work. He tried sitting again, the room spinning like a top, his stomach churning. Gagging, he leapt out of bed and raced to the bathroom, just making it to the toilet before tossing his stomach. After five minutes of retching, he flushed the toilet and wiped his mouth on a hand towel, then looked in the mirror. His skin was pasty yellow, dark circles puffing up his cheeks, and his eyes were watery and crisscrossed with broken blood vessels. He looked like he'd just gone ten rounds with Muhammad Ali.

Sarah walked into the bathroom with a glass of water and three Motrins. "Take these. It'll help."

"Not sure I can keep them down."

"Take them. We need to get going."

"Where?"

"To see Dr. Schwartz."

"But we're not scheduled until tomorrow," Ethan said, taking the pills, gagging again, but managing to keep them down. "I can't go. I was late yesterday working the murder scene. Can't be late again today. Peter will throw a fit."

"I don't care about fucking Peter Sampson or your damn job anymore. You have no choice," she said, still agitated. "I called Dr. Schwartz early this morning and told him about last night. He wants to see you, find out what happened, and doesn't want to wait until tomorrow."

"But Sarah—"

"Don't 'but Sarah' me. We're going." She turned on the shower. "Get in. We're leaving in fifteen minutes."

*****

Dr. Fred Schwartz's office was on the tenth floor of 125 Central Park West, an old prewar building on the northeast corner of Seventy-Third Street. It was large and airy with breathtaking views of *Strawberry Fields*, the beautiful garden memorial to John Lennon who'd been murdered down the block in front of the Dakota, one of the most exclusive apartment buildings on the Upper West Side. Ethan paced the waiting room staring at his watch, still dizzy, his head pounding. He grabbed three more Motrin from his coat pocket and popped them into his mouth. Now he was going to overdose on painkillers, like he almost did on the Scotch. He kept staring at his iPhone, worrying about a series of phone messages he hadn't returned from Paul and Peter.

Something had happened.

Something important.

But what?

Sarah had insisted he wait until after he talked to Dr. Schwartz before worrying about work. Now he'd be in even more trouble. He lit a cigarette and sat down on a beige couch next to her, but couldn't relax—his teeth clenched, his jaw muscles tight, his foot tapping the floor uncontrollably. He took several quick puffs on his Marlboro, stared at his watch, and started to get up, Sarah pushing him down, growing more and more obdurate.

"Sit still, Ethan. I can't take your impatience another second. Dr. Schwartz will see us soon."

Five more minutes.

Still no Dr. Schwartz.

Ethan thought he was about to explode.

Then the door opened, and Dr. Schwartz walked into the waiting room. In his late sixties, diminutive, with a paunch hanging over his belt, he had long gray hair parted on the side, ruddy skin, and bushy white eyebrows. He was wearing gray flannel pants, a yellow cotton shirt, a blue tie, and a matching blue cashmere sweater.

"Good morning," he said cheerfully. "Sounds like you've had a couple of rough days, Ethan. Come. Let's talk."

They all sat, Ethan next to Sarah, Dr. Schwartz across from them. He turned on a tape recorder and grabbed a yellow pad and pencil, then stared deeply into Ethan's eyes and said in a soft but probing voice, "So, Ethan, what triggered this episode?"

Ethan glanced at an ashtray sitting on the table next to him then fumbled a Marlboro from a pack in his shirt pocket.

"You really need that, Ethan? Before we get started?"

"Yes," he said sharply, striking the cigarette with a match, inhaling deeply and blowing a stream of white smoke out his nose.

"Better?" Dr. Schwartz said, watching his hands shake.

Ethan still didn't answer.

"You've got tremors, Ethan."

"So? They'll go away."

"Have you had them before?"

"First time—I think?"

"Sarah?"

"I've never seen them before, but I've never seen Ethan go on a bender like this one."

"So tell me. What happened, Ethan? You haven't answered my question."

"I dunno. Just a bad day."

"That's not a real answer," Dr. Schwartz said, jotting a note on his pad. "Why did you lose control of your drinking?"

Ethan stubbed out his cigarette, still evasive.

He turned to Sarah. "What's going on with Ethan?"

Sarah hesitated then said, anger in her voice, "Everything was pretty much under control the past few months. He'd drink a glass of Scotch every now and then, but nothing excessive. And the two of us had been real good together, talking about everything and doing things as a family. He's been playing ball with Luke, taking him along when he walks Holly, and reading to him every night at bedtime. He's closer to Luke than he's ever been."

"So what triggered the binge?" Dr. Schwartz said, steering the conversation back to Ethan. "You ready to talk about it?"

Ethan lit another cigarette but refused to answer.

Dr. Schwartz jotted another note on his pad. "What do you think touched off the episode, Sarah?"

She peered over at Ethan then said, eyes downcast, "The grind of work mostly. Ethan finds the phone calls and the meetings with Peter Sampson very frustrating. He goes to the office, spends all day fixing other people's problems, then comes home and the phone starts ringing. Peter. Peter. Peter. And more Peter. The guy never lets up. Never makes a decision without first consulting Ethan. Never leaves him alone."

"Ethan?"

"Goes deeper than that," he said reluctantly. "But Sarah's told you the nub of it."

"So you find your job tedious, boring, taxing?" Dr. Schwartz said. "Is that why you lost control of your drinking?"

"Not fair. I just had a bad day yesterday," he said belligerently. "I was up all night on location working a new story, a process piece about how the police are investigating a series of murders. Then I went to the office and had a full day of very contentious meetings with Peter. So I went out after work to blow off steam."

"I thought you weren't producing stories anymore."

"I haven't in a long time."

"So why are you doing this one?"

"Because I miss being out in the field, and I miss telling stories."

"But won't that make your job more difficult?" Dr. Schwartz said. "You already feel pressure working as Peter Sampson's senior producer."

"That's what I tell him, over and over," Sarah said testily, facing Ethan. "But no, you won't listen to me. You never listen to me. You just do whatever you want." She grew angry. "This goddamn story is adding more pressure to your already-pressure-filled life. And you can't handle it, Ethan. You started drinking and haven't stopped since the moment you learned about the story. A couple of Scotches that morning when you met with the private investigator at McGlades. Moe called me about that. Christ, Ethan, it wasn't even ten o'clock. Then when you met the lead detective. Then more Scotch after you got home and started reading that fucking murder book. And then again after your all-nighter at the crime scene when you went back to McGlades with Mindy and got really shit-faced. Do you drink all day at the office too?"

"Not fair," Ethan said, pounding on the table. "I've been under a lot of pressure lately. You know that."

"Let's take a deep breath. Getting angry at each other isn't going to help," Dr. Schwartz said, checking his notes. "A lot has spilled out the past few minutes, and if I heard the two of you correctly, Ethan's drinking has been building for a couple of weeks and has become acute since he took on this new story."

"Correct," Sarah said flatly.

"But you haven't said anything at our sessions until today."

"No," Ethan said, ashamed.

"And neither have you, Sarah."

"I should have—right away, because Ethan's a drunk. And has been for most of our relationship. But since he started this story, he's been on a fucking five alarm fire. I can't take it anymore. And I won't."

There was a moment of ugly silence. Then Dr. Schwartz addressed Ethan. "Maybe you should consider taking some time off, spending a couple of weeks in rehab so you can really dry out."

"No way."

"But you need to focus on your drinking without the pressures of your job."

"No!"

"But you can't go on like this," Dr. Schwartz said quietly. "You're never going to get better."

"I can handle it."

"See, he won't listen," Sarah said furiously. "Not to you and definitely not to me. He's hopeless."

Ethan stood, paced the room, then looked out the picture window at Central Park, still covered in deep snow glistening in the sunshine. He lit a cigarette and remained circumspect.

"Then maybe you should give up your new murder story," Dr. Schwartz said. "Lighten your workload. Alleviate some of the stress."

He whipped around. "Not gonna happen," Ethan said, staring from Dr. Schwartz to Sarah. "Maybe, instead, I should just pass on being a senior producer and go back to being a full-time producer."

"You can't be serious, Ethan," Sarah said, aghast.

"I'm dead serious," he said sullenly. "Chuck the title. Chuck the salary. I hate Peter Sampson. I hate the job."

All the air was sucked out of the room as Dr. Schwartz put his pad and pencil in his lap and leaned forward. "Why, Ethan?"

"Because that's not who I am. I need to tell stories. I need to work in the field. I can't sit around in an office and rearrange widgets. It's suffocating. It's slowly killing me. I can't do it anymore. And I won't."

"Are you sure, Ethan? You've been able to handle Peter Sampson and the pressures in the past?"

"It's different now," he said.

"Why?"

"I don't know. It just is."

"He's not telling you the whole truth," Sarah said, her voice shaky. "He won't talk about it, but he can't fool me. It's different now not just because of his job but because of the story he's producing. It's dredging up all these bad memories."

Ethan turned ashen gray.

"Is she right, Ethan?"

"Tell him, Ethan," Sarah said. "Admit it."

Ethan slumped in his chair but didn't answer.

"Tell me what, Ethan?"

"Nothing."

"Christ, Ethan. You're so fucking weak." She turned from Ethan to Dr. Schwartz. "His new story is about dead little girls. Four dead little girls. Older than the baby we lost, but nonetheless, little girls, and they're bringing back memories of our dead baby and the fact that he ignored my cries for help when I needed him. Right, Ethan?"

Ethan remained perfectly still.

"Am I right, Ethan?"

Ethan shook his head up and down.

"Okay, now it's out in the open," she said, her voice cutting like a knife. "Now you know why I want him to say no to this fucking story and go back to being Peter Sampson's senior producer."

"Not gonna happen," Ethan screamed. "Never."

"Then you won't stop drinking," she said, her voice now cold, distant. "You're gonna keep trying to run away from the memories, the ones that haunt you, and bury them in that fucking Scotch. You've made *that* decision perfectly clear this morning."

A heavy silence hung over the room as Dr. Schwartz turned off his tape recorder.

"I've got another patient, so I'm afraid we have to stop." He looked at the two of them. "A lot was said today that's been simmering for what appears a very long time. There's much anger and resentment, not only about your drinking, Ethan, but about the way you leave Sarah out of your decision making. I want the two of you to talk to each other, to help each other without yelling and name-calling. It's the only way you're going to stop drinking, Ethan, the only way you're going to get your marriage back on track."

CHAPTER 12

Ethan exited the no. 104 bus on the corner of Broadway and Fifty-Seventh Street and headed west toward his office. The Global Broadcasting System had been housed in an eighteen-story Gothic structure since the late 1960s, and Ethan had been working for the news division for almost twenty years—since his first job as a desk assistant. He paused and lit a cigarette when he reached the revolving door leading into the cavernous lobby and stared up at the row of gargoyles perched atop the big Romanesque portico, wondering how he'd reached this crossroad in his life. His career was in crisis, his marriage slipping away, his future in doubt. He felt alone and helpless—and all he wanted was a hit of Scotch to alleviate the pain. Taking one last puff on his cigarette, he stubbed it out on the sidewalk and walked into the building.

As he flashed his ID badge to the security guard and pushed through the x-ray machine, his iPhone pinged. He quickly checked the LCD screen. Shit. It was Paul. Again. He'd been leaving Ethan voice mail messages all morning—messages he'd ignored. Did somebody tell him about McGlades? That he'd drunk himself into oblivion and blacked out the night before? James. It had to be James. Taking a deep breath, he sat down in a Naugahyde armchair not far from the elevator bank and answered the phone.

"Where have you been?" Paul said, short-tempered.

"At my shrink," Ethan said, not missing a beat.

"But it's Tuesday. I thought your weekly session was on Wednesday?"

Christ.

He knows my schedule.

"I did an extra hour this morning."

A short pause. "Anything wrong?"

"No."

"So why didn't you tell me you were going to be late? Could have avoided a big headache."

"My mistake. Won't happen again."

"Well, get your ass up here. I have an office full of people waiting for you."

Ethan clicked off the phone and sighed. He sensed there was a problem by the tone in Paul's voice, but he didn't think it was his drinking. That was a relief.

*****

He walked down the long red hallway still wearing his overcoat and earmuffs and stopped in front of Monica's desk. She barely acknowledged his presence.

"The shit's hitting the fan. They're down in the conference room waiting for you. Just go right on in."

Draping his coat over his arm, he pulled off his earmuffs and combed his hair with his fingers then slowly ambled the thirty feet down the corridor—past Paul's office, his screening room, and a group of day-of-air production assistants organizing the scripts for Sampson's studio bridges, scheduled to be taped later that morning. He paused when he got to the conference room, took a deep breath, and walked in.

"Close the door and sit down, Ethan," Paul said, checking his watch. "We've been here the better part of an hour waiting for you."

Ethan sat at the end of the table, placed his briefcase on the floor and his overcoat on the back of his chair, and scanned the room. It was filled with company executives—Douglas Fitzgerald, the president of the news division; Jamie Summers, the chief counsel for the network; Horace Pewter, the senior vice president of affiliate relations; and Georgina Wannager, the news director at WGBS.

"Good morning," he said cheerfully. "Sorry I kept everyone waiting."

"You should be," Paul said, snapping at Ethan. "All of us are busy. Your behavior is downright rude."

Ethan held his tongue, fuming on the inside. "Well, I'm here, and I've apologized—that's the second time to you, Paul. Where's Peter? Shouldn't he be here?"

"He was," Paul said angrily. "But he couldn't wait for you any longer. He's getting ready for the studio. You and I will have to brief him after the taping."

Shit, he was going to miss the taping. "Okay, why are we here?" he said, already sensing the problem.

"Patricia Highland held a press conference yesterday afternoon," Paul said. "And the story's become very big, just as you predicted."

Ethan had completely forgotten about the press conference, too busy working with Peter after pulling the all-nighter, then getting drunk and passing out. Man, how could he be so stupid. He should've known. It was part of his story. Part of his job. Part of his responsibility to himself. He wasn't just failing as a senior producer; he was failing as a producer.

"And I got a call early this morning from George Pierce, the chairman of the board of our illustrious company," Douglas Fitzgerald said sarcastically. "He got a formal complaint from Horace, here, about your shoot at the crime scene yesterday. Every affiliate in the network is clamoring for the video."

Ethan quickly glanced at Paul.

But got no reaction.

"He wants you to give a copy to WGBS and to cut a piece for today's news feed to the rest of the network," Fitzgerald continued. "Paul has already explained the ground rules laid out by the District Attorney's Office, and I, in turn, made them perfectly clear to both George and Horace, but they're insisting we share your video."

"Can't do it," Ethan said without hesitation.

"But we have four dead girls—kids—sadistically tortured in what appears to be a ritualistic ceremony then left in a playground. This story is huge, the biggest story of the day, the month, maybe the entire year," Georgina Wannager said. "It's front-page headlines in the *New York Times*, the *Daily News*, and the *New York Post,* and it's about to go national. We need your crime scene video to stay ahead of the competition. You shot something nobody else has, and WGBS has an obligation to share it with our viewers."

"What obligation?" Ethan said, stupefied.

"That should be obvious," Horace Pewter said. "Our job as journalists is to report the news, and my office started getting requests for your video from dozens of our affiliates as soon as the story hit the wires."

"Look, Mr. Benson," Georgina Wannager said forcefully. "We have a killer loose in our city. He's murdered four little girls, and in all likelihood, will murder again. You have to share your video, and you have to keep us in the loop as you learn more about the investigation. It's a chance for WGBS to build ratings and bury our competition."

"But I just told you, if I give you the video or any inside information before the killer is arrested, then there won't be any video or any inside information, because I won't have a story. ADA Highland has made that perfectly clear. She'll pull the project and give it to another network, and then their affiliates will pull in the big ratings. Not you."

"Is there any wiggle room?" Paul said, trying to diffuse the tension in the room.

"No."

"And you can't go back and ask her?" Douglas Fitzgerald said.

"No."

"Jamie?" Fitzgerald said, turning to the chief counsel. "Can you approach the district attorney directly. See if you can strike some kind of deal?"

"Risky," Summers said. "The DA is not going to overrule his ADA. This is her case, her task force, and she's calling the shots. We've agreed to her terms, and a telephone call from me is going to muddy the waters. It may backfire and cost *The Weekly Reporter* a very big story."

"We've got to make the call," Wannager said. "We need the footage."

Paul pulled out a pen and started doodling on a yellow pad then looked up and said, "You can't have it. I want this story, and Ethan has landed it on the pretext that we'll hold the video to protect the integrity of the police investigation. End of argument."

"This is outrageous," Wannager said, pounding on the table. "We all work for the same company."

"And that's why I'm sitting here," Douglas Fitzgerald said, his tone signaling the end of the discussion. "George sent me to see if there was any way to free up the video for broadcast, and there obviously isn't. Ethan will share as much as he can to help you stay ahead of the competition editorially, but no images."

"Anything else?" Paul said, staring around the room.

Nobody said a word. Then they all stood.

"I'll call you if George has any more questions," Fitzgerald said. Then they left one after the other.

"Stay a minute, Ethan," Paul said, motioning for him to sit back down. "We need to talk."

Ethan hesitated then put his briefcase back on the floor and his overcoat on the chair. *Now what?* he thought, eager to return the half-dozen phone calls that had stacked up since he got to the office.

"What's going on with you?" Paul said, standing and closing the door.

"Nothing," Ethan said defensively. "I just worked around the clock. I'm fried."

"I can see that. But you've been off your game the past few weeks. What else is goin' on? Is it Peter?"

Ethan hesitated. Did Paul sense he didn't want to work with the anchorman anymore. He heard Dr. Schwartz's admonition ringing in his head then said half-heartedly, "Everything is fine with Peter."

"And you're not tired of being his senior producer?"

"No."

"Well, you're not acting that way."

"Come again," Ethan said, trying desperately to contain what he was feeling.

Paul resumed his doodling. "Peter came to me last night." He looked up at Ethan. "And said he wants to make a change. That he doesn't think you're committed to working for him anymore."

Ethan tried to sound shocked. "Why?"

"Your attitude. The way you approach being his senior producer. And because you want to produce this crime story even though he's told you he doesn't want you in the field. He says that's more important to you than working for him." Paul paused, letting it all sink in. "Is he correct?"

"Well—"

"Don't say anything. I know what you really want to do. That's obvious from your behavior. But do you understand the implications if I have to remove you as his senior producer."

"But—"

Paul held up his hand. "Not another word. I just want you to think about it. You're damn good at your job, and there's nobody better on my staff. So I told Peter I won't replace you at the moment, and he's accepted my decision. But don't push your luck and force my hand. If he comes to me again with this, I'll pull the trigger, and you'll be gone."

*****

Ethan slowly walked down to his office, shoulders slumped, and unlocked the door, James following as he sat in the leather chair behind his desk.

"Here are your messages," he said, handing him a list of phone calls. "Do you want coffee?"

"I'm fine, James," Ethan said quietly. "Is Peter back?"

"He's still in the studio."

Ethan looked at his watch. Damn, he should've been in the control room supervising the taping. Peter always leaned on him for support, to help him tweak the script, to correct mistakes in his delivery. It was a big part of his job, and he had blown it off because he'd been hungover. No wonder Peter had gone to Paul asking for a new senior producer. Ethan was shirking his responsibilities. Badly.

"Did he ask where I was?" he said, worry in his voice.

"He knew you were in with Paul and the network brass."

"Was he pissed?"

"I guess so, but Dirk Fulton went with him to supervise the pages."

Ethan rubbed the bridge of his nose, his hangover raising its ugly head again. "Let me know when he's back. I need to talk to him."

"No problem, Ethan." He started to leave then turned and said, "Sure you don't want coffee?"

"I'm good, really. Just give me fifteen minutes and then tell Mindy and David to come up to my office."

Ethan swiveled in his chair as James left and stared out the big picture window. Ominous gray clouds were building, floating across the western horizon, signaling more snow. He clasped his hands behind his head and closed his eyes, trying to decide what to do. His decision to step down as Sampson's senior producer, a decision that seemed so clear earlier that morning, was clouded in doubt and uncertainty now that he was confronted with the possibility that he might lose his job. How would Sarah react to that? Would she understand? Would she stand by him? Ethan didn't want to think of the possibilities.

Sighing, he pushed it out of his mind.

Like he always did.

When he worried about Sarah.

Then he scanned his messages. Leslie Cohen was over-budget on a three-day shoot for her gun-control story, Dirk Fulton wanted to meet after the taping to discuss new story ideas, and Peter's co–anchor, Julie Piedmont, needed a few minutes to discuss her ever-diminishing role on the show.

All busy work.

Managerial.

Ethan thought he'd explode.

He opened a desk drawer and stared at a pint bottle of Black Label hidden beneath a stack of file folders. A short nip would take off the edge, dull his insecurities, get him back on track. He picked up the bottle, licked his lips, then buried it back under the folders. What the hell was he thinking? He was in the office. Everyone would smell booze on his breath. Standing, he paced the room, back and forth, then poked his head out the door.

"Changed my mind, James. Get me a cup of black coffee."

He sat down on the couch and took a series of calming breaths, trying to relax, trying to will away the pounding in his temples, trying to control the urge for a drink. As he spilled three Motrin into the palm of his hand, Mindy and David dropped into two swivel chairs across from him.

"Does anybody know about last night?" he said tentatively.

Mindy shook her head. "David and I have kept it quiet."

"And James?"

"He says he hasn't mentioned it to anybody."

"Paul didn't seem to know," Ethan said, relaxing.

"Are you sure you're okay, Ethan?" David said. "Haven't seen you hit the Scotch so hard since we worked together on the Rufus Wellington story. And that was a year ago."

Ethan shrugged.

"Jeez, Ethan, you gotta take this seriously. You're gonna slip up and—"

James walked into the office carrying a pot of coffee and four mugs.

"Am I interrupting," he said sheepishly.

"You're fine, James," Ethan said. "Put the tray down and pull up a chair. I wanna talk about our story." He poured himself a cup of coffee and sipped the scalding liquid, sending a jolt of caffeine through his system. "What have we heard from the District Attorney's Office?"

"All five murder books are ready," Mindy said.

"Can they e-mail us the files?"

"Not a chance," David said. "We talked to both Randall Newton and Gloria Alvarez while you were meeting with Paul. They won't put the evidence online. Too worried we'll get hacked and the info will land in the wrong hands. They're sending us hard copies. Should be here by midafternoon."

Ethan spun around to James. "Make four copies, one for each of us, keep the original, and ship one to my apartment. That's where I do my best thinking."

James nodded okay.

"What else?" Ethan was beginning to feel in control again—working a story, doing what he loved.

"Just set up a meeting with Newton and Alvarez and the second lead detective, Henry Dinkus," Mindy said.

"The guy from the Sixth Precinct?"

"That's the guy."

"Where we meeting?" Ethan asked.

"At the Special Victims Unit up on a Hundred Twenty-Third Street in Harlem," David said.

"Makes sense," Ethan said, now totally focused. "That's where Gloria Alvarez is based. What time?"

"Seven o'clock. James says your last meeting with Peter is at five. So there won't be a conflict."

"Is Lloyd joining us?"

David dropped a folder on his desk. "His consulting contract and retainer. I ran it through the business office."

"Same fee?"

"Five thousand plus expenses. Need your signature."

Ethan grabbed a pen and wrote his John Hancock in the three places highlighted in yellow then passed the documents back to David.

"So can he make the meeting?"

"He'll be there," David said, scooping up the paperwork.

Ethan turned to James. "I need the murder books as soon as possible. Make sure the documents are shipped to my apartment no later than tomorrow."

"No problem, Mr. Benson."

"Are we back to Mr. Benson?"

"No. No. I mean Ethan."

They all laughed and then heard Peter bellowing in the hallway.

"That's your cue to take off, guys," Ethan said. "Time to see what the old boy has in store for me the rest of the day."

CHAPTER 13

The Manhattan Special Victims Unit was housed in an old 1950s brick-and-cement structure at 221 East 123rd Street in Harlem. It shared space with Police Service Area 5—a small, tactical unit that policed a ten-block area around the station house. SVU's detectives were an elite force within the NYPD, responsible for investigating sex crimes in the borough—all rape, gang rape, torture, pornography, and sexually motivated murders. It also investigated abuse against the very old and the very young. In its heyday, it was well staffed and well budgeted with all the latest toys and technology. But with budget cuts and the reorganization of the NYPD under the de Blasio administration, Special Victims had been reduced to handling the same workload of sex crimes without the manpower or the necessary firepower.

In short, it was operating on a shoestring budget.

Ethan and Mindy were sitting in a taxi heading up First Avenue, Ethan scrolling through his iPad reading stories on the Patricia Highland press conference, while Mindy tweaked the settings on a Panasonic 2-Chip digital camera she'd requisitioned from the tech office and planned to use to record the meeting.

"Highland didn't give them much," he said, buried in a *New York Times* article. "Just the basics. Four murders. All kids. All tortured and posed in the same way. But no specifics on the actual investigation."

"Did you get to the section on GBS?" she said, tweaking the exposure.

"She didn't give them my name, did she?"

"Just that the show is working on the inside, and that she would schedule briefings for everybody else as the investigation progressed."

"Our colleagues at the other networks can't be happy about that."

"That's an understatement. Scroll down to the end of the story," she said, staring at the tiny monitor on the back of the camera.

"Christ. Scott Pelley at CBS News is lobbying the mayor for full access, just like us."

"Won't happen," Mindy said. "I asked Randall about it, and he laughed. Said the mayor is taking his cues from the DA's Office, and we've got the exclusive, because ADA Highland thinks she can control the coverage better with only us, and they want *you* and your input into the investigation."

"That's probably the only reason Peter agreed to the story," Ethan said cynically. "He's hoping some of the spotlight will rub off on him."

The cab approached Martin Luther King Jr. Boulevard and turned left, heading west toward the center of the city. It sloshed through the melting snow and past one burned-out building after another, the windows broken, the facades crumbling, the doors boarded up with plywood. A homeless man was sleeping on a Con Ed steam grate trying to stay warm, a drunk was drinking beer in a doorway, his oversized trench coat hanging open despite the frigid temperatures, while a group of gangbangers—some no older than ten or twelve—were peddling drugs to passing cars on the corner of Second Avenue. They stared at Ethan warily until the cab crawled by then began hustling again as soon as the coast was clear.

They continued driving, turning on a series of side streets, inching through huge puddles of water, until they made a left onto One Hundred Twenty-Third Street and pulled up in front of the precinct.

"Where we meeting everybody?" Ethan asked.

"Supposed to be right here—in front of the precinct."

"Are we early?"

"We're right on time."

"Well, they aren't here, and we certainly aren't gonna wait outside, not in this neighborhood." He grabbed his iPhone and punched in a number. "Where are you, David?" There was a pause. "Smart. Are you with James?" Another pause. "And Lloyd?" A third pause. "Okay, we'll sit tight."

"What's goin' on?" Mindy said.

"He told me to stay in the car. There was a gun battle a half hour ago just around the corner. Rival gangs trying to control the drug trade. One of the shooters was shot and killed. There's an army of cops canvassing the area and investigating the crime scene. We must've driven around them. That's why we didn't see all the commotion. Lloyd's on his way down to get us." Ethan explained the situation to the cabbie, paid the fare, and then they all waited.

Two minutes later, Lloyd walked out the front door and down the steps—just ahead of Gloria Alvarez. They were both carrying firearms—Lloyd a Glock 9mm and Alvarez her Sig Sauer P226—their safety locks off, their weapons pointing at the ground. When they were sure it was safe, they holstered their handguns, approached the cab, and opened the doors for Ethan and Mindy.

"Bullets were flying everywhere just a while ago, *amigo.* Big fucking mess," Alvarez said, pointing to a fresh bullet hole to the left of the front door of the station house. "Come pretty close, how you say it, for comfort, *sí*? I almost cancel our meeting. Thought it too dangerous for you guys, *no*? But then, poof, no more gun battle. Coast clear."

"You expecting any more shooting tonight?" Ethan asked.

"Maybe. Gangs sometimes get even, *sí*? So can't walk streets, until we sure everything's under fucking control."

"Where's the body?" Ethan said as a coroner's van raced down One Hundred Twenty-Third Street, accompanied by two patrol cars, lights flashing, sirens blaring.

"One block north on First Avenue."

"And the shooters?"

"Gone, *amigo.* Hiding in buildings. Come. Forget about drug shooting. Not your concern. Time to work on Child Sex Murders."

Ethan got out of the back seat, the cab already moving as he closed the door, exhaustion from the night before catching up with him. He thought about calling Sarah, telling her where he was, that he was working and not drinking. But then he thought about the tension in Dr. Schwartz's office and the way they'd left without saying a word—distant, combative—and decided to wait until he got home.

"Start recording, Mindy. I wanna document the entire evening, beginning with a shot of us walking up the steps. Make sure to pan over to the bullet hole and back to us as we head into the station."

He fell in line behind Alvarez as she pushed open the door. Mindy tracked them with the digital camera as they entered a small vestibule with a middle-aged African American sergeant perched behind an old wooden desk typing on a computer as the telephones rang off the hook.

"They're with me, Cyrus," Alvarez said. "Ethan Benson and Mindy Herman from Global Broadcasting. Ignore camera. They're doing a story on the Child Sex Murders, and the DA's Office says they can shoot anything they want. Not my call. Big politicians' call."

"What's goin' on out there," he said, checking their names on a computer. "Just heard more sirens."

"Coroner. Getting ready to take goddamn body back to morgue. The guys stuck all night processing crime scene. Lucky son-of-a bitches, *no*? We good to go?"

The desk sergeant nodded, and Alvarez led them into a huge room, maybe forty feet square, crammed with old metal desks, file cabinets, and evidence boxes. There were plainclothes detectives working the phones, typing police reports, and taking statements from a slew of victims, mostly women, some battered, some bleeding, some crying hysterically. A young man with a gash over his right eye, accused of raping his girlfriend and beating her within inches of her life, was sitting in a small lockup next to an empty office. He was chain-smoking a cigarette, discarded butts on the floor all around him. He stood and leaned up against the bars, staring, his eyes locked on Mindy, then grabbed his crotch, and started hissing as she zoomed in to a tight shot.

"No pictures, man. No pictures. Or I give you some of this." He thrust his hips forward. "Get the fucking bitch away from me. I no wanna talk. I wanna lawyer."

Mindy slowly backed away, unfazed, as he started violently shaking the bars then panned across the rest of the precinct. Some of the abused women stared into the lens shell-shocked, others hid their faces, others waved her away—but the detectives kept asking their questions, typing on their computers, ignoring the camera.

"You have to get releases before you can air this shit," Alvarez said curtly.

"James will take care of that. Otherwise, we'll blur their faces in the edit room," Ethan said, peering around the room. "Who's working the Child Sex Murders case?"

"Not here," Alvarez said. "Upstairs."

They went through a steel door behind Alvarez that led to a stairwell littered with Styrofoam cups, candy wrappers, and dead cigarettes.

"I know what you're thinking," Alvarez said as she turned and looked down at Ethan two steps below. "Fucking Mayor de Blasio keeps cutting budget. Less money for cleaning. Less money for overtime. Less money for cops. Barely got enough to do our jobs. That's why you here, *amigo*. To get us big publicity. Big money. More *manpower*. So we catch fucking killer, *no*?"

"But there was just another kid murdered," Ethan said. "It was plastered on the front page of every newspaper. The police commissioner didn't beef up the investigation?"

Alvarez's face grew hard. "You think we have big task force now that fourth *chiquita* raped, tortured, murdered? Today, is bigger. 'Cause big suits at City Hall breathin' down our necks screamin' for results. But you wait, tomorrow drug dealer up street get big headlines in papers. And suits, they forget us. Money and manpower go there and task force shrink again, *sí*? That's way it works. That's why we work around clock. That's why I stuck with you, *Mr. Investigator-Producer*. So big suits no forget. *Comprendes*?" She stared probingly into Ethan's eyes. "Come, almost there. I show you."

Alvarez opened another steel door and pressed into a nearly empty room. The atmosphere was quiet, subdued, a handful of detectives huddled in a small group, flipping through documents, staring at crime scene photos.

"Brain center," she said. "Lemme introduce you to *big* team."

Ethan motioned for Mindy to keep shooting, then entered a small, cluttered conference room with a round table, a large pegboard crowded with photos of the four dead girls in situ, and two detectives dressed in black suits, white shirts, and ties. David was labeling a stack of video disks and handing them to James who was carefully placing them in his backpack, while Lloyd, standing next to Randall Newton, was studying the photos of the girls.

"This is Ethan Benson, the producer of *The Weekly Reporter*," Alvarez said formally. "And the lady shooting pictures is Mindy Herman, his associate producer. Say hello to new members of team."

The two detectives nodded.

"The big guy with no hair is Henry Dinkus out of Sixth Precinct," Alvarez said, continuing the introductions. "And young lady sitting next to him is Kathy Bowman from Twelfth. She join task force this morning after the last Jane Doe found at Dry Dock Playground. She's gonna lead that end of investigation. Now three detectives assigned to case. Task force much bigger, *no*?" She shook her head disgustedly.

Both detectives acknowledged Ethan but remained silent.

"So now that we dispense with formalities, down to business," she said officiously. "You got murder books, *sí*?"

"Already making copies," James said, continuing to catalogue disks.

"And crime scene videos?"

"That's what I just gave them," Dinkus said. "The three murders at Pier 51 and all the shit Kathy's team shot last night."

"I'll need copies to take home," Ethan said, turning to David.

"You got it, boss," he said, affixing the last label to a disk. "I'll have an Avid editor send you a link."

Ethan scanned the room. "So bring us up to speed. Last night's victim was staged in a different location. The killer changed his MO. Are you sure it's the same guy and not a copycat?"

"Gotto be the same guy," Lloyd said, pointing to the latest victim. "Her body's posed in exactly the same position as the other three girls."

"And the torture wounds are all the same," Bowman said, sliding a document to Ethan. "The coroner's report."

Ethan quickly scanned the five pages. "Cigarette burns, bruising around her vagina, slashes up and down her arms, a thin gash around her neck. From the same kind of garrote?"

"ME says it's a dead match," Bowman said flatly. "A synthetic. Polyethylene fiber. One quarter inch diameter."

"All four murders?"

"Identical," Alvarez said.

More proof it's the same guy, Ethan thought. *Is it important?* He turned to Alvarez. "And you can't ID the new victim, because the killer pulled her teeth and cut off her fingers like the others?"

"*Si.* We running DNA and fingerprints on body," Alvarez said. "But don't hold breath. If like other murders, we get nothin'."

"And nobody's come forward looking for a missing child?"

"*No.*"

"What about alcohol or drugs in the kid's system?" Lloyd said, eyeballing the coroner's report over Ethan's shoulder.

"The new Jane Doe appears to be clean," Bowman said emphatically.

"Can I see the tox reports?" Ethan said.

Bowman slid another file across the table. "They're preliminary, but from the initial results and the lack of track marks, the kid didn't do drugs or drink."

"What about semen?"

Bowman slid another lab report across the table. "Swabs showed multiple sex partners."

"So this kid was sexually active too?"

"Looks that way," Dinkus said.

"And how old was she?"

"Coroner says ten. Maybe eleven."

Ethan leaned back in his chair. So all four girls had barely reached puberty and were having sex with lots of guys. How was that possible? Were they runaways? Were they living on the streets? Were they kid whores? There was something gnawing in the back of his mind. Something he had felt the moment Lloyd had first told him about the story. But what was it? Then the nub of the thought vanished.

"And I take it," he said, "that we can't ID the killer from the semen samples?"

"Keep dreaming, Benson," Alvarez said sardonically. "This one smart killer, *si*?"

Ethan ignored her flip comment. "So we're still working under the same assumption even though we have no concrete proof," he said, standing and carefully peering at the photos of the four dead girls pinned next to each other on the pegboard. "It's the same killer."

The three detectives nodded.

"Why'd he pick an Asian girl this time? The other three were Latinas."

"No theories," Alvarez said cautiously. "Our profiler's working on it."

"What's his name?" David said, pulling out a pen and paper from his backpack.

"Leon Fennimore."

"FBI, right?" Ethan said.

"Out of Quantico."

"Can we talk to him?"

Alvarez nodded, pulled out her cell phone, and forwarded Fennimore's contact information to Ethan. "I'll give Leon a heads-up you gonna call."

Ethan nodded then turned back to the photos of the four dead girls. "Any luck with the security cameras around the playground?"

"Only a handful and none of them worked," Bowman said. "Not surprising. The neighborhood is a fucking ghetto."

"Eyewitnesses?"

Alvarez chuckled. "We canvass each building, and everybody yell and scream that police lazy, don't do job, let neighborhood go to shit. But no, nobody saw nothin'. They hate police as much as bad guys. Wouldn't tell us nothin' even if they see whole goddamn murder."

"And cell phone videos?" Ethan asked.

"I'll send you what we got," Bowman said, jotting herself a note. "But it's all aftermath, video of the crime scene guys canvassing the murder site. Nobody had anything of the killer, or the murder."

"What about the tire tracks?" Ethan said.

"One set was from a utility vehicle and the other from a van. Can't get more specific than that."

"And the footprints?"

"Two sets. One was combat boot, size 16," Alvarez said, dropping a photo on the table. "So some big guy was there. And the other we see before at Pier 51." She lined up four photos, one from each crime scene. "They all match—a small footprint, size 7, and check out irregularity in tread at big toe. Same pattern, *si*?"

More proof the same guy was involved in all four murders, Ethan thought. *But now there are two sets of footprints. Did the killer have an accomplice?*

"Could there be two killers?" he said.

"Possibly. But we're still leaning to one guy committing all four murders," Dinkus said.

Ethan paced the room then peered at the four dead girls on the pegboard again. "What are these?" he said, pointing to the square of skin removed from each of the girl's ankles. "They look exactly the same."

"They are," Bowman said. "Same size. Same shape."

"Any idea what they mean?" Ethan said.

"Your guess is as good as mine," Bowman said. "The profiler is trying to figure it out. Could be symbolic of something. Of what, he ain't sure yet."

"Did the killer use the same knife to cut out the squares?" Ethan said, pulling a photo from the pegboard. "And these slash marks on her arm. They're all even and precise."

"You smart, Benson," Alvarez said. "Coroner thinks they all came from same kinda blade."

"A Karl Storz surgical knife? Like the one you found last night?"

"That's his theory," Alvarez said stoically, turning to Bowman. "What did coroner say in his report on yesterday's murder?"

"I've still got it," Lloyd said, flipping through the document and handing a page to Ethan. "Read the first paragraph."

Ethan scanned the document then read out loud, "The square of skin and the slash marks found on Jane Doe number four appear to match the other three victims and are consistent with incisions made by a Karl Storz No. 6 surgical blade or another brand of surgical knife roughly two inches long, a half inch wide, and an eighth of an inch thick. He whipped around to Alvarez. "And you found a Karl Storz surgical blade at Pier 51, right?"

"That's what lab guy says in evidence report, *si*?"

"Any fingerprints on the blades?"

Alvarez shook her head. "Killer used Latex gloves. Lab found residue on both knives."

"So that's a dead end," Ethan said, frowning. "Any idea where you can buy them? Maybe the killer used the same medical supply house?"

"That's a fucking long shot," Randall Newton said, speaking for the first time from the corner of the room.

"Glad you paying attention, Randall."

"Fuck-off, Gloria."

"Well, we got no other shit on this guy at moment except fucking footprints," Alvarez said. "Benson's got good idea. We need to check sales records from medical supply houses in city. That'll take time, but maybe it give us name. Give us lead, *si*."

"And who's gonna do that?" Newton said harshly. "We still got a bare-bones team working the murders."

"Well, you hot shit prosecutor. Go to ADA Highland and get me more people."

"Waste of time," Newton said, digging in. "We should use our resources more wisely."

"I run police investigation and you manage politics, and this, Randall, is best lead at moment. Get me foot soldiers while we still on front page of newspapers. We need to go through sales reports. Otherwise, I do it myself, or maybe, I give copy to Benson and let him do it. Now that won't look good to big boss lady if she finds out you refuse to help task force, *si*? 'Cause that's your job, *RANDALL*. To get me more people and more money so I can do my job, *no*?"

"Fuck-off, Gloria."

Ethan watched the exchange silently. There was simmering tension between the two of them, genuine animosity. He turned and faced Mindy who was peering into the camera as she pulled back to a two-shot of Alvarez and Newton. Hopefully, she'd captured the sequence and was still rolling as Newton pushed back his chair and stood.

"I'll see what I can do," he said angrily. "Just hope you know what you're doing, Alvarez. It's a big waste of time if you ask me. Big waste." He peered at his wristwatch. "Let's pick up in the morning. It's been a long day, and I gotta get some sleep." Then he faced Ethan and said caustically, "Making waves already, Benson. Just what Patricia Highland said you'd do when she brought you on board. Except in this case, you're sending us down a dead end."

Ethan watched as he turned and disappeared down the staircase.

Something was amiss with Randall Newton.

And Ethan needed to know what it was.

CHAPTER 14

Ethan walked into his apartment and locked the door then placed his briefcase on the floor underneath the side table and hung his overcoat in the closet. The lights were dimmed in the center hallway as he made his way to the living room, following the muffled sound of the television playing quietly in the background. He had avoided talking to Sarah since they'd left his psychiatrist's office—too worried she'd grill him about his drinking and his off-the-cuff comment to step down as Peter Sampson's senior producer. It was the first time the words had ever slipped out of his mouth. Now it was out in the open, an albatross hanging around his neck, waiting to be discussed and dissected like a festering sore.

Steeling himself, he slipped into the living room and found her lying on the couch in a bathrobe, her feet bare, her hair neatly washed and combed. The TV was tuned to local news, but Ethan could see she wasn't watching, that she was quietly seething and ready for a fight. Before he could utter a word, she sat up and said coldly, "How could you, Ethan?"

He sat next to her and tried to kiss her cheek.

"Don't," she said, turning and pushing him away. "I've been worried sick all day, waiting for you to call, but no, you didn't bother. Not even once." She glared at him, her eyes fierce. "Don't you care about me, Ethan? Don't I mean anything at all to you anymore?"

"Babe, let me explain."

She leaned over and smelt his breath. "At least you weren't out drinking in that fucking bar, McGlades. Where the fuck were you?"

"Working," he said, a little too sharply.

"But you didn't bother to tell me you'd be home late, knowing I was pissed after we'd met with Dr. Schwartz." She sat silently—livid, taciturn. "And what the fuck did you mean when you said you don't want to be Peter's senior producer anymore. Have you lost your mind?"

Ethan lit a cigarette, taking a long pull, hoping the nicotine would mask his racing heart. "I've been meaning to tell you for a long time."

"So why didn't you?"

He took another drag on his cigarette. "I dunno, babe. I couldn't find the right words, I couldn't bring myself to admit it, I couldn't—"

"Find the courage."

"That's not fair, Sarah."

"But it's true."

"Well—"

"Say it. That you were scared to tell me."

"Come on, babe."

"Don't 'come on' me, Ethan. I have a right to know. Are you going to quit your job?"

He lit another cigarette with the one he'd just finished and moved to a wing chair opposite her. The rift between them had grown into a canyon, and deep down he knew Sarah would never understand what he was feeling. That even with his constant complaining about the endless meetings and the endless phone calls, she believed he'd never walk away from the money and prestige that came with being Peter Sampson's senior producer. Now everything was out in the open, front and center, no longer a secret tucked away in the recesses of his mind. But instead of being honest and explaining, he said nothing, keeping his feelings buried deep inside.

"So you won't talk about it," she said gruffly.

"I haven't made up my mind yet."

"Horseshit." Her tone was sharp, caustic. "And you won't tell me why?"

He lowered his eyes.

"Be that way," she said, standing and walking to the door, before stopping and wheeling around. "Go make love to your Scotch. You don't care about me anymore. You only care about yourself."

Ethan kept staring at the floor.

"Say no more. You just answered my question." She backed down the center hallway, never taking her eyes off him, then disappeared into their bedroom, locking the door behind her.

*****

Ethan pushed into his study and made a beeline to the wet bar. He hadn't had a drink all day, controlling the urge for a taste, for a glass of Scotch to ease the pain building inside him. Oh, the relief. The warmth. The oblivion it would bring. All his problems would vanish. All his cares would disappear. All his fears would melt away in the euphoria of the alcohol as it spilled through his body. He grabbed the bottle of Black Label and lifted it to his lips, downing a long pull, the Scotch biting his insides, melting his anxieties. He wiped his mouth on his sleeve and poured three fingers into a glass. Better. Much better. He'd deal with Sarah later, when he had more courage. She was his wife. They were a family. And he knew she loved him.

It would be okay.

It had to be.

Carrying his drink and the bottle to his desk, he took another belt and turned on his laptop. He glanced at the annotated version of the murder book and thought about reading it, then decided to wait until James sent him copies of the originals so he could evaluate the raw evidence without any spin from the task force.

He lit a cigarette. Why hadn't he told Sarah the truth? Why couldn't he discuss his feelings? Why was he pushing her away? Maybe he shouldn't work anymore tonight? Maybe he should rush down to the bedroom and talk to her? Hold her? Make love to her? Maybe he was a fool.

Instead, he remained anchored to his desk clutching his Scotch, staring blankly at the wall in front of him, until he finished the last drop and poured another glass. Grabbing his iPhone in a panic, he punched in Mindy's number.

"You still awake?"

"Jeez, Ethan," she said, mildly irritated, "don't you ever sleep?"

"Only when I'm forced to," he said, slurring his words.

"You're drunk."

"That's my business, Mindy."

"No, it's not. It's affecting all of us who love you. You need to get help."

"I'm goin' to a shrink."

"Not enough anymore. You need to go somewhere and dry out."

Shit. She thinks I need rehab like Dr. Schwartz. How much longer can I run away from it? "Look, I don't wanna talk about it," he said belligerently. "I wanna screen the footage you shot tonight."

"All of it?"

"The whole thing."

"And it can't wait until the morning?"

"No."

"You're hopeless, Ethan. Give me a minute. Gotta upload the data from the camera into my computer. Then I'll post it on WeTransfer so you can download it." He listened as she put down the phone and began fumbling in the background. Five minutes later she was back on the line. "Just sent everything. Runs about an hour. Let me know when you've got it."

Ethan punched on the icon for his e-mail and waited for her message to hit his box.

"Just landed," he said. "Hold on while I check the attachment." He clicked the link to WeTransfer—marked Special Victims Unit and dated that day—then clicked on download.

"Well?" Mindy said.

"Should have it in a few minutes."

"What are you looking for?" she said.

"Randall Newton."

"Why?"

"A hunch."

"What does that mean?"

"Can't say at the moment."

"Well, he didn't say much, so I didn't get a lot. But I got the sequence at the end of the meeting."

"Good. Good," he said, slurring his words badly.

"Ethan, lay off the damn bottle before it kills you. And if you want my advice, go to bed and sleep it off. I'll ring you in the morning."

Ethan punched off the phone and poured another Scotch as he waited for the video to finish downloading. He drank it all at once, capped the bottle, and blurted out loud, "Enough, Mr. Benson. You've had quite enough tonight." Then he started laughing hysterically, before tears welled in his eyes. "Man, I'm totally loaded. Totally out of control. Nothing more than a damn stinking drunk."

He started shaking.

Wiped the tears on his shirtsleeve.

And stared blankly at the computer until an image filled the screen.

Then he hit Play, the sound kicking in almost immediately as the camera settled on a wide shot of Ethan and Detective

Alvarez ascending the steps and entering the building. He tried to focus, but his vision was blurred. Shaking his head, he stared at the computer until his mind gradually cleared. Then he checked the time. 1:00 a.m. He'd been awake for two days and his body was crashing, so he puffed away on his cigarette, punched a command into his laptop and fast-forwarded at double speed, the images blowing through the screen—a battered woman with a black eye crying in the corner, a cop furiously taking notes, the crazy man in lockup shaking the bars and screaming. The clock kept ticking, the night slipping away, so Ethan pushed the video faster, the images now flying, until the camera settled at the top of the staircase and zoomed into the conference room.

The task force at the table.

Randall Newton in the background.

He stubbed out his cigarette and lit another, his mouth parched, and peered at the bottle of Black Label. One more. For a quick burst of energy so he could finish screening. No harm in that. It would do him good. Any thoughts of Sarah and his job and his life falling apart vanishing in the never-ending pull of the Scotch. Pausing the video, he poured two inches, drank, and licked his lips, the alcohol tingling his throat. Now he could keep going. He placed the glass next to the ashtray, the smoke from his cigarette curling around him, and hit Play, screening another twenty minutes of the tape—hoping to catch a glimpse of Randall Newton that would confirm his suspicions.

Mindy had captured the meeting from a series of different angles, never stopping the camera, and as she had warned him, there was little of Randall Newton—only a handful of tight shots and a couple of wide shots where he blended into the background. Frustrated, Ethan checked the footage counter—only five minutes until the end. Gulping the rest of his drink, he watched the footage stream by—Lloyd standing at the pegboard staring at the photos of the dead girls, Kathy Bowman sliding the file folder with the new autopsy report across the table, Ethan reading the line about the Karl Storz surgical blades. Then the argument between Alvarez and Newton over committing manpower to canvass the medical supply houses. Was that unusual? With all the tension from the case? Maybe not.

Ethan replayed the argument.

It still seemed unimportant. Just a difference of opinion between two people who'd been working for months, unable to track down a killer. He let the video run to the end and poured another finger of Scotch.

Standing, he peered at the monitor, the room spinning as Mindy tracked around the table, pausing at each member of the team—Alvarez, Bowman, Dinkus, Lloyd, David, James—before ending on Randall Newton, hunched over and quietly scribbling on a piece of paper. Ethan paused the shot. Mindy had positioned the camera just over Newton's shoulder, the slip of paper clearly sitting at the bottom of the screen. He hit Play, listening as Newton said it was time to go home then folded the paper and placed it in his coat pocket. He replayed the sequence, pausing just before the camera settled on Newton. Then he punched a set of commands on the keyboard and ran it frame by frame until he could clearly see the handwriting.

He stared at the image.

What the hell?

He zoomed in tighter then opened the top drawer of his desk, rifled through a stack of papers, and pulled out a magnifying glass. He grabbed a pen and paper and wrote down the following words: *Make the call as soon as the meeting is over. Urgent.*

What the fuck did that mean?

And who did Newton need to speak to?

Patricia Highland?

Somebody else?

He leaned back in his chair and finished his Scotch, wondering what he should do next. It was too late to call Mindy, too late to call Lloyd—but he had this nagging suspicion about

Randall Newton, that he was playing both sides of the coin, so he shot them a short e-mail:

> *Just finished screening tonight's footage. There's an interesting moment at the end of Randall Newton writing himself a note to call somebody. No idea who it is, and I'm sure there's no way to find out, but there's something off about this guy. I can feel it in my bones. First thing tomorrow, I want both of you to run a background check on Newton. I want to know everything about him—where he went to college, how long he's been working at the Manhattan District Attorney's Office, how much money he makes, and how much cash he has in the bank. I may be barking up the wrong tree, but I don't think so. Regroup in the morning.*

Then he turned off his computer, poured one last Scotch, and drank it. Standing, his legs unsteady, he fell back into his chair. Maybe he'd rest a minute, just a minute, until he felt better; then he'd get up and go to bed. He put his head down on his desk, closed his eyes, and within seconds, passed out.

CHAPTER 15

Ethan opened his eyes and stared at the bottle of Black Label, an empty glass overturned, Scotch soaking the documents on the corner of his desk. *What time is it? Where am I? Why am I sitting in a chair and not in bed with Sarah? And what the fuck smells so bad?* He tried to stand then noticed the pool of dried vomit covering his shirt and pants. Shit, I must've puked in the middle of the night. Gotta get out of these clothes and into the shower then come back and clean up this mess. He rubbed his eyes and lit a cigarette and thought about a quick eye-opener to straighten his head, dismissing the thought before stripping down to his boxer shorts and staggering down the hallway to his bedroom.

Sarah was sitting in front of the mirror in her vanity, applying lipstick and fussing with her hair. She spotted him through the glass, her eyes cold, her expression hard.

"You disgust me, Ethan. You're a stinking drunk. A shell of the man I once loved. Don't come near me."

Ethan hesitated then slowly moved toward her.

"Stop. Now. Don't you dare touch me."

"Sarah, babe—"

"Don't 'babe' me, Ethan. You stink of vomit."

"But, Sarah—"

"Enough," she said, holding up her hand. "I have nothing to say to you, and there is nothing you can say to me to make things better. Go get some coffee. And then get into the shower. Maybe that will sober you up."

Ethan hesitated, unsure of himself, trying to find the right words to ease the pain they were both feeling. "I love you, Sarah, you know that."

"Fuck that. Fuck you. Love isn't enough anymore. I can't stand to be around you. Just go and leave me alone. I'll be gone in a few minutes."

"Sarah, please—"

"No more talking. Just get out of my sight and leave me alone."

He stood stock still and noticed the single tear dripping down her cheek, smudging her makeup, then turned and strode out of the room.

*****

Randall Newton pushed through the door and down the steps of One Hogan Place. The temperature was hovering about twenty degrees, and he was chilled to the bone as he hiked the collar of his Brooks Brothers trench coat snuggly around his neck. By the time he reached the sidewalk, he was shaking all over. He checked his watch. Almost 9:00 a.m. He was taking a big risk ducking out of the office, even though he'd been sitting at his desk for two hours, pouring through the murder books, searching for references to the Karl Storz No. 6 surgical knives, hoping to bury their importance and deflect the task force from pursuing a search for their owner.

After last night's meeting with Benson, that might be impossible.

He stood on a snowbank, now covered in filth, and checked to make sure nobody had seen him leave, then hailed a yellow cab and slipped into the back seat.

"Chinatown. The corner of Mott and Canal Streets," he said, still wary he'd been spotted. The driver hit his meter and began weaving through the crowded streets, the rush-hour traffic crawling.

He wiped his brow.

He was covered in nervous sweat, even though the temperature inside the cab was as cold as on the street. He flipped open his briefcase, rifled through half a dozen files, until he found the one marked *Karl Storz Surgical Knives* containing police reports from the third and fourth murders and autopsy reports confirming the knives had been used on all four victims. He was deep in thought when the cabbie pulled to the curb and said, "Eleven dollars, even."

"Hold on a sec," Newton said, quickly stuffing the file back into his briefcase and reaching for his wallet. He pulled out a ten and four ones, handed the cash to the driver, and said, "Keep the change."

Slipping on his gloves, he opened the door and stepped into six inches of slush, his shoes instantly soaked. Shaking his feet furiously, he cursed and started down Mott Street, the sidewalks clogged with Chinese immigrants, some dressed in traditional *Tangzhuang*, some dressed in the latest Western fashions. He passed one outdoor market after another—a store selling exotic fruits and vegetables, another displaying Peking-style ducks hanging from hooks in neat rows, and yet another with dozens of Eastern teas in open-air vats on a table taking up most of the sidewalk. His feet became numb as he limped down to Hester Street, looked over his shoulder one last time, then ducked into a small restaurant—*Hung Chow Delicacies.*

He waved to a bartender wearing a silk *Ba Gua Kungfu* shirt and past three elderly Chinese men sipping tea and counting numbers slips. They nodded as he walked to the back of the restaurant and picked the darkest booth along the far wall. Facing the door, he sat and unbuttoned his overcoat, leaving it draped over his shoulders to keep warm. He waited five minutes, tapping his fingers impatiently on the table, then ordered a pot of *Golden Monkey* tea and pulled out his cell phone. He stared reluctantly at the LCD screen then punched in the now-familiar number. He waited—three rings, five rings, seven rings—until a gravelly voice answered.

"Are you on a burner?"

"Yes."

"Alone?"

"I'm not in the DA's Office, if that's what you mean."

There was a short pause, the only sound the hiss of the telephone line. Then the man said, "What happened last night?"

"We all met at SVU," Newton said nervously.

"Benson?"

"And three of his assistants."

"Names."

"James Lapidus, David Livingston, and that girl, Mindy Herman."

"The lady at the Patricia Highland meeting?"

"Same one, and she was shooting a video camera."

"What about the private investigator, Lloyd Howard?"

"He was there too."

There was another long pause. Newton could hear the man striking a match and then inhaling a cigarette.

"Well, this is not part of our deal," he said, hissing through the phone. "You were supposed to make sure nothing like this ever happened. That the task force would never get publicity. Now your boss is holding press conferences. And this guy, Benson, is doing a story about the investigation. This is a problem."

"Well—"

"Can you get Benson off the case?"

"Well—"

"Shut up, you coward. I'll take care of it myself. You're a useless piece of goat dung."

Newton's hands began shaking. "We've got another problem."

"What now?"

Newton hesitated.

"Tell me, asshole," the man said, screaming into the phone.

"Benson is obsessed about the surgical knives, the ones the Butcher left at the crime scenes.

"You told me that wouldn't be a problem."

"It wasn't until the second one showed up at the Dry Dock Playground. Now he's convinced the task force to focus on where they came from and to search medical supply houses for people who might have purchased them."

"A long shot," the man said dismissively.

"But what if they get lucky and connect them to your boy?"

"Then it becomes your problem, Randall. You're on the inside. You're supposed to make sure the investigation goes nowhere. That's what I'm paying you for. If you fuck this thing up, I'll tip off the cops to your little secret, or maybe, I'll let the Butcher have his way with you. That won't be pretty, will it?"

Newton's Adam's apple started bobbing in his throat like a ping-pong ball.

"I want to see the evidence on the knives," the man said coldly. "Did you bring it."

Newton clicked open his briefcase then said, stuttering. "I got-got-got—"

"Shut up and listen to me. I'm sending someone to get it. And he'll have a package for you to give to our guy at City Hall. Maybe we can get him to work his magic and cut off any new money for that fucking task force now that the pigs in the press are all over the story. Maybe we can even get him to shut it down entirely. You at the usual place?"

"I-I-I—"

"I'll take that as a yes. Don't leave."

"But-but-but, I've got a meeting with Patricia Highland."

"So you'll be late. Make an excuse."

The man clicked off the phone, Newton holding the burner pressed to his ear, listening to silence. Slowly, he placed the cell phone back in his briefcase, picked up the pot of tea, his hands trembling, and spilled it all over the table as he tried to refill his cup.

*****

Ethan paid the cabbie and got out of a taxi in front of the broadcast center. His face was drawn, his eyes bloodshot, his head pounding, his hangover worse than he could ever remember. He was still reeling from his confrontation with Sarah. She had never been so distant, so cruel. She had never made him feel so broken. And what did she mean love wasn't enough anymore? Was she about to leave him? Was she about to take Luke and go? Fearful, he pulled his woolen cap over his ears to ward off the chill and headed to the revolving door leading into the lobby where a man dressed in a heavy down coat and silk scarf stepped in front of him.

Winston Peabody.

The WGBS reporter who had spotted him at the crime scene.

"Ethan, how you doing?" he said cheerfully. "Got a minute?"

Ethan immediately stiffened. He'd known Peabody for years, bumping into him occasionally at company parties, but never working or collaborating on a story.

"Not now, Winston. I'm running late."

"Come on, Ethan, just got a few questions."

Ethan hesitated then said, "Not here. Walk with me to Starbucks."

They crossed Fifty-Seventh Street in silence, dodging the heavy traffic, and pushed through the door, where they were met with the scent of fresh coffee.

"Looks like you need a jolt of caffeine," Peabody said. "Late night?"

"Didn't sleep much."

"Out working your story?"

"Come on, Winston, my boss made it perfectly clear to your boss," he said contemptuously. "We can't share any information about the Child Sex Murders investigation. My hands are tied. That ground rule was laid down by the ADA in charge of the case." They reached the head of the line. "What do you wanna drink?"

"A large black coffee."

He turned to the barista. "Two Venti coffees."

Peabody continued pushing. "I'm not asking for details, Ethan. I just need a feel for what's going on. This story is big. It's screaming headlines in all the papers. It's leading all the local newscasts. Christ, the entire city is on edge. There's a maniac out there killing little girls, displaying them like artwork in playgrounds, and you're at the center of the investigation. We work for the same company. Can you give me anything?"

"No," Ethan said flatly. He grabbed the two coffees, paid the bill, and handed one to Peabody. "I can't release anything until the case is solved."

"Just a little background to give us an edge over the competition?"

"Won't do it," Ethan said, hurrying out of the Starbucks. "Take a hike, Winston. I got a meeting with Peter Sampson."

Peabody followed Ethan across the street and stopped him in front of the broadcast center. "I'm not looking to give you a hard time, but I wanna know first if you release any info on the investigation."

Ethan nodded then said abruptly, "I'll get back to you."

"Be that way," Peabody said. "And, Ethan, I got a tip for you. Pick up some mouthwash before you go to your meeting. Your breath stinks of alcohol."

*****

Randall Newton checked the time. Ten thirty. His first task force meeting with Patricia Highland was about to get under way in the conference room at the DA's Office, and he was going to miss it. What excuse would he give her? She ran the schedule with an iron fist, so he needed to come up with a plausible story; otherwise, she'd ream him a new asshole. He ordered a fresh pot of *Golden Monkey* tea, and right on schedule, his office cell phone buzzed in his coat pocket. The ADA. He ignored the call. Two minutes later, she rang again. He turned off the power and slipped the phone back into his pocket.

He waited.

Five minutes.

Ten minutes.

Fifteen minutes.

Then the front door swung open, and an enormous Chinese man stormed into the restaurant—the same Chinese man who had delivered Jane Doe number four to the Butcher. Newton watched him scan the restaurant, his eyes darting back and forth, before he came up to the booth and wedged his big body into the banquet across from him. Without asking, he grabbed Newton's cup of tea and slowly began to sip.

"The boss is pissed."

Newton wiped his brow, beads of sweat pooling on his skin.

"And you know the reason why," he said, staring, his face impassive.

Newton squirmed. "But it's not my fault, Bingwen."

"Shut up and give me the documents."

Newton clicked open his briefcase and pulled out the folder containing the evidence on the Karl Storz surgical knives. The big man grabbed it and, as fast as a streak of lightning, slapped him hard across the face.

"Now you listen to me, Randall, you piece of cow dung. The boss wants you to make sure the cops never connect the knives to the Butcher." He waved the file in his face. "He doesn't care how you do it, just make sure it doesn't happen. Ever. Because if the task force pins the murders on our boy, and he sings to the cops to save his skin, then you know what that means, don't you?"

"I'll do the best I—"

"Shut up." The big man slid an envelope across the table. "You know what to do with this."

Newton grabbed the envelope, his hands trembling, sweat pouring down his brow, and slipped it into his coat pocket. "They're gonna find me out, Bingwen. I can't do this anymore."

"You sniveling dog," Bingwen said, spitting in his face. "Just do it and don't make yourself scarce. The boss wants to know everything you're doing." Then he climbed out of the booth and disappeared onto the street, leaving Newton mopping up a glob of mucous dribbling down his chin with a napkin.

*****

Ethan unlocked the door to his office, tossed his overcoat on the couch, and dropped into the leather chair behind his desk. He'd stopped at the Duane Reade on Fifty-Seventh Street and Seventh Avenue, purchased a small bottle of mouthwash, then headed straight to the men's room on the eleventh floor. He'd quickly gargled and splashed water on his face, stunned by his pallid color and the deep lines under his eyes. *I'm falling apart, and everybody's gonna know—like that fucking Winston Peabody. I gotta get a grip. I gotta stop drinking. Before I lose Sarah. Before I lose everything.* Combing his hair and straightening his tie, he marched down to his office and past his assistant, James, not making eye contact.

He guzzled half his coffee then booted up his computer as James knocked on the open door and walked into his office. "It's after eleven, Ethan. Peter's furious."

"Tell him I'm here."

"He knows that. He's waiting for you to go see him. What should I say?"

"That I'll be there in a moment," he said offhandedly as Peter suddenly stormed through the door and waved James away.

"Where the hell have you been?" he said furiously, placing both hands on the edge of the desk and looming over Ethan. "No telephone call. No e-mail. Not a word. I've been here for almost three hours. You missed every meeting." He paced around the room. "Don't you read your schedule. I know you got a copy. James said he e-mailed you before he left last night."

"No excuses, Peter," Ethan said, carefully choosing his words. "I worked late on our Child Sex Murders story and didn't get to sleep until about five, then slept through my alarm clock. Won't happen again."

"You're damn straight it won't," Peter said, pointing his finger. "You're on thin ice. I've already talked to Paul, and the only reason you're still working for me is that he's not ready to fire you. But that can change and it will, so help me God, if you pull one more stunt like this morning, we're finished."

Ethan wanted to quit on the spot, but held his tongue as Paul walked into his office.

"I could hear you yelling all the way down the hall. What's going on?"

"You know what's going on," Peter said belligerently. "Ethan was late again and didn't have the common courtesy to tell me he was bailing on our entire morning schedule. I already told you I was pissed."

Paul sat down. "We talked about this yesterday, Ethan," he said, his voice calm but stern.

"I know. I know. I worked much later than I should have."

"Mindy told me," Paul said. "I bumped into her in the hallway, and she told me about the meeting with the task force. Did you fill in Peter?"

"Of course not," Peter said gruffly. "I'm the last person Ethan tells anything."

"Tell him," Paul said gently.

Ethan spent the next ten minutes bringing Peter up to speed—concentrating on the Karl Storz surgical knives and his recommendation that Gloria Alvarez canvass the medical supply companies in the city to come up with names of people who had recently purchased the No. 6 blades.

"It's a long shot, but it may be our first big lead."

"Anything else I should know?" Peter said sharply.

Ethan thought about Randall Newton, but decided not to mention his suspicions, not until he had something more concrete. "Nothing else significant."

"So are you going to disappear again today?" Peter said. "Or are you going to do your job?"

Ethan hesitated then said testily, "Look, I'm here, right. And I just told you. It won't happen again."

"Enough," Paul said, raising his hands. "Let's table this until later, Peter. We have a lunch meeting with Fred Pierce. Can't keep the chairman waiting."

They both stood, but before reaching the door, Peter said disdainfully, "Last warning, Ethan, and don't you forget it."

Ethan sat quietly as they headed to Paul's office. It could have been worse. Much worse. Neither asked if he'd been drinking, or if he was hungover. If that was the real reason he'd been late. That would have been the end of him for sure. He had to get his drinking under control. He had to. Otherwise, his whole world would come crashing down around him.

CHAPTER 16

Maria opened her eyes, the crate that was her prison rocking back and forth. She could hear men shouting, engines droning below, ship horns blaring in the background. Where were they taking her now? Had she arrived in New York? She'd been locked in the crate for what seemed an eternity, on a journey that never ended, with no one to talk to, no one to comfort her. *I want my momma and papa.* And those terrible, horrible men on the boat—the men who had brought her food, changed her slop buckets, given her a new set of rags every few days, and murdered Juanita. *Poor, poor Juanita. Why did they do it? Why did they kill you? Why? Why? Why?*

She was physically exhausted, but the cuts and bruises on her body had started to heal. There'd been no new beatings and no more men doing those disgusting things to her. That had all abruptly stopped after the two men had stuffed Juanita's little body in the plastic bag, leaving her alone in this godforsaken place.

She was scared.

Hungry.

Abandoned.

The crate suddenly stopped swaying, thumping on the ground, as two heavy chains were draped over the top of the container. Maria stood and listened, taking in every sound, searing it into her memory. It began moving—bouncing, bouncing, bouncing—picking up speed. The crate must be on a truck.

What else could it be? Then an engine roared, Maria looking for purchase on the wood walls as she was tossed around like on the playground, when the boys got too rough with their games. She curled into a ball and started to scream, "I wanna go home. Momma, Papa, come save me. Where are they taking me?"

Tears began flowing down her cheeks, her face contorting in terror, until she suddenly snapped and fell silent, forgetting her parents, her home in her little village, her old way of life. There was no more screaming, no more hysteria, no feelings at all.

She stared into the darkness,

Her mind disappearing somewhere else.

*****

Bingwen stood in the doorway of the Allied Shipping Company, a warehouse facility tucked away amongst other nondescript buildings at the eastern end of the Red Hook Container Terminal in Brooklyn. He was staring through a pair of binoculars at the Argentinean frigate the *Spanish Conquistador*, as a one hundred-foot gantry, painted red like the color of blood, hoisted one crate after another off the back of the ship, swinging them through the air and stacking them on the back of a flatbed truck. He counted six crates in all, did a quick calculation in his head, and then peered over to the box truck parked in the loading area with "Allied Shipping" painted in big black letters on the side.

It's too small.

Way too small.

He refocused the binoculars on the flatbed as the last crate was positioned and chained into place and the truck began the half-mile trip from the offloading facility, through the busy terminal, and over to the warehouse. Then he called his boss.

"The merchandise is here."

"How many?" the man said without emotion.

"The fat priest says he shipped twenty."

"How old?"

"Younger than fifteen."

"Wire him the money as soon as you get the merchandise."

"I'll transfer the cash so it can't be traced."

"Excellent, and, Bingwen, call me when you get back to the Lower East Side."

Bingwen hung up and walked over to the box truck, angled with the cargo compartment facing out. It was three in the morning, and light snow was falling, leaving a fresh coat of white powder on the ground. He rolled up the door and peered inside, then powered his three hundred pounds into the back, straightened the half-dozen dirty mattresses lining the floor, dumped several sacks of old clothes in the corner, and watched as the flatbed, lights blazing through the snowflakes, slowed, turned, and backed down the street between the rows of warehouses until it pulled to a stop five feet from the box truck.

A slight man in his midtwenties named Honghui with a pronounced Mandarin accent climbed out of the cab and walked around the flatbed.

"Flucking cold tonight," he said, hopping from one foot to the next, trying to keep the circulation flowing in his extremities.

"Any trouble with customs?" Bingwen said, checking to make sure no other crews were unloading containers at the other warehouses.

"Gleased the asshole, and he look other way," Honghui said, lighting a cigarette. "Here's for record keeping." He handed Bingwen the shipping manifest and climbed onto the flatbed.

Bingwen went through the document. Everything seemed in order. Allied was allegedly receiving five thousand cases of *Don Miguel Gascon Malbec* from Buenos Aires destined for restaurants and liquor stores in New York, Philadelphia, and Boston. It was the perfect cover and had fooled US Customs for years. He placed the document into a folder and locked it in his alligator-skin briefcase then turned to the small, wiry man and said, "Unload the fucking girls."

Honghui laid a wooden plank from the flatbed to the box truck, grabbed a key ring, and unlocked the padlock on the first crate, swinging open the door and revealing three little girls—all thirteen or fourteen years old—who were huddled against the back wall. They were dirty, dressed in rags, and scared.

"Get out," he said threateningly. "Hurry up. Hurry up. Hurry up. Into the truck with you."

The girls stood, still huddled together, and slowly crossed into the box truck, eyes transfixed, moving like zombies.

"Put on the clothes. They'll keep you warm, and don't say a word or scream for help, you bitches," Bingwen said, scowling, "or I'll give you a whooping you'll never forget." He shoved the last girl up against the wall with his massive foot and wheeled around to Honghui. "Unload the rest of them. And do it quickly. There's a security van making the rounds. It's scheduled to be here soon."

One after another, the small man opened the locks and the girls in twos and threes stumbled out of the crates, across the wooden plank, and into the box truck. When he pried open the final one, Maria was sprawled on the floor, curled in a ball, her hands locked together covering her face.

"Out," he said harshly. But Maria didn't move. "Get fluck out and into truck with other girls. Now." She still didn't move. Bingwen nodded, and in a flash, Honghui pounced on Maria, slapped her across the face, then dragged her by the hair into the box truck—the other girls surrounding her, trying to protect her.

"Leave her alone," said a small girl with teeth as white as ivory and eyes as blue as the Caribbean Sea.

"Fluck you, bitch," he said, hauling off and punching her full in the face, the girl crumbling in a heap, blood pouring from her broken nose and split lip.

Bingwen roared, “You stupid shit. You’ve messed up her face. She’s no use to us all smashed up like that.”

“She’s got big mouth. She had comin’.”

“No more beating on my girls,” he said, shoving Honghui to the ground, then stomping on his hand, the bones in his fingers crunching as they shattered. “I’m gonna have to get a doc to patch her up before she’s any use to us.”

“You’ve smashed my hand,” Honghui said, wailing, as he scampered away from the big man, cradling his broken limb. “It’s flucking ruined. Give me money. I deliver girls, now want get paid.”

“Here’s your money, asshole,” Bingwen said, glaring, then pulling five hundred dollars out of an envelope and tossing the bills in the air. The little man hesitated then crawled on his good hand and picked up the cash, Bingwen kicking him in the side one more time for good measure. “Now don’t you ever forget, motherfucker, it’s my job to discipline the girls, not yours. If you ever lay a finger on them again, without me telling you, I’ll whoop your ass so bad you’ll never drive for me or anyone else again.”

“Okay. Okay,” Honghui said, standing and stuffing the money in his pocket.

Bingwen thought about kicking him one more time then backed off and stared at the girls. “There’s only nineteen. We’re missing one. What the hell happened?”

“One died on the boat,” Honghui said, still clutching his hand as it swelled to the size of a baseball glove. “My guys toss bitch overboard.”

“Well, fuck me,” Bingwen said, raging. He reached for his burner, punched in a sixteen-digit number, and waited.

A sleepy voice finally answered hello.

“Wake up, you fat fuck.”

“Who is this?”

“You know who this is, priest. We’re short one girl.”

"Not my fault. I shipped twenty," Pedro Juan Ignacio Rodriguez said belligerently. "That was the plan."

"Fuck you, priest. Your operation lost one in transit. I'm deducting the money from your payment. That's five thousand dollars."

"You can't do that. I lived up to my end of the bargain. I snatched twenty girls."

"But we're missing one, and the big boss ain't paying. You got a problem with that?"

"Well—"

"Well what, motherfucker."

There was a short pause. "Wire me the money," Pedro Juan Ignacio Rodriguez said. "I'll eat the cost of the missing girl."

"That's a smart man," Bingwen said, satisfied. "And there's one more thing. The big boss needs fifteen more."

"That'll take a little time."

"One week. That's all you got to secure the product. Otherwise, we use another supplier."

"Come on, Bingwen. I need more time. I got Mass to celebrate and responsibilities at the *basilica.* The cardinal is already suspicious."

"Fuck the cardinal. Figure it out," he said, out of control. *We should terminate that guy,* he thought. G*et our product from a Chinese distributor, not a foreign infidel with ugly Latinas.* He clicked off the phone and turned to the wiry man, still cradling his smashed hand. "You know what to do."

"Shit, Bingwen, I no drive like this. Hurts like hell. Go to hospital."

"Later. Get the girls out of here and do it now. Take the long way—through the Hugh L. Carey Tunnel, then make your way to Houston Street using the back roads and over to Avenue D in Alphabet City. I'll meet you at the tenement."

*****

Maria lay on an old mattress shivering as the box truck started moving, the other girls stripping off her dirty rags and dressing her in a pair of worn pants, a cotton shirt, socks, and shoes. They pulled a woolen hat over her head, covering her ears, and draped a threadbare shawl over her shoulders. She didn't move as they clothed her. Didn't answer their questions. Didn't say a single word—her face impassive, her expression lost, her mind all but shattered.

"What's wrong with her," said a little girl who was staring, her eyes opened wide like saucers.

"I don't know," a slightly older girl said. "Maybe she's hungry. Maybe she's tired. Maybe she just needs to sleep."

"Maybe she's broken," a third girl named Valentina said, sitting down next to Maria and cradling her in her arms. "Maybe if I hold her, make her warm, make her feel good, she'll come back to us."

The other girls scattered, leaving the two sitting alone in the corner, Valentina stroking Maria's face, gently rocking her back and forth, quietly singing her a make-believe lullaby. *Be brave, my sweet new friend. I'll take good care of you until your mama and papa come and rescue you and take you back home to the place where you belong.* Valentina kept singing the verse over and over, holding her hand tightly, kissing her lovingly all over her face. But Maria remained motionless, her mind a jumble of disconnected thoughts.

She'd shut out the world.

And climbed into a space where nobody could hurt her.

CHAPTER 17

Ethan blinked several times, the clock on his desk ticking in the background, mimicking the sound of water dripping in a basin—over and over and over. He opened his eyes, the light from his desk lamp burning brightly, and gazed at an empty bottle of Black Label lying on its side. Shit. He'd fallen asleep in his study again. How many times did that make this week? Two? Three? He licked his lips, his mouth thick with the taste of Scotch and cigarettes. He sat back in his chair and yawned, stretching his arms over his head, trying to get the kinks out of his neck, then checked the time. Seven o'clock. At least he hadn't overslept. He pushed through piles of papers, found the pack of Marlboros, and lit a cigarette, taking a long, deep pull before reaching for his iPad.

Coffee.

He needed a cup of coffee.

Heading down the center hallway, he bumped into Luke and Holly heading to the kitchen, the little boy dragging a blanket, the Labrador retriever hanging on for dear life, playing a game of tug of war.

"Hey, Lukie," Ethan said, swinging him off the ground and into his arms, Holly still clinging to the end of the blanket. "What are you up to this morning?"

"Holly's hungry. She wants breakfast. I'm gonna feed her."

"You hungry too, Lukie?"

"Kinda."

"How about breakfast with your dad?"

"Yay. That would be great," Luke said, excitement in his voice. He squirmed out of Ethan's arms. "Race you to the kitchen." He took off, Holly on his heels.

Ethan smiled.

He loved that little guy.

He found Luke lugging a bag of Purina Dog Chow out of the cabinet and filling Holly's bowl, spilling almost as much on the floor as into the dish.

"How about some Honey Nut Cheerios? That sound good to you?"

"I want a big bowl with lots of milk," Luke said, grabbing a Darth Vader action figure from under the table and climbing into his chair. Ethan turned on the automatic coffeemaker, pulled the Cheerios out of the cabinet, poured two big bowls and added milk. Then he waited for the coffee to finish brewing, poured a piping hot mug, and sat down next to Luke, hoping his little boy couldn't tell he was hungover. "Taste good?"

"Scrumptiliotious," Luke said, shoveling a spoonful into his mouth, a stream of milk dribbling down his chin. He wiped it away with the sleeve of his pajamas, smiled, and said, "What we gonna do today, Dad?"

Ethan hesitated, staring into his bright eyes, at the expectant look on his face, then said, "Daddy has to work today, Luke."

"All day?" he said, his demeanor deflating.

"Maybe."

"But it's Saturday?"

"Of course, it's Saturday," Sarah said, padding into the kitchen, her tone still cold, distant. They were talking, but barely—the shadow of their constant fighting hanging over them. "And it's the beginning of winter vacation, Luke, even though that doesn't mean anything to your father."

The little boy paused, sensing the tension, then said tepidly. "I forgot. No school for a week." A smile spread across his face. "Can I go watch TV?"

"You finished eating?"

"All done, Mom."

"Go ahead then," she said. "I need to talk to your dad. Maybe we'll go to the park and have a snowball fight with Holly."

"Hooray. That'll be fun. Maybe you can come too, Dad." He pushed away from the table and raced out of the kitchen, Holly barking at the excitement as she tore down the hall behind him.

Sarah poured a cup of coffee and sat down across from Ethan.

"What are we gonna do, Ethan?"

"I dunno, babe," he said, sensing he was skating on thin ice.

"So make a decision. Me or your job."

There was a long silence. Then Ethan said, staring into his half-empty cup of coffee, "We've been over this, Sarah. I'll shrivel up on the inside if I continue working for Peter. I need to work on my own story. That's who I am. It's an obsession deep inside me. I can't stop once I get started."

"So you won't give up the story."

"No."

"And you're gonna step down as Peter's senior producer."

Ethan squirmed, but didn't answer.

"So you still won't tell me," she said.

"Enough, Sarah."

"You're just gonna keep on drinking until it kills you."

"Enough," he said, realizing he was shouting.

She pushed away from the table, scratching the floor with the chair, the sound punctuating her anger. "This isn't working."

"What do you mean?" he said defensively.

"I'm done. I can't take it anymore."

"What does that mean?"

"Please. You know what it means."

"I don't. We're making progress with Dr. Schwartz," he said, desperation creeping into his voice.

"No longer enough," she said bitterly. "I'm leaving you."

"What?"

"This has been coming for a long time. I need to get away from here. And away from you."

"That's ridiculous, Sarah, sit down."

"My mind's made up. I'm taking Luke and going to my sister's in Cleveland. We'll stay there during his vacation. Then I'll decide what to do."

"You can't be serious, Sarah. Things aren't that bad between us."

She stared at him, her lips quivering. "Listen to yourself. You can't face the truth. That we've got serious problems. That you hide from them in that fucking bottle of Scotch. Maybe we can work things out if we separate. Maybe you can take a deep look at yourself and start talking to me like you used to." She started shaking uncontrollably as she made her way to the kitchen door. "I haven't told Luke yet, though I suspect he already knows. I said we were going on a short vacation without you. That you couldn't get time off from the office. He got upset, but he's a kid, and he'll get over it. I don't want to worry him any more than I have to until I make a decision about you. A decision about us."

*****

Ethan gulped a glass of Scotch and topped off another as he listened to Sarah packing in their bedroom, trying to numb the pain spreading through his body like wildfire. He had pleaded with her for over an hour after she'd returned from Central Park, telling her he wouldn't hide his feelings anymore, telling her he'd be more open with her, telling her he'd stop drinking. But it was all to no avail. She was taking Luke and leaving. Swishing the Scotch in the tumbler, he heard her chatting with Luke, laughing, telling him they were going to have a good time at her sister's. Then she called the doorman to come up for the luggage.

He stood, but hesitated, wondering if he should go down the hall and beg her to stay one last time. But he was tied up in knots, totally at his wit's end, and feared he would break down in tears if he watched her leave. So instead, he sat back down and finished his Scotch as Sarah, her high heels clicking on the floor, made her way to his study.

"Keep drinking. It's what you do," she said, aggrieved. "I get into Cleveland at five o'clock. Anita's picking us up at the airport. I'll call you in a day or two. Give your dad a kiss," she said, brushing her hand through Luke's hair, standing quietly next to her.

Luke skipped over, stared at the Scotch in his hand, and gave him a big hug. "Sure you can't come, Dad?"

"Not this week, Lukie. Be a good boy and listen to your mother. I'll see you when you get back."

Then the doorbell rang, and without another word, Sarah grabbed Luke's hand, made her way to the front door, and left—leaving Ethan alone at his desk, drowning in Scotch.

*****

Ethan could hear his iPhone buzzing, rattling, as he opened his eyes and sat forward on the couch. He looked at his watch. Almost two o'clock. He must've drunk himself into a stupor after Sarah walked out. God. He had to keep it together. His cell phone continued buzzing, now pounding, ripping through his head like a jackhammer. He peered down at the LCD screen. It was Lloyd. Work. But he couldn't face the world, not yet.

Sarah.

She'd taken Luke and left him.

Maybe forever.

He let the phone go to voice mail, then stood, wobbly, almost tripping over Holly who was lying at his feet. He patted her head absentmindedly and stumbled down to the kitchen for coffee. There was half a cup left from the morning. Cold. A layer of grinds floating on top. He drank it anyway, then made his way to the bedroom, Holly tagging along beside him, frowning. Did she sense they were gone? That he was all alone? He stripped off his dirty clothes, leaving them in a pile on the floor, and climbed into the shower, the water ice-cold, stabbing his skin like pinpricks, digging deep into his soul.

Sarah.

She'd taken Luke and left him.

Maybe forever.

He toweled himself dry, shaved, and got dressed, his mood heavy, his emotions all over the place. He made his way to the kitchen, brewed a fresh pot of coffee, and headed back to his study, pouring a cup and placing the pot on his desk. Work. He had to work. Maybe that would make things better. He flipped on his laptop and picked up his iPhone, calming himself before punching in Lloyd's number.

"Hey, Lloyd, it's me. Sorry I missed your call," he said, trying to make himself sound like everything was okay.

"No problem. I knew you'd get back to me."

"What do you got?"

"Probably not what you want to hear. I did a preliminary background check on Randall Newton. Placed a couple of phone calls. Talked to a couple of sources in the District Attorney's Office."

"And?"

"He's a straight shooter. Stellar reputation. Highly credentialed. Admired by the other lawyers. The new district attorney, Joshua Cunningham, handpicked him to work under Patricia Highland. He's supposed to have exceptional organizational and leadership skills. Rumor has it he's on the fast track to becoming Cunningham's number two. Afraid I've heard nothing but praise about him."

"And his finances?" Ethan said.

"Mindy's working on that," Lloyd said. "But so far she's found nothing out of the norm."

There was a moment of silence as Ethan banged notes on his iPad. "Any idea who he called after our meeting the other night?"

"Could've been anybody."

Ethan hesitated. Maybe he'd misjudged Randall Newton. Maybe he was reading into something that wasn't there.

"I don't know, Lloyd," Ethan said, trying to control the tremor in his voice. "There's something off about the guy."

"So what do you want me to do?"

"Not sure yet," he said.

"Want me to follow him? That's what I do for a living. I find out stuff about people who seem squeaky clean."

Ethan hesitated again. *Trust your instincts, Ethan.* "Go ahead, Lloyd. Tail him. See where he goes. Who he meets. Give it a day or two, and if nothing pans out, we'll move on."

"Do you want surveillance pictures?"

"Yeah. And let me know what you find out."

"That's a ten-four."

Ethan clicked off the phone, relieved. Lloyd hadn't sensed what was really going on, that Sarah had left him. How long could he keep it a secret? How long could he keep up the charade? He stared at the wet bar. He could feel the sensual pull of the Scotch. It would blur his emotions, hide his shame, make his problems go away. *No. Not now. Maybe later.* He brushed the sweat from his forehead with the back of his hand and poured another cup of coffee then peered at the stack of notebooks sitting on a chair under the window—the five murder books James had copied and shipped to his apartment.

No better time than now to start plowing through them.

He had to stay busy.

Standing, he walked across the room, peering out the window at the overcast sky matching his mood. He grabbed the first notebook and opened it to the front page. It was labeled the Child Sex Murders and signed by Gloria Alvarez and Henry Dinkus. The first murder had taken place two years earlier, and the murder had become a cold case long before the district attorney had created a task force to oversee the investigation. That hadn't happened until sometime after the second little girl had been found over a year later. *Curious,* Ethan thought, *why didn't it warrant more manpower right from the beginning, even without press coverage? Other child murders had caused outrage in the city and mobilized every investigative agency—the police, child services, the US Attorney, the FBI, the entire might of law enforcement. Why was this case different?* He walked back to his desk with the murder book, picked up his iPad, and jotted himself a note to ask Patricia Highland once again why she couldn't muster resources and manpower.

After sipping his coffee, Ethan flipped down to the page listing all the personnel assigned to the original case. Gloria Alvarez out of SVU was at the top of the list, then Henry Dinkus out of the Sixth Precinct, and a small complement of lab technicians.

A skeleton crew.

He lit a cigarette, walked back to the chair, and picked up the second notebook, dated November 6, 2018, and skimmed down the personnel list. There was Patricia Highland, the two original detectives, plus the same handful of lab technicians. Still a skeleton crew even though the task force had been created. Then he picked up the third book. No new list of personnel. Just spillover documents from books 1 and 2. That made sense. The urgency to find the killer had vanished once again with the lack of press coverage. He placed the notebook back on the chair and picked up the fourth book—dated March 24, 2019 —the date of the third murder. Just four months after the second little girl had been butchered. The killer had moved up his timeline. Ethan put out his cigarette then flipped to the personnel page and ran his finger down the list. Bingo. There was Randall

Newton prominently displayed right after Patricia Highland. Why had a second ADA been assigned to the case? Why at this particular moment? Had the district attorney been pressured by higher-ups to make it look like they were doing everything they could to find the killer? But that didn't make sense either. There were still only a handful of cops working the killings. Why was a second ADA assigned and not additional detectives?

Ethan made a mental note to find out.

After lighting another cigarette, he walked the fourth murder book back to his desk and sat down, thumbing through the three-page index until he found a section marked personnel bios. He found Randall Newton right after Highland. No surprise there. He was second in command. Ethan pulled the bio out of the notebook. It read like a press release. First in his class at Harvard University. First at Stanford Law School. A prestigious clerkship in the US Supreme Court. A coveted position in the mayor's office in charge of terrorism. Chief investigator in the criminal division in the US Attorney's Office. And now assistant district attorney in charge of online pornography and organized crime in Manhattan.

Shit.

He was barking up the wrong tree.

Randall Newton was a rising star.

Ethan highlighted the bullet points with a yellow marker and then punched Lloyd Howard's number into his iPhone.

Lloyd answered on the third ring. "Was just about to call you back, Ethan. I'm sitting with Mindy in her office. Let me put you on speaker."

Ethan reached for another cigarette then decided he'd already smoked too many and slipped it back into the pack.

"Can you hear me?" Mindy said, her voice faint in the background.

"You need to speak louder," he said.

"How's this?"

"Better." He stared at the pack of Marlboros. Fuck it. Better than a glass of Scotch. He lit up and inhaled. "What do you have for me?"

Lloyd cleared his throat. "I called my contact at the IRS, and he e-mailed me Newton's tax filings for the past five years."

"Anything unusual."

"Not a thing. He only declares his salary. There are no 1099s for interest or dividend payments, so he doesn't have a big stock portfolio other than his 401K, and he takes few if any business deductions from one year to the next. The returns are pretty straightforward, and the guy's never been audited."

"And his spending habits?" Ethan said, taking notes on his iPad.

"Got a banker friend to slip me his account information," Mindy said. "He's got a small savings account, twenty-three thousand four hundred fifty-two dollars and twenty-seven cents to be exact, and a checking account with a balance of about seven thousand dollars."

"Credit cards?"

"American Express and Master Card," Lloyd said. "Which he pays off each month."

"Where does he live?"

"In a large two-bedroom condo on the Upper East Side," Mindy said, chiming in. "Got a pretty big mortgage, but makes the payments every month on time. Comes right out of his checking account."

Ethan wrote a single line in his notes. *Newton's financial portfolio squeaky clean.* He underlined *squeaky*. "Anything unusual in his private life?"

"He lives by himself, rarely travels, and doesn't date," Mindy said. "Seems to spend all his time working."

"Lloyd?"

"Guy's completely above the board. Straight as an arrow, except for one thing. Hold on a second." Ethan could hear Lloyd rustling through a bunch of documents. "Got it."

"Got what?"

"A list of credit card payments to a private car service called *Charge-A-Ride*."

"What does that prove?" Ethan said, perplexed.

"Not sure," Lloyd said. "Every week on the same day, Saturday, at about the same time, eleven at night, he calls for a car and pays the same amount of money, seventy-five dollars."

"Where does he go?" Ethan said, now curious.

"Pickup is always at his apartment," Mindy said, "and drop-off is always at some tenement on Avenue D on the Lower East Side."

"How do you know?"

"Computer records," Lloyd said. "I hacked into the *Charge-A-Ride* system."

"That legal?"

"What do you think?"

"Okay. Got it. Any idea what he's doing in Alphabet City?"

"Not the faintest," Lloyd said. "But I'll start following him tonight as we planned," Lloyd said. "See where he goes."

"Can you go with him, Mindy?"

"Jeez, Ethan. Wouldn't miss it."

"Lemme know what you find out."

Ethan clicked off and spent the next hour leafing through the first murder book, not finding much he didn't already know, then decided he needed to get out of the apartment. It was lonely without Sarah and Luke. Maybe he'd check out Pier 51, get a mental picture of where the cops found the first three bodies. That always helped him piece together loose ends. He checked the time. 3:00 p.m. There were still two hours of daylight. He picked up the phone and called Gloria Alvarez.

"Afternoon, Detective."

"Benson, you solve case yet?"

Ethan chuckled. "Not yet."

"So what can I do for you, *amigo*?"

"Need to take a look at Pier 51."

"Aren't the photos good enough?"

"Might be helpful if I looked myself. You know, a fresh set of eyes," he said, not missing a beat. "Got time to show me?"

"When?"

"Now?"

"Can't do it," she said firmly. "But I send Detective Dinkus, *sí*?"

"Thanks." Ethan clicked off the phone then immediately punched in David Livingston's number. It rang ten times before he picked up. "What are you doing?"

"It's Saturday. I'm watching the Knicks/Lakers game."

"Turn off the TV. I need you to meet me at Pier 51. Henry Dinkus is giving us a tour of the crime scene. Can you get a camera?"

"I can bring the one Mindy used to shoot at SVU."

"Excellent. Meet in an hour."

He hung up and grabbed the first murder book, packed it in his briefcase alongside his Canon G20—in case he needed a second camera—wrapped himself in his hat, gloves, and navy blue down parka, then headed to the door. With a little luck, he'd be home by dinner with plenty of time to call Sarah. Maybe by then he could talk some sense into her, make things right, get her to come home with Luke.

A plan.

A good plan.

He had no idea how wrong he could be.

CHAPTER 18

Ethan got into a taxi on the corner of Fifth Avenue and Ninety-First Street and told the driver to drop him on Jane and West Street in Greenwich Village, about a block from Pier 51. The traffic was heavy heading downtown, the sidewalks filled with people—young couples walking their dogs, families heading into Central Park, children running up and down the snow-covered paths, laughing and playing hide-and-seek. The temperature was warm for late February, the sun shining brightly overhead, melting the snow and ice, foreshadowing springtime just around the corner. Ethan cranked down his window a notch and inhaled the fresh air, happy to be out of his apartment and away from the crisis tearing his life apart.

He grabbed the murder book from his briefcase and flipped to a map and a series of Xerox photos of the Pier 51 playground. They were taken several days after the first murder—all the police tape removed, all the chalk marks washed away, all the evidence cones and markers collected. The playground appeared brand-new, almost pristine, a state-of-the-art facility with swings, a junior hump climber, a horizontal ladder, a merry-go-round, plenty of rubber padding to cushion little-kid spills, and of course, the bow of the wooden ship where the dead girls had been found. The playground measured a hundred feet square, was completely enclosed by an eight-foot-high iron fence, and accessed by one entrance that was padlocked with a heavy chain when it closed at dusk.

Ethan stared long and hard at the fortress-like setting.

Why had the killer dumped the bodies here?

What was he missing?

He leaned back and stared out the window. They'd already driven through Central Park on the Sixty-Sixth Street Transverse, passed the ABC News headquarters, and made a left onto West End Avenue, heading toward Fifty-Seventh Street and the entrance to the West Side Highway. He wanted a smoke—but tapped down the craving. He flipped through the pictures again, studying every square inch of the playground, looking at details, searching for clues. But nothing jumped out at him, nothing obvious, nothing with insight into the mind of the killer. He continued thumbing through the book, through the hundreds of detailed pages of evidence, the hundreds of false leads and dead ends. Then Ethan came across a picture of Jane Doe number one, the same picture Lloyd Howard had shown him that first morning at McGlades. He stared long and hard at the image then read a detailed analysis of the staging, written by Detective Dinkus:

> *The body was tied to a folding chair and carefully placed at the far end of the playground in an area made of wood planks and designed to look like a boat. It was sitting on the third tier of a triangular shaped deck, completely unencumbered with the Hudson River in the background and nothing blocking the body in the foreground. There was a clear line of sight from every square inch of the playground, guaranteeing the body would be discovered as soon as the gate was opened and children streamed into the facility.*

Did the killer want the body to be found?

By little kids?

Shit.

What did that mean?

He scribbled himself a note in his iPad to call Leon Fennimore, the FBI profiler assigned to the task force, then stuffed the murder book back into his briefcase and checked his bearings. The cab had stopped at a red light on the corner of Gansevoort and Greenwich Street, just a couple of blocks from Pier 51. He banged on the Plexiglas partition.

"This is good," he said and paid the fare.

He got out of the cab. The sky had turned overcast, the temperature still hovering in the forties. Much of the snow had melted, but there were still pools of water running along the curb. Overheated, he stopped and unzipped his down jacket, thinking he should have worn something lighter. The neighborhood was much more upscale than Alphabet City, where the killer had staged the body after the last murder. There were boutiques and fancy restaurants lining the streets, wealthy young couples sauntering from one shop to the next, laden with shopping bags full of clothes and shoes and other high-end goodies. Dozens of nannies pushed strollers and walked hand in hand with young children, many coming from the playground, from Pier 51.

Ethan followed Google Maps on his iPad, heading west on Gansevoort toward the Hudson River. Mixed between old brownstones were pizza parlors and souvenir shops and upscale nightspots already teeming with people he could see through the windows. When he reached the Whitney Museum of American Art on the corner of West Street, he saw the elevated Highline, crowded with people enjoying the unusually warm weather, and continued walking toward the Hudson and Pier 51.

He waited for the light to turn green then crossed West Street. It was backed up for blocks with cars and taxis and delivery trucks. How did the killer manage to elaborately stage the bodies with traffic and so many potential eyewitnesses this close, even in the middle of the night?

He crossed the Hudson River Greenway, a pedestrian and bike path and passed a two-story maintenance building with bathrooms and snowplows parked out front. He turned back to West Street. He could hear car engines, but the traffic was mostly blocked by the building and the thickly planted trees and shrubs. Now he could see how the killer might go unnoticed. Drivers couldn't see the playground clearly, especially after dark.

The perfect spot to dump the bodies.

Ethan continued walking north, another hundred feet or so, until he reached the open gate leading into the playground. The warm weather had brought out dozens of little kids scampering about, screaming for joy as they played on the outdoor equipment. There was the new World Trade Center looming a mile away toward the south and the glittering glass towers in Jersey City across the river. He pulled out the murder book and went through the photos one more time then headed toward the three-tiered wooden ship where the dead girls had been found. As he walked, he looked for David. Must be running late. Then he spotted Henry Dinkus, leaning against the chain-link fence, staring out over the Hudson.

Ethan lit a cigarette and walked up to the detective.

"Thanks for meeting me on such short notice," he said, shaking his hand.

"Can't see how this is gonna help."

Ethan was taken aback by the coldness in his voice. Maybe all the detectives resented his presence on the task force.

"Always find it useful to see the murder site. Anyway, only got an hour before sunset. So we gotta do this quickly." He inhaled his cigarette, flicked it into the Hudson, and checked for David. Still no sign of him. "I'd like to shoot pictures."

"Be my guest. I've been told you can take your camera anywhere you want."

Ethan nodded and pulled his Canon from his backpack and turned it on. "If you want to tell me anything as we go, feel free."

They spent the next forty-five minutes combing through the playground—Dinkus pointing out the exact spot where the killer had staged the bodies, its position relative to the playground equipment, and a crevice between two slats of wood in the ship's deck where the CSI found the Karl Storz No. 6 surgical knife after the third murder.

"Could be the guy got careless?" he said, crouching and putting his finger into the crack. "Only mistake he's made so far, and he's made it twice now. Otherwise we'd have jack-shit on him."

"Is the task force canvassing the medical supply houses, looking for leads on who might have purchased the surgical knives?"

"That was a good idea, Benson," Dinkus said without emotion. "We've got a half-dozen plainclothes we wrangled from SVU knocking on the doors of the twenty-three companies in the city that sell the No. 6 blades. We're compiling lists of names and addresses and dates the knives were sold, dating back a year. Most of them were purchased by hospitals, outpatient clinics, and plastic surgeons. It's gonna take a couple of days to get it into a computer and sift through everybody and see if any potential buyers look out of the norm. Then we'll make a few house calls and see if we come up with anything."

"You don't seem too enthusiastic, Detective," Ethan said, pulling the lens into a medium shot.

"That's because there were thousands of those damn blades sold during the past twelve months. So it's a long shot we'll find anybody."

"Do you think it's a waste of time?"

"No. We're running down every possible lead, even though it's like looking for a needle in a haystack."

"Randall Newton thinks it's a waste of time."

"That guy puts up a fuss whenever we dedicate manpower that takes us away from policing in the field."

"What does that mean?" Ethan said, puzzled.

"Nothing against Randall. He just thinks we can use our slim resources better, maybe circulate more undercover cops in a five-block radius around the playground. Do the same thing at the Dry Dock Playground."

"How's that helpful?"

"Sometimes you get lucky and nail the son-of-bitch in the act."

"You mean, if he happens to murder another girl and dumps her body at one of the two sites."

"That's the reality, but so far we've got bubkes."

Ethan pulled back to a wide shot and panned across the playground. He'd been so busy talking to the cop he hadn't noticed they were all by themselves, that the playground was about to close and that the kids had headed home with their nannies and parents. He swung around and refocused on a medium shot of Dinkus.

"Is this what happens every afternoon?"

"Yup. The park is locked at five o'clock sharp this time of the year. That's in fifteen minutes," Dinkus said, checking his watch. "So after dark, well, the playground's basically deserted."

As he was about to ask his next question, he spotted David racing up to them.

"Sorry, Ethan. Was a bitch getting here. The subways were all backed up."

"Don't sweat it." Ethan said, reintroducing David to the detective.

"Do you want me to finish shooting with my camera?"

"No. Just got a few more questions. I'll finish up with—"

A sharp blast rang out, echoing over the Hudson, and a bullet ripped off the top of Dinkus's head, smashing it like a melon—bone and blood and brain matter splattering Ethan's hands and face as the detective's eyes bulged for a split second before he crumpled to the ground arms spread to his sides, legs splayed. Instinctively, Ethan kept rolling as another shot exploded, and the whiff of a high-powered projectile whirred over his head. Panicking, he hit the wooden deck and scampered down the steps, hiding behind a trash can at the bottom.

"David?" he said, screaming.

No answer.

"Are you hit?"

Still no answer.

"David? David?" Ethan said, now desperate.

"I'm okay, Ethan. Scared shitless, but okay."

"Where are you?"

"On the ground, stretched out next to the bottom step."

"Don't move in case the asshole fires again."

"Is he dead?" David said, his voice trembling.

Ethan peered back at the detective, motionless, most of his face obliterated, an open gory mess, parts of his skull blinking through his skin, blood pooling in a circle around his body.

"Yeah, he's dead, and I got the whole thing on camera."

"Shit, man. You okay, Ethan?"

"My heart's pounding," he said, taking three deep breaths, "but I'm no worse for wear." Then he eased back behind the trash can, trying to make his body smaller, pulled out his iPhone and called 911. "This is Ethan Benson. There's been a shooting on the playground at Pier 51. There's a cop down. Detective Henry Dinkus. He's dead."

"Are you hurt?" a woman said, her voice flat.

"No. But the asshole shot at me too. The bullet missed by an inch." He pulled out a cigarette, his hands shaking uncontrollably.

"Are you by yourself?"

"There's another person with me."

"He hurt?'

"No. No," he said, shrieking at the top of his lungs.

"Are you safe?"

"Who the hell knows. I'm mostly exposed in the middle of a deserted children's playground."

"Stay calm, Mr. Benson, and don't hang up the phone."

Ethan listened as the 911 operator called in a 10-54—*cop down, possibly dead*—and gave the location of the Dry Dock Playground. Then she got back on the line. "Any more shooting?"

"For God's sake, no," Ethan said as he took three quick puffs on his Marlboro, trying to control his runaway emotions.

"Stay on the line, Mr. Benson. Cops on the way. Should be there any minute."

He gulped down three more quick hits of nicotine and realized his whole body felt cold and numb. As he hastily zipped up his coat, sirens began screaming in the distance.

"Still no more shooting?" the dispatcher said.

"No. No. No. I just told you that."

"Calm, Mr. Benson." Then she said in a clear voice over the transit, "No more shots fired. Eyewitnesses safe. Emergency medical services en route."

Police cruisers flooded into the Hudson River Greenway, screeching to a halt, doors flying open, dozens of cops pouring out in full riot gear, guns drawn. Barricades immediately went up, blocking off both directions of West Street. Two ambulances arrived and were kept at a distance as cops carefully inched forward, holding polycarbonate shields, sweeping long guns from side to side. Powerful flashlights sprayed beams of light, illuminating the near darkness in front of them. Ethan started to stand but froze in place as a cop yelled through a bullhorn, "Down. Stay down. Until we sweep the area."

Soon Ethan and David were surrounded by cops, kneeling and placing the polycarbonate shields all around them. They were handed bulletproof vests, which they quickly slipped over their coats and were told not to move. There was a crackle of sound on a walkie-talkie, before Gloria Alvarez's voice came booming through the speaker.

"Benson. Ethan Benson. Find him for me."

A cop, Captain Benjamin Butler from the Sixth Precinct, who was leading the investigation, bellowed through a bullhorn, "Which one of you guys is Benson?"

"That's me," Ethan said, his voice still shaky. Then he was given the walkie-talkie.

"What the fuck happened, Benson?"

"Two shots. The first one hit the top of Detective Dinkus's head."

"Sure he's dead?" Alvarez said, the sound crackling over the walkie-talkie as she paused, waiting for an answer.

A cop hovering over Dinkus yelled from the top tier of the wooden ship, "No pulse. Not much left of his face. He's dead."

"I heard that," she said, her singsong voice flat. "Any idea where shots came from, *sí*?"

"I was looking through my viewfinder, doing an interview with Dinkus when he was shot," Ethan said.

"So you saw nothing?"

"I saw where the shots were fired."

"Who the hell is that?" Alvarez screamed.

"My researcher, David Livingston. You met him the other night."

"Why's he there?"

"Helping me produce my story."

"And he see where shots fired, *no*?"

"I saw," David said loudly. "Two quick flashes, one after another, from a construction site along the river—some complex being torn down about ten blocks uptown from here."

"You're sure?" Alvarez said. "That's the abandoned Sanitation Department salt shed at Pier 52."

"Sure as shit," David said, pointing wildly.

"A sniper," Alvarez said urgently. "And he may still be somewhere in that complex. "Captain, dispatch a tactical team in full riot gear and start search for gunman. And get those two newsman out of there. Take them inside maintenance building. I'll be there in five minutes."

"You heard the lady," Captain Butler said, bellowing. "Get them to safety."

Ethan and David, still surrounded by a half-dozen cops holding shields, were hustled across the Greenway toward the empty maintenance building. Ethan turned on his camera and started shooting again, making a point-of-view shot and sweeping wide shots of the chaos all around him, the beams of light from the flashlights flaring in his lens, making the images surrealistic. *Unbelievable footage*, he thought. *Fuck an egg, I just captured a murder on camera.* Then he started thinking about the second bullet.

Man.

That was close.

The fucker almost nailed me.

CHAPTER 19

Ethan dusted off a thin layer of snow coating his down jacket as he and David huddled in the corner of the maintenance building. The temperature had fallen near freezing, and an unexpected squall had suddenly dropped an inch of slushy snow on the ground. Ethan hadn't noticed until he'd started hustling through the playground, his feet slipping on the pavement, the wet snow clinging to his shoes, numbing his toes. Two cops were stationed, holding high-powered rifles, on either side of the only door leading into a small office. It was dark. The lights turned off to make sure the gunman couldn't see them and pull off another kill.

Ethan whispered into David's ear, "Do you have a laptop?"

"In my backpack with the 2-Chip."

"Can you download the images from my camera?"

"Not a problem, Ethan. Why?"

"Cause it's evidence in a murder investigation, and Alvarez is going to take it when she gets here. I need a copy of what I shot. We may never get it back from the task force. How long will it take?"

"A couple of minutes."

He gave David the Canon and waited impatiently as David transferred all the video to a file in his laptop.

"Done," he said as he handed Ethan the camera and packed his laptop next to the 2-Chip—just as Detective Alvarez pushed through the door, followed closely by Randall Newton.

Why is he here?

"Shit, Benson, you're bad luck," Newton said.

"Where camera?" Alvarez said. "It's evidence."

He held up the Canon. "When can I get it back?"

"Not until I say so," she said. "Maybe when investigation is over, and asshole who killed Dinkus is behind bars." Alvarez slipped into Latex gloves, pulled out an evidence bag, and dropped the camera inside. Then she handed it to a CSI, dressed from head to toe in protective white clothing, so the chain of evidence wouldn't be broken.

"Now since I stuck with you, *si*?" she said disgustedly, "and I can't change that, you can follow over to Pier 52 as we search for evidence—if that's what you wanna do. The shooter's probably gone, but I take no responsibility if something happens to you or sidekick, David. Got that?" She paused for emphasis then continued, "Or you can stay here with Captain Butler. He's leading investigation at playground, trying to find second bullet and map out trajectory so we pinpoint where shooter pull trigger. Your choice, Benson."

"We'll follow you," Ethan said without hesitation. "And I wanna record everything you do."

"You have another camera?" Newton said, visibly annoyed.

"David has one in his backpack," Ethan said.

"Was it rolling during the shooting?" Alvarez said.

"No," David said emphatically.

"And you're not lying to us?" Newton said rudely.

"No way," David said.

"Show me," Alvarez said.

David pulled out the Panasonic 2-Chip and rolled the video. There was nothing on the disk. After a minute, she barked, "Okay, believe you. Shoot new camera."

"Bad decision," Newton said, almost in Alvarez's face. "They can't go with us. Too fucking dangerous, and that camera is going to get in the way. What if the shooter is still there? What if he comes after us and opens fire? Then what? Benson's gonna fuck things up, be a drag on our investigation. They should stay here with Captain Butler."

"I no like either, but not my call," Alvarez said, throwing up her hands, angry. "Highland say Benson wanna go, shoot pictures, risk life, he go—shoot anything and everything he want. That deal, *sí*? You no like, *Randall,* you call big boss. Say no. Not me."

*****

Ethan hung back with David a few feet behind Alvarez as they trudged through the fresh layer of slush on the Greenway, Newton walking just ahead of them surrounded by part of the tactical police unit accompanying Alvarez. *What the fuck just happened?* Ethan thought. *Newton just tried to boot me off the shoot. Like the other night at SVU. But why? Is he hiding something?* That sixth sense that Randall Newton was somehow involved in the murders was rumbling just below the surface, trying to break free, but clouded in uncertainty. He tapped David on the shoulder and whispered, "Make sure to include Newton in the sequence."

"Why?"

"Just do it."

David nodded and started shooting.

The derelict sanitation depot was a quarter of a mile uptown, and all six lanes of West Street were cleared of traffic as far as the eye could see. Cops were positioned every ten feet controlling the gawking onlookers who lined the far side of the Greenway and blocking the press core, their remote trucks parked along the side streets, their reporters and camera crews angling for position, trying to capture the pandemonium. The local stations were going live to the network, feeding images and commentary, the murder now the lead story on the six o'clock newscasts, adding to the growing fear gripping the city. Ethan spotted Winston Peabody, mic in one hand, motioning his cameraman with the other to capture him on camera as they proceeded toward the depot.

He wondered if they had a clean shot.

And were broadcasting his image over the airwaves.

His emotions were boiling like a cauldron—images of Detective Dinkus's shattered face searing his memory, his thirst for alcohol raising its ugly head like a venomous viper.

Scotch.

Jonnie Walker Black.

The antidote to his problems.

Taking a deep breath, he told David to move closer to Alvarez and make a series of wide shots as they made their way to the depot. Then he pulled out his cell phone and texted a short message to Lloyd Howard:

> *There's been another murder at the first kill site. I'm with David and Gloria Alvarez heading to the old Sanitation Salt Depot where a sniper fired a long gun that killed Henry Dinkus. Randall Newton is with us—lobbying to boot me off the story. The guy is trouble. I still want to make sure you follow him tonight, see where he goes. I'll let you know when he cuts out of here.*

Ethan got an immediate response: *Already waiting at his apartment. You be careful.* He shoved his iPhone into his pocket and realized his coat was spotted with blood, as were his hands and face. He shuddered and tried to wipe it away, but the fresh blood, now shades of maroon and stygian black, was crusted like a new layer of skin.

Scotch.

He needed a scotch.

Soon.

He picked up his pace and caught up to Alvarez as they approached a barricade blocking the entrance to the depot.

"Open it," Alvarez said commandingly. "We're going in."

Ethan motioned to David to move into a tight shot as a cop severed the thick chain with a bolt cutter. They all crouched, Alvarez and her crack tactical team sweeping rifles and handguns out front, pushing ahead of Ethan and Newton and their bodyguards as they entered the complex. The depot was massive, jutting out at least fifty acres over the Hudson, man-made a half century ago to house the city's sanitation trucks and millions of tons of salt used to clean the streets after a snowstorm. Being demolished to make way for a new city park, there were originally seven huge buildings standing on the site. Some had already been torn down by heavy equipment now sitting idle, waiting for the courts to throw out a lawsuit filed by an environmental group that had halted demolition. There was a patchwork of dirt roads traversing mountains of steel and bricks and garbage that had yet to be hauled away.

"Here's how he got in!" yelled a Latino cop kneeling on the outside of a chain-link fence about a hundred feet from the gate. "He cut a hole and slipped through. But I don't see any tools. Maybe he took them or heaved them into the river."

"How'd he get all the way down there lugging assault weapon," Alvarez said as she approached the opening from the inside. "You're standing on a three-foot-wide cement wall. Big drop down to river. Maybe twenty feet, *no*?"

"Guy must be Spider-Man," the cop said jokingly.

Nobody laughed.

"Mark spot and get lab guy here to lift fingerprints and look for shoe prints," she said forcefully. "And get dive team in water as soon as we clear site. Maybe we get lucky and find evidence, anything to nail motherfucker."

They continued walking toward the larger of the two remaining structures, David hustling to keep up after finishing the sequence at the fence. Alvarez's walkie-talkie squawked again, the sound piercing the near silence.

"What do you got, Captain?"

"Found the second bullet embedded in a fucking piece of wood to the left of the bow of that fucking ship."

"What caliber?" Ethan said surreptitiously.

"Who was that?" the captain fired back.

"Nobody," Alvarez said, glaring at Ethan.

"A Parabellum hollow point 9mm. Exploded on impact. Nasty. I'm surprised the top half of Dinkus's entire body wasn't blown to kingdom come."

"Any idea what kind of rifle?" Alvarez asked.

"My tech guys aren't a hundred percent sure. But maybe a 300 Win Mag or a Remington Long Action. That's their best guess at the moment, until they get the bullet back to the lab."

"Where was motherfucker?"

"Just finished the calculations. Best guess? The big building closest to the highway. Top floor. Second or third window on the left."

"How sure?" Alvarez said, peering at the three-story brown brick building with most of the glass blown out and a huge hole in the front wall from the demolition.

"Ninety percent, according to the techs."

"We go there," she said, pointing.

"Look, Alvarez," the captain said commandingly, "the perp might still be in there. Sure it's prudent to take those press guys with you? Maybe you should do your sweep first then bring them in."

"I second that," Randall Newton said dismissively. "Too dangerous. I'll check with Highland."

"Too late, *NEWTON*," Alvarez screamed. "Can't wait for big boss lady to change mind, *sí*? Gotta go in now, in case shooter still hiding in there. Unlikely. But maybe, *no*? Benson?"

He peered at David who nodded, then turned to Alvarez. "We understand the risks."

"Heard that loud and clear," the captain said. "But it's your ass, Alvarez, not mine, if something happens to them."

"Copy that," Alvarez said then clicked off the walkie-talkie.

"I still object," Newton said insistently.

"Fuck off, *Randall*, you were at meeting when *loca* deal made with Benson. Full access." She wheeled around to Ethan. "Last chance, *amigo*."

"We're going."

"Thought you'd say that. Just stay behind tactical team and don't do anything stupid."

Then they started moving, slowly, rotating their weapons from side to side, dodging around crumpled steel girders and huge dumpsters stuffed to the brim with refuse, using the abandoned heavy equipment for cover. Alvarez pointed to the other buildings, about a hundred yards from the shoreline, the river currents raging as the wind picked up, the snow coming down harder.

"Half you guys sweep in there. Rest, come with me."

Ethan watched a dozen cops peel out and followed Alvarez behind two plainclothes detectives, both in body armor, who'd been unofficially deputized to protect him. He felt exhilarated, buoyed, alive for the first time since Sarah had walked out, the insipient fear he might lose her buried deep inside, forgotten by the thrill of the hunt, of being out in the field. Then he realized his story was masking what was really important, and anxiety rippled through him again, the need to talk to her, to tell someone she'd left him, clouding his judgment. He had to get a grip. He had to get to the Scotch. Turning to David who was shooting back toward the gate, his legs spread, his arms extended steadying the camera, he noticed Randall Newton hightailing back to the Greenway.

"Where's he going?" Ethan said as David panned back to Alvarez and the tactical team.

"Dunno," he said, still rolling. "He just got off the phone."

"Who'd he call?"

"I was too far away, but the camera has a good built-in directional mic. Maybe we got somethin' on the video."

Ethan nodded, hurried to catch up to Alvarez, the two plainclothes detectives sticking to him like glue. Carefully, he moved a few short steps at a time, using whatever he could find for protection, then stopped behind a front loader, and quickly punched a number into his iPhone.

"Lloyd, it's me. He just left."

"Any idea where?"

"Don't know. David said he made a phone call and took off."

"You still at the murder scene?"

Ethan checked to make sure Alvarez and the tactical squad hadn't moved too far ahead of him, then said, "About to go into an abandoned building where the cops think the shots might have been fired."

"Any sign of the shooter?"

"He's probably gone."

"He'd be an amateur if he wasn't."

"Look, I gotta get off. The two guys babysitting me wanna get moving. Stay put at Newton's building. Call me if he shows up."

He clicked off without waiting for a response then looked for David who was right behind Alvarez, surrounded by his own bodyguards, panning his camera back and forth, alternating the angle of his shots, then moving hurriedly to catch up. Feeling chilled to the bone, he zippered his down coat up to his chin and pulled on his wool hat. He was shaking. His teeth chattering. But not from the cold. The snow had turned to a misty rain, the temperature still hovering about freezing. What was wrong with him?

Sarah.

Had to be Sarah.

She had left him with Luke.

Detective Alvarez suddenly began screaming and waving for him to hurry over. So he buried his emotions and hustled toward her. One of the cops, his rifle slung over his shoulder, was placing an orange cone on the ground.

"Thought you should see this," she said pointing.

Ethan kneeled over and stared at a trail of footprints in the slushy snow—some heading into the building and some leaving.

"The shooter?"

"Has to be," she said excitedly. "There's been nobody in here for months. And they're fresh. See?" She pointed. "Within last hour, maybe two, which was time of shooting." Alvarez clicked on her walkie-talkie and ordered a full CSI team to begin searching the depot for evidence. "They start here, make mold of shoe prints before snow melts, then head into building."

Ethan spun around. "Where's David?" he said excitedly. "I want him to shoot this."

"He already shoot footprints. He now follow part of my tactical team into building. They're doing a full sweep to make sure killer isn't hiding somewhere in there." She pointed to the derelict structure. "He make more pictures."

"Sure it's safe?" Ethan said, alarmed.

"We know in few minutes." She smiled half-heartedly. "You guys got balls. There's just been murder. By sniper. Maybe hit man. And instead of shoot pictures of poor Henry, may his soul rest in peace," she said, crossing herself, "you guys follow me with camera, look for bad guy. Balls. *Benson.* Big balls."

Sarah.

If Alvarez only knew what was going on in his private life.

Then what would she think of me?

Static again on Alvarez's walkie-talkie. "Just found the location the sniper used to shoot Detective Dinkus."

"Where?"

"Captain was right—last window to the left next to the wall, after you walk through the door on the third floor."

"My researcher still shooting?" Ethan said, hard focused on his story again.

"He's right in there with his camera," the voice said over the walkie-talkie.

"Copy that," Alvarez said, motioning for part of her tactical team to follow, ordering the others to keep searching the perimeter of the building, careful not to disturb any evidence they might stumble across. She raised her rifle, a thin, bright beam of light emanating from her shoulder harness, then carefully slinked through the crater in the brick wall and into the building. "Stay behind me, Benson, and do what I say "

Ethan followed, light beams crisscrossing the exposed pipes, metal girders, bricks, and cement blocks, some haphazardly piled in mountains that reached three stories up to the roof, as Alvarez's tactical team canvassed the derelict building, constantly yelling back and forth, "Clear."

Water was leaking from the rain and melting snow, soaking much of the debris, the detective carefully picking her way up the steps, Ethan close behind. When they passed through the door leading to the top floor, Alvarez raised her hand and said, "Everybody watch where walk. Don't want anybody disappearing through floor, falling down basement. That wouldn't be pretty, *no*?"

Ethan chuckled at a rare moment of levity from the detective. Then a text came in on his phone: Peter Sampson was trying to find him. Not now. He jammed the phone into his pocket and looked for David, who was crouched on one knee, shooting through what was once a window but now just an empty hole. A team of crime scene investigators flooded over to Alvarez, was issued orders, and then began the painstaking task of searching for evidence.

"That's where he made the shots?" Ethan said, motioning for the detective to turn off her shoulder light and waving his hand in a circle, alerting David he wanted to do a short on-camera interview.

"Won't know for sure until guys finish up. Gonna take couple a hours."

"How was it possible to make a kill shot from up here?" he said, glancing at the gaping hole. "We're pretty far from the playground."

Alvarez walked to the window and pointed to the ground below, David swinging around to his right, pressing against the wall, keeping her in frame. "Take good look, Benson. We only a couple a thousand feet from playground. Won't know exactly how far until guys complete measurements, but the killer had clean shot down to boat deck. A marksman with high-powered rifle and good scope would have no problem making kill, *no*?"

"So why did he shoot twice?" Ethan said.

"Make sure he no miss."

"But why did he shoot Detective Dinkus?"

"Maybe warning."

"What warning?"

"Maybe get task force back off investigation. Maybe."

Ethan nodded to David that he was finished and peered down at the crime scene. There were now a series of floodlights illuminating a fifty-foot circle around Detective Dinkus's body, still sprawled on the ground where he had fallen, a dozen tech guys poring over the site. An ambulance was parked thirty feet from the body, and two guys from the coroner's office were holding a black body bag, getting ready to take Detective Dinkus to Bellevue Hospital for an autopsy.

Well, there won't be a manpower issue now, he thought, staring at the circle of cops standing listlessly around the body. *If it's the same guy who's killing the kids, man, he just nailed a member of the task force. The cops gotta get the asshole and quick. 'Cause nobody's safe anymore. Nobody.*

CHAPTER 20

"Got him," Lloyd Howard said, framing his new Nikon D5 DSLR camera, fitted with a Nikkor 300 mm telephoto lens, a little tighter. Click. Click. Click. "He's heading our way. Can you see his face in the binoculars?"

"Just barely," Mindy said, fiddling with the focus.

"Well, I can see every detail, and man, he's really stressed." Click. Click. Click. "His eyes are darting all over the place, he's checking out everybody he passes, and keeps looking over his shoulder."

"He thinks he's being followed?"

"Seems like it." Click. Click. Click. "And he's fucking paranoid about something."

They were sitting in the back of Lloyd's state-of-the-art white surveillance van, parked on the east side of the street, just south of Seventy-Third, close enough to see Randall Newton's sleek high-rise on the northwest corner of Seventy-Fourth Street, but far enough away so they wouldn't be spotted. The ADA was standing on the corner of Seventy-Sixth Street, waiting for the light to change. He was soaked from the rain, his overcoat drenched, his pants sticking like glue to his legs.

"He just punched a number into his cell phone." Click. Click. Click. "He's yelling and waving his free hand. Somebody's giving him a hard time."

They waited patiently to see what Newton would do next then watched as the light turned green and he crossed the street heading south, continuing to check everybody he passed, gesturing frantically, talking on the phone excitedly. Lloyd kept Newton in the center of the frame, staying tight on his upper body as he snapped off a burst of pictures—click, click, click—until Newton reached the front door of his building, breezed by the doorman without saying a word, and disappeared into the lobby. Lloyd lowered the camera and fished a Red Bull from an ice chest then checked the little screen on the side of the camera.

"How do the pix look?" Mindy said, still scanning up and down the street.

"Perfect. Every detail. Every facial expression. The guy looks like he's in some really deep shit."

"What time is it?" Mindy said, still peering at the front of Newton's building through her binoculars.

"Exactly eight thirty."

"If he sticks to his pattern," she said, "the *Charge-A-Ride* won't pick him up for another two and a half hours."

"Always a possibility that he isn't going after the cop was killed tonight," Lloyd said, draining the Red Bull and crunching the can with his hand. "Text Ethan. Tell him to get his ass over here right now."

*****

Ethan read the message one more time then turned and faced Detective Alvarez.

"I gotta go," he said hurriedly. "Can you spare one of your detectives to get me through the police barricade and past the crowds?"

Alvarez studied his face discerningly. "What's the rush, Benson? I can take you in a little while, *no*? Aren't you gonna shoot my meeting at DA's Office? I gotta give Highland a big briefing on new murder and investigation. Maybe change our strategy, get more people, now that crazy killer, maybe same sicko who's doing little girls, is going after us."

Ethan turned rapidly to David. "Can you go?"

"On it," he said without hesitating as he continued shooting a CSI painstakingly search every square inch of the floorboards around the opening in the wall where the shots had been fired.

"That work for you?" Ethan said, rotating back to Alvarez.

"Whatever," she said, nodding to a beefy detective with broad shoulders who was jotting notes in a small pocket notebook. "Simmons, run block for Benson. He's got somewhere important to go."

Ethan thanked her and whispered to David, "Shoot as much as you can at the task force meeting then send me a detailed e-mail when you finish."

"Where you going?"

"Following a hunch."

David gave him the high sign and resumed shooting as Ethan followed Detective Simmons, weaving around the dozens of cops, crime scene investigators, and tactical police units poking around the building, then down the debris-filled staircase, and out into the open air. They walked briskly through the mounds of rubble piled on the ground and past more CSI still searching for evidence at the opening in the chain-link fence where the killer had cut his way into the complex. The crowd had thinned on West Street, but the press corps was still camped a half block away on the far side of the barriers, waiting for a statement from anyone leaving the crime scene. Ethan made his way down Jane Street, pulling his wool cap across his forehead, hoping to slip by the remote trucks, their broadcast antennas pointing to satellite uplinks. But he didn't get far before he was mobbed by reporters pointing cameras and microphones.

"What's happening in there?" the WABC reporter yelled, pushing her way in front of Ethan, trying to block his path through the melee.

"What did you see?" another reporter said.

"Did they find the killer?" yet a third reporter screamed.

Ethan ducked behind Detective Simmons to no avail, finally stopping and looking into the bank of lenses. "No comment. No comment."

"YOU HEARD THE MAN," Simmons said, bellowing. "LET HIM THROUGH."

A narrow passageway was created, the press corps reluctantly backing away, still rolling their cameras and firing questions. Ethan slowly pushed through the mob, behind the detective, when he was confronted one last time by Winston Peabody.

"Frame up the shot," Peabody said to his cameraman before shoving a microphone into Ethan's face. "I knew it was you, Benson. Who else would the cops take in there. A quick statement for WGBS, *your* sister station."

Ethan glared but kept walking, Peabody and his cameraman on his heels.

"Just answer one quick question. Who was murdered in there?"

Ethan stopped and turned, composing himself. "We've been over this, Winston. I can't make a statement, not at the moment. You'll have to wait for Patricia Highland's press conference. That's all I'm gonna say."

"So why are you covered in blood?"

"I can't say anymore."

"Is it your blood?"

"Not mine."

"Another little girl's?" Peabody said, continuing to fire away.

Ethan pushed forward, Detective Simmons blocking Peabody, who yelled as Ethan got into a taxi, "So are you confirming this is another Child Sex Murder? Just a simple yes or no, Benson."

Ethan ignored him, slammed the door, and leaned back against the seat, then gave the driver Randall Newton's home address. He exhaled deeply through his nose, trying to stop his heart, racing like a thoroughbred, before checking his messages. Nothing new from Lloyd or Mindy. Just another irate voice mail from Peter Sampson demanding to know where he was, plus a terse text from Sarah: *At my sister's. Luke's fine. Don't call.* He stared long and hard at his cell phone, then slowly dialed her number, hesitated, and abruptly punched off. She'd asked for space. A little time to think. To get away from their marriage. Better wait, maybe until tomorrow. He shoved the phone back into his pocket and opened his briefcase. A new pint bottle of Black Label was sitting on the bottom in a brown paper bag. He ripped off the wrapping, began unscrewing the cap, then closed his eyes, sweat pouring down his brow, and put it back in the briefcase.

Later.

He needed to stay sober.

Had to work.

*****

Fifteen minutes later, the cab pulled to a stop at Third Avenue and Seventy-Second Street. Ethan paid the fare, pushed open the door, and eased himself out. He headed north on the west side of the street and spotted Lloyd's surveillance van catty-corner one block ahead. He crossed the street then walked up to the rear door of the van and climbed in.

"Is he still here?" he said, out of breath.

"I would've called if he wasn't," Lloyd said frankly.

"How long?"

"About an hour," Mindy said, staring through the binoculars, fixed on Newton's building.

"Pictures?"

"Dozens. Shot him coming down the block and walking into his lobby. He was a wreck. Not the same guy we met at the District Attorney's Office."

"What time is it now?" Ethan said, beads of sweat pooling on his face.

"Nine fifteen." Mindy said, staring at his visage. "Jeez, Ethan, you look like shit. You been drinking?"

"Hell no," he said, although he'd almost downed a quick pop in the taxi.

"So what's wrong?"

"Nothin'," he said evasively.

"Dinkus's murder?" Howard said, as concerned as Mindy. "He took the bullet right in front of you. That would rattle me to the core."

Ethan didn't answer, feeling nothing about Dinkus, but totaled by Sarah. Should he say something? Tell them she'd walked out on him? No. Better to wait a couple of days and see if she came home. Then he could pretend nothing had happened. So what should he say? He was about to make an excuse, to blame his disheveled appearance on the detective's murder as Lloyd had suggested, when Mindy suddenly shushed him.

"A black car just pulled up to Newton's building."

"Is it Newton's car service?" Lloyd said, raising his camera and snapping away.

"Looks like it."

"But it's too early to fit the pattern?" Ethan said urgently. "Any sign of him?"

"Not yet," Lloyd said.

"Maybe the car's for somebody else?"

"Wait. Here he comes." Click. Click. Click. "He's cleaned up his act and is in a suit and tie, and he's holding a briefcase. Everything looks expensive." Click. Click. Click. "Okay, the doorman's hovering at the curb. Newton just tipped him. Now the driver's opening the rear passenger door, and he's getting in." Click. Click. Click.

"What kinda car?" Ethan said.

"A black Mercedes SUV," Mindy said, staring through the binoculars.

"License plate?"

"NY64643," she said, jotting it on a slip of paper. "Why?"

"So we can cross-check it in his computer records and see if he uses the same driver every Saturday night."

"Gotch-ya."

"Wasn't one of the tire tracks from the Dry Dock Playground murder an SUV?" Lloyd said, still snapping pictures.

"I forgot about that," Ethan said.

"Hand Ethan the binoculars and drive. They're pulling away from the curb, and I wanna keep shooting. Ethan, you need to run point so we don't lose him."

Ethan crawled into the front seat next to Mindy as she hastily turned on the engine, flipped the gearshift into drive, and pulled out into traffic, settling in about a half block behind the Mercedes.

Time to rock and roll.

*****

Newton hefted a deep sigh, lit a cigarette. He didn't notice the white van, about five car lengths behind, that was shadowing their every move as they drove up to Seventy-Ninth Street, turned right, and headed across town. He wasn't a smoker, only occasionally grabbing a cigarette at a cocktail party or when hitting on a girl at a bar, but tonight was different. He'd been pushed close to the edge, beginning when he got the call about Detective Dinkus in Patricia Highland's office, then when the ADA dispatched him to the crime scene to be her eyes and ears and to supervise the task force investigation. At first he hoped it was just a coincidence, a random act of violence—a police officer gunned down while confronting a suspect. But when he got to the Pier 51 playground and found that asshole producer, Ethan Benson, he knew the killing wasn't random. Then when he'd gotten the call from the big boss himself and was told that Dinkus hadn't been the target, that he was just a tragic bystander, he knew he was in big trouble. Somehow the big boss had found out that Benson would be at the playground and had decided to dispatch one of his goons to kill him and derail the press coverage of the case. Now all hell was breaking loose, and *he* was in the shitter—ordered to clean up the mess.

Newton puffed twice on his cigarette, coughed, then leaned over to the driver. "Bernie, a different address tonight."

"Not headed to the usual place?"

"Not tonight."

"Where to then, sir?"

"Smith and Wollensky Steakhouse on Third Avenue."

"On the corner of Forty-Ninth Street?"

"That's it."

"No problem, sir. Should be there in about fifteen minutes, depending on traffic."

"Thanks, Bernie."

He slumped in his seat and lit another cigarette with the end of the one he'd just smoked to the filter. Nervously, he glanced out the side window, then out the back, flicking his eyes into every passing car, worried someone was tailing him. Fuck. Fuck. Fuck. Then his office cell phone pinged. A short message from ADA Highland: "Where are you? I need an update." He lied, firing back a quick reply, telling her he was still at the crime scene, that he'd call when he came up for air. God. Did she suspect? Had she figured out who he really was? How much longer before his cover was blown? He closed his eyes and tried to clear his head. Then his burner vibrated noisily in his briefcase.

The big boss.

"Almost there, Randall?"

"On my way."

"How long?"

He quickly glanced out the window, not sure where he was. "Maybe another five minutes."

"Good. Because our friend is waiting."

"But—"

"Just listen, asshole. Do you have the package?"

"In my briefcase."

"Give it to him and then come see me."

The connection went dead.

*****

Mindy carefully followed the black Mercedes, always hanging back a couple of car lengths, letting a yellow cab cut in front of her at Seventy-Ninth Street, then catching up as they slowly made the right onto Second Avenue into bumper-to-bumper traffic.

"Where the fuck's he going?" she said, shifting to the left lane, the Mercedes three car lengths ahead in the right lane.

"Beats me," Lloyd said, snapping more pictures on his Nikon. "But it sure ain't Alphabet City."

"Don't let him see you, Mindy," Ethan said, his eyes glued to the Mercedes's taillights.

"Jeez, Ethan, get a grip. I've done this before."

The driver turned on his blinker and made a right onto Forty-Ninth Street then cruised down the block until it reached the near corner, where it pulled into a space next to a fire hydrant on the right side of the street in front of a two-story green and white building.

"Pull over and don't get too close," Ethan said.

Mindy slowed and eased into an empty space on the left side of the street, about half a block from Third Avenue.

"Can you see him through the lens, Lloyd?"

"Got him."

"What's he doing?"

"He's talking to the driver." Click. Click. Click. "Now he's getting out of the car." Click. Click. Click. "He's still acting very cautious, checking out everybody around him. Now he's just standing quietly, and there, he just walked into Smith and Wollensky."

"Fuck me," Ethan said, vexed. "He's going to a fancy dinner? With all the shit that's hitting the fan at the moment?"

"Maybe he's meeting somebody?"

"Still doesn't make sense," Ethan said. "ADA Highland is holding a task force meeting to go over Dinkus's killing. Shouldn't he be there?" He tapped Mindy on the shoulder. "Get a bit closer. Pull through the intersection and double-park eight or ten car lengths from the corner." Then he turned to Lloyd. "You still have a clean shot of the restaurant."

"Full frame on the front door."

"Good. Now we wait. See if he walks out with somebody."

*****

Newton pushed through the door and walked up to the maitre d' who was just returning to his reservation book after sitting a young couple at a table near the bar. The restaurant was packed with people, mostly attorneys and wealthy businessmen, all partying, letting off steam after a busy day cutting deals. Newton scanned the room, looking at faces, searching for anyone he might know. He instantly relaxed. *Good. Nobody here who can ID me.* The maitre d', dressed in a formal black tuxedo, stared into his face, smiling from ear to ear.

"Good evening. How can I assist you, sir?"

"Randall Newton."

"Ah, Mr. Newton. I've already seated your dinner guest. Follow me. Right this way."

They weaved around tables, the ornate room dark and intimate, the white walls trimmed with freshly stained mahogany paneling and lined with glass cases of expensive French wines, the ceilings affixed with elaborately-colored Tiffany chandeliers.

There were freshly starched white tablecloths, crystal wineglasses, and fancy stainless steel cutlery, the best accoutrements money can buy. Newton kept his eyes fixed straight ahead as he weaved around the tables, avoiding the crowds of onlookers, still paranoid he'd be recognized as he approached a man sitting by himself at a table in the back of the restaurant.

"Sit, you're late," the man said, pouring Randall a glass of Chateau Margaux.

"Couldn't be helped," Newton said, inhaling the bouquet of the red wine then taking a sip. "Had a tough time extracting myself from the murder investigation."

"Detective Dinkus. Tragic loss. I need to stop by Bellevue Hospital and then make a statement to the press. But that can wait until we finish up here." He cut a small piece of porterhouse steak and plopped it into his mouth, chewing slowly, savoring the rich flavor of the prime cut of meat. "You going to order, Randall?"

"No time. Have another meeting downtown."

"Well, did you bring it?"

Newton flipped open his briefcase and pulled out an envelope, placing it on the table. "It's all there."

The man casually picked up the package, briefly thumbed through the one hundred dollar bills, and slipped it into the pocket of his suit jacket.

"Excellent. I'll make sure to take care of our problem."

Newton nodded and started to get up.

"Leaving already?"

"I gotta go."

"Sit with me a moment while I finish my dinner. And don't waste the wine. The bottle cost me close to a thousand dollars."

CHAPTER 21

"Anything happening?" Ethan said impatiently.

"He's still in there," Lloyd said, his camera fixed to the front door of the restaurant.

"Christ. It's been almost an hour. What the fuck's he doing in there?"

"Chill, Ethan," Mindy said, her hands fixed on the steering wheel. "It's only ten thirty. He's still got a half hour to get downtown."

"But maybe he's not going to the Lower East Side. Maybe we're wasting our time."

"Hold on. Here he comes," Lloyd said, rolling off a series of shots.

"Is he by himself?" Ethan said, leaning forward in the passenger seat, straining to find Newton in the crowd of revelers waiting for the traffic light to change.

"He's alone." Click. Click. Click. "And the *Charge-A-Ride* just pulled up. He's getting in."

"Quick, Mindy," Ethan said excitedly, "back up onto Third Avenue in case he heads uptown."

"I'll be damned," Lloyd said, continuing to take pictures. "Police Commissioner Jordan Langely just walked out of the restaurant. He just nodded to Newton in the back seat of the Mercedes and got into his own car." Click. Click. Click."

"Think that's the guy he called from the Dinkus crime scene?" Ethan said. "To set up a dinner?"

"That would certainly ratchet things up," Mindy said, easing the surveillance van into an empty space on the corner and waiting to see where Newton went next.

"But why would Newton take time to eat a fancy dinner with the commissioner? After a cop killing? They both have shit to do. Especially the police commissioner. He's the face of the NYC Police Department. He's gotta meet the mayor, visit Dinkus's family, make a statement to the press. This makes no sense. I want you guys to hit your sources. See if we can connect Newton to Langely. Find out anything you can about their relationship. Maybe this was just a harmless dinner, but my gut tells me there's something else going on here."

"He's on the move again," Lloyd said, rolling off a series of pictures.

"Follow him, Mindy."

She eased into Third Avenue traffic, hanging back a block as they headed uptown. At Seventy-Ninth Street she ran a red light and tailed the Mercedes east—past Second Avenue, then First, before stopping a safe distance behind at York.

"He's getting onto the FDR Drive, heading south," Lloyd said, tracking the Mercedes through the lens of his camera.

"Don't lose him. Maybe he's finally on his way to the Lower East Side," Ethan said, leaning against the dashboard.

Mindy gunned the engine, sped onto the Drive, signaled, and pulled across a lane of traffic. "Damn, I don't see him."

"Still got him on a tight shot." Click. Click. Click. "Ethan, find the car with the binoculars."

Ethan panned randomly, desperate, panicked. Then he locked in on the Mercedes. "Left lane, Mindy, maybe nine or ten cars ahead."

Mindy scanned for an opening then cut off a red Toyota in the right lane and accelerated. She pulled up five car lengths then got boxed in by an old junker in front of her and a muscle car to her left.

"Shit. Shit. Shit."

"He's pulling away. He's got clear sailing for a quarter of a mile. Do something, Mindy," Ethan said, gripping the binoculars like a vise.

"Easy, easy, Mindy," Lloyd said softly, "it's okay if he pulls a short ways ahead of us. We don't want him to spot us." Click. Click. Click. "There, he's slowing down, stuck in another bottleneck. Just stay where you are. We won't lose him."

They held pace for a half mile, the Mercedes stopping and starting in the traffic, Mindy still following in the right lane—four car lengths behind. Then traffic eased in front of her, and she said, "Should I pass him?"

"Hell no. The last thing you want is to get in front of him," Lloyd said. "If he exits suddenly, he'll be gone for good."

"So what should she do?" Ethan said, his heart thumping in his chest.

"Pull up alongside."

"But there's a cabby tailgating me," Mindy said.

"Ignore him. He'll pull around you. I wanna see what he's doing." Click. Click. Click.

Mindy softly braked until she was sitting next to the Mercedes, a lane of cars still between them. "Can you see him?"

"Clear as day. He's on his cell phone. Animated. Like he's scared of something," Click. Click. Click. "Try to keep the van steady, Mindy. My lens is bouncing. Can't get off a clean shot." He kept shooting as Mindy concentrated on the road, trying to avoid potholes, taking the curves smoothly. "Hold it like that a few seconds. Hold it. Hold it. Hold it." Click. Click. Click. He stopped shooting and began scrolling through the images.

Impatiently, Ethan said, "What do you got, Lloyd?"

"Give me a sec."

"Come on—"

"The cell phone looks funny. Take a look, Ethan."

He grabbed the camera and stared at the small monitor. Randall Newton filled the frame, licking his lips, twisting a lock of hair, his eyebrows furrowed as he talked to somebody.

"Okay, what am I looking at?"

"What kind of phone does Newton use?"

"Some kind of heavily-encrypted smartphone. That's standard issue at the District Attorney's Office."

"Does that look like a smartphone?"

"No. It's the wrong shape and size. So what is it?"

"It could be a burner."

"Why does an ADA have a burner?" Mindy said taciturnly as she dropped a few car lengths behind the Mercedes.

"Good question," Ethan said, "and who the hell is he talking to? Can't be the task force. He'd be using his smartphone." He tried to process this nugget of information then punched David Livingston's number into his iPhone. It rang for a long time before he picked up.

"Ethan, can't talk. I'm at the DA's Office shooting the task force meeting. Lots happening. Can I call you back?"

"Need to talk now." Ethan could hear David sigh, walk several steps, and close a door.

"In the hallway. What gives?"

"First, tell me what's happening there."

"The CSI found a shell casing between two floorboards about thirty feet from the window," he said hurriedly. "The sniper must've missed it in his haste to get out of there. It's already at forensics. They've got a good thumbprint and are running it through CODES, looking for a match."

"So maybe they caught a break in the case?"

"That's what Alvarez thinks. A big one."

"Anything else?"

"The mold from the shoe print in the snow. Won't know for sure until they compare it to what they've got at the lab, but it looks like a match to the prints they lifted at the four murder scenes.

"The size 7 sneakers with the irregularity in the big toe?"

"Uh-huh."

"So the same guy killed Dinkus?"

"Could be."

"Any luck on tracking the No. 6 surgical blades?"

"Nothin' yet. A team of detectives is still cross-referencing names. Won't know for a couple of days."

"And who's replacing Dinkus?"

"Some detective named Victor Nottingdale. Also out of the Sixth Precinct."

"And you got all this on camera?"

"Every word," David said. There was a sudden commotion in the background. "Ethan, I gotta go back in there. The shit's hitting the fan."

"What shit?" Ethan said insistently.

"Randall Newton is AWOL. He hasn't checked in with Patricia Highland since he left the crime scene. She's been trying his cell over and over, but it goes straight to voice mail. And it sounds like this isn't the first time he's inexplicably disappeared."

Ethan fell silent, processing this new piece of information.

"Gotta start shooting, Ethan. This is the kind of process stuff nobody ever gets. What was your question, by the way?"

"You just answered it. Thanks." He turned to Mindy and Lloyd. "Well, Newton's not talking to the task force. He's definitely talking to somebody else on the burner."

*****

Randall Newton sat quietly in the Mercedes, staring absentmindedly out the front window, tapping his fingers softly on the plush leather armrest at his side—one, two, one two, one two—keeping time to an imaginary drum beat only he could hear. He had stopped answering the telephone, both his burner and his office cell phone, avoiding his two masters, trying to stifle a growing sense of dread pouring into every fiber of his being. He was out of excuses for Patricia Highland. She'd already heard them all. And he was dreading his meeting with the big boss, scared of what might happen now that the task force was running whipsaw out of control. Maybe that's why he was sent to bribe the police commissioner—to get him to pull some strings and rein in the investigation. And then there was Ethan Benson. The guy never gave up like a rabid pit bull, picking up on leads he had successfully managed to bury, sniffing closer to the truth, threatening to destroy everything he'd spent all those years building one agonizing step at a time.

Benson.

He hated Ethan Benson.

Hated him.

Pounding on the armrest in frustration, he said, a little too harshly, "Bernie, put on some music."

"Preference?"

"Classical. Maybe Mozart."

Bernie shuffled through the music catalogue on his smartphone and tapped on the *String Quartet No. 14 in G Major,* a violin sonata filling the car with the sounds of springtime on a clear country day.

Newton could feel the music—soothing, mellowing, enchanting, calming. Then his burner buzzed again, destroying any hope of easing his mushrooming anxiety, and after staring at the LCD screen, he punched the icon for Call.

"Hold on for the *Jiaofu,* Mr. Newton," a thin, female voice said in singsong Mandarin.

He waited, pulling nervously on his lower lip, the streetlights along the FDR Drive alternately throwing patterns of bright light and then darkness across the back seat of the Mercedes.

"Mr. Newton," said an elderly man with a gravelly voice, "you disappoint me. You haven't held up your side of my very generous deal. And now look at the problems you've caused me. Ah, what a pity. I'm forced to take things into my own hands to clean up your mess."

"But—"

"The commissioner will help, but the burden still rests on you."

"But—"

"You enjoy my special business, don't you, Mr. Newton? It gives you much pleasure, doesn't it, Mr. Newton?"

"Well—"

"Quiet, Mr. Newton," the old man ordered sharply. "I want to relish the fear I hear in your voice." He paused. "How long until you get here?"

"We're coming up to Houston Street on the Drive," he said listlessly. "I should be there in a few minutes."

"Good. I just wanted to make sure you were still coming. You've been ignoring my phone calls since we last talked. I thought, maybe, you'd decided to run."

"But—"

"*Gou!*" the old man said harshly. "We'll talk more when you get here. Then I'll decide what to do with you."

*****

"His right blinker is flashing," Ethan said, his binoculars pressed up against the windshield. "Looks like he's getting off at Houston Street."

"Right on the money," Mindy said, pumping her fist as she followed the Mercedes down the off ramp and up to a red light. "Right blinker still flashing. He's definitely headed to the Lower East Side."

"Check the address?" Lloyd said, still peering through the viewfinder of his Nikon DSLR, snapping one picture after another.

"The reporter's notebook in the glove compartment, Ethan. Bottom of the first page," she said, the light turning green, the Mercedes pulling onto Houston four car lengths ahead of them.

Fumbling with the small spiral notebook, his hands visibly shaking, he ran his finger down the page until he found the address carefully printed in big, block letters.

"148 Avenue D. Shit. That's only a couple of blocks from the Dry Dock Playground where the killer dumped the last girl."

"Coincidence?" she said.

"Don't believe in coincidences."

"Punch the address into the GPS," Lloyd said, never taking his eye off the camera lens. "That way we can track him if we lose him at a red light."

Mindy hung back another two car lengths, now a full half block, as Ethan fiddled with the computer on the dashboard. So far, they were winning the cat-and-mouse game, the black car making no erratic moves, showing no signs it knew it was being followed. Houston Street was alive with people walking with purpose, ducking into sleazy bars and restaurants, drinking beer buried in brown paper bags, hustling for a handout.

"He comes here every Saturday night?" Ethan wondered out loud.

"That's the pattern," Lloyd said. "Leaves from his apartment at eleven o'clock sharp and gets dropped off at the same place on Avenue D. Except tonight, of course. The pit stop at the steak house is definitely not part of his routine. Shit. He just picked up the burner again." Click. Click. Click. "His eyes are bulging. He looks agitated."

They passed an all-night McDonald's, a liquor store with heavy bars crisscrossing the windows, and a Laundromat filled with people washing their clothes. Then they got caught in a traffic tie-up, six cars behind the Mercedes, one lane to the left. They waited for a Budweiser delivery truck to finish unloading a keg of beer then started moving again, now just a few car lengths behind.

"Still got him in my lens," Lloyd said. Click. Click. Click. "He just got off the burner and pounded it back into his briefcase. He's freaking out about something."

Ethan ran through everything he'd observed about Randall Newton since they'd first met at the DA's Office. The guy was a certifiable asshole, who'd been on his back, trying to kick him off the Child Sex Murders case since the moment they'd met. There was something terribly wrong with him. Something really bad. And now this? A weekly trip to the Lower East Side? To one of the most dangerous neighborhoods in the city? What was he doing here? And how did it play into the investigation? Or did it?

What was he missing?

"Pull in closer behind him, Mindy," he said. "We're almost at Avenue D."

She hit the blinker, waited for an opening behind a yellow Porsche Carrera, and eased in three cars behind the Mercedes.

"He's not turning," Lloyd said, still perfectly calm. "He's going somewhere else tonight."

Ethan ran his fingers through his hair. "What the fuck?"

"He's signaling," Lloyd said, "making a left onto Chrystie Street."

Mindy eased into the turn and followed. One block. Two blocks. Three blocks.

"Now a right onto Grand Street," Lloyd said, lowering his camera. "Looks like he's headed somewhere in Chinatown."

They followed another five minutes, traversing a web of narrow, clogged side streets, before the black car hung a quick left onto Hester and stopped in front of a dingy, hole-in-the wall restaurant called *Hung Chow Delicacies.*

Ethan scanned the block. "Pull into the space next to the fire hydrant. Let's see what he does next."

CHAPTER 22

Newton sat a moment, trying to compose himself, then grabbed his briefcase and stepped out of the car.

"I don't know how long I'll be, Bernie, but can you come back, let's say, in about two hours, and pick me up?"

"Sure thing, Mr. Newton. That's our arrangement. I drop everything when you need me. Be back by one thirty."

"I'll call if I need you earlier."

The Mercedes pulled away, leaving Newton standing on the sidewalk, surrounded by Chinese families with small children still shopping for groceries like it was the middle of the day, watching as the black car turned right and disappeared onto Mott Street. Then he took a long and hard look at the modern building directly across the street, nestled in amongst the run-down tenements, shrugged his shoulders longingly, and marched to the front door of the restaurant, stopping to quickly glance left and right before pushing through the door. The dining room was just as dingy as the last time he'd been there, but packed with tourists eating dinner, waiters hustling back and forth with big trays propped on their shoulders filled with steaming-hot Chinese delicacies—Peking duck, shrimp in black bean sauce, Yeung Chow fried rice. He pushed his way through the crowd of young people drinking at the bar and walked up to the same Chinese bartender wearing the same silk *Ba Gua Kungfu* shirt who always seemed to be there.

"Back room?" he said as confidently as he could.

The bartender didn't speak, gestured toward a curtain across from the bar, and watched as Newton weaved around tables, checking that his hair was neatly in place, pushed behind the curtain, and rapped three times on a door. A sliding wood panel creaked open, and a large Chinese man with inscrutable eyes looked him over, opened the door, and silently waved him in. He started to perspire. The man in a black T-shirt, the fabric stretched tightly by his broad frame, stepped aside and motioned him down a dark passageway. Taking a deep breath, he proceeded and paused at another door then walked through. There was a steep staircase leading underground, lit by a series of bare light bulbs hanging from wires and a tunnel that stretched under Hester Street with more exposed light bulbs positioned every ten or so feet along the way.

Newton hesitated.

Why were they meeting over there?

And not in the usual place?

He wiped the sweat off his brow.

His heart pounding uncontrollably in his chest.

He followed the passageway, as he'd done so many times before to sample the secret pleasures that made him who he was, but instead of feeling the usual excitement, there was only a deep sense of dread. He reached a third door, this one more elaborately decorated than the others, rapped three times, and was greeted by a petite Chinese woman dressed as a *yi-zhe* concubine in an elegant floral red velvet *yukata*, wooden *geta* sandals on her feet, and two ancient ivory needles laced through her long black hair. She offered him a glass of Dom Pérignon in a champagne flute and escorted him down a sleek, modern hallway with expensive marble floors, up a spiral staircase adorned with elegant Murano chandeliers hanging from a hand-painted fresco ceiling. He sipped the champagne too fast, his head buzzing, and was ushered into a large vestibule decorated in sensual red, pink, and lavender silk fabrics. There were two doors, both closed. Taking a quick peek at the one in front of him, the one he usually passed through, he was motioned by the pretty *yi-zhe* to the one on the left.

He finished what was left of his champagne.

Steeled himself.

And walked into the room.

*****

They sat quietly in the back of the surveillance van, the frigid night air chilling them to the bone, peering through a small window, camouflaged with a layer of dark plastic matting—making it nigh on impossible to see in from the outside. Ethan wrung his hands, trying to improve his circulation.

"Mind if I smoke?" he said.

"You crazy, Ethan?" Mindy said, aghast. "There's no air in here, and it's too fucking cold to crank down a window. No. You can't smoke."

Ethan shoved the cigarette back in the pack and leaned up against the side of the van. He hated stakeouts. They always made him tense, irritable. He checked his messages. Nothing he had to worry about from David, Paul, or Peter Sampson. But there was also nothing from Sarah. No text. No e-mail. No voice mail. He stared vacantly at the screen, his fingers hovering over the keyboard. What should he do? Should he shoot her a brief message? Tell her he loved her? Tell her to come home? Closing his eyes, he tried to control his urge to reach out—then texted her three short words: "Please call me."

He waited.

Hoping she'd answer.

Hoping.

But after five long minutes, he put away his iPhone.

Closing his eyes, he tried to tap down his desperation. How could he live without her? Without Luke? He thought about the pint bottle of Scotch in his briefcase. *A short pull, that's all I need. The warmth sliding down my throat. The soothing calm it'll bring. The courage it will give me to get through the rest of tonight. Fuck. I need a drink. I need one. Badly.* He squeezed his eyes tightly, tears dripping down his cheeks, trying to will away the pull of the Scotch.

"Anything?" he said, turning to Lloyd.

"All quiet."

"How long's it been?"

"Over a half hour," Mindy said, peering through the darkened window next to Lloyd. "How long should we give him?"

"Until he comes out."

Lloyd continued watching then scrolled through the images on his Nikon until he reached the sequence of Newton walking toward the restaurant. Something caught his eye.

"Curious," he said, handing Ethan the camera. "Take a look. What do you think he glanced at just before he walked through the door?"

Ethan clicked through the pictures then looked up at Lloyd. "I don't see anything."

"Give me the camera," Lloyd said." He backed up to the beginning of the sequence, slowly advanced through the images, then handed the camera back to Ethan. "Look at his face in this one."

It was a medium shot, Newton's body twisted sharply to the right, his gaze clearly transfixed away from the Chinese restaurant and across the street. Ethan scooted to the other side of the van and peered through a second camouflaged window. None of the buildings looked different, all built a century ago, all run-down, except one sitting in the middle of the block—a new town house with a richly patterned stone and marble facade. Ethan stared down at the picture then over to Lloyd.

"Anything showing more of the other side of the street?"

"That's it. I was concentrating on Newton."

He studied the picture and glanced through the window. "There's nothing except that new building. Think that's what he was looking at?"

"Who the fuck knows?" Lloyd said half-heartedly.

"Roll off a dozen pictures of the town house and give me a lot of angles." Then he whipped around to Mindy. "Find out who owns that building and what he or she uses it for. Can you do it right now?"

Mindy rolled her eyes. "At one in the morning?"

"Right. Right."

"I'll make some calls first thing tomorrow."

Then they all went back to waiting for Newton, but now they were watching, not one, but two buildings.

*****

Newton entered a dimly lit room with plush red carpeting and priceless Oriental silk screens finely crafted with dragons and warriors and traditional Chinese landscapes. A thick layer of smoke hung like a cloud below the ceiling, a pungent but sweet odor filling his nostrils, heightening his senses to their very core. Lounging on a plush layer of silk cushions, surrounded by a small army of Chinese bodyguards, was Chang Kai Shu—the big boss, the godfather, the *Jiaofu*—the most powerful man in the Chinese underworld and the head of the most notorious *Tong* in the city. He was smoking an opium pipe—a long wooden cylinder covered with ornate spirals, a small barrel in the middle, and the head of a fierce dragon carved in front. He inhaled three quick puffs and blew the smoke out his nose, a stream of light-brown mist floating into the thick cloud hanging above.

"Would you like a taste?" he said in a soft, melodic tone as he offered the pipe.

Newton licked his lips, stepped forward, his hands outstretched, his face eager. The *Jiaofu* smiled and pulled the pipe away, cradling it in his arms.

"Not yet, Mr. Newton. Not until we finish our pressing business. Is that satisfactory, Mr. Newton?"

He nodded.

Not sure what to say.

The *Jiaofu* placed the pipe back in his mouth, inhaled deeply, then stood and approached Newton, his eyes heavy, his expression unreadable. He was ancient, somewhere in his eighties, maybe nineties, with long white hair pulled back in a braided Chinese queue that hung halfway down his back and thin rasps of white hair on his chin. His posture was crooked from arthritis and old age, his skin pasty and wrinkled like coarse leather. Wearing a long silk robe tied at the waist with a sash, he told Newton to sit on a chair propped in front of him.

"Are you comfortable, Mr. Newton," he said, waving a hand with long, painted fingernails.

Newton nodded.

Still unsure what to say.

"Good. I always want my guests to feel honored when they're in my presence. Some tea, maybe? Something a little stronger?"

Newton shook his head no, bile rising from his gut.

The *Jiaofu* sat back on his silk cushions and puffed on the opium, his eyes growing redder, heavier. Handing the pipe to a *yi-zhe* who materialized from the shadows, he glanced at a man standing patiently in the corner. Bingwen Ho slowly made his way to the back of Newton's chair and placed his big hands firmly on his shoulders. The *Jiaofu* smiled, and Bingwen squeezed.

Newton cried out in pain.

The *Jiaofu* snapped his fingers, and Bingwen released his grip.

"Do you enjoy pain, Mr. Newton?"

"No, no, no," he said, whimpering.

"Then why do you continue to disappoint me?"

"I'm doing the best I can, Mr. Chang."

The *Jiaofu* smiled again, and Bingwen squeezed even harder. Newton writhing, twisting, trying to wrestle away from his grip, his fingers digging ever deeper into Newton's muscles, sending shock waves of pain down his arms and into his legs.

"Enough. Please. Enough," he begged, his head lolling forward, his eyes glazing.

The old man stared piercingly, Bingwen continuing to squeeze, harder, harder, harder, the *Jiaofu* knitting his brow. "I think my dear guest has endured enough pain for the moment." Bingwen loosened his grip, and Newton collapsed to the floor. "Prop him back up," he said bitterly.

The big man grabbed him by the scruff of his collar and slammed him back into the chair.

Then there was silence.

The only sound, soft music coming from somewhere else in the building.

Newton lifted his head and wiped a stream of drool coating his chin with the back of his hand, pain coursing through his body like shock waves, his legs prickling, his arms numb, his hands dead.

The *Jiaofu* stood and stepped toward Newton, crouching eye to eye, six inches from his face.

"The art of traditional Chinese torture, Mr. Newton, learned decades ago in my small village outside Beijing and taught to my associate, who's learned the body's pressure points like a master craftsman. The pain will persist for most of the night, then leave you aching from your head to your toes for at least another day. Maybe two. I hope you enjoyed your punishment, Mr. Newton. Enlightening, wasn't it?"

Newton was horrified.

Grabbing him by the ears, the old man's wrinkled face twisted in a mask of rage, he said, "I want Benson dead. The task force investigation must come to an end. And you, my dear, Mr. Newton, have to figure out some way to make both those things happen. I tried helping you today, but my associate here, the Butcher—please, come say hello to my dear friend, Randall—was just too far away. He killed the detective instead of the producer, my intended target. No great loss. The detective had to go anyway."

Quay Chaoxiang stepped forward, his shifty eyes gleaming, his tattoos shimmering, and kneeled in front of Newton next to the *Jiaofu*, a wry smile twisting his face.

"So here's what I'm going to do, you worthless pig. I'm going to give you one more chance to earn my respect, to carry out my wishes, to redeem your honor—or I'm going to give you to the Butcher and let him have his way with you. And that, as you know, won't be pleasant. Understand, Mr. Newton?"

Randall looked from the old man to Quay, his eyes flashing back and forth, the crippling pain from the old man's claw-like grip clouding his mind. So he simply nodded and slumped in his chair, the *Jiaofu* releasing his ears, a trickle of blood dripping onto his collar.

"I'll take that as a yes," he said, grinning. Then he patted Newton's cheek and turned to the *yi-zhe*. "Give him the pipe and as much opium as he wants. Let him experience what he craves, what he loves so much, but don't, under any circumstances, take him down the hall. No *pootange* for him tonight. Maybe next time he graces our humble abode—after he completes his end of our bargain." He clapped his hands three quick times and turned to Bingwen. "Escort him out of the building when he's finished, dump him in his car, and send him home like the insidious mongrel that he is."

Then he bowed and left the room.

Surrounded by his *Tong* bodyguards.

*****

"Shit. He's been in there for three hours. What the hell is he doing?" Ethan said, his craving for Scotch hammering every cell in his body. He unzipped his down coat, the heat clawing, his throat closing. "I can't take it anymore. I gotta get outta here. I gotta go home."

Mindy peered at him, worried, then shot a quick glance at Lloyd. She'd been watching him all evening, seeing signs that something was wrong.

"We can't leave, Ethan," she said soothingly. "We've been tracking Newton all night. Something's going on in that restaurant. He's bound to come out soon."

"But I can't be cooped up any longer. I can't breathe. I need fresh air."

Alarmed, Mindy scooted across the van and sat next to him. "Ethan, what the fuck's going on?"

"It's stress from the story, from watching somebody get his head blown off right in front of my eyes."

"No. It's not Dinkus's murder. It's something else," Mindy said, scrutinizing the pain on his face. "You've been checking your cell phone every few minutes since we got here. Who are you waiting to hear from?"

"Nobody."

"Bullshit, Ethan."

"I'm telling you everything's fine."

"I don't' believe you, Ethan. Is Sampson riding up your ass?"

"No."

"Paul?"

"No. No."

"Then who? What?" Mindy said, not letting up.

"It's nothing," Ethan said, deflating, the tension leaching from his body.

Mindy's face grew softer, her voice gentler. "Is it something at home?"

"Christ, back off," he said, quietly.

"Sarah?"

Ethan shrank into himself, his hopes, his resolve, his deep-seated fear that Sarah had left him forever a breath away from spilling out in the open. "Mindy, please, I'm begging you. Take me home. We're not gonna find out anything else tonight."

"No. That'll blow the whole evening."

"He's coming," Lloyd said suddenly. "Table it until later."

Ethan snapped to attention, locking Sarah back inside, and shuffled over to the window facing the Chinese restaurant. "Where? I don't see him."

"Neither do I," Mindy said, straining over his shoulder.

"That's because he's leaving from across the street, from that new building," Lloyd said quietly, pointing across the van as he lifted his Nikon. They crowded around him, not getting in his way, as Lloyd rolled off a continuous burst of pictures. Click. Click. Click.

"Jeez, how did he get over there?" Mindy said, whispering.

"And what the hell's wrong with him?" Ethan said.

"He looks drunk," Lloyd said.

"Or stoned on drugs," Ethan said. "He can't stand. Those two guys are literally dragging him out of the building. And who the fuck are they?"

Lloyd zoomed in tighter, first snapping a series of shots of the huge Chinese man with the eye patch on Newton's left, and then the smaller man covered in tattoos and face piercings on his right.

"Ever seen them before, Lloyd?"

"Never," he said, concentrating on the images. "But they aren't the kind of guys you'd find at a Park Avenue cocktail party."

"Do you have clean shots?"

"Plenty."

"E-mail me the photos and tap your sources, Lloyd. Maybe at the FBI or the Justice Department. See if anybody can ID them. But do it quietly."

"You're not giving the pics to the task force?" Mindy asked.

"Not right away," Ethan said candidly. "Not until I figure out what to do about Newton. I think he's the key to breaking the Child Sex Murders case."

"Bit of a leap," Mindy said, "don't you think?"

"Maybe. But maybe not."

Lloyd tapped Ethan on the shoulder. "They just dumped Newton on the street and left in a hurry—in a new black Escalade."

"Did you get it on camera?"

"The whole sequence."

"The license plate?"

"Clear as a bell."

"Run that too, Lloyd. See if you can find out who owns it."

"We can't leave him there," Mindy said. "He'll freeze to death."

"We don't have to worry about that," Lloyd said, still shooting. "The Mercedes's back and just pulled up to the curb next to him."

They all watched as the same driver hurried around the front of the car and kneeled next to Newton. Cradling his head, he quickly looked around, hoisted him to his feet, and deposited him into the back seat of the car. Then he raced around the front, still checking to make sure they hadn't been seen, climbed into the driver's seat, and roared down the now-deserted street.

"Fuck me," Mindy said, a little too forcefully. "What just happened?"

Ethan ignored her and turned to Lloyd. "Did you get a clean shot of the driver's face?"

"Yep," Lloyd said, peering at the monitor. "Want me to check him out too?"

"Do it."

Lloyd climbed behind the wheel. "They're not too far ahead, should I follow them?"

Ethan hesitated then said, "Let 'em go. We're not gonna learn anything more from Newton tonight. Take me home. It's been a long day." He crawled into the passenger seat and massaged the bridge of his nose. He could feel the bottle of Scotch in his briefcase, calling to him, beckoning him. *Soon,* he thought, *very soon.*

Then his mind drifted to Sarah, and he cried silently to himself.

CHAPTER 23

Bingwen Ho was sitting in the back seat, brooding, lost in thought, as his black Escalade weaved through traffic on the congested streets of Lower Manhattan. Yesterday had been an unmitigated disaster. First, the sicko, the Butcher, had blown the hit on Benson and killed a member of the task force. That was going to ratchet up the investigation into the murdered girls and bring more heat on the *Tong*. Then the *Jiaofu* had been too easy on Randall Newton and sent him off to screw up something else. Why didn't he just cut his losses and let Bingwen slash the asshole's throat and bury him in some landfill where nobody would find him?

He shook his head and lit a Cuban Cohiba.

Inhaling the rich tobacco.

Exhaling it through his nose.

And what was he going to do about the Butcher? He was out of control, a liability, a bigger threat to the *Tong* than even Newton. What did the *Jiaofu* see in the guy? Sure, he'd get rid of a used-up girl on a moment's notice. He loved the art of killing, to look into his victim's eyes and see the terror, before methodically torturing and butchering them. But now he was going too far. Displaying them like artwork for the world to see. This was not good. It was going to be the end of their very profitable business.

Maybe it was time to take matters into his own hands.

Take care of the Butcher.

And get rid of the girls himself.

That lifted his spirits.

But soon he remembered the Butcher's eyes, the evil in his soul, and shelved the thought of killing him—because he didn't have the nerve to do it himself. He glanced out the window. The Escalade was turning left onto Avenue D. Ten more short blocks, and they'd be there. He salivated and puffed on his Cohiba. Tapping the shoulder of the *Tong* bodyguard who accompanied him wherever he went, he said, "Are the girls cleaned up?"

The *Tong* stared back at him, his slanty eyes dead, and nodded silently. Bingwen leaned back in the leather seat, admiring the rich appointments of his Escalade, the status it brought him, and flicked an ash from his cigar out the rolled-down window, oblivious to the freezing temperature, as the SUV pulled to a stop in front of 148 Avenue D. He nodded to the *Tong*, and they both alighted, leaving the driver and another Tong bodyguard, double-parked and waiting for them.

He stared at the front of the building—a five-story tenement, old, weary, a relic from the city's past. There was a wino slumped on the ground snoring, his mouth open, a bottle of cheap booze lying empty next to him. Bingwen kicked him in the gut as he passed, a violent blow, laughed to himself as the burnout groaned in pain. He hiked up a short flight of crumbling steps and turned to face the street as his *Tong* bodyguard opened the unlocked front door. Garbage was frozen into the ice from a leaky pipe, and discarded condoms and needles and empty packets of heroin littered the small portico where he stood, reminding him of the refuse of society who lived in the derelict building. He smiled to himself. It was the perfect place to stash the girls, to hide them from prying eyes until they were ready to be moved and put to work.

He pushed past the *Tong* and walked into the darkened hall of the vestibule.

*****

Ethan stirred in his bed. All the blinds were wide open, and the sun was streaming into the room, the beams of light electric, sending shock waves through his head. He moaned and reached over to touch Sarah, then remembered she was gone. God. What was he going to do? He knocked over his alarm clock as he reached for his cigarettes, flipped a Marlboro from the near-empty pack, and struck it with a match. Closing his eyes, he took a deep pull, then sat up, little men pounding with sledgehammers in his head, and grabbed his iPhone hidden in the tussle of rumpled sheets. He quickly scanned his LED screen. Fourteen phone calls since he'd last checked, before he'd drunk himself into oblivion. Paul. Paul. Peter. Paul. Peter. Peter. Peter. Paul. Mindy. David. Mindy. Mindy. Lloyd. James. He leaned back on his pillow.

Nothing from Sarah.

Nothing.

He checked his voice mail. Seven messages. All from Mindy, David, Paul, and Peter, and the last one from James. Something was wrong at the office.

He tried getting out of bed, but was too dizzy. What the hell time was it? From the position of the sun blaring through the window, it looked like it was late. He fumbled for the clock on the floor, and his heart sank. Christ. It was almost two in the afternoon. He'd been out cold for hours. What had happened after he'd gotten home? Had he eaten anything? Had he taken Holly for a walk? The dog. Holly. He hadn't fed or walked her since yesterday morning. He spotted the half-empty bottle of Black Label lying on the floor, unscrewed the top, and took a short pull to clear his head. Then he wiped his mouth and placed it on the bedside table.

No more.

Not today.

He was going to take a day off from drinking.

He kicked off the covers and stood, wobbly, the Scotch beginning to level him off. He stared down at his feet. He was still wearing his shoes, his clothes caked in mud from the sanitation depot. Then he spotted the blood, Detective Dinkus's blood, on his pants and shirtsleeves. He stripped out of his clothes, disgusted with himself, and slipped into his bathrobe, pocketing his iPhone, lighting another cigarette. Heading out of his bedroom in search of Holly, he peeked into the mirror in the hallway and stopped dead in his tracks. His face was drawn, his eyes bloodshot, and his two-day stubble was as dark as his mood. Running his fingers through his hair—dirty and matted to his forehead—he picked at the flecks of blood splatter dotting his face. Had Mindy or Lloyd told him he was covered in blood, that he looked a wreck in the surveillance van? Maybe. But he couldn't remember.

Where was Holly?

He whistled.

But she didn't come.

He checked each room as he headed down the center hallway and found her lying on the floor, curled in a ball at the foot of Luke's bed, sad, lonely. His heart sank. Lukie. His little boy. Gone. With Sarah. He bent down next to the retriever and stroked her muzzle then clapped and headed to the kitchen, Holly slinking along behind him. Reaching for the kibble, he poured her a big bowl, stroking her head and her flank as she gobbled her breakfast.

"Sorry, girl, I know I haven't been around. I'll take better care of you until they come home. And they will. I promise."

But would they?

Pull yourself together, Ethan. Everything's gonna be okay. She'll forgive you. She always does, he thought, doubting his own words. He scooped a pot's worth of ground coffee into the automatic coffeemaker and turned it on, the machine stirring to life. He waited for the coffee to brew then poured a big cup. Maybe this would kick-start his day. As he headed back to his bedroom, his iPhone buzzed in his pocket. Sarah, finally, Sarah. She missed him as much as he missed her.

"Babe, I'm sorry. I love you."

But it wasn't Sarah.

It was James.

"I thought it was my wife," he blurted out.

James sounded flustered. "Ethan, where have you been? Everybody's been trying to find you. They're all furious, including my uncle. You better get your ass in here. They've been waiting for you for hours."

"Did you say anything to Paul?" he said icily.

"About what?"

Ethan sighed. James hadn't said a word about his drinking. It was paranoia. "Forget it."

"How long before you get here?"

"Gotta shave and shower. Give me forty five minutes."

*****

The hallways were crumbling, exposed electrical wires dangling from the ceiling, wallpaper peeling, armies of roaches scampering across the floor as Bingwen headed up a back staircase to the top floor, pushed through a broken fire door, and approached apartment 5A. He rapped three times on the door, then once, then three more times. The signal. Then he waited, listening to the patter of hurried footsteps approaching, the dead bolt being thrown, and the door swinging partially open, the chain still stretched in place. Honghui, the box truck driver, his left arm in a plaster cast from his fingers to his elbow, peered through the slit in the door.

"Open up, asshole," Bingwen said, bellowing.

Honghui flinched then threw the chain and stepped back as the big man and his *Tong* bodyguard stepped through the door.

"Honghui, this is Yo Min. Yo Min, meet Honghui, the brave soul who delivered the last shipment of merchandise here to our little safe house."

"Fluck you, Bingwen."

"Fuck yourself," he said, annoyed.

"You broke almost every bone in my hand, motherflucker, when you stomped on it. Doctors said it's gonna take months to heal and months more until I can use it. So fluck you, asshole."

Bingwen smiled, sensing fear in the man. The *Tong* bodyguard remained silent as always. "Where are they?"

"Where do you think?" Honghui said, a bit too curtly. Bingwen loomed over him and raised his fist, the box truck driver cowering. "In the back getting cleaned up."

"Are they dressed?"

"Some of them."

"Fed?"

"What do you think, Bingwen? That we're animals?"

"Not animals, just fools," he said dismissively. "Has the doctor checked them out?"

"We sobered him up just long enough so he could examine each girl and pronounce them ready to work. Then we gave him another bottle, cheap wine, and now, well, he's passed out on the couch in the living room."

"And that's where he'll stay until we need him again." Bingwen glanced around the apartment. It was a bigger shithole than he remembered. "Are they sorted into groups?"

"The fifteen year olds are in the last room on the left." He pointed down a long hallway.

"How many?"

"Six."

"And the others," Bingwen said, calculating how much they could charge their rich, sicko clientele.

"Nine fourteen year olds in the first room on the right and three thirteen year olds across the hall."

"The young ones will pay top dollar. The *Jiaofu* will be pleased. English?"

"Most of them pretty good, like the fat *Padre* promised."

Bingwen nodded. He hated the fat Spanish *Padre*. They should get rid of him too—snuff him out—and buy their girls from a Chinese distributor. That's what he'd do if he was the *Jaiofu*. Chinese girls were far more delicate, more pleasing to the eye. They'd give much more pleasure to the perverts who paid for them. Then he started down the hall, stopping abruptly and swinging back around.

"That's only eighteen by my count. We're missing one, Honghui. What the fuck happened?"

"Not my fault. I didn't do anything," he said, worried the big man was about to take out his wrath on him again.

"What's not your fault?" he said, his voice raging.

"The girl, Maria, the real pretty one. There's something wrong with her."

"What do you mean?" Bingwen said, screaming, the walls in the apartment shaking around him.

"See for yourself. I stashed her away from the others. Last room on the right."

"Bet your ass I will," he shrieked. "Go get the truck and pull around to the front of the building. Time to move the girls to Hester Street."

The wiry man scampered by the *Tong* bodyguard and the drunk doctor still snoring on the couch and through the front door, Bingwen sighing heavily as he moved as swift as a cat, motioning to the bodyguard to remain where he was. The girl was perched on the edge of a bed, dressed in a clean pink frock, her hair neatly washed and combed and tied in a ponytail, her countenance drawn, expressionless, dead. Her once-beautiful blue eyes now vacant, listless. Bingwen walked up to her and called her name. Maria. Nothing. He snapped his thick fingers in front of her face. Still nothing. He grabbed her shoulder and shook. Not even a flinch.

Shit. Gone in the ozone. Useless. A liability.

He punched the *Jiaofu's* number into a new burner he'd grabbed from a stack under lock and key in the town house and waited.

"Speak, Bingwen," the old man said, his voice floating like the wind.

"We gotta problem, Mr. Chang," he said respectfully as he waited for a response, listening to the old man breathing rhythmically. The *Jaiofu* was high on opium again. He was always high on opium.

"Go on, I don't have all day," he quipped.

The big man hesitated then said, "One of the girls is too damaged to be of any use to us."

"Traumatized?"

"Yes, sir."

"No way to bring her back?"

"I don't think so, Mr. Chang."

"Then give her to the Butcher," he said commandingly, pulling in another lungful of opium. "And tell him to get rid of her."

"But the city's crawling with cops since we hit the detective?"

"Don't question my authority. I can't sell the girl. Nobody will pay to fuck a lump of dead meat. Make her go away. And do it now."

CHAPTER 24

Ethan departed the elevator on the management floor and stubbed out the cigarette he wasn't supposed to be smoking. He'd stopped at the Starbucks across the street and downed a black coffee then ordered a second he was now carrying in his hand. The caffeine hadn't touched his headache, hadn't smoothed out his hangover, or mollified his fear about what Paul was about to tell him. He sat on the couch in the empty glass waiting room and punched Sarah's number into his cell phone. He needed to speak to her. To hear her voice again. It rang five times and went to voice mail. *This is Sarah. Can't come to the phone. Leave a message.* Beep.

He hung up.

Her voice haunting.

Sighing, he picked up his briefcase, unlocked the glass door, and pushed through. Shoulders slumped, eyes downcast, he maneuvered through the hallways, feeling lost, and stopped when he reached James sitting at his desk across from Consuela. Neither said a word.

"Can't be that bad, can it?" he said, his eyes shooting from one to the other.

"They're in your office, Ethan," James said timidly. "You better go in."

Ethan removed his hat and gloves and folded his overcoat over his arm. He was wearing a white shirt, red tie, and his blue blazer, hoping it would assuage his ghastly appearance and make him more presentable. Pushing by both of them, he walked in. Paul was sitting on the couch next to Peter, Mindy in one of the leather chairs. The mood was somber.

"Sorry nobody could find me," he said sheepishly. "We had a long night. I couldn't wake up this morning."

"Mindy filled us in, Ethan," Paul said soberly. "Please, sit. We need to talk."

Ethan hung his coat on a hanger on the back of the door and sat behind his desk. "Look, I can explain," he said with little conviction.

Paul nodded. Then Peter said unexpectedly, "We all saw the video of the detective's murder. We called in Joel Zimmerman, and he played it for us in one of the Avid Rooms." He paused, Ethan trying to read the expression on his face to no avail. Peter continued, "How are you handling it. The images were pretty shocking. You okay?"

Ethan peered around the room then back to Peter. "Rattled, of course, but I'll get over it."

There was an another awkward silence. Then Paul said in a comforting voice, "This isn't the only reason we're here, even though it is an important one." He paused, obviously choosing his words carefully. "Ethan, why didn't you call us after the shooting yesterday? Why did we have to find out you were there at the crime scene in the middle of everything from Winston Peabody who interviewed you on camera during a special report on our local programming? Everyone saw it all the way up to George Pierce, the chairman of this company, who called personally wanting to know what had happened."

"No excuse, Paul," Ethan said, hoping a mea culpa would be enough to satisfy the executive producer.

Paul leaned back on the couch and let a few seconds pass. "Look, Ethan, we know what's going on."

Ethan was taken aback.

"After Peter and I couldn't reach you, we called Mindy hoping she knew where you were. What time was that, Peter?"

"Eight o'clock this morning."

"Right. And she told us in detail about the murder and the stakeout and the fact that you were completely at wit's end last night."

Ethan vaguely remembered Mindy asking him if something was wrong—beyond the trauma of seeing somebody being blown apart in front of his eyes. What had she really suspected, and what else had she told Paul?

The executive producer held up his hand. "Don't say a word, Ethan. Let me finish. We asked Mindy to try Sarah on her cell phone. But she didn't answer either. Then she gave me the number, and I called six or seven times before she finally picked up." Paul took a sympathetic breath. "She told me everything that's going on at home. That you've been drinking again. That your behavior has been increasingly more erratic. And that she couldn't handle it any longer, needed to take a break from your marriage, and is staying with her sister in Cleveland."

Ethan began to protest, to explain his side of the story, when Peter interrupted.

"Let Paul finish. We've been talking about this all morning and have made a decision about how to proceed."

"That's the main reason we're here this afternoon."

Ethan shot Mindy a quick glance pleadingly, hoping she'd step in and offer an explanation, any explanation. But she lowered her eyes and remained silent.

"Paul, give me a chance, and I'll explain."

He held up his hand again to silence him. "I've decided to suspend you, to give you and Sarah time to sort things out."

"I don't need time off. I need to work. That's all that's holding me together."

Paul stared probingly into his eyes then said, "I don't think that's going to help. I've discussed this at length with Peter and Mindy and the head of HR. You need time to work on your marriage and your drinking without the stresses of the office."

"Yes," Peter said, almost kindly. "I feel strongly that I can't depend on you any longer to function effectively as my senior producer. There are just too many variables, too much responsibility for someone with your problems. We've already set the wheels in motion and asked Dirk Fulton to step in and work with me, until you're better."

Ethan felt his whole world crash around him.

"I gotta work," he said, pleading. "Don't you see. It's the only thing I have left. It gives me purpose. A reason to go on while I deal with my personal problems. You can't throw me out on my ass. It'll be the absolute end of me."

Paul shot Peter a quick glance—then Mindy, then Ethan. "Do you have a proposal?"

Ethan nodded.

"Tell me."

"I'll give up my responsibilities as Peter's senior producer. That'll relieve me of at least some stress and give Peter the support he desperately needs, and that I'm obviously neglecting." He paused, knowing he was fighting for his life. "But please, I beg you. Keep me on the Child Sex Murders story. Don't give it to another producer. I have to finish it. Please."

"What about your family?" Paul said, still not convinced. "You need the time."

"I'll make the time."

"Peter?"

"I won't work with him," Peter said firmly.

"I understand that, really, I do," Ethan said hopefully. "I know I've been a terrible senior producer, and that you don't want to do the story with me. That's a given. So let's assign it to another on-air person. Maybe Julie Piedmont. She's wanted to work with me for a long time."

Paul grabbed a yellow pad from the coffee table and started doodling, writing the co-anchor's name in a series of swirls and flourishes. Then he looked up at Ethan.

"Sarah pleaded with me not to send you away when I told her I was going to suspend you. She said it would make things much worse, and the last thing I want is to push you, both of you, beyond the point of no return. I couldn't live with myself if I did that. So I'll make a deal with you, Ethan."

"Anything," he said deprecatingly.

"You agree to get help, more help, from your psychiatrist, Dr. Schwartz."

"Agreed."

"And stay sober."

"Agreed."

"And start working on your marriage."

"I'll make that my priority."

"That's what Sarah wants too. I'll call HR and give them my decision, that I've changed my mind about suspending you, at least for the moment." He turned to Peter. "Last chance. You don't want to keep the story?"

"Give it to Julie," he said, preoccupied with answering messages on his iPhone, the matter settled in his mind.

"So here's the deal," Paul said, sounding like the boss. "I'll explain the situation to Julie, all of it, your drinking, the problems in your personal life, and the reason you're no longer working with Peter. And if she agrees to pick up your story, under the circumstances, I'll let you finish the project. Understood?"

Ethan nodded, remaining silent.

"And one more thing," Paul said, unwavering. "I'm gonna watch your behavior like a hawk, ask lots questions to everybody working with you, and if I decide this is a mistake, for any reason, the deal's off, and you're gonna take some time away from the office and get your life back together before you can work again on my show."

Ethan nodded and said, "Thank you, Paul."

Mindy waited until they'd both left and were out of earshot then said, "I'm not sure I agree with this decision. I've been watching you the past few weeks. All of us have. David. Lloyd. Even James. And we all think you're sinking down a destructive path. Sarah cried hysterically when she was on the phone with Paul. He got so upset he handed it to me to calm her down."

"But—"

"Just listen, Ethan, for God's sake. She fucking loves you more than you can imagine. But she's scared shitless. She's angry. At her wit's end. She said you've been a closet alcoholic for a very long time, since you lost your first baby."

"She told you about the baby?" he said, ashamed.

"It all came spilling out. Everything. She unloaded to me for an hour, while we waited for you to show up. I had no idea how fucked up things had gotten."

"Did you tell Paul?"

"Yes.

"And Peter."

"Yes. All of us know."

He sat pensively, relieved his secret was out in the open, that he didn't have to hide it anymore. "Think she'll come home? She won't pick up the phone when I call."

Mindy stood and walked to the door, then stopped and said sympathetically, "Call her, Ethan. I think she'll talk to you now. I'll come back when you're done. We've got lots to discuss about the murders."

*****

Ethan closed the door after she left and lit a cigarette, needing the nicotine to build his confidence, not caring about company policy. He sat back down at his desk and stared at his cell phone. Steeling himself, he punched in Sarah's number. It went directly to voice mail. Shit. Then he tried his sister-in-law's home phone. It rang one, two, three times before she picked up.

"Anita, it's me, Ethan."

There was a long pause.

"I told her not to talk to you," she said coldly. "I've never seen her so distraught."

"Please. Put her on the phone."

No response as the phone was slammed onto a counter.

Ethan could feel his nerves fraying, his resolve waning. Then Sarah picked up the telephone.

"Ethan, did he fire you?" she said, no emotion in her voice.

He hesitated, gulping. "No, babe, he didn't suspend me."

"What about Peter?"

"I'm no longer his senior producer, at least for the moment."

"Well, that's what you wanted, right?" she said accusatorily.

"Please, babe, let's not quarrel. We need to talk about us. I miss you. I miss Luke. When are you coming home?"

He waited. The silence deafening.

"I don't know, Ethan," she said, quivering. "I can't face you and all your problems, our problems, not yet."

"What can I say? What can I do to make you forgive me? I'll do anything, babe. Anything."

Her voice was firm. "There's nothing, Ethan, nothing until I sort out my feelings. We've been trying for a long time to make things right. To get you to stop drinking."

"I'll do better, I promise," he said, feeling her slipping away.

"You've been saying that for years. I don't believe you."

"But what about Luke? He needs us together as a family."

Sarah began to sob. "Please, I can't talk anymore, Ethan. I'm glad Paul didn't throw you under the bus, because I know you need to work. I know that's all you care about."

"Not fair, Sarah," Ethan said, pausing to get a grip on his emotions. "I love you. And I love Luke. I need you to come home."

"I can't."

"When?"

"I don't know. Take care of yourself, Ethan, I gotta go."

She hung up the phone, and he began to cry.

CHAPTER 25

Ethan remained motionless, staring vacantly out the big picture window overlooking Central Park—the sky gray, shrouded in snowflakes blowing aimlessly in gusts of wind as they covered the landscape in a fresh layer of white powder. It had been fifteen minutes since Sarah had hung up, smashing his hopes, ending his prayers of reconciliation. All he could think about was his empty apartment—no Sarah, no Luke, no family, no nothing.

He was alone.

Maybe forever.

He stood, trying to find his inner equilibrium, and opened the door. Consuela had left for the day with Sampson, but James was still there, patiently waiting. He waved him into his office.

"Can I get you anything?" James said. "Maybe some food? Coffee?"

"Nothin', thanks," Ethan said, pointing to a chair in front of his desk. "Sit. We need to talk." He waited for James to get comfortable and said, "Do you still work for me, or is Paul moving you to another job?"

"He hasn't said anything about that."

"Do I need to pack up my office? I'm no longer Peter's senior producer."

"Peter said to me as he was leaving that there's no rush. Not until things were sorted out. He said we should leave everything just the way it is until he decides whether you'll be working for him again or not."

Well, that's a plus, Ethan thought, though he knew his days as Peter's senior producer were over. Wasn't that what he really wanted? He cleared his throat.

"And what about you, James? Do you still want to work for me, under the circumstances?"

No hesitation. "Yes. You're a good boss."

"Okay. Let's see what happens. Maybe I can pull myself together and do my job," he said, having doubts. "Where's Mindy?"

"In her office waiting for me to let her know you're okay."

"And David?"

"He's with her."

"Lloyd?"

"Not here."

"Well, tell them to come up."

*****

Ten minutes later, they paraded into his office, Mindy holding a cardboard tray with four cups of coffee from Starbucks. She handed one to Ethan, distributed the rest then sat down on the couch.

"So everybody knows what's goin' on?"

"We've been discussing it all morning, Ethan," she said soothingly.

"Any need for me to explain anything at all about my behavior? About the personal crisis in my life?"

They shook their heads no.

"Look, Ethan," David said, taking the lead, "we know you're struggling, that you're going through a rough patch. We're all here to help, to give you whatever support you need, and to work together on our story. That's not gonna change. The last thing we want is for you to start worrying about what we think."

"We got your back," Mindy said. "Jeez, you should know that by now. So do you want an update on our story? Or do you need more time to lick your wounds and crawl into your shell."

Ethan shook his head and laughed. Leave it to Mindy to find the right words to lighten the mood.

"Okay, hit me with it."

Mindy rattled off the latest developments in detail—that there'd been no movement on the Karl Storz No. 6 surgical blades, that the evidence collected at the sanitation depot, while promising, hadn't led to any fresh leads on either Detective Dinkus's murder or the murder of the four girls, that they were still digging, but hadn't found anything unusual in Randall Newton's background or his relationship with the police commissioner, and that he'd called in sick and missed the daily task force meeting at the DA's Office again.

"Does Patricia Highland suspect anything?" Ethan said.

"Not when I talked to her," Mindy said. "She's pissed that he's not there, but that's about it."

"Do we know where he is at the moment?" Ethan said earnestly.

"Took the liberty of calling Lloyd when we couldn't find you this morning. He's parked outside Newton's building in his surveillance van."

"And?"

"Newton's holed up in his apartment," David said, jumping in. "He left shortly after Lloyd arrived, looking pretty beat up. He went to the Duane Reade on his corner, then walked back into his building holding a package from the pharmacy. Hasn't left since he got back."

"Pictures?"

"Lloyd's been shooting everything," Mindy said.

"And the plan moving forward?" Ethan said.

"Lloyd's going to keep watch on his building. Follow him if and when he's on the move again," she said.

"Any idea who he called from the sanitation depot?"

"We checked," David said, scanning his notes on an iPad. "Lloyd pulled his telephone records from yesterday. Nothing. He must've used his burner."

"What about those two guys who dumped him on the street last night?"

"Could've been one of them he called," Mindy said. "But we can't prove it."

"Have we ID'd either one of them?"

"We're working our contacts," David said emphatically. "Both Mindy and me. Nothing yet. We'll let you know as soon as we have anything."

"What about the limousine driver."

"Bernie Sokoloff. Lloyd tracked him down from his license plate number."

"Any record?"

"He's clean," Mindy said.

"And you're digging quietly?" Ethan said, staring at both of them. "We can't let the task force know what we've got until we're sure it means something."

"Come on, Ethan," Mindy said pointedly. "We know Newton was up to something last night, that those two guys, how should I put it, are no Goody Two-shoes. We'll be careful." She paused briefly. "And what about Highland. You going to give her a heads-up about Newton, at least privately?"

"I have to," Ethan said. "It might have a bearing on the investigation and the murders and the reason they've got nothing. We can't prove it, but we can't ignore our suspicions any longer. I'll stop down there and tell her in person as soon as we're finished here."

"Do you need the JPEGs?"

"Good idea."

"I'll have Joel isolate the best and make sure he forwards them to you."

"And what do you want us to do while you're gone?" David asked.

"James, I want you to come with me to the DA's Office. Maybe you can shoot some video on your iPhone. And Mindy, David, here's what you need to work on." Then he spent the next ten minutes carefully outlining, step by step, how to move their story forward.

*****

Sitting in a yellow cab as it weaved through traffic on the FDR Drive en route to One Hogan Place, Ethan carefully reread his story notes on his iPad as he blocked out the best strategy to brief the ADA. He wanted to make sure he was upfront about Randall Newton, to tell her enough, but not too much, so he didn't lose momentum as he followed Newton on his secret excursions around the city. As he passed the exit to Forty-Second Street, the snow began falling harder, making the roads slick. He turned to James who was sitting quietly staring out the window.

"Do you know about the town house?"

"Mindy filled me in, showed me the JPEGs."

"Think you're up to doing a little research on your own?"

"Anything."

"Okay, Mindy doesn't have time to find out who owns that building where Newton spent last night. Think you can figure it out?"

"I can try."

"How?"

"I'll start at the zoning board. See who filed the paperwork to get approval for construction. Then I'll track the builder, architect, and who actually paid for everything. That should lead me to the owner, I think?"

"That's a jumping off point," Ethan said, satisfied. "Run with it, James. Let's see what you can do."

"Thanks, Ethan."

"Don't sweat it," he said, burying himself back in his notes, before pulling up the latest newspaper stories on Detective Dinkus's murder and a long piece in the *New York Post* summarizing Patricia Highland's early-morning press conference. There was nothing new in the story, nothing he hadn't seen firsthand at the crime scene the day before—except that his name was now front and center as an embed in the investigation. Shit. He was going to be hounded by the press. Deep in thought, ticking through loose ends, his iPhone buzzed.

"Ethan, it's me," Paul said, all business. "Just got off the phone with Julie Piedmont. She wasn't thrilled after I explained what's going on, but she's willing to talk to you. She says she doesn't care that Sampson won't work with you anymore or about replacing him on your story, but she is worried about your drinking. So talk to her. See if you can convince her to pick up the Child Sex Murders. Call me back and let me know what happens. We'll go from there."

He hung up.

Not waiting for a response.

Ethan sighed, prepared himself psychologically, then looked up Julie Piedmont's cell phone number in the company directory on his iPhone. As the junior anchor on *The Weekly Reporter*, Piedmont was constantly hovering in Peter Sampson's shadow—fighting for airtime, scrambling for recognition. At thirty-five, she'd established herself as a serious journalist who did her homework, worked well as part of a production team, and delivered hard-hitting and insightful interviews. She was petite and photogenic, with pale skin, luminous green eyes that sparkled on camera, and long, straight auburn hair. She prided herself on her wardrobe, always impeccably dressed in the height of fashion, never wearing the same costume on camera more than once. But what impressed Ethan the most was her dogged determination to cover a story and get to the truth.

He dialed her number.

She picked up immediately.

"That was quick. Just got off the phone with Paul."

"Is this a good time to talk?"

"I'll make time. So tell me, what's going on with you?"

Ethan spent the next five minutes telling her everything, not leaving out a single detail, not smoothing over a single fact. He was open, honest, and contrite. When he finished, he waited calmly for her reaction.

"Well, that's pretty much everything Paul told me, no worse, but certainly no better. But I still don't understand. Why do you want to hang on to this story? Shouldn't you step back and spend time working on your marriage? I don't know you real well, but if I was in your shoes, I'd certainly drop everything and focus on my family and on my drinking problem."

Ethan hesitated, his mind scrambling, all his emotions, all the turmoil in his life flooding to the surface. He took a deep breath.

"Sarah and Luke are more important to me than anything, and I plan to fight like hell to bring us back together as a family. But I need to work. I need that foothold in my life. That stability. Otherwise, I don't stand a chance to repair the damage I've inflicted on the two of them."

"I understand that. I'm the same in a lot of ways. But what about the Scotch?"

"I'm working on—"

She interrupted. "Am I going to find you drunk on the job?"

"Well, I—"

"Can't guarantee you'll remain sober."

Ethan paused then said emotionally, "I'm determined to change, to get better, but I'm an alcoholic." There, he'd said it. "And I can't predict what's going to happen. I just know I want to get my life back on track."

"That's an honest answer. I respect that."

"So will you work on my story?"

He waited anxiously. Then she said delicately, “My first reaction after I talked to Paul was to take a pass. Not worth the risk. There are other producers and other good stories out there. But I know your reputation, Ethan. You are one of the best in the business. So I’m going to roll the dice and take a chance. Put together a research book and send it to me. I’ll read it tonight, and let’s meet tomorrow, say ten o’clock in my office. I’ll see you then.”

Ethan clicked off the phone and put it back in his pocket.

“Sounds like Ms. Piedmont wants to do your story,” James said.

“Yeah. She’s agreed. Can you work late tonight?”

“Anything you need, Ethan,” he said buoyantly.

“Put together a research book for her. She likes to read everything. So don’t worry about how big it is. Give her the police reports on each murder for starters then everything you can find in the newspapers since Patricia Highland gave her first press conference and Henry Dinkus was gunned down. That should give her a good foundation. We’ll fill her in on the rest when we meet tomorrow. Oh, yeah, right. Send everybody an e-mail, including Lloyd, and tell them ten o’clock sharp in her office.”

“Consider it done.”

“And get her the book by eight o’clock tonight.”

“I’ll head back to the broadcast center as soon as we leave the task force meeting.”

“No. You’ll drop me off and take the cab straight back. That’ll give you enough time to organize everything.”

“What about shooting the meeting?”

“Not as important as getting Julie the research. I’ll do it myself.” He paused and searched James’s face. “Sure you’re up to this. Maybe I should call David?”

“I got it, Ethan.”

“Yeah. I believe you do.”

They sat in silence for the rest of the trip, Ethan composing a long e-mail to Sarah, pouring out his soul, determined to make things right. He hit Send and waited, hoping she'd read it and respond, hoping it was a first step in repairing their fractured relationship.

But there was no response.

Nothing.

Not a single word.

*****

The mood was somber as Ethan pushed through the door and entered the war room. Patricia Highland was sitting at the head of the conference room table surrounded by documents, her head buried in a memo. There were other team members—Gloria Alvarez, Kathy Bowman, a detective Ethan didn't recognize, and a tiny man with gold-rimmed spectacles, a perfectly bald head, and his sleeves rolled up to his elbows—all huddled across from the ADA. Highland stood when she spotted Ethan, poured herself a cup of coffee from a pot sitting on a credenza, and walked over, her usual impeccable appearance far off its game—her clothes rumpled, her hair unkempt, her face pasty.

"Ethan, didn't expect to see you here today," she said, shaking his hand. "That was quite an experience you had at the playground. I screened your video. Are you all right? My entire team is devastated by the ruthlessness of Detective Dinkus's murder."

"Same guy who committed the Child Sex Murders?"

"We think so from the little evidence we've gathered. The shoe prints from the sanitation depot are a perfect match to what we found at both the Dry Dock Playground and at Pier 51. The lab guys gave us the confirmation this morning. It's the same killer," she said, sipping her coffee. "This stuff is nasty. Somebody make me a fresh pot. Oh, Ethan, how rude of me. Let me introduce you."

She pointed a thin finger—the crimson nail polish chipped—to the detective sitting next to Alvarez. "That's Victor Nottingdale out of the Sixth Precinct. He's been on and off the case since the beginning. Now he's taking over Dinkus's responsibilities." The detective nodded and went back to work. "The other guy with the glasses, you haven't met him either. That's our FBI profiler, Leon Fennimore. He flew up from Washington early this morning to go over the details of yesterday's shooting and to alter the killer's profile now that we think the child sex killer is also our sniper. The personality types don't go hand in hand, at least on the surface, but Fennimore says there's precedence in his casework, that they could indeed be one and the same person."

Ethan shook hands with both the detective and the profiler.

"Any idea who we're looking for?" Ethan said, directing his question to Fennimore.

The profiler leaned back in his chair and cleaned his eyeglasses. "My best guess, the guy is small in stature, that's based on his shoe size and nothing else. He probably hates women, especially little girls from the pattern of killings. Since he's now butchered four kids—all under fifteen plus Detective Dinkus—he's showing the classic signs of a serial killer, probably a sociopath who carefully plans and executes each murder, because he enjoys the act of killing."

"Why a sociopath?" Ethan said, sitting down at the table across from the profiler. "Hold on. I wanna record this." He pulled his Canon digital camera from his briefcase, checked the electronics, and began rolling, zooming into a tight shot of the profiler's face. "Let me reask that question. Why a sociopath?"

"Because he's organized, careful, and systematic in the way he tortures his victims before he kills them. He's extremely violent and has no conscience, but his methodology isn't scattered or unpredictable. He tortures each one exactly the same way. He cuts them, burns them with cigarettes, strangles them with the same kind of synthetic rope, and them removes their teeth and fingertips to conceal their identities. He knows exactly what he's doing, enjoys it, and probably achieves sexual arousal and orgasm from his conquests. The guy's a classic sociopath."

"Any significance to the piece of skin he removes from his victim's ankles?" Ethan said, holding a tight shot on the profiler.

Fennimore thought a moment before answering. "Could be a trophy, but it's not the kind of body part most serial killers collect. Skin is fragile and breaks down, even when carefully preserved in formaldehyde. Maybe it's part of his MO. Maybe he's removing something he doesn't want us to know about. Maybe it's something else. I'm not really sure. It's just not clear yet."

"And why little girls?" Ethan asked.

The profiler sighed. "Most serial killers, especially those that torture and sexually abuse their victims, have suffered some kind of traumatic experience as a child. Maybe he was socially awkward growing up. Maybe he was rejected by girls he fantasized about. Maybe his mother diddled him when he was very young. Who knows? But something happened to him, something that scarred his psyche and rattled his inner core, his very sense of being, and he snapped. So the only way he feels good about himself is to dominate women—and in this case, little kids—and to take out his sexual aggression on them before he tortures and murders them."

Ethan pulled back to a medium shot, revealing ADA Highland and the detectives taking notes as Fennimore spoke.

"And how does the ritualistic posing of the bodies play into our killer's motivation?"

"Ah, now we're getting into the nub of our dilemma with this guy." He leaned over the table and stared into the camera. "This killer not only wants to punish the kids he's murdering, he wants to scare the living shit out of every little kid who enters his sick world. It's an obsession with this guy. It's what drives him. It's why he leaves the bodies in playgrounds. And I can guarantee you he's not gonna stop at four."

"So you think he's gonna kill again," Ethan said, zooming back into a tight shot of Fennimore.

"Positive. And I'm almost certain he's murdered other little kids we don't know about yet. So that's our guy, Mr. Benson, in a nutshell."

Ethan lowered the camera and thought about the small man with the tattoos and piercings who had helped drag Newton from the town house on Hester Street. Could he be the killer? Probably not.

"But why would this guy kill Detective Dinkus?" Ethan said. "It doesn't seem to fit his pattern."

"That bullet was for you, Benson, not Henry," Alvarez said nastily.

"Now we don't know that for sure," the ADA said. "That's one of the theories we're discussing. That he wants you out of the picture, because you work for the press. But it's only a supposition at the moment."

"But he missed," Ethan said, glancing from Highland to Alvarez. "So he can't be much of a sniper, can he?"

"Probably no military training, *amigo*," the detective said. "Otherwise, Benson, *you'd* be dead and no longer part of *this* investigation."

"Enough," Highland said commandingly. "Ethan's here for a reason, and I want all of you to stop the hostility immediately."

There was a moment of awkward silence. Then Ethan said, "Can I have a few words in private, Patricia?"

"Everybody stay put," she said, still glaring around the table. "And who's brewing my coffee? I need a cup now. And bring one for Ethan, please, somebody." Then she marched out of the war room, looking more like her dignified self, and led him to her office in the corner of the bullpen. "Sit," she commanded as she pointed to a black swivel chair across from her desk. "Sorry you had to endure that, Ethan. As I said, everybody's nerves are frayed since Detective Dinkus was murdered."

"Understood. No offense taken," he said. "Look, I want to talk a little about Randall Newton."

"Not here today. Said he was ill. Also rattled by Dinkus. Should be back tomorrow."

"That's not what I mean," Ethan said carefully. "We've been tracking him."

Highland raised an eyebrow. "Explain."

Ethan reached into his briefcase and pulled out a file, dropping it on her desk.

"What's this?"

"His credit card statements."

Highland fixed her hawk-like gaze on Ethan. "Why do you have his credit card statements?"

"I've highlighted in a yellow marker the expenditures that, let me find the right words, sent up a red flag to my team."

Highland opened the file and poured through the pages. Then she peered up and said, "Okay. I still don't understand."

"They're car service payments."

"So?"

Ethan handed her a second file. She opened it and poured through the document—more entries highlighted with a yellow marker. "Records from the private car service called *Charge-A-Ride*."

"How'd you get your hands on this stuff? Don't tell me. Has to be Lloyd. He's the only person with the contacts to secure this kind of information. Okay, what does this all mean?"

Ethan spent the next five minutes explaining—that each Saturday night at eleven o'clock, Randall Newton used the same driver to go to the same location in Alphabet City on the Lower East Side.

"Why the same driver?"

"Newton must have struck a deal with him."

"Why didn't he just use the car service available here to all the ADAs?" Highland said, still skeptical.

"Because he didn't want you to know where he was going," Ethan said bluntly.

"And how do you know that?"

"Hunch."

"Okay, I'm a prosecutor who likes facts," she said, still not convinced it meant anything. "Why is this important?"

"On the surface, it isn't. But last night after he disappeared from the Dinkus crime scene, we tailed him in Lloyd's surveillance van."

"Go on."

Then he explained everything that had happened from the time Newton was picked up at his apartment to the moment he was dumped in the gutter in front of the town house on Hester Street.

"Let me get this straight. Somebody, for the lack of a better word, beat him up in Chinatown, then dumped him on the sidewalk like a piece of trash. Any idea who the two guys are?"

Ethan waited for a cop to bring two cups of coffee into Highland's office and leave then said quietly, "This might be best if it stayed between the two of us for the moment, but I've got surveillance pictures."

He reached into his briefcase again and pulled out his iPad with the color photos Joel Zimmerman had e-mailed him. He passed it to Highland.

She scrolled through the JPEGs—the first a three-shot of Newton, the huge Chinese man with the eye patch, and the much smaller Chinese man covered in tattoos; the second and third tight shots of each thug; and the last a wide shot of the town house.

"The big guy is Bingwen Ho," she said, "an enforcer for the Chinese underworld who I put away a few years back for drug trafficking. He's a real piece of work. Ruthless. I didn't know he was out of prison." She picked up the picture of the wiry man with the tattoos. "No idea who this is. Never seen him before."

Then she leaned back in her chair, sipped her coffee, and sighed. "So let me get this straight. You think those two guys beat up Randall inside that town house, but you don't know why?"

Ethan nodded.

Highland scrolled silently through the photos again.

"There's something else I need to show you." He grabbed the iPad and leafed to another set of photos. "Take a look. They, too, were taken last night after Detective Dinkus was murdered, just before Newton went to Chinatown."

He passed Highland the iPad, and she looked at the series of photos then stared up at Ethan, gobsmacked.

"What was he doing with the police commissioner?" Ethan asked.

"Hell do I know," she said furiously. "He has no jurisdiction to meet with the commissioner as part of this task force unless I say so. And believe me, I didn't authorize a meeting. Christ, I couldn't even find Randall last night. He was AWOL. Just like today." She stood and walked to the door and screamed "More coffee" then returned to her desk and picked up the phone and buzzed Gloria Alvarez. "Find Randall Newton and—"

"Can I make a suggestion," he said boldly.

"Hold on, Gloria." She covered the mouthpiece. "What?"

"Don't do anything about Newton for the moment."

She glared at Ethan then said, "Hold off on Randall, Gloria. I'll call you right back." She dropped the phone into the cradle. "Why shouldn't I bring in Newton? He might be leaking information about the investigation," she said before standing and walking back to the door. "Where the fuck is my coffee. Somebody bring me another cup." She sat back down. "So what are you proposing?"

"Lloyd's parked in his surveillance van outside Newton's apartment building. He's been holed up all day licking his wounds. Let's wait and see what he does next. We already know he missed his rendezvous in Alphabet City last night. Something changed his pattern. Could be Detective Dinkus's murder. Could be something else. But we taped him on the phone with somebody at the sanitation depot yesterday. Then he abruptly disappeared from the crime scene."

"Could've been anybody, Ethan," she said dismissively. "You can't prove that's somehow connected to this case, can you?"

"Not yet," he said without blinking an eye. "But let me play it out and see where it leads us. It may have a bearing on the investigation."

The ADA stared into his eyes, processing. "Against my better judgment, you have twenty-four hours, no more. I'll get my team to trace the phone call, and I wanna send Detective Bowman to stake out his apartment with you—since it's her precinct he's been sneaking off to. Then I'm gonna arrest his sorry ass and find out what he's doing."

CHAPTER 26

Ethan spent the next forty-five minutes listening to the detectives in the war room, shooting video on his Canon as they worked on the killer's profile. The more he listened, the more he wondered about the small man with the tattoos. Was it just a coincidence? He seemed to fit the bill—at least in his diminutive stature. As he was standing on a chair making a wide shot, his iPhone beeped. A text message from Lloyd: "Newton on the move in the Mercedes. Following him. Will keep you posted." Ethan placed his phone in his pocket, bundled up in his down jacket, and collected his briefcase. He slowly moved through the tangle of people now surrounding ADA Highland. He waited for the right moment then said, "Patricia, I shot plenty for my story and need to go."

She looked up, clearly preoccupied with the task at hand. "Kathy. Go with him, and let me know what happens with Randall."

"I'll make sure we keep you posted," Ethan said, exiting the war room with Bowman.

They weaved through the near-empty bullpen and rode the elevator to the lobby. It was already dark when they pushed through the revolving doors and headed down the snow-covered steps. The storm had intensified, the temperature falling well below freezing, the icy snow blowing against Ethan's face, stinging his cheeks. His iPhone pinged again. Another text message from Lloyd: "The Mercedes just exited the FDR Drive and is traveling west on Houston Street. Find a cab and head toward the Lower East Side. Will keep you updated." Ethan texted Lloyd back, told him about Bowman, then turned to the detective.

"You've been briefed about Newton?"

"Patricia told all of us."

"And you know we need to keep a lid on this until we figure out what he's up to."

"Come on, Benson, what do you take me for? An idiot? I'll play your game. We'll all play your game—until the ADA says otherwise."

Ethan ignored the sarcasm and told her about Lloyd's text message then hailed the first cab that approached.

"Lower East Side," he said, scrambling into the back seat.

"Got an address?" the cabbie said.

"Soon," he said, out of breath from the cold. "And can you put on some heat, please?"

The driver hit the meter and turned up the blower then skidded from the curb and headed north on Centre Street. The roads were nearly deserted, most of the government office buildings closed, the snowstorm chasing the rest of the city indoors. They drove three blocks, hung a quick left onto Canal, the snowpack making it difficult to navigate, and then a right onto Lafayette, the storm pelting the windshield even harder. Ethan sat quietly, holding his iPhone. He'd run through his e-mails. Nothing from his production team. Nothing from Paul. Nothing from Sarah.

Why doesn't she call? Why won't she talk to me? He felt hurt, angry, confused—and decided to schedule an emergency appointment with Dr. Schwartz first thing in the morning. Then another text message wafted into his phone from Lloyd: "He's definitely headed to Alphabet City. Just turned right onto Avenue D. Hanging back a block. Don't want to be spotted. Give you an exact address soon."

He showed Bowman the text message and tapped the Plexiglas partition until the driver slid open the window.

"Avenue D."

"Where on Avenue D?" the cabbie asked, his response short and gruff.

"Need a few more minutes, and I'll tell you," Ethan said.

"Shit. We're driving in a snowstorm. Make up your mind." He slammed the window, skidded right onto Lafayette Street, and gunned the engine.

*****

Randall Newton sat in the Mercedes chain-smoking. His whole body still ached from the thrashing he'd experienced at the whim of the *Jiaofu* and the hands of his henchman, Bingwen Ho. All day long, he'd been downing painkillers, massive doses of Oxicodone, huddled in bed, waiting for the shooting pains to subside, avoiding Patricia Highland and the task force. But his agony had only grown worse, not better. Now he was heading downtown to check on the merchandise, and to make matters worse, he was meeting the big Chinese man at the apartment. That could only mean trouble. He stubbed out his cigarette and lit another one. The nicotine was getting the better of him. After all these years of abstaining, he was addicted once again.

"Are you all right, sir?" the driver said, staring through the rearview mirror.

"Fine. Fine, Bernie," he said, waving him off. "Put on some music. Maybe the *Kremlin Chamber Orchestra.* Do you have that on your iPhone?"

"Certainly, sir."

"How about Tchaikovsky? His *Serenade for Strings*. They play it so beautifully. Maybe it will lift my mood."

"Right away, sir."

"And, Bernie, where are we?"

"Headed up Avenue D. Should be there in a few minutes. Got to be careful in the snow. The city isn't plowing yet. The roads are almost undrivable."

Newton puffed away on his cigarette then swung around and peered out the back window. There were still headlights several blocks back, but he couldn't tell if it was the same car he'd seen earlier.

"Are we being followed, Bernie?"

"Not that I can see," Mr. Newton.

"What about the headlights behind us?"

"What headlights?"

Newton turned back around. The lights were gone. No sign of another car. *Must be nerves,* he thought. *Maybe it's time for me to pack up and disappear for a while.* He grabbed another cigarette, then changed his mind and shoved it back into the pack—his mouth dry like sandpaper. He checked his messages. A whole series from Patricia Highland wondering if he'd be back in the office tomorrow. At least she wasn't giving him a hard time. Then his mind flashed to the *Jiaofu* and his subtle but dangerous threat. The *Tong* boss blamed him for all his problems with the task force, with Benson, with the rest of the press. What was he going to do? If he didn't make things right, the *Jiaofu* would take his vengeance out on him. Yup. He had to disappear—no ifs, ands, or buts. Closing his eyes, he listened to the music, the melodic violin opus only fueling the fire in his head.

Then his burner buzzed, and he was paralyzed by fear. "Bingwen?"

"Where the fuck are you? We have a job to do."

"Five more minutes."

"That's all the time you've got, or I'll whip your fucking ass."

Newton's burner went dead, and he held it in his hand like a talisman foreshadowing his doom. Then he started to pray, even though he didn't believe in God.

*****

Lloyd shut off his lights and dropped back another block, the only car behind the Mercedes. He stopped for a red light at East Fourth Street, the limo still moving a quarter of a mile ahead. The light turned green, and he pulled through the intersection, his eyes glued to the car's taillights. Increasing his speed, he closed the distance between them then punched Ethan's telephone number into his cell.

"He's headed to 148 Avenue D."

"You sure?" Ethan said.

"Positive. The Mercedes just passed the Dry Dock Playground. If I'm correct, it's another block or two ahead on the right."

"Has he spotted you?"

"Don't think so. The driver's not acting as if he knows I'm behind him. Hold on a second." He placed his phone in the cup holder affixed to the dashboard and eased the van to a stop next to the Franklin Delano Roosevelt School, a block north of the playground. Turning off the engine, he grabbed his Nikon and snapped a series of pictures—click, click, click—as Randall Newton climbed out of the back seat, rolled up the collar of his overcoat, and slid in the snow as he climbed the steps and disappeared into the front door of the building. "Still there, Ethan?"

"What's goin' on?"

"He just walked into No. 148."

"Pictures?" Ethan said anxiously.

"Still pix. Can't get off a clean shot with my video camera. Too much snow. Blurs the moving image. And, Ethan, guess what?"

"I'm waiting, Lloyd, with bated breath."

"The Mercedes pulled up behind a black Escalade."

"The same one as Hester Street?"

"Bingo. License plate No. NY66-BOSS.

"Any idea who it's registered to?"

"Just heard from my contact at the DMV. Some guy named Bingwen Ho."

"Patricia Highland just ID'd him from the photos you shot last night. That's the big Chinese guy. What the hell's he doing here with Newton?"

*****

The hallway was pitched in utter darkness, the overhead lights not working, as Newton passed one apartment after another on the first floor. He found the elevator bank and pressed the button. Nothing happened. *Jesus, the elevators are out of order like the rest of this shithole.* He flicked on a penlight and saw the door leading to the emergency stairwell. His neck throbbing, his legs rubbery from the painkillers, he started climbing the four long flights until he reached the top floor, bending over and placing his hands on his knees, trying to catch his breath. Damn, why had he started smoking again?

Apartment 5A. He'd been there a million times before to check on the merchandise for the *Jiaofu,* but why did this trip feel different? He rapped three times, then once, then three times more and waited. The door slowly creaked open, the apartment as dark as the rest of the building, and he walked over the threshold and right into a fist.

Lights out.

He hit the floor with a thud.

*****

Ethan got out of the cab with Detective Bowman two blocks south of the surveillance van. He trudged through six inches of fresh snow, the wind howling, the storm raging. He wrapped a scarf around his face, bent forward, and battled his way to the passenger door, then hustled into the warmth of the front seat, Detective Bowman climbing into the back next to Lloyd.

"Fuck, we haven't had a winter like this in a long time. Feels like the North Pole."

He brushed off the snow clinging to his clothes and removed his gloves, placing his hands in front of the heater. Lloyd was huddled behind the camouflaged window on the side of the van, his Nikon in hand, snapping pictures of the Escalade and the Mercedes.

"Where you guys been?"

"Very funny, Lloyd. Cab got stuck in the snow three times. Almost didn't make it at all." He checked his messages on his iPhone again. Lots of spam from the assignment desk. Still nothing from Sarah.

"How long has Newton been in there?" Bowman said, peering through the window next to Lloyd.

"Maybe fifteen minutes."

"And Bingwen Ho?"

"Haven't seen him. He was already inside the building when I got here. But I did shoot something very interesting. Hold on, I'll show you." Lloyd screened through a series of photos on the back of the camera, and handed the Nikon to Ethan, Bowman scooting into the driver's seat and leaning over Ethan's shoulder. "There are two of them sitting in the Escalade. One in the driver's seat. One in the back."

Ethan looked at the pictures. "They're Chinese?"

"They're *Tong*. I already e-mailed the best shots to a couple of sources."

"*Tong*?"

"Go figure," Lloyd said, "but if they're in the system, I'll get positive IDs, then we can figure out if they have a record."

Ethan turned to Detective Bowman. "Call Patricia. She knows about Bingwen Ho, but she doesn't know about the *Tong*."

Bowman placed the call.

Ethan handed Lloyd the camera and eased back in his seat. *Newton's in that building with Bingwen Ho, and two Chinese thugs, maybe members of the Tong, are waiting in the Escalade,* he ruminated. *What are they all doing, and how does it play into the murders? Or does it?*

"Lloyd, what about Newton?"

"He was all fucked up. Hunched over when he left the Mercedes, barely able to move. He slipped on the sidewalk as he lumbered through the snow, his eyes wandering back and forth like a crazed animal. Here, take a look." He handed Ethan the camera—a tight shot of Newton's face, unshaven, his hair askew, a physical and emotional wreck. "He looks like he's unraveling," Lloyd said, peering out the window at the Escalade, nearly hidden by the snow. "And knee-deep into whatever illegal shit those Chinese guys are running in that building."

*****

Newton opened his eyes as a bucket of cold water was splashed in his face. His nose was broken, blood oozing over his lips and down his chin and onto his wrinkled white shirt, a big pool spreading on his chest. He tried sitting, the room spinning, his equilibrium shot to hell. Scanning the room, he spotted Bingwen perched in a torn wing chair about ten feet away, puffing smoke toward the ceiling from a cigar that looked a mile long.

"Another," Bingwen said, nodding to his *Tong* bodyguard. A second bucket of cold water was thrown in Newton's face, soaking his overcoat and pants. "Get up, asshole. Work to do."

He tried to lift his body off the floor, the throbbing from his smashed nose too much to bear. When he slumped back down, the big man stood and kicked him violently, breaking a rib, then lifted him off the ground and propped him up against the wall. A roach skittered down his face and disappeared inside his ruined white shirt.

"What's wrong with you, dumbass?" Bingwen said, screaming. "You couldn't even make it here on time? I waited patiently for seven whole minutes, and when you walked through the door, well, sorry, I just lost it. No harm done. The docs in the emergency room will fix your nose, and in a few days, it'll be as good as new, except for maybe the bruising around your eyes. That might take a bit longer to heal. So you might have some explaining to do at the office." He roared with laughter.

Newton gingerly touched his nose. Excruciating pain. It was perfectly flat and squished to the left. "Why am I here, Bingwen," he said, blood gurgling in his throat. "I thought you already delivered the new shipment to the town house?"

"I did, all except one too damaged to sell. "

"Wait a minute. I know where this is headed. I'm the old man's eyes and ears. I do damage control at the DA's Office. I don't get involved in the dirty work."

Bingwen took a long drag on his cigar and blew the smoke into Newton's face. "We ain't gonna kill her, not yet. I talked sense into the *Jiaofu.* We're gonna hide her in the town house until things cool down. Too much heat from the cops, thanks to you. So I deputized you as a member of the waste removal team. You're gonna help me transport the girl to Hester Street."

"That's your job, Bingwen," Newton said, whimpering. "I don't ever get involved in the logistics."

"Should I tell the *Jaiofu* you refused?" he said, his eyes gleaming as he pulled an eight-inch combat knife from a sheath on his belt and waved it in Newton's face. "Or would you like a taste of what my girlfriend here can do?"

"Okay. Okay. Put that thing away. I'll do what you want."

"I thought she might persuade you," he said, waving the knife one more time. He pointed to the last door at the end of the hall. "This way. I'll introduce you to the sweet Maria. She's actually quite luscious. Doesn't talk much, but she's a great fuck. I've already had the pleasure. Do you want to take a turn with her?"

"No. No. No. No. No!"

*****

"How long's he been in there?" Detective Bowman said, checking her watch.

"An hour," Lloyd said, peering through the viewfinder of his Nikon.

She punched a number into her cell phone. "What do you wanna do. He's still in there with those Chinese guys." A moment of silence. "Okay." More silence. "And where are they parked." Silence. "I'll tell Benson." She clicked off and faced Ethan. "ADA Highland has three patrol cars and a tactical unit stationed up on Thirteenth Street. You've got fifteen more minutes, and then she wants to take down Randall. She's worried about playing this cat-and-mouse game and wants to know what he's up to."

"Shit. I'm gonna call her," Ethan said, shivering in the passenger seat, the temperature down to twenty, the heater unable to keep up with the cold.

"Hold on. Hold on. The two Chinese guys just got out of the Escalade. One's standing next to the front passenger door. The other's opening the tailgate." Click. Click. Click.

"Any sign of Newton?"

"Not yet."

"You getting this on camera?" Ethan said, huddling at the window next to Lloyd, Bowman right behind him, the visibility reduced to a hundred feet by the snow.

"I got it, but it's not great." He eased the camera to his right and adjusted the focal length, zooming into the front door of the tenement. "They're coming out."

"Newton?" Ethan said, flummoxed.

"Yeah. He's carrying something heavy with another Chinese guy we haven't seen yet." Click. Click. Click. "Bingwen is trailing just behind them."

"Shit. I can't see through the snow," Bowman said.

"It looks like a burlap bag," Lloyd said.

"Any idea what's inside?"

"Not a clue." Lloyd continued shooting. "They're making their way to the Escalade. The Chinese guy at the tailgate is waving furiously. Can you see, Ethan?"

"Barely."

"They just tossed the sack into the cargo compartment. It's heavy. Now Bingwen is talking to Newton. Shit, man, he just slugged him in the stomach. Three rapid bursts out of nowhere. Newton's flat on his back." Click. Click. Click. "The Chinese guys just got into the Escalade. It's pulling away from the curb. Should I follow them?"

"No. Stay with Newton," Ethan said, whipping around to Detective Bowman. "Call your guys up on Thirteenth Street. Tell them the black Escalade is heading their way and to follow it. Make sure those assholes don't see them. We need to know where they're going." Then he turned to Lloyd and shrieked, "What's happening with Newton?"

"The driver's out of the Mercedes," he said as he jumped into the driver's seat, still rolling off pictures. "He's helping Newton into his car." Click. Click. Click. "Now they're pulling away, also heading uptown."

He gunned the engine and shot into the snowstorm.

"Don't lose them, whatever you do," Ethan screamed. "I'm calling Patricia Highland. She's right. It's time to arrest Randall Newton and find out what the fuck he's up to."

CHAPTER 27

It was eight in the morning, and Ethan was sitting in his shrink's waiting room staring vacantly at a magazine, smoking a cigarette, worrying. He'd followed Randall Newton in the surveillance van to the emergency room at Lenox Hill Hospital where the doctors had patched together his broken nose and bound his broken rib then back home to his apartment on Third Avenue, where Newton had stumbled out of the back seat of the Mercedes and disappeared into the lobby. It was almost 4:00 a.m. when Lloyd dropped Ethan at Ninety-First Street after depositing Detective Bowman at One Hogan Place, and instead of going to sleep, he had walked Holly down Fifth Avenue in the snow, fed her dinner, and parked himself in his study—where he'd sent a long e-mail to Patricia Highland explaining everything that had happened since they'd last talked. It hadn't taken long before she'd zinged him a reply—the task force would arrest Randall Newton the following day as soon as Ethan built a production crew to capture the moment on camera. Then he had showered and shaved, and made a big breakfast—bacon, eggs, toast, and coffee—his first meal in twenty-four hours—and headed straight to Dr. Schwartz's office.

Now he was having a panic attack.

Wondering how he'd get through another day.

Without Sarah and Luke.

"Ethan, I'm ready," Dr. Schwartz said kindly as he stood in the doorway leading into his inner office.

Ethan followed, and instead of sitting in an armchair, he lay down on the couch, his head propped on a pillow, his eyes staring at the pale yellow ceiling. "I'll be more comfortable here today," he said, striking a fresh cigarette. "Thank you for seeing me on such short notice."

"You sounded in crisis this morning. I only wish you'd called over the weekend after Sarah left with Luke. I would have made time for you then." He flipped on his tape recorder and grabbed a pen and paper. "Start from the beginning, Ethan, what happened?"

He sat silently smoking, his left forearm draped over his eyes, Dr. Schwartz waiting patiently.

"We had a huge fight after our last session. It was nasty, one of the worst we've ever had. And we kept fighting over everything all week long—my job, my story, my decision to go back to producing. And I guess, I kept drinking to feel better, to make the pain go away, to hide from Sarah."

"How much, Ethan?"

"A lot."

"You got drunk?"

"Probably," he admitted reluctantly.

"Every day?"

"Yeah. Yeah. Yeah." He took a long pull on his cigarette.

"How about right now? You been drinking this morning?"

"I had one pop in the middle of the night. Nothing else since then."

Dr. Schwartz scribbled a note on his yellow pad. "So what happened during your fight—the one that came after our last session?"

Ethan sighed, took a final hit on his cigarette, and lit another one. "Sarah was furious I hadn't called all day, and that I'd gotten home really late. I was holding a glass of Scotch when she came into my study, but I'd been drinking all evening, and she knew I'd had one too many. She told me she could smell it on my breath. Then she chastised me about my drinking, said I was hopeless, and we started screaming at each other."

"We talked about this at our last session. All three of us. And Sarah was very clear about how she felt, that she wanted you to stop drinking."

Ethan nodded, his eyes fixed on the ceiling, but said nothing.

"Did you argue about anything else, besides your drinking?"

He frowned and took a deep breath. "She was hurt that I hadn't told her I was thinking of giving up my position as Peter's senior producer, that she had to hear it here for the first time." He paused to blow his nose. "She was pissed, really pissed, that I was planning to walk away from the prestige and all the money and go back to producing full-time. After a few minutes of yelling and screaming, she stormed back to our bedroom."

"Did you go after her? Try to continue the discussion?"

"No."

"Why not, Ethan?"

He swung his feet off the couch and faced the psychiatrist. "I don't know, Dr. Schwartz. I keep playing the argument over and over in my head, and I have no answers."

"You're not dealing openly with your feelings, Ethan. You're hiding from yourself and from what's really important."

"I know. I know."

He jotted another note on his pad. "So what happened the rest of the week?"

Tears filled Ethan's eyes. "We avoided each other like the plague. I went to work, and I didn't call, and didn't come home until very late every night."

"And you got drunk?"

"Smashed."

"And you argued."

"Yes."

"About the same things?"

'Yes."

"Did Luke hear you?"

Ethan hesitated then said, "He must have. We were really going after each other."

"Is that it?"

Ethan sighed. "No. Sarah said he cried. That he thought we were angry with him."

"That's a typical reaction from a seven year old. And how did that make you feel when you found out?"

"Like a failure as a father."

"Did you talk to him about it?"

"No. I didn't, Dr. Schwartz."

"Don't you think you should have?"

Ethan closed his eyes. "Of course, but I didn't."

Dr. Schwartz jotted another note then looked up and said candidly, "Anything else happen that pushed her away from you?"

"The night before she left, I drank half a bottle of Scotch after we fought. I never went to bed and passed out at my desk. That's where I spent the night." He stood and paced the room, visibly shaken. "The next morning she walked out with Luke, told me she had to get away, that she needed a break from our marriage, and would be staying with her sister in Cleveland." He sat back down and stared blankly at the wall. "Now she's gone and won't talk to me."

"So she left two days ago. Do I have the timeline correct, Ethan?"

"Yes."

"And yesterday morning, Sunday, Paul removed you from your job as a senior producer. Still on the timeline?"

"Yes."

"Why, Ethan?"

He heaved his shoulders.

"I was shirking my responsibilities with Peter, spending all my time on my Child Sex Murders story, drinking until I was smashed, coming in late. Then Saturday I worked all night and overslept. Late again. I guess they got worried, so Paul called Sarah looking for me, and she told him and Peter everything. That I was getting drunk and that she'd separated from me."

"How did that make you feel?"

Ethan exploded. "Really pissed, furious, betrayed."

"By Sarah?"

"Who else?" he said, realizing he was out of control.

"Does she know what you're feeling?"

"How could she? She won't talk to me, remember, except for a two-minute conversation after Peter removed me as his senior producer."

"What did she say?"

"What do you think? That I'd gotten what I wanted—*no more Peter Sampson*—and that she was all but through with me."

"And?"

"And what?"

"What do you plan to do, Ethan?"

"Who the fuck knows."

Dr. Schwartz turned off his tape recorder and put down his pad and pen.

"I have another patient, Ethan. All I can say is keep reaching out to her and let her know what you're feeling. You've hurt her, and she feels wounded, and she's withdrawing to protect herself and Luke. She needs time to heal." He placed his hand on Ethan's shoulder. "I'll see you Wednesday at our next session. If you need to talk before then, call me, and I'll get back to you. And, Ethan, stay sober. That's critical for Sarah. She won't come home with Luke until she believes you've stopped drinking."

*****

Mindy fell in right behind him as he hustled down the hallway to his office. "I got your e-mail about Newton. We've got two staff crews on standby."

"Who?"

"Bobby Raffalo and Herb Glickstein and their two sound people."

"Good. Now I don't have to worry about the production."

"When is Highland going to arrest him?" she said, trying to keep up.

"One o'clock. That's when I said we'd be ready. Do we know where he is?"

"He called out sick again."

"Not surprising. He spent hours in the emergency room last night being patched up. He's probably totaled. Lloyd watching his building?"

"In his surveillance van. Newton hasn't stepped out since he got home."

"Does Patricia Highland know?"

"Lloyd's been on the phone with her, acting as her eyes and ears too."

"Good. Good. Everybody's working together on this. That's our deal with the DA's Office. Full cooperation. Keep checking with Lloyd. If Newton doesn't leave. That's where we'll link with Highland and the task force."

Mindy stepped in front of him, forcing him to stop before he reached his office.

"Any word from Sarah?" she said, refusing to let him avoid what really mattered.

"Nothing," he said, anger and melancholy in his voice at the same time.

"What are you gonna do, Ethan?"

"Fight like hell to win her back."

"How?"

He tried mustering a smile, but failed. "I don't know, Mindy, I really don't. Let's discuss this later, please. We only have a few minutes until our meeting with Julie. I don't wanna be late the first time. Are the guys here?"

"Ready and waiting."

*****

Julie Piedmont's office was down the hall from Sampson's—farther away from the executive producer's—befitting her status as the second banana on the show. Ethan, followed by his production team, nodded good morning to her assistant, an older man in his midfifties named Jerome Bishop, who told them to go on in. Julie was sitting at her desk—a modern teak affair with a tabletop computer and printer—looking bright and cheerful, a pleasant surprise after Sampson. She motioned them to sit on a comfortable feather couch and joined them on a matching high-back chair, holding the thick black notebook with the research James had put together the day before.

"Jerome, call Paul and alert him that Ethan has arrived, right on time."

"Paul's joining us?" Ethan said, annoyed.

"He wants to sit in on our first meeting," she said as Paul hustled through the door and sat down next to her.

"Morning all," he said, rushed. Then he stared long and hard at Ethan. "You look like shit."

"I was up all night working on our story."

He kept peering into Ethan's eyes, looking for telltale signs. "You sober?"

"I'm fine, Paul," he said testily.

"Just making sure."

"Now that we've cleared that up," Julie said, "let's get started." Then she dropped the black notebook on the coffee table in front of her. "Read this last night before I went to sleep. An impressive backgrounder on the Child Sex Murders. So I'm up to speed on the storyline and the key characters."

"James put that together," Ethan said, glancing at Paul.

The executive producer smiled.

"So where do we go from here?" she said. "I'm ready to dive right in."

Ethan spent the next thirty minutes thoroughly laying out everything that had happened the past forty-eight hours—Henry Dinkus's murder, Randall Newton's clandestine trips to Smith and Wollensky, Chinatown, and Alphabet City, and his connection to Bingwen Ho, the *Tong* with a rap sheet half a mile long.

"What's the guy into? Drugs? Prostitution? Illegal gambling?" Paul said, thoroughly drawn into the new twist to the story.

"I don't know yet," Ethan said truthfully. "But I've got pictures of Bingwen Ho with Newton that I took the last two nights as I was tailing him around the city. I also have pictures of Newton with Police Commissioner Jordan Langley the night Detective Dinkus was killed."

"Why's that important?" Paul said.

"Don't know if it is. We're still digging."

"Okay. Go on. What video do you have?" Julie asked.

"Task force meetings, the police investigation after they found the last girl's body, and Detective Henry Dinkus's murder."

"You were there?" Julie said incredulously.

"I was doing an interview with him when he was shot."

"Think we can we air it?" Paul said, almost to himself.

Ethan nodded to David. "You screened it with Joel. What does he think?"

"If we tone down the colors and distort the image, we can probably get away with it."

"My sentiments exactly. Should help spike the ratings," Paul said, pleased. "Now let's get to the question sitting in the room like a white elephant. Is the task force making progress solving the murders? All this footage is great television, but only if they catch the killer. I won't run the story if they don't."

Ethan thought a moment, trying to frame his answer.

"The investigation is moving forward, Paul, and I can't promise you anything until I know more, but I'm pretty sure Randall Newton is leaking inside information. He may even be involved in the murders. That's the current thinking at the task force—at least by Patricia Highland." He scanned from Paul to Julie, making sure he had their full attention. "We can't prove any of that yet, but the task force is going to bust him this afternoon and then interrogate him. I'll have my cameras there for the whole thing."

Paul beamed. "Wonderful. Wonderful. Wonderful. But I still don't have a shooting budget. Who approved the camera crews?"

"I did. I'm still technically a senior producer."

"I'll let that slide for the moment, but I want a story budget on my desk today." He whipped from Ethan to Julie. "Are you going?"

"Bet your ass I'll be there."

CHAPTER 28

It was twelve thirty, and Ethan and Julie and his A-crew, Herb Glickstein and Zoe Whitfield, were putting the finishing touches on the game plan in the back of Lloyd's surveillance van a half block north of Randall Newton's apartment building. He'd just gotten off the phone with Mindy who was accompanying Patricia Highland in a Crown Victoria that was leading a motorcade of cop cars heading north from One Hogan Place.

"The B-crew, Bobby Raffalo and Eli Hobbs, are shooting in the ADA's car," he said, mapping out everything on a pad of white paper. "They're capturing footage of her and the chatter on the police radio as well as a visual sequence of the motorcade as it heads uptown. Mindy is going to direct that crew when they get here and cover the shit out of Highland."

"What's your plan for me?" Julie said eagerly.

"We'll exit the van as soon as we see the flashing lights. I want you to wait until the ADA gets out of her car and then accompany her through the building and up to Newton's apartment. Talk to her, ask her questions about Newton and the bust, like a short shotgun interview highlighting the event."

"Does she know it's me and not Peter Sampson?" Julie said, a competitive edge in her voice.

"Discussed it with her on the telephone before we left. She's cool."

Julie nodded, satisfied.

"Herb, I want you to shoot the cops as they arrive—spilling out of their cars, drawing their guns, a complete visual sequence with energy and excitement. When you've got enough, peel off and concentrate on Julie and the ADA. I've told Mindy to pull the B-crew as soon as Julie is talking to Highland and to shoot everything that happens once the cops enter the building, so you won't have to worry about that. Just focus on Julie. I'll be right behind you directing." Then he turned to Lloyd and said without taking a breath, "You hang with the cops and give me a heads-up if they find anything that requires us to shift gears. And, Zoe, is Julie mic'd?"

"Done."

"And you'll use a boom for the secondary sound."

"That's my plan?" she said, tinkering with her Nagra sound mixer.

"So everybody understand their assignments?"

They all nodded.

"Good. So now we wait."

*****

At one o'clock Lloyd signaled Ethan from the back of the van.

"Here they come. About four blocks away. An army of blue-and-white police cars, lights flashing, moving single file up Third Avenue."

"Everybody hit the street," Ethan said, the doors sliding open and his team pouring out onto the sidewalk. The doorman, standing outside the building, was startled when he saw Herb Glickstein mount his Sony 2-Chip on a steel harness designed to stabilize the small camera and then start rolling on the motorcade of cop cars as it screeched to a halt, blocking traffic on Third Avenue, their bubble gum machines flashing blue-and-white over everything. Several dozen cops piled out all at once, some wearing riot gear, some dressed in NYPD blue, all with nightsticks and guns drawn.

Gloria Alvarez took the lead, flashing her badge and telling the doorman who had shriveled against the wall to clear the lobby because they were heading into the building to make an arrest. Then she dispatched half a dozen cops to barricade the sidewalk and push back the crowds who were forming around the building. As Mindy and her crew exited the lead car with ADA Highland, Ethan signaled Glickstein to break off and follow Julie as she made her way over and shook hands with the ADA.

"I'm Julie Piedmont," she said in her anchorwoman voice.

"My pleasure," Highland said, eager to get into the building.

"Why are you arresting Randall Newton?"

"Because he's now a suspect in the murders."

"Do you think he killed those girls?"

"He's a person of interest."

"And a member of your task force."

"Indeed he is. All the more reason to arrest him, so we can find out who, if anyone, he's working for, whether he's passing information to somebody who doesn't want us to solve the case, and if and how he's involved in these murders." She paused and waved to Alvarez. "We ready to go in?" The detective nodded, and she turned back to Julie. "You're welcome to accompany me up to Newton's apartment. Keep asking me questions if you want, and I'll keep answering as long as it doesn't compromise my investigation."

Herb Glickstein positioned himself in front of the two of them and began gliding backward, Zoe Whitfield guiding him with a hand on his back, Julie firing away one question after another as they made their way into the lobby. Ethan was observing from a distance, listening to their conversation, pleased with Julie and her fluid style—a natural-born interviewer who put her subject at ease, so different from Peter Sampson, distant and aloof. He pivoted to Mindy and the B-crew, motioning for them to continue shooting the chaos, pointing to different images he wanted them to capture. Then he caught up to Julie and ADA Highland as they moved briskly past the doorman and through the lobby, surrounded by Alvarez and a dozen tactical police units. They all stopped at the elevator bank, Alvarez pointing to a back stairwell and leading most of the cops up the five flights of stairs to Newton's apartment. Mindy and the Raffalo crew followed, Herb Glickstein continuing to roll on Julie and Highland as an elevator door slid open and a young couple, terrified by the police and their weapons, exited as fast as they could.

Then they rode up in silence and regrouped fifty feet from Randall Newton's apartment, the Raffalo crew making a master shot of everybody silently marching down the hallway and surrounding his door.

"What's the plan from here?" Julie whispered, showing no signs of fear, Herb Glickstein swinging his camera to a tight shot of ADA Highland.

"Hopefully, Randall will come along without a fuss," she said dubiously, "but I have my doubts. He's been ignoring my phone calls all morning."

"Get that, Herb?" Ethan said, tapping his shoulder.

His cameraman nodded and kept rolling.

"Okay, everybody, stand back," the ADA said commandingly. "Time to take him down."

"Julie, hang with me and Lloyd and let the cops do their thing," Ethan said, barking his own set of orders. "Mindy, take Bobby and follow Highland when she goes in, but for God's sake, be careful. Herb, you keep shooting Julie. Then shoot the shit out of the arrest and make sure to include Julie in your shots." He wheeled around to his anchorwoman. "No more questions until we get the all clear from Highland. I promised her we wouldn't get in the way."

Julie nodded, showing the first signs of trepidation, as Ethan checked to make sure his cameramen were rolling, then waited silently as Alvarez signaled her team, poised in front of the door, guns at the ready, and shook her head up and down to ADA Highland, who took a deep breath and rapped on the door.

"Randall, it's me, Patricia. Open up. We need to talk."

Nothing happened.

The ADA banged on the door again. "Open up, Randall."

Still nothing but silence.

She looked at Alvarez who mouthed, "One more time."

"Last chance. I know you're in there. Open the door and let me in. We need to talk about the investigation."

They all waited one, two, three seconds.

No response.

Then Detective Alvarez glanced at each member of her team, now crowded in a tight circle and said, "Break it down."

A cop holding a steel battering ram pushed to the front, took aim at the lock, and slammed the door. It splintered on the first thrust, then caved in on the second, ripping the locking mechanism out of the wall. Alvarez and her tactical team stormed in ahead of Highland, all screaming, Mindy and Raffalo following at a safe distance.

"All clear in the kitchen."

"Clear in the library."

"Clear in the living room."

"And the spare bedroom."

Then silence, Ethan motioning to Julie and proceeding cautiously into the apartment. A phalanx of cops was standing outside Newton's bedroom—a Franz Joseph Hayden Concerto for Cello and Orchestra blasting in the background. Highland was standing in the doorway, Bobby Raffalo next to her as she gestured wildly and ordered a uniformed cop to kill the music.

"I want this treated as a crime scene. Get CSI to sweep the apartment. And nobody touch anything until they get here." Then she turned to Ethan. "Wanna take a look?"

Ethan waved to Herb and Julie, standing a short distance away, dispatched Mindy and the second crew to start shooting the cops pouring through each room, then said to Highland, "Can we do a short interview with Newton?"

The ADA sighed heavily. "You can try, but I don't think you'll get much out of him. Not today. Come, I'll show you why."

He followed her into the bedroom, Julie by his side, Herb circling with his camera, then zooming into Newton, who was lounging in a chair, dressed in red silk pajamas. His face was swollen to the size of a basketball and deeply bruised, a nasty gash sutured over his right eye, his nose bandaged and soaked with blood. A milky white substance had leaked from his mouth and dribbled down his chin, his eyes red and teary, his gaze fixed on something nobody else could see.

"What's wrong with him?" Julie said, turning to Highland, Glickstein framing on a two-shot.

Highland pointed to a long wooden pipe sitting on his lap. "He's stoned."

"On marijuana?"

"No. Opium," she said, pointing to a bag of brown paste on the floor. "Won't know for sure until we get it back to the lab."

"Did you know he was an addict?" Julie said, pressing the ADA.

Herb zoomed into a tight shot. "The answer, young lady, is no. An unmitigated no. Randall Newton was part of my task force, an up-and-comer in the District Attorney's Office. Until last week, he was a trusted ally in this investigation. I never in a million years thought he was addicted to opium."

"Do you think he compromised your case?"

"I don't know what to think. Ethan certainly thinks he has, and let me tell you, when he sobers up, I certainly aim to find out. Now, no more questions. I have to work."

Highland signaled two detectives who lifted Newton from the chair and strapped him onto a hospital gurney—paramedics dressed in protective clothing and booties having just arrived with a full team of crime scene investigators, now scouring the apartment for evidence. Once Newton was chained in manacles, still off in his dream world, he was wheeled through the apartment to the front door.

"Where they taking him?" Julie said to ADA Highland, Herb Glickstein right there with his camera.

"To a locked ward at Bellevue Hospital for detox."

"Can we follow him with our cameras?" Ethan said.

"Be my guest. You've got full access. All part of our deal."

"Julie, go with them. It'll make a great visual." Then he searched for Mindy and found her in the living room. "Julie's accompanying the cops to Bellevue with Newton. Take Bobby and shoot it. Julie's still wired. Pick up as many interviews as you can—the cops, EMTs, emergency room doctors, whoever will give us information on Newton and what they're doing to clean him up. I'll finish shooting here with Herb."

Ethan watched as the EMTs pushed Newton down the hall, neighbors poking their heads out their doors, gawking, wondering why their nice neighbor was being escorted out of the building by the police. Patricia Highland had buttoned her overcoat and was leaving with two detectives.

"Ethan, I'm headed to One Hogan Place. Gotta hold a press conference so I can spin this the right way, so the newspapers and TV stations don't have a field day speculating on how a member of my task force compromised my investigation. Gloria will finish up here with the CSIs. Stay and shoot as much as you want, then call me, and we'll figure out what to do about Newton. Not sure at the moment whether I'm gonna let you interview him on camera or not."

"But I need him for my story."

"I know," she said, waving her hand. "I just need to figure out if an interview will compromise my case. Need to mull it over with my team and with the district attorney. I'll make a decision by the end of the day." Then she slipped on a pair of gloves, buttoned her overcoat, and left.

*****

Ethan began directing furiously, instructing Herb to make a wide shot of the crime scene investigators turning over every square inch of the apartment, then to shoot as they searched through closets and cabinets, bagged the pipe and opium, dusted for fingerprints, and collected other evidence. He tapped Herb on the shoulder and whispered, "Only planning a short sequence here, so I don't need much. As soon as you have it, give me a heads-up, and we'll wrap." Then he scanned the apartment for Lloyd Howard and found him standing in the doorway of the library, quietly motioning.

"Ethan, I need to show you something."

He followed him to a window along the far wall, the room trashed, documents strewn haphazardly on the floor, a large pail filled with shredded documents. There were wads of cash spilling out of an open floor safe and a passport peeking out from under a stack of file folders.

"What the fuck was he doing?" Ethan said.

"Destroying incriminating evidence and getting ready to run."

"The guy must've been knee-deep in this shit," Ethan said, thinking about the big Chinese man with the eye patch and the small Chinese man covered in tattoos and piercings.

"The question is how," Lloyd said, whispering.

Ethan spotted an open file folder sitting on the desk. It contained a list of the medical supply companies that sold *Karl Storz* surgical knives. There was a short handwritten note on the inside cover. It said "Passed a copy to the big boss."

"Check this out, Lloyd," Ethan said, holding up the folder.

"Shouldn't touch that," Lloyd said. "It's evidence."

"I know that," he said, "but what does the note mean?"

Lloyd stared at the scribblings. "No fucking clue, Ethan."

"I think he gave it to somebody who isn't supposed to have it."

"You can't prove that," Lloyd said incredulously. "Besides, we have no idea if the information in there is incriminating in any way."

"Well, I'm gonna find out," Ethan said, shoving the file inside his briefcase.

"I didn't see you do that," Lloyd said, rolling his eyes. Then he walked to the door and peeked out, making sure nobody was coming. "There's something else I need to show you." He walked to a chair standing askew in the corner and pointed. "A burner, maybe the same burner I photographed when Newton was in the Mercedes."

Ethan crouched and reached for the phone.

"You gonna take that too?" Lloyd said, grabbing his arm.

"Think I'll leave it for Alvarez. She has more tools to trace the calls than we do." He grabbed his iPhone, punched the camera icon, zoomed in tight on the burner, and snapped a half-dozen shots. "It's an Ultra Mobile. Ever hear of that?"

"Costs about thirty bucks. You can make domestic and international calls and change the SIM card, or you can smash the phone into smithereens and buy a new one whenever you want."

Ethan stood, signaling to Herb, then searched for Alvarez.

"Detective," he said, shouting over all the noise in the apartment, "got something you need to see."

Alvarez disentangled herself from a group of plainclothes detectives and made her way into the library, Herb following with his camera, Zoe Whitfield next to him booming the sound.

"What's got your knickers in a bunch, *BENSON*? I was about to start processing this room, *amigo*."

Ethan pointed to the far corner, ignoring her sarcasm. "Come, take a look for yourself."

He led her to the chair, and she cursed in Spanish, "*Mierda*. A goddamn burner. What the holy fuck was *RANDALL* doing with burner?" She leaned down, slipped on a pair of Latex gloves, then dropped the phone into an evidence bag.

"He was using it the other night."

"And how the fuck do you know that, *Benson*?"

"I've got pictures."

"What? You holding out on me?" she said, scowling.

"Of course not," he said, tapping down a slow burn. "I showed them to ADA Highland."

"So why the fuck don't I have them?"

"Maybe it's because I haven't sent them to you yet."

"*Gringos*. All fuckin' *gringos* are the same. Fuckin' not trustworthy."

"Cut the crap, Detective. I'm sick of your running bullshit." Ethan's anger was spilling over. "If I didn't want you to know about the burner, I would've pocketed that damn thing and never told you."

"But—"

"No buts, Detective. If you want my help, then you start treating me as part of your team and not as your enemy." Ethan paused, silence wafting through the apartment, the entire task force listening to their conversation.

Alvarez flicked her eyes to the living room and back to Ethan, then smiled.

"You one tough cookie, *Benson*." Then she stuck out her hand. "No more bullshit between you and me, *si*? Work together." All the tension in the room evaporated, the task force getting back to work, the noise level once again deafening." So when do I get pictures?"

"As soon as I get back to my office," he said, "and you'll share whatever you find on the burner?"

"I'll do better than that," she said contritely. "Task force meeting at SVU tonight. Eight o'clock sharp. Join us, and I make sure you get all the latest on investigation."

CHAPTER 29

Bingwen Ho pushed through the partially concealed door in the back of *Hung Chow Delicacies* and descended the rickety staircase to the underground passageway, his massive bulk barely fitting in the narrow corridor. For the first time since he'd joined the *Tong* as the *Jiaofu*'s number two, he was questioning the big boss's decisions. He'd left Randall Newton's apartment earlier in the day after watching the ADA unraveling. High on opium, he was unable to function, unable to provide him with the latest task force information, and unable to accompany him to meet with the old man. Bingwen cursed himself for not eliminating Newton on the spot. He could've sliced the guy's throat, or even better, spiked the opium with strychnine, killing the worthless son of a bitch in a matter of seconds. The cops, when they found the body, thinking the opium was tainted by his pushers, would never have suspected it was foul play.

He proceeded through the tunnel, climbed the second set of stairs, thundering heavily on each one, and opened the door into the lobby of the town house. Not a penny had been spared in decorating the building—marble floors imported from Italy, expensive tongue and groove wood paneling, elaborate plaster reliefs on the ceiling crafted by skilled artisans from Europe, and modern artwork by Jeff Koons, Jasper Jones, Robert Ryman, and Cady Noland purchased at the best galleries in the city. The building was leased to an upscale spa called Lost Horizons, a clothing designer, an antique dealer specializing in nineteenth-century Italian furniture, and the *Tong*'s dummy corporation, the Allied Shipping Company. To the public, this new town house on Hester Street was the first step in rebuilding one of the oldest and most dilapidated neighborhoods in Manhattan.

Nobody suspected it was a front.

For an illegal empire run by the *Tong*.

Bingwen nodded to the Chinese doorman, dressed in a gray uniform and top hat, then walked to a recessed vestibule next to a bank of elevators. He stopped in front of a priceless landscape painted by Jasper Francis Cropsey, a well-known Hudson River School master, checked to make sure he was alone, found a lever hidden in the wood paneling, and pushed his way through a secret door, closing it quietly behind him. Then he proceeded down a series of underground hallways, before passing through a carved wooden door into the *Jiaofu*'s inner chambers. The big boss was sitting in a comfortable red velvet chair, his long ponytail neatly groomed and hanging down his back, his opium pipe perched in his mouth.

"Ah, Bingwen, would you like a taste," he said, offering him a toke. "The opium is smooth and very powerful."

Bingwen shook his head no.

"Whatever you desire," the old man said, inhaling the drug and blowing the smoke in a long stream out his nose. "Very, very good. Sure you don't want to sample my product? It will take you to a special place that's simply unimaginable."

The big man didn't move.

"I guess not," he said cynically. "So now to the business at hand," his mood suddenly shifting, his face growing hard. "Did you pay a visit to Mr. Newton?"

Bingwen nodded but remained silent.

"And?"

"He acts like a sniveling woman."

"Did you give him the opium?"

"As you instructed. He got stoned out of his mind."

"Good. Good," the *Jiaofu* said, slowly pulling on the pipe. "And you left him enough of the product to make it look like he's an addict?"

"More than enough." The big man bowed his head.

"But what, Bingwen? There is something you are reluctant to tell me," the old man said, his eyes piercing.

"May I speak freely, sir?"

The *Jiaofu* smiled and handed the pipe to a concubine. "Of course, Bingwen. It's what I expect from a loyal servant."

"I should've killed the motherfucker."

"But why?" he said gleefully. "That would've ruined all the fun."

"Because Newton was arrested by that bitch, Patricia Highland, as soon as I left, and that guy, Ethan Benson, was there with his cameras," he said, rattled. "Newton knows too much, and he's gonna talk and blow everything."

The *Jaiofu* waved his hand, and Bingwen fell silent. Then he stood and walked over to the big man, staring up into his eyes with daggers. "Do you doubt me, Bingwen, after all these years? Don't you trust me to know what I'm doing? Randall Newton was a very useful source, eager and well paid. But he was weak. A mistake. My mistake. And he was growing too fond of my opium. So we had to make it look like he was an addict to discredit him. So Patricia Highland would no longer trust him." He puffed on his opium pipe. "But just to be safe, I will make sure that Randall never talks. I have friends, lots of friends, wherever the police decide to cage him. Rikers. Bellevue. The New York City Department of Corrections. Everywhere. I will stalk him like an angry tiger, and then, he'll be long dead before he says a single word to the authorities about our lucrative business empire."

The *Jaiofu* clapped his hands.

Bingwen lowered his eyes.

And the big boss headed toward another secret door surrounded by bodyguards.

"One more small detail, Bingwen. That sweet little Spanish girl, Maria, has given this old man much pleasure. She's been well trained in the art of lovemaking by her captors. But alas, I have grown tired of her. So I want you to find the Butcher and make the necessary arrangements for her disposal as we planned. It's time to get rid of her."

*****

Ethan sat behind the driver in a yellow cab, staring out the window as the skyscrapers on Fifth Avenue blew by one at a time, tweaking his tentative shooting schedule to launch his production, organizing his next steps on his iPad. ADA Highland had consulted with District Attorney Cunningham and decided to allow Ethan to interview Randall Newton as soon as he recovered from his injuries, and from the reports he'd received from Mindy and Julie after they'd shot the mad scene at Bellevue Hospital, that would take place in maybe a day or two. He listed on-camera interviews with Highland, Gloria Alvarez, Victor Nottingdale, Kathy Bowman, Leon Fennimore, as well as Newton. He added visuals—the police photos, the task force meetings at Special Victims and One Hogan Place, the dead girl at the Dry Dock Playground, Detective Dinkus's murder and the investigation that followed, and of course, Randall Newton's arrest and admission to the prison ward at Bellevue Hospital. All great stuff, but not enough to build a story.

There was still no killer.

As the cabbie turned onto One Hundred Twenty-Third Street and pulled up to the station house, he hastily reviewed the e-mail with the story elements and the proposed budget and pressed Send. *This will get Paul off my back at least for a little while.* He paid the driver, hustled up the steps and into the building, waving to the same desk sergeant juggling phone calls, then made his way through the first-floor bullpen, more subdued than the last time he'd been there, up the back staircase, still littered with garbage, and into the task force conference room on the second floor.

Sitting around the table were Gloria Alvarez, Kathy Bowman, and Victor Nottingdale.

Before Ethan had a chance to sit, Alvarez said, "Got JPEGs shot by your undercover investigator as promised. Thank you, *BENSON*. But still no ID on little Chinese man. Already run photo through databases, see if digital face match, but so far we got shit. No nothin'."

Ethan pulled off his hat and coat and sat. "What about the town house?"

"What about it, *BENSON*?"

"I know who owns it," he said, pointing to the JPEG of the modern building on Hester Street now filling the computer screen in the center of the table. "A company called Allied Shipping."

"Why the fuck is that important?" Nottingdale said.

"Not sure yet."

"So why we even talking about it?" Bowman said.

"Because the night I followed Newton to Chinatown, he went into the restaurant across the street and came out of that town house with those two Chinese guys who beat the shit out of him. The guys in the photos."

"How the fuck did he pull that off?"

"My guess, there's a tunnel under the street connecting the two buildings," Ethan said pointedly.

"So you think town house is important to Child Sex Murders?" Alvarez said, perplexed.

"Yes."

She peered long and hard at the JPEG. "What kind of business is Allied Shipping?"

"Import/export—mostly wines from Argentina."

Alvarez turned to Bowman. "Run background on Allied. Find out who runs company. How big business—sales, revenues, profits, taxes. See if there are any outstanding audits, lawsuits, warrants against owners. See if Allied is *legitimate*." She turned to Benson, "Maybe new lead, *no*?"

Ethan leaned back in his chair. He hadn't had a Scotch all day, and the urge was rearing its ugly head.

"Maybe. I think Allied is a front for something else, that it's being used by those two Chinese guys—who are both probably *Tong*—to cover up something illegal that Randall Newton is somehow a part of."

"And how's that connected to the Child Sex Murders?" Bowman asked.

"That's what we need to find out."

"*Mr. Investigator-Producer* full of ideas tonight," Alvarez said with hubris. "Victor, stake out building. Two people. Three shifts. Twenty-four hours a day. Let's see who goes in and out of that fucking town house."

"And where do I get the plainclothes?" Detective Nottingdale said. "The police commissioner pulled our manpower to work on the Dinkus murder, remember?"

Ethan looked from Nottingdale to Alvarez. "But I thought the Dinkus murder was part of the task force investigation."

"No more, *amigo*," Alvarez said. "Commissioner Langley says Dinkus murder *separate* from Child Sex Murders. Wants own team to investigate. So he moves people from our investigation. No manpower again."

Ethan leaned back in his chair and wondered about the dinner at Smith and Wollensky, now convinced the police commissioner was somehow linked to the murders and obstructing the investigation. The question was, Why?

"So how can you stake out the town house—if you just have a skeleton crew working the case."

"I talk to Patricia," Alvarez said. "We find way to build stakeout team. Steal manpower maybe from SVU. Maybe somewhere else." She reached for a file folder. "One last piece of business, *BENSON*. This is for you." She pushed a document across the table. "A list of all Karl Storz No. 6 surgical knives bought at big medical supply houses during past year. I know you wanted it. The sales are mixed with other equipment purchased by doctors, clinics, and hospitals all over city."

Ethan picked up the document, thinking about the copy he'd taken from Randall Newton's apartment but decided not to mention it. Maybe it was better not to let her know he'd lifted evidence from the Randall Newton crime scene. That would all but destroy their fragile working relationship. Then he thumbed through the pages.

"There are thousands of transactions," he said. "Names, credit card numbers, and in some cases, addresses. Has your team finished going through this?"

Alvarez laughed cynically. "No, *BENSON*. Big job. Take time. Not enough people."

"Any leads—at all?"

"Nothing. Just shit," Nottingdale said.

"And what about the burner I found at Randall Newton's apartment?"

"Don't hold your breath," Detective Bowman said, jumping in. "Our tech guys are analyzing the SIM card, and they found two telephone numbers that Randall called multiple times. But we can't trace them. They're probably other burners. Whoever he was working for is fucking smart."

"And you'll let me know if you find anything?"

"Bet your ass we will. But at the moment, it's just a dead end," she said disgustedly.

"And to make matters worse, the press is having a field day with our investigation," Nottingdale said. "One screaming headline after another. *No Leads on Child Sex Murders Case. Task*

Force Floundering. And the mayor is now breathing up our asses, demanding an arrest."

"What about Randall Newton? Maybe he'll give us a lead when he comes out of his stupor?" Ethan said.

"Or maybe he plead Fifth," Alvarez said, looking around the table. "We just sucking wind at the moment. Sucking goddamn wind."

*****

Ethan opened the door to his apartment and entered the foyer. It was quiet, depressing, haunting. He flipped on the light, and Holly scampered out of Luke's bedroom, rubbing against his leg, her tail wagging. He knelt, scratched her under the chin.

"How about some dinner and a long walk," he said soothingly. "That'll make you feel better. Won't it, girl?"

In the kitchen, he filled her bowl with kibble and peered around at the chaos. Dirty dishes were piled in the sink, pots and pans on the stove, leftover food on the counters. Sarah had been gone for less than a week, and he'd let the apartment go to hell.

Like the rest of his life.

He waited for Holly to finish eating then led her to the front door, attached her leash, and headed to the street. The sky was clear, the moon full, casting long shadows over the mostly empty sidewalks. Ethan could see his breath as he proceeded down Fifth Avenue and zipped his parka up to his chin. He passed a handful of dog walkers, waved hello, and proceeded to Eighty-Sixth Street, where he waited for the light to turn green, lost in his grief about Sarah and Luke, then crossed over to the Neue Gallery on the southeast corner and headed back uptown. When he got to Eighty-Eighth Street, his iPhone pinged. *Sarah. It's gotta be my Sarah,* he thought, barely able to contain his excitement. Fumbling for his cell, his fingers numb from the cold, he checked the LCD screen and his heart sank.

"Paul, I wasn't expecting to hear from you again tonight."

"Get used to it, Ethan," he said gruffly. "I'm gonna check in with you every night." There was a momentary awkwardness. "I talked with Julie late this afternoon. She said the shoot went well."

"Got the bust and the aftermath and Julie did a nice job shot-gunning interviews with both ADA Highland and Detective Alvarez."

"Nothing from Newton?"

"Unable to talk."

"Do they think he's the killer?"

"No," Ethan said. "But we think he knows who is."

"How much longer do we wait for an arrest?"

"Come on, Paul, you know I can't answer that."

"Don't bullshit me, Ethan. You're already on thin ice.

"I just need more time."

"I can't wait much longer." A long pause. "Why's the budget so fucking expensive."

"Do you want the long or short answer."

"Very funny. Lay it out in an e-mail then we'll talk." Another long pause. "And when is Julie interviewing Newton?"

"As soon as the ADA gives me the okay."

"That's not an answer."

"Best I can do at the moment, Paul."

"Well, I'm gonna pull the plug in the next day or two, so help me God, if you don't give me concrete answers and something, anything, to make this into a good story that I'll air," he said contemptuously. "Are you drinking?"

"Is that the real reason you called, Paul? "

"Are you sober, Ethan?"

"Yes."

"Good. That's what Julie said. Keep me posted."

CHAPTER 30

When Ethan arrived back at his building, still fuming over his phone call with Paul, he waved to Winston the Doorman who jumped out of his seat and followed him to the elevator bank.

"Mr. Benson, did you run into your friend?"

"I didn't see anyone."

"He was just here looking for you."

"Who was it?" Ethan said, confused.

"Small man with a thin mustache. I told him you were walking your dog, probably on Fifth Avenue. I assumed he went out to find you."

"Did he say what he wanted?"

"No. But he left you a package. I've got it at the front desk. Give me a second."

Winston rummaged through a pile of boxes and came back with a thick, nine-by-twelve manila envelope.

Ethan looked at the package. His name was hand-printed in bold letters on the front, the flap sealing the contents neatly scotch-taped. He turned it over several times, but there were no other markings—no name, no return address, no telephone number.

Ethan nodded thank you to Winston and rode the elevator up to his floor. After opening his door, he hastily pulled off his hat, gloves, and parka, and slipped off Holly's leash. She ran down the center hallway and into Luke's bedroom. God, she missed him as much as Ethan did. Grabbing his briefcase off a chair in the foyer where he'd left it, he headed straight to his study and sat down at his desk, making space for the manila envelope. Then he reached for a bottle of Johnny Walker Black, poured a finger into a dirty glass, and drank it all at once.

"Fuck you, Paul," he said out loud. "You can't tell me what to do when I'm off the clock." Then he poured another glass, searched for scissors in the top drawer of his desk, and picked up the envelope.

Carefully, he slit open the top and pulled out the contents. It was a stack of color photos of the Dry Dock Playground shot during the last Child Sex Murder with a hand-scribbled note affixed to the top. He adjusted the desk lamp, throwing more light on the photos, and read the note:

> *You don't know me, Mr. Benson, but I certainly know you from all the TV coverage of the murders. Let's just say I'm an observer who was wide-awake the night that poor little girl, the fourth victim of the maniac, was murdered and dumped in my lovely little playground. Not sure these will help, but I refused to cooperate with the police when they knocked on my door because they beat on poor souls like me, and thought you, the big television producer, might find these enlightening. Now don't try to track me down, because I ain't gonna talk to you and don't plan to give you anything else. Maybe these photos will help you catch your killer.*

Who the hell was this guy? Should he try to find him even though he was warned to stay away? Ethan downed his Scotch, dismissed his musings for the moment, and focused on the images, spreading them out on his desk. There were nine in total, all shot with a telephoto lens. Ethan peered from one to another, pausing briefly, until he spotted a medium shot of the murdered girl. He picked up the photo: Jane Doe number four, propped on the shoulder of a small, slightly built man whose face was turned away from the camera. He could see the slashes up and down her arms, the cigarette burns on her breasts, and the thin red line around her neck made by the garrote. He placed the photo on his desk and reached for the bottle of Scotch then stopped. *No more. Not tonight. I can't let myself get wasted.*

Then he took three quick puffs on his cigarette, stubbed it out in an ashtray, and studied the rest of the photos, until he came to one where the small man was facing the camera. It was slightly out of focus, but Ethan could make out his features. An Asian with a shiny bald head and tattoos all over his face and neck. He flipped open his briefcase and grabbed the photos Lloyd had shot in Chinatown and found the one of the two men dragging Randall Newton out of the town house. Then he looked back. It was the same small, wiry man who had dumped Newton unceremoniously on the sidewalk with Bingwen Ho.

Shit.

He had just found the killer.

And he was definitely connected to Randall Newton.

As he was about to text Mindy and David with the news, he saw the picture of a run-down yellow Ford Econoline Van. The license plate was visible in the lower left-hand corner: *66 LPE 490.* Maybe he could track down the killer's name. He checked the time. 1:00 a.m. Was it too late to call Lloyd? Fuck it. He'd wake him up if Lloyd was asleep. He punched in his cell number and waited. Lloyd answered after the fourth ring, sleepy.

"It's me."

"What the fuck time is it?"

"Late. Look, I got a license plate number—*66 LPE 490*—from a yellow van." He told Lloyd about the images dropped off by the mystery man. "May be the killer's. Can you run it for me."

"Give me fifteen minutes."

Ethan hung up and reached for the bottle of Black Label. *No more. No more. NO MORE.* He started pacing, the minutes ticking by. Fifteen. Thirty. Forty five. Then his iPhone buzzed.

"Name on the registration is Quay Chaoxiang. 27 Regatta Place in Douglaston, Queens. Ritzy neighborhood on the north shore of Long Island. This our guy?"

"Maybe."

"Anything else you want me to check?"

"Later."

He hung up and reached into his briefcase, pulling out the two computer printouts of medical supply companies—the one he was given by Detective Alvarez and the one he'd pilfered from Randall Newton's library. He checked the time. 2:00 a.m. He'd give himself one hour and then call it a night. He needed at least a few hours of sleep or his hangover would be a bitch in the morning.

Then he thumbed through the pages of Gloria Alvarez's printout.

Thousands upon thousands of names.

Then he checked Randall Newton's copy.

It looked the same.

Lighting a cigarette, he decided he needed coffee and headed to the kitchen, Holly scooting out of Luke's bedroom and following him. *At least you still love me,* he thought. Turning on the coffeemaker, he made a pot then walked back to his desk, Holly still on his heels. Then he glanced at the first few pages of Randall Newton's printout, trying to get a feel for the information. The names were organized in alphabetical order by the buyer and provided information on the medical equipment purchased—from MRI scanners to scalpels, forcipes, CPAP supplies, and home oxygen equipment—plus the cost, manner of payment, telephone number, and occasionally the address. Now he understood why Gloria Alvarez had insisted it was like looking for a needle in a haystack. He flipped down to the Qs and found another handwritten note in the right-hand margin. *His name is plain as day in the middle of the page. The task force is going to figure out who's been murdering the girls.*

So this was why Newton didn't want Gloria Alvarez to assign detectives to canvas the medical supply houses for the names of their customers. He was worried they'd get too close to the killer.

He poured another cup of coffee.

Lit another cigarette.

And dove in.

Running a ruler down the first page of *Q*s.

Qadir. Qamar. Qaqish. Qazim. Qiang. Qiao. Qin. Qing. Quaal.

And then he spotted the killer.

Quay Chaoxiang.

Excitement rippled through his body as he double-checked the information Lloyd had just given him on the yellow van's registration. Same name at the same address. And he had purchased a dozen Karl Storz No. 6 surgical knives, the same knives the task force had found at both murder scenes, at *Murray's Medical Equipment* on Canal Street in March of last year, after the first killing but long before the second, third, and fourth bodies were dumped. Ethan could now link Quay Chaoxiang to physical evidence and had proof that ADA Randall Newton was obstructing the task force investigation and passing inside information to somebody he called the big boss. Grabbing his iPad, he quickly jotted a list of questions. Who the hell was the *big boss*, and how was he or she connected to Newton and the killer? Why were they murdering little girls? Was there a conspiracy? A cover-up? And was somebody else, maybe the police commissioner, privy to all this information?

Exhausted, he shut down his computer and made his way to the bedroom, kicked off his shoes and got undressed, then climbed under the covers. Then he thought about Sarah and Luke, and a profound loneliness poured through his soul. He grabbed his iPhone and texted her: "Good night, babe. I love you. I love Luke. And miss the two of you terribly. Please call me. Please come home. Please." Then he closed his eyes and listened to the seconds tick by, sleep elusive, a faraway dream.

CHAPTER 31

The sun was just peaking over the horizon, the moon setting over Central Park, the sky still speckled with a handful of stars fading in the morning light when Ethan unlocked his office door and dropped his briefcase on the couch. He had tossed and turned for two hours, never falling asleep, not for a single moment, then climbed out of bed, shaved and showered, walked and fed Holly, and cabbed to work. Ironically, he felt refreshed, no fatigue, no hangover from all the Scotch he'd consumed while working in his study, his head clear, his mind razor-sharp. Sipping a black coffee he'd purchased at Starbucks, he booted up his desktop computer and pulled the folder with the clandestine photos from his briefcase.

Then an e-mail landed in his mailbox.

And a feeling of dread overwhelmed him.

He stared at the message. Sarah, finally, Sarah. A response to the e-mail he'd zipped off in the middle of the night. Why hadn't she just called as he'd asked? Timorously, he read the missive:

> *Ethan, I know I should tell you this on the telephone, but I couldn't bear to talk to you. My emotions are raw, and I couldn't face another angry argument.*
>
> *I've just made the hardest decision of my life after much soul-searching. You are my*

best friend, my lover, and our years of happiness together will always fill my heart. Please try to understand that I made this decision based on what I felt was the right thing to do, not just for me and Luke, but also for you. I can't come home, not yet. We need more time apart to sort out our lives. We have lived for too many years in the shadow of our baby girl's death. It's been hard for both of us, impossible to get over, partly because you've been unable to face the reality of what happened and have drowned your feelings and sorrows in that damn bottle of Scotch. I decided, by the way, it was time to tell Luke, so I did, and all he said was, "That's terrible, Mom. It must've made you and Daddy very sad," and then he ran off to play in Anita's backyard as if I'd told him nothing but a fairy tale. So you don't need to worry anymore about how Luke will take the news. He knows about the baby, and he's fine.

Now the hard part. I've taken an apartment here in Cleveland not too far from Anita and have already enrolled Luke in the local public school. He was upset when I told him we weren't going home and started to cry. So I tried to explain that you and I are having problems, that we still love each other and are still his mommy and daddy and always will be, but that we need to live apart for a while while we try to sort out our feelings for each other. I can imagine you are quite upset reading this, and believe me, I am upset too. But this is my decision, the only

> *way I can save myself from the heartache I've experienced the past few years watching you pull away from me, unable to reach you, unable to cope with your drinking. PLEASE, Ethan, don't hate me. This is the right decision for both of us. We've tried very hard to work through our problems, but it just hasn't happened. Maybe over time we can find each other again. That is my hope. That is what I am praying for.*
>
> *I promise to call you as soon as I feel strong enough, but that may take a couple of weeks. PLEASE, Ethan, don't stop going to Dr. Schwartz. You need to talk to him. It's the only way you're going to get better. And don't forget about Luke. You're his father, and he needs you, and maybe now that we're separated, you'll make the time to call and talk to him. I love you, Ethan. Don't stop loving us. Sarah.*

A single tear rolled down Ethan's cheek as he looked out over Central Park, the sun now a fireball over the city, his world crashing around him. He hit Reply on his computer and tried to compose a response, but then froze.

Too late.

Sarah's gone.

He'd already lost her.

When his iPhone rang, his voice was hollow, distant, shallow. "Yes."

"Ethan, it's Patricia Highland. Hope I didn't wake you?"

"I'm already in the office, Patricia."

"Good. We've been sweating Randall Newton in his hospital room. He won't talk. Not to us. And believe me we've tried. He's got a lawyer. A guy named Morris Allworth. Very high-powered. Represents a lot of big-time white-collar criminals. Guy's a prick. Allworth's been trying to cut a deal with us all night. He wants us to drop any murder charges against Newton. Then maybe he'll talk."

"So cut the deal, Patricia," Ethan said, wondering where this was headed.

"It's not as simple as that."

"Explain."

"Newton will only talk to you, Ethan. In fact, he's insisting it's you. He says he wants to make sure the public hears his side of the story, and he doesn't trust us, me, to give him a platform to do that. You wanna do your on-camera interview? Take a crack at him? You have the magic touch with dirtbags. Maybe you'll have better luck than we've had."

"When?"

"Right now, if that's possible."

"Can't do. It's gonna take me a couple of hours to pull together a production team."

"Yeah. Yeah. When can you be ready?"

Ethan checked the time. Eight thirty. The office wouldn't come to life for another half hour.

"Lunchtime at the earliest. Why don't we plan for one o'clock?" He hesitated, trying to decide if he should tell the ADA about the photos and the anonymous source, that he'd ID'd the killer, Quay Chaoxiang, the wiry Chinese man in Lloyd Howard's surveillance photos, then decided to wait until he'd discussed it with Paul. Maybe he could use it to his advantage when interviewing Newton. Get to the bigger picture. Find out about the *Tong*. Who the big boss was. Why they were murdering the girls. What they were hiding. "Does that work for you, Patricia?"

"I'll get you permission to shoot on the prison ward at Bellevue. Call me if anything changes."

Ethan hung up and immediately typed a short e-mail to Paul:

> *There's been a big break in the Child Sex Murders. I have a probable killer. We need to strategize the best way to proceed. Let's say, nine o'clock in my office.*

Fifteen seconds later, a response zinged into his mailbox:

> *About time. See you at nine sharp.*

*****

Paul Lang strode into Ethan's office, poured a cup of coffee from a service James had prepared for the meeting, and sat at the small conference room table across from him. He slid the stack of photos across the desk to his executive producer.

"What am I looking at?"

"The killer."

He picked up the top photo "Where did the task force get this?"

"They didn't. I did." He spread the rest of the photos across the table and stared at Paul. "They were delivered to my apartment building around midnight. I have no idea by whom. He didn't leave his calling card."

"And the task force agrees with you?"

Ethan hesitated for a split second, "They don't know yet."

"Why not?"

Ethan laid his plan out.

"I'm not sure I like this," Paul said, tapping his fingers on the table. "Where's James?"

"Can you join us, James?" Ethan said, yelling across the room.

He came in and waited.

"Get me Jamie Summers on the phone," Paul barked. "As the keeper of standards and practices, I want to discuss what Ethan, here, is proposing before I decide whether it's a hare-brained idea or not. Do it."

James grabbed the telephone on the table and dialed Summers's extension. "Please hold for Paul Lang," he said, handing the phone to his uncle.

"Sit, James, you may learn something," Paul said gruffly as he waited for Summers to come on the line. "I've got a policy question for you, Jamie." He then laid out in detail everything Ethan had just told him. "You're sure we're not liable for withholding evidence from the District Attorney's Office?" He listened, furrowing his brow. "Yes, we plan to tell them in a couple of hours." Silence. "And we'll pass on all the evidence Ethan has collected." Paul listened and concluded the call. "Okay, I'll go over the risks with him."

Paul hissed through his nose.

"I'm gonna roll the dice on this, Ethan. Do the interview with Randall Newton. The risk we face is if another little girl is murdered by this guy you've fingered as the killer. The show could face obstruction of justice charges, or worse, accessory to murder charges for not telling the authorities about Quay Chaoxiang and giving the task force the opportunity to arrest him. Our brothers in the press, especially that damn reporter, Winston Peabody at our affiliate, will have a field day with you and *The Weekly Reporter.* I'm willing to take the risk, and so is Jamie Summers, since you think withholding the information will help you determine if there's a bigger conspiracy and a cover-up behind the murders. But you can't hold the evidence one second beyond the interview with Randall Newton."

"I won't."

"You understand the risks?"

"There are none, Paul," Ethan said calmly.

"What the hell does that mean?"

"I've already taken care of Quay Chaoxiang. I dispatched Mindy and Lloyd Howard to his home in Douglaston, Queens, before I left for work this morning. Quay's there. His yellow van, the same one in the photo, is parked in the driveway. Lloyd's watching his house from his surveillance van, shooting pictures of everything. And if he leaves, I'll know, because Lloyd's gonna tail him everywhere he goes and keep me posted on his movements."

"And you'll alert ADA Highland if that happens?"

"Yes."

Paul stood and adjusted his wire-rim glasses. "You've thought of everything, haven't you, Ethan? You sober?"

"That again?"

"Are you?"

"Yes, for Christ's sake. Anything else?"

"Call Julie and tell her everything we just discussed. Make sure she understands the risks and that Jamie Summers has been consulted and given us the go-ahead. Then call your team and make the interview happen."

Paul disappeared down the red hallway.

"James, call David. I want him in my office in fifteen minutes." Then he picked up the phone and called Julie Piedmont.

*****

It was almost twelve o'clock, and Ethan sat poised in the back seat of a limousine next to Julie as it sped down the FDR Drive to Bellevue Hospital on Twenty-Sixth Street and First Avenue. He had dispatched David and his two crews to begin the arduous setup in Randall Newton's hospital room with explicit instructions on how to light and place the cameras, while he spent the morning briefing Julie and writing questions. At first, she had balked at doing the interview, insisting it would force her to cancel a shoot with one of her other producers that had been scheduled for weeks. But once Ethan explained that he'd ID'd the killer and could prove his connection to Newton, Julie had acquiesced, called her assistant, and canceled her entire day's schedule. Now they were huddled together, tweaking the questions for a full-blown three-camera interview with ADA Newton.

"You sure he's gonna talk to us?"

"All we can do is try. Show him the pictures of Quay Chaoxiang and tell him we know that he helped kill the girls with him."

"What if he stonewalls—like he's stonewalling the task force?"

"Then hammer him until he breaks down and talks."

They sat in silence the rest of the trip, Julie continuing to prep for the interview, Ethan texting back and forth with Lloyd and Mindy, Quay Chaoxiang's yellow van sitting in his driveway, the killer still holed up in his house. Then the limousine arrived at the sprawling Bellevue Hospital complex.

Ethan shot her an anxious look.

"For heaven's sake, Ethan, I've virtually memorized the questions. Stop sweating it."

They pushed through a revolving door and went into the grand three-story lobby. The building was less than a decade old with six floors of offices and hospital beds, an all-glass facade, and a lattice of decorative but functional steel beams crisscrossing the front. A series of marble hallways branched from the lobby linking a handful of separate buildings, some dating back to the nineteenth century.

Gloria Alvarez was waiting for them.

"This way," she said, and they walked toward the prison psych ward.

Two city policemen dressed in blue and holding nightsticks and long guns stood in front of a heavy steel door. Gloria

Alvarez flashed her gold shield. They knew to expect her. One of the cops keyed in a code, opening the doors leading into the interior of the prison hospital. Then they followed the detective through a maze of short corridors, stopping at a second security checkpoint, and down an even dingier hallway with yellowing linoleum floors and an x-ray machine where two correction officers ordered them to empty their pockets; place their shoes, briefcases, and shoulder bags on a conveyor belt; and walk through. They continued, passing a phalanx of heavily armed prison guards positioned in front of a series of closed doors, listening to inmates yell and scream.

"Some of these prisoners are downright *feura de tu mente*," Alvarez said, circling the air with her finger. "Some stoned on drugs like our boy, *Newton*, others recovering from beatings, knifings, gunshot wounds—you name, we got it in this fuckin' place. That's why building is armed fortress, *no*? You gotta always be on guard." She pushed an elevator button. "Randall's up on fifth floor."

They rode up the rickety elevator and exited at the psych ward, Alvarez leading them past more closed doors, doctors and nurses running in and out, treating one hysterical inmate after another. Ethan's soundwoman, Zoe Whitfield, was tinkering with a mixing board outside the last door at the end of the hall, flanked by Detectives Kathy Bowman and Victor Nottingdale.

"That's Newton's room?" he said, turning to Alvarez.

"Room 522. Biggest and quietest on ward. Best we could do on short notice," she said ironically. "Of course, we had no idea you'd be turning room into TV studio, *si*?"

Ethan smiled at her subtle attempt at humor then turned to David who was sitting in front of a bank of monitors. "How do the cameras look?"

"Getting there," David said, waving hello to Julie. "Herb and Bobby are tweaking the lights."

"Is there enough space?"

"Barely, but the guys are pros. It's gonna look great when they're done."

"Can we set up an extra digital camera to capture Julie passing Newton the photos?" Ethan said, whispering.

"Afraid not. There's no place to jam in a fourth camera."

"So how we gonna make the shot?"

"Leave it to Herb."

Satisfied, Ethan turned to Detective Alvarez. "I want to introduce Julie to Randall Newton. Can we go in?"

"His fuckin' lawyer, Morris Allworth, is still in there. Good luck. He's piece of work."

CHAPTER 32

The beautiful nurse with blue eyes and long blond hair fixed in a bun, wearing a white dress, white shoes, and white stockings, got off the elevator on the fifth floor, pushing a cart filled with medicine. Her name was Alice Walters, and her prison identification tag was draped around her neck as she rolled down the hall and stopped at room 500, the first inmate on her afternoon rounds, a heroin addict arrested for dealing to schoolchildren in East Harlem. After checking his vital signs—noting his blood pressure, heart rate, and oxygen levels—she pulled out a syringe, filled it, and injected a clear liquid into his IV line, administering a dose of methadone. Noting the time of the injection on a clipboard attached to the foot of the bed, she straightened his bedding, made sure he was sleeping soundly from the tranquilizers the doctor had also prescribed to manage his anger, then slipped out of the room, punched her ID code into a keypad, registering she'd been into room 500 on schedule, then walked across the hall to her next stop, room 501, where she showed her ID to a correction officer and began the same routine all over again.

*****

Ethan entered Randall Newton's room and walked into a makeshift television studio. It was sparsely decorated and threadbare—the walls a dull, flat yellow, the floor a pasty green linoleum. Herb Glickstein and Bobby Raffalo had set up a traditional one-on-one interview with three Sony HD cameras mounted on tripods—the A-camera shooting Randall Newton, the B-camera focused on Julie Piedmont, and the C-camera making a wide shot. There were half a dozen Kino Flo lights filling the room with a soft, warm glow, the one small, barred window near the ceiling covered with a layer of gray translucent plastic to filter the sunshine so it wouldn't interfere with the indoor lighting on the set.

Newton was perched in a hospital bed elevated so he was sitting upright. There were tubes and wires running out of his arms and legs and attached to equipment measuring his heart rate, blood pressure, and brain waves—squiggly red and green lines dancing across monitors, alerting doctors to any changes in his vital signs. An IV was taped to his wrist, a clear liquid dripping into his arm, medication for his broken nose and the lacerations on his face. He was chained to steel rails on either side of his bed, and his nose was covered in a thick white bandage, hiding the damage and the deep purple bruises under his eyes.

Patricia Highland stood with Allworth, a small, heavyset man—no more than five feet tall—who was dressed in a tailor-made blue pin-striped suit, a heavily starched white shirt, polished black Gucci loafers, and a blue-and-white striped tie.

"Randall's attorney, Morris Allworth," the ADA said to Ethan.

"My pleasure," Ethan said agreeably.

Allworth shook Ethan's hand and turned to Julie Piedmont. "I watch you on *The Weekly Reporter* every week. Never miss a show." He pivoted back to Ethan. "I've changed my mind, Mr. Benson. I don't like the terms of the agreement and advised my client not to talk to you or ADA Highland. So I'm afraid you're wasting your time."

"I've made my best offer, Mr. Allworth," Patricia Highland said, clearly frustrated. "Take it or leave it."

"Then there's no television interview."

"Does your client agree with you?" Ethan asked calmly.

Randall Newton nodded from his hospital bed, licking his chafed lips.

"And there's no wiggle room," Ethan said, looking for a way to reopen the negotiations. "Maybe setting some ground rules to protect your client's rights during the interview?"

"I've been working on that all morning," the ADA said. "We were hoping to convince Mr. Allworth that Randall would be helping himself if he turned evidence and answered our questions. But we're going around in circles."

"What if you were to drop the murder charge and change it to manslaughter or accessory to murder or obstruction of justice," Julie Piedmont said, turning to Highland, "and offer Mr. Newton partial immunity from prosecution."

"Full immunity," Allworth said. "That's the only deal we'll accept."

"No can do," Highland said emphatically. "I've already told you that's not gonna happen."

Ethan stared at both attorneys, feeling the interview slipping away, then said to ADA Highland. "What if you drop all the charges and offer Randall witness protection if he turns evidence and gives us the name of the killer and the people he's working for."

"A new name, a new identity, a new life, nothing less," Morris Allworth insisted.

"Maybe I can work with that," Highland said.

They all turned to Newton who was listening intently. "Can I keep my law license?" he said, his voice strong, in spite of the residual effects of the opium and the injuries to his face."

"That I can't promise, Randall. You know how the system works. A legal review board is going to make that decision."

"So do we have a deal?" Ethan said hopefully.

"Clear the room and let me talk to my client," Allworth said, puffing up his chest. "I need a few minutes in private to discuss your proposal."

*****

The nurse dressed in all white continued to make her rounds, stopping in rooms 502, 503, and then 504, chatting amiably with the prison guards and inmates as she charted their vital signs and injected their medications into IV lines. When she finished in room 504, she slipped through the door, punched her ID code into the security keypad, and was met by frantic yelling and screaming from her next patient in 505—a crack addict who had stolen an old lady's purse and beaten her within inches of death. Alice Walters leaned up against the wall and chatted with another guard and waited patiently as a doctor accompanied by two nurses streaked from the security checkpoint at the end of the hall and into room 505, immediately strapping more restraints on the unruly inmate screaming for a fix to ameliorate the demons in his head. One minute. Two minutes. Three minutes. The nurses still struggling to control their patient, the doctor grabbing a syringe off a tray table, and injecting the addict with a strong dose of Thorazine.

Alice Walters, still standing and chatting, quickly glanced at the television crew hovering anxiously outside ADA Randall Newton's door. She checked the time and waited for the chaos across the hall to subside, peeking at the television crew then her wristwatch then back to the television crew.

She saw a bright light snap on, then another.

Time was running out.

She had to hurry.

*****

Ethan paced in the hallway. *What the fuck's taking so long. This is a no-brainer. He's been offered a sweet deal. Why doesn't he just take it?* He took a calming breath, peered over David's shoulder at the three camera shots, relieved they were ready to go, then checked his iPhone. Mindy. He'd missed a call from Mindy. Hiking a short distance down the hall out of earshot from ADA Highland, he punched in her number.

"Is he still there?"

"Yup," Mindy said, whispering. "Quay went out to his van a little while ago, opened the back door, and rummaged around inside. Lloyd had a clean shot on his Nikon and took a bunch of still pictures. Jeez, Ethan, the guy's got a virtual operating room in that stinking truck."

"You gotta be kidding."

"Looks like a house of horrors—a stainless steel table, fancy lights, medical equipment, grappling hooks, and lots of knives and scalpels."

"Think that's where he kills the girls?"

"Maybe. And there's one more thing. Lloyd made a shot of a Karl Storz surgical blade. Not the greatest, but you can clearly read the label. It's a No. 6."

"*Dynamite*!" Ethan yelled, before lowering his voice. "More proof Quay's our guy. E-mail me the JPEGs. I wanna take a look, maybe show them to Newton, along with the other photos."

"Done."

Ethan waited for the e-mail to ping into his iPhone, scanned through the images, then said, "What's Quay doing now?"

"We thought he was leaving after he closed up the van. He climbed into the driver's seat, started the engine, and talked on what looked like a burner for about ten minutes, before turning off the engine and going back into his house. He's been in there ever since."

"Lloyd got pictures of that too?"

"Snapping away. Hasn't missed a thing."

"Good. Good," Ethan said as Morris Allworth walked out of Newton's room. "Gotta go, Mindy. Trying to work through a sticky problem with Newton's attorney. Keep me posted on Quay. I wanna know everything, and I mean everything he does."

He disconnected without waiting for a response, was momentarily startled by the commotion at the far end of the hall—an inmate screaming, a doctor running in and out of a room, a correction officer holding a gun, and a nurse waiting with a cartful of medicine—then made a beeline over to Allworth.

"Decision?"

"He'll do the interview as soon as we have a written guarantee from the district attorney."

"Thought you might want that," ADA Highland said, shooting him an e-mail. "Already talked to DA Cunningham, and he's put our deal on paper. Take a moment and read it. We should be good to go."

"Give me a second," Allworth said, walking back into Newton's room, his eyes glued to his iPhone.

Ethan waited patiently, occasionally glancing up the hallway, the yelling and screaming now over, the nurse pushing the cart, punching a keypad, and walking into another inmate's room.

Fifteen minutes slipped by.

Still no green light from Newton.

"What are they doing in there?" Julie said forcefully. "Writing a counterproposal for the ADA?"

"Let's hope not. This could take all afternoon."

Another five minutes, then Morris Allworth reappeared in the doorway. "My client will do the interview if I can sit by his side and give him advice. He also wants a guarantee that if I don't like a line of questioning, I can stop the interview without forfeiting our agreement. That's nonnegotiable."

They turned to ADA Highland. "Nope. If you can't guarantee that Randall will answer all of our questions, then we don't have a deal."

"Then there's no interview."

"Take the fucking deal, Morris," Newton said limply from his hospital bed. "I can't go to jail. It'll be the end of me."

*****

Alice Walters exited room 520, ten feet from Randall Newton's room, careful not to draw attention as she punched her security code into the keypad, smiled at the correction officer in the hallway, checked her medication list, and rolled her cart down to her next patient. Pausing just outside room 521, she noted the exchange between Benson and the attorneys and watched as the two camera crews poured into Newton's room to put the finishing touches on the makeshift studio they'd spent all morning designing, then listened as Benson told his anchorwoman they were about to begin the interview.

Just enough time to finish up with the inmate ahead of Newton.

She pushed into room 521.

And slipped a special vial of medicine out of her pocket and onto her cart.

CHAPTER 33

David was sitting in front of a monitor, cutting back and forth between the three shots with a toggle switch as Ethan leaned over his shoulder.

"Let me see Newton."

David clicked the shot into the monitor.

"Give me your headset," Ethan said. "Herb, you got a kick in your lens."

"Nothing I can do about it. Can't move the light stand and eliminate the problem without creating a whole new set of problems."

"Don't worry about it," Ethan said, turning back to David. "Show me Bobby's camera."

David quickly punched it in.

"Julie looks great. Now show me the wide shot."

David clicked the third camera into the monitor. It showed the entire room with all the equipment and was positioned perfectly to capture the photos as Julie passed them to Newton.

Good to go, Ethan thought as he handed David the headset. "Let me know if you see a problem." Then he rushed back into the room. "Nice job, guys." He turned to Julie Piedmont. "You ready?"

She fluffed her hair with her fingers as she checked a monitor on the floor in front of her and nodded.

"Ready."

"Quiet on the set and turn off all handheld devices," Ethan said, putting on his headset. "Roll the cameras."

"Speed on the A- and C-cameras," Herb said.

"Speed on the B-camera," Bobby said, scooting over to Julie, straightening an errant cable in his shot, and stepping back behind the camera.

"Got synch?"

"Locked and loaded," Herb said, peering through his lens at Randall Newton.

"All yours, Julie," Ethan said, nodding. "Whenever you're ready."

Julie glanced down at her questions then back to Newton. "Are your injuries very painful, Mr. Newton?"

Randall cleared his throat, shot a quick glance at his attorney, and said, "They ache a bit, but they're much better. The doctor says I'll be as good as new in a couple of weeks."

"Glad to hear it," Julie said, glancing at her questions. "Let's cut to the chase, Mr. Newton, did you murder the girls?"

"No."

"Were you involved in any way with the murder of the girls?"

"No. I swear. It wasn't me."

"What about Detective Henry Dinkus?" Julie said, leaning forward in her chair. "Did you murder him?"

"How could I? I was there. At the crime scene. Part of the investigation."

"So you had nothing to do with the Child Sex Murders or the killing of Detective Dinkus?"

"Well—"

"Did you plan them?" Julie said forcefully.

"My client has already answered that question," Allworth said, leaning into the shot. "Move on to something else."

"Our deal is he answer all our questions," ADA Highland said icily.

"That's all right, Patricia," Ethan said, leaning over and whispering into Julie's ear "Go to question 21."

She scanned down her questions and stared into Randall Newton's eyes. "You made a phone call just before you left Detective Dinkus's murder scene. Who did you call, Mr. Newton?"

"I can't remember," Newton said, his arm restraints rattling on the side of his bed.

Herb Glickstein zoomed into a tight shot of his face.

"You sure, Mr. Newton?"

"Positive."

"Maybe I can refresh your memory." She pulled a photo from a file on her lap. "My producer followed you after you left the crime scene, and yes, he took photos of you from a surveillance van." She waited as all the color drained from Newton's face. "You made a number of stops that night after you cleaned up at your apartment. The first was at the steakhouse, Smith and Wollensky. Do you remember that, Mr. Newton?"

There was stony silence in the room.

"Did you meet somebody for dinner there?"

More silence.

"Is that who you called from the crime scene?"

More silence.

"Still can't remember?" Julie said, raising an eyebrow. "Well, maybe this will help jog your memory." She held out the photo.

Morris Allworth plucked it from her hand, peered at it disbelievingly, then showed Randall Newton.

"Is that who you had dinner with?"

"Well—"

"Answer her question, Randall," ADA Highland said.

A bead of sweat dripped down his forehead. "Yes."

"Why did you have dinner that particular night, the night of Detective Dinkus's murder, with Police Commissioner James Langely."

Newton licked his lips and peered at his attorney before answering quietly, "To give him a bribe."

"A bribe? How much?"

"Ten thousand dollars."

"What for?"

"Do I have to answer that, Morris?"

"Yes."

Newton squirmed. "To get Langely to pull resources from the task force."

"To obstruct the investigation."

"Yes."

"To make sure the task force wouldn't find the child sex killer."

Newton nodded but didn't answer.

"Who told you to bribe the police commissioner?"

Newton shook his head, fear on his face.

Ethan pulled off his headset, walked over to Julie, flipped through the photos in her file, and handed her the one he wanted her to show Newton. Then he sat back down.

"I have another photo my producer wants you to look at." She passed the photo to Allworth who showed it to Newton. "The big guy who's dragging you out of that town house. Bingwen Ho. He's a member of the *Tong*. Did he give you the money to bribe Commissioner Langely?"

"Please," Newton said, "he'll kill me."

"Did he give you the money?"

Newton closed his eyes. "Yes."

Now ask him about the smaller man in the photo, Ethan thought. *Get him to finger Quay Chaoxiang.*

"And what about the other man, the guy with the piercings and the tattoos. Who is he?"

"I won't answer that."

"Who is he?" Julie Piedmont repeated, more forcefully.

"I can't—"

But before Newton could finish, a correction officer poked his head through the door, David Livingston on his heels. "I tried to stop them, Ethan, but they wouldn't listen."

"The duty nurse is here," the officer said belligerently. "She says the doctor is insisting Mr. Newton take his afternoon medicines."

"My client can't miss his meds," Morris Allworth said. "Please stop the cameras."

Frustrated, Ethan pulled off his headset, but motioned to his two cameramen to keep rolling.

The correction officer held open the door, and Alice Walters pushed her cart into the room.

"This won't take long," she said, checking Newton's blood pressure, heart rate, and oxygen levels, before walking back to her cart and double-checking a computer printout. "He's scheduled for a dose of *Naltrexone* to counter the effects of the opium." She filled a syringe from a vial, squirted to make sure there was no air bubble, then injected the medication into a port in Newton's IV line. "Another minute for a mild painkiller, and I'll be on my way."

She grabbed the vial she'd slipped onto the cart, checked the color of the yellow liquid in the light, emptied it into a syringe, then quickly shoved the vial into her pocket. After injecting the painkiller, she apologized again and left the room with the correction officer.

Ethan put on his headset, waited for Herb and Bobby to tweak their shots, then motioned to Julie. "Ready."

She checked her monitor, smoothed the makeup under her eyes, and stared down at her questions. "Where was I, Ethan?"

"The second man in the photo."

"Right. Right. Mr. Newton, who is—"

'Hold on a sec," David said over the headset. "The ADA is sweating profusely. We need to dab his forehead before we start the interview again."

Then Randall Newton began to convulse, violently, his eyes rolling into the back of his head, his jaw locking on his tongue, blood dripping down his chin.

"What the fuck's happening?" Ethan said, panicking, as all the medical equipment in the room began beeping.

Everybody froze as a doctor raced into the room with a team of nurses. "He's crashing. Get me a defibrillator. Go. Go. Go." The nurses flew into action, lifting Newton's body, now slumped on the bed, as the doctor listened for a heartbeat. "Adrenaline," he said. "We're losing him." He was handed a syringe, which he jammed into Newton's heart. "Where's the crash cart." Then he turned to Ethan. "What happened?"

"A nurse," Ethan said, rattled. "She gave him two shots of medication in his IV line."

"Find her."

"She's left the floor," the correction officer said. "I already checked the computer."

"What's her name?"

"Alice Walter and her ID number is 666773224."

"Anybody know her?" the doctor said, still listening for a heartbeat, the monitors no longer registering any sign of life. "See where she went. I need to talk to her right away." The correction officer hurried from the room as the defibrillator rolled in. "Everybody back." He placed two paddles on the sides of Newton's heart and sent a current of electricity through his body. He listened for a heartbeat. Nothing. Then he shocked him again. Still nothing. He handed the paddles back to a nurse. "Time of death 2:06 p.m. Did we find the duty nurse?"

"No record of an Alice Walters in the system," the correction officer said, standing in the doorway.

"So how the fuck did she get in here?" Ethan said, glancing at Herb who was circling the room, capturing the scene with his camera.

He zoomed into the doctor.

"This man may have been murdered," he said, pointing to the thick mucus dripping from Newton's mouth. "His lungs are flooded with body fluids. Need to find out what that nurse gave him."

Patricia Highland wheeled around to her detectives. "Alvarez, lock down the entire hospital complex. Bowman, call prison security and double the manpower on this floor. Nottingdale, take a team of correction officers and search the building. She can't have gotten too far. She was just here fifteen minutes ago. We gotta take her down before she gets away."

*****

Patricia Highland faced the cameras outside the entrance to Bellevue Hospital clearly upset, Julie and Ethan standing beside her, his two cameramen recording the mob of reporters who had assembled after word of the murder had leaked from the staff.

"I have a short statement," she said, raising her hand as she waited for the hubbub to die down. "A short while ago, Randall Newton, a member of my task force, who'd been arrested and taken into custody for questioning, was murdered in his hospital room. Ethan Benson—many of you know Mr. Benson from the other high-profile cases he's covered for Global Broadcasting—was present with a production crew, recording an on-camera interview with ADA Newton. There's currently a manhunt under way for the killer, and as soon as we have more information, there'll be another statement issued by my office."

A chorus of questions rang out all at once.

"Ms. Highland—"

"Ms. Highland—"

"How was he murdered?" a reporter said.

"Who is the killer?" another reporter yelled.

"Is there video?" Winston Peabody screamed, pushing to the front of the pack with his WGBS camera crew. "The public has the right to know what happened. Benson needs to make the video available to all of us."

"Please. No questions."

"But, Ms. Highland—

"No more. That's it for the moment," she said, turning and motioning to Ethan and Julie before leading them through the revolving doors, a half-dozen cops blocking the mob from stampeding into the hospital after them.

CHAPTER 34

The *Jiaofu* was lounging on his bed of cushions in his private chamber in the Hester Street town house, surrounded by his usual entourage of bodyguards and *yi-zhe* concubines, smoking his ceremonial opium pipe, blowing clouds of pungent smoke through his nose, giving everybody in the room a contact high. He was drifting in a dream world, his senses heightened, his body floating like a feather dancing in the wind. He snapped his fingers and pointed to the door. A *yi-zhe* clasped her hands together and bowed, then turned and exited the room, apparently understanding exactly what her master wanted. Five minutes later, she reemerged, stuffed a second pipe with the pasty brown substance and exchanged it for the one the *Jiaofu* had just finished. He nodded to the concubine and inhaled deeply.

"Where is Bingwen?" he said to nobody in particular.

"He just entered the building," one of his bodyguards said.

"Ah, right on time," the *Jiaofu* said, raising the opium pipe to his lips and inhaling deeply.

Two minutes later, the big man entered the room and waited for the big boss to acknowledge his presence.

"Well, Bingwen?" the *Jiaofu* said, taking one last pull and passing the opium pipe to the *yi-zhe.*

"Randall Newton is dead as you ordered."

"And Alice Walters, our assassin, left no trace of evidence that might compromise our position?"

"She used the false identity we provided her."

"The task force?"

"They're searching, but they will never find her. I took care of her as you wished."

"How?" the *Jiaofu* said, snapping his fingers for his opium pipe.

"I broke her neck like a twig."

"And the body?"

Bingwen broke into a broad smile. "Ground into hamburger in our warehouse at the Red Hook Container Terminal and fed her to the stray dogs that plague the port."

"Very good," the *Jiaofu* said impassively. "Taste?" He offered Bingwen the pipe.

Bingwen lowered his eyes and shook his head no.

"Cautious as always. You never let your guard down around me. Very smart, Bingwen. You know your place." The *Jiaofu* smoked quietly for a few minutes, inhaling deeply, blowing clouds of smoke up to the ceiling, his eyes heavy. "What about the sweet Maria?"

"Tonight."

"And she's no longer here?" He puffed more opium.

"We're holding her at the apartment on Avenue D as you ordered."

"And the Butcher?"

"The exchange will take place in the middle of the night." Bingwen raised his eyes. "May I speak freely?"

The *Jiaofu* nodded.

"We should instruct the Butcher to dispose the girl in a subtler way. The police and that producer, Ethan Benson, are getting too close to you, my master, and now that Randall Newton is dead, we have no inside access to the workings of the task force and no idea what they're planning."

He lowered his eyes.

The *Jiaofu* stood.

"The Butcher works in strange ways. He is *zahn shi,* a warrior, trained in the ancient art of death by Chinese masters. He's eliminated countless girls for me over the years, far more than the empty-headed police can possibly imagine, so we should not tamper with his methods, not at the moment. Besides, Bingwen, I doubt you want to tell him how to do his killing. You are no match for his special skills—even with your great size. Let the Butcher take care of Maria as he desires. That's my gift to him for his loyalty." The *Jiaofu* took one last drag on his opium pipe, handed it back to the *yi-zhe*, and walked toward the door. "One more thing, Bingwen."

Bingwen bowed.

"Call in a favor with our organization in Buenos Aires and make that fat priest disappear. We'll find a new contact somewhere else. Maybe it's time to offer only Asian girls. Maybe that would better fit the tastes of my clients."

"As you wish," Bingwen said as the *Jiaofu* opened the door and disappeared into another room in the inner sanctum of his town house.

*****

Ethan followed Patricia Highland through the bullpen on the tenth floor of One Hogan Place and into her office. He had sent Julie and David back to the broadcast center to brief Paul and show him the footage, Randall Newton's murder already making headlines, gripping the city in fear. The tabloids and the ratings-starved local news stations had pieced together the details of his murder from unnamed sources and were blasting the task force for allowing a killer to gain access to his hospital room and then to escape. Winston Peabody had done a particularly devastating story from outside Bellevue Hospital on the six o'clock news, not holding back any of the particulars and demanding, once again, that Ethan release the footage. Paul had downloaded Peabody's story and e-mailed it to Ethan along with a short message:

> *Already slammed the WGBS news director. She's going to rein in Peabody so he won't be*

> *a problem for you anymore. Excellent job, Ethan. Julie said she loves working with you. Keep me posted.*

Relieved, Ethan now had to face the music and break the news to ADA Highland that he'd fingered the Child Sex Murderer and withheld his name from the task force.

"Patricia, we need to talk."

She looked at him impatiently.

He snapped open his briefcase and reached for a file. "My plan was to drop these on Newton during the interview."

"These what?" she said as he handed her a stack of photos, her jaw dropping as she glanced at the top one.

"Go through all the pictures, and I'll explain."

Highland slowly studied each photo, spreading them in a row on her desk, her expression growing more and more incredulous. "Who shot these?"

"I don't know. They appeared at my apartment building late last night."

"Why the hell didn't you show me immediately?"

"I thought if we held them until the interview with Newton, maybe, we could've shocked him into revealing all the players in the murders."

She stared at the photo of the killer holding the dead girl. "It's the same guy, isn't it?"

Ethan grabbed another file, rifled through it, and slid one of Lloyd's surveillance photos across the desk."

Highland studied the image. "Definitely the same guy with Bingwen Ho dragging Randall across the sidewalk. Christ, that fucker was knee-deep in the murders and steering us away from this guy who you say is the killer."

"My theory about Newton? He was providing both those guys with information about the task force so they could stay one step ahead of you. Was there anybody else involved? We know from the interview that the police commissioner was taking bribes to interfere with your investigation."

"The district attorney is already preparing an arrest warrant. We'll have him in custody in the next hour or two."

"But we still don't know who was providing the bribe money," Ethan said.

"Got any ideas, Benson? You seem to have all the answers."

"Gut instinct. There's a full-blown conspiracy behind the child sex killings and a massive cover-up, probably orchestrated by somebody high up in the *Tong*."

"And that's why Randall Newton was murdered?"

"He knew too much."

"But who's calling the shots? Can't be those two guys in the photo. They look like hit men."

"Whoever owns Allied Shipping and that town house."

"Why?"

"Because they're hiding something illegal in there, something that's very lucrative."

ADA Highland picked up a picture of the town house and phoned the war room. "What's the status from the surveillance team at the Hester Street town house?" She listened patiently. "Okay. Don't knock it down. Anything changes, I wanna know immediately. And one more thing. Call Organized Crime and find out who runs the *Tong* in Chinatown and if they own the Allied Shipping Company." She hung up and turned to Ethan. "They're seeing some very rich people heading to that upscale spa on the second floor of that building."

"Lost Horizons?"

"That's the place."

"Think something illegal is going on there?" Ethan said.

"Maybe it's more than just a spa." She picked up the photo of the Chinese man carrying Jane Doe number four. "Who the fuck is this guy?"

"His name is Quay Chaoxiang."

"How do you know that?"

Ethan spent the next ten minutes explaining how he'd discovered the killer's name then said, "He lives in a mansion in Douglaston, Queens."

"I should lock you in jail and throw away the key for withholding all this information from the task force," she said harshly. "You've known who the killer is and his whereabouts for close to twenty-four hours and have said nothing. Nothing. NOTHING." She banged on her desk. "We could've nailed his sorry ass and put an end to all this madness. What if he kills another girl? That would be on you, Benson."

"Lloyd's watching him," Ethan said calmly.

"You're tailing him?" she said, exploding. "And you're first telling me?"

"Couldn't risk him slipping through our fingers."

Patricia stared, her expression morphing from anger to contempt. "I'll deal with you later." Then she picked up the telephone and called Detective Alvarez. "I'll fill you in on details, but fucking Benson has fingered the killer. Put together a SWAT team. We're gonna bring him in."

"Better hurry," Ethan said, reading a text on his iPhone. "Quay Chaoxiang is on the move. He just left his house in his yellow van."

*****

Bingwen Ho entered the apartment at 148 Avenue D. He lit a Cohiba, puffing away until he'd blown a thick cloud of smoke, and pulled a small flashlight from his coat pocket—too risky to flip on the lights, too many cops patrolling the neighborhood. He poked his head into every room, making sure he was alone, then dropped his overcoat on a chair, and headed down the hall, stopping at the last door on the left. *What shall I do while I wait for the Butcher?* he thought, salivating. *Ah, Maria, such a beautiful little thing, small hands, small feet, round eyes, milky brown skin. So much like a young Chinese maiden, yet so different, so exotic.* He puffed the Cohiba and slowly entered the room. She was lying where he'd left her, sprawled on the floor under the window, chained to a bed. The *Jiaofu* had dressed her as a young *yi-zhe* whore while he was fucking her—her face painted with white makeup, her eyes heavily shadowed, her lips smeared with deep red lipstick. Now her clothes were torn, her traditional Chinese wig missing, her cheeks smudged by tears, but to Bingwen, she still looked like a goddess.

He stripped down to his underwear, flexing the massive muscles in his arms and chest, and advanced ominously. *Might as well have one last go at her,* he thought, already excited, *before I give her to the Butcher.* As he started to pull off her dress, her eyes shot open, and she recoiled, scooting as far away as her chains would allow.

"Now, what do we have here? Our little flower has finally awakened."

Maria raked her fingernails down the side of his face, drawing blood. "Stay away from me, or I'll kill you," she said defiantly.

Bingwen backed away, flicked off the blood, and laughed. "She talks, and our little maiden has turned into a dragon." He hauled off and punched her, splitting her lower lip and opening a deep gash under her eye. "Do you want more of that, or will you be a good little girl and submit to my wishes?"

She spat in his face, a wad of phlegm dripping down his chin.

He hit her again, smashing her nose, blackening her eye, blood spraying the peeling paint on the wall.

"A tigress. I like that in a girl," he said, salivating with anticipation.

Maria continued clawing his face, kicking him with her tiny feet, ignoring her pain. "Kill me now, you monster, but don't touch me like that dirty old man and all those other demons. Kill me. Kill me. *Kill me.*"

She bit his arm as he climbed on top of her, his huge body covering her small frame like a blanket. Rearing up, he struck her—once, twice, three times—her face now misshapen as she gasped for air and passed out beneath him.

Then he laughed and entered her.

Pumping away.

Until he was sated and satisfied.

CHAPTER 35

The Butcher backed out of his driveway, his eyes darting up and down the quiet street at the million-dollar mansions, seeing nothing but manicured lawns, expensive cars, and pleasure boats sitting on trailers in every driveway. He was so different from his pretentious neighbors with his tattoos and face piercings and his penchant for death, but with the influx of Chinese and Korean immigrants in Douglaston and the surrounding villages, he had managed to lose himself in the flood of yellow faces. Quay Chaoxiang had gotten the call from Bingwen Ho earlier that evening and had spent the past two hours getting his tools ready for his next victim, the yellow van laid out with all his instruments of death—including a brand-new Karl Storz No. 6 surgical knife. He pulled to a stop for a red light at the corner of Regatta Place and Northern Boulevard, an east-west thoroughfare connecting Manhattan with Nassau and Suffolk Counties on Long Island, opened the glove compartment, and grabbed the leather notebook with the pictures of all his girls. He flipped to the last page and the new photo of Maria—number seventeen in his gallery of conquests—and maybe, the most beautiful of all with her long black hair, green eyes, and delicate brown skin.

He licked his lips.

And got an erection.

Oh, he could see the blood.

The smoke from the cigarette burns.

And the sparkle of life draining from her terrified eyes.

The light turned green, and he slipped the notebook back into the glove compartment, then made the right onto Northern Boulevard and drifted into traffic. It was midnight. Two hours from his rendezvous with fate. Three hours from the magic hour with its blood, pain, and death. A broad smile filled his face. He could taste Maria's essence. So precious. So beautiful. So luscious. And his, all his. He felt electrified, intoxicated with anticipation, and ready to fulfill his destiny.

*****

"He's heading west toward the city," Mindy said, hanging back a quarter of a mile and making the right turn onto Northern Boulevard as she followed. "Shit. I've lost him in the traffic. Do you have him in your shot?"

"Dead center," Lloyd said, adjusting the small camera perched on his shoulder. "The video looks eerie. With all the headlights and taillights, the color jets are going absolutely wild, flaring through the shot like bolts of lightning."

"Don't lose him. We're fucked if he gets away."

"Pull a little closer. His right blinker's flashing. I think he's gonna pull onto the Cross Island Parkway."

Mindy hit the gas pedal and weaved in and out of traffic like a Formula One driver, passing fast-food restaurants, an all-night carwash, and a driving range, before following the yellow van onto the parkway and closing the gap between them.

"Where the fuck's he going?" she said, stressed. "Not sure how long I can stay with him in all this goddamn traffic."

"He ain't gonna get away."

Mindy eased into the center lane, pulling closer to the yellow van now a few hundred feet ahead of her as she passed one large home after another overlooking Little Neck Bay, Alley Pond Park, and the entrance to the Throgs Neck Bridge connecting Queens with the Bronx. Traffic began to thin out, forcing Mindy to hang back a little farther.

"Call Ethan and put him on speakerphone," Lloyd said as he turned off his small video camera and grabbed his Nikon.

Mindy autodialed Ethan and pulled into the left lane. "Where is he? I don't see him, Lloyd. Shit. I've lost him."

"Steady. Steady. I got him." Click. Click. Click. "He's about ten cars ahead of you in the right lane. Get closer."

"Where the fuck are you?" Ethan's voice boomed over the speaker.

"Hello to you too," Lloyd said. "We're having a blast following Mr. Quay. He just turned onto the Whitestone Expressway."

"Mindy," Ethan said, "how're you doing?"

"Jeez, Ethan, how do you think? I'm having a blast following this asshole. Christ," she wailed as an eighteen-wheeler cut her off, forcing her to slow down.

"We ain't gonna lose him, Mindy. Chill out. He's just passing City Field and slowing down. Looks like he's getting ready to exit onto the Grand Central Parkway."

"I'm following," she said, turning on her blinker and exiting three car lengths behind him.

"Ethan, we need a plan," Lloyd said, continuing to snap pictures with his Nikon. "He's just approaching LaGuardia Airport, and unless I'm really off base, he'll be in the city soon."

"Hang tight, guys. I'll get right back to you."

*****

Ethan clicked off his iPhone and shoved it into his pants pocket. He was sitting between Patricia Highland and Julie Piedmont in the back seat of an unmarked Crown Victoria, Gloria Alvarez in the driver's seat, Kathy Bowman in the front passenger seat. He hadn't slept or eaten in almost two days, his skin clammy, his body wracked by fatigue, but his mind racing as they zeroed in on the killer. He turned to ADA Highland.

"Quay appears to be headed to New York," he said, glancing at a new text message from Lloyd. "He's on the Triborough Bridge, about to exit onto the FDR Drive." He leaned forward and tapped Gloria Alvarez on the shoulder. "You got teams in place, ready to move as soon as we figure out where he's going?"

"Many units on standby, Benson," she said. "Detective Nottingdale is in war room coordinating troops, dispatching manpower. We ain't gonna let this motherfucker get away." Alvarez glared at Ethan then turned to the ADA. "I don't get why we let Benson call shots. Let's set up roadblock on FDR and arrest asshole, *no*?"

"This is Unit 11. Over."

"Go ahead," Detective Bowman said on the police radio.

"The yellow van just passed One Hundred Tenth Street. He's still heading south. Should I get on the drive and follow him?"

"Affirmative, Unit 11," Bowman said. "All other units on this frequency hold your positions and no flashers, no sirens. Copy."

A half-dozen voices acknowledged in unison.

"This is crazy," Alvarez said, pressing the ADA. "We know where killer is. Let's nail son of a bitch before he slips away."

"No," the ADA said firmly. "Ethan's right. We gotta find out where he's going. See who he's meeting. Something's about to go down. I can feel it in my bones."

"And why is she here?" Alvarez said, pointing to Julie.

"Because I'm the anchorwoman on this story," Julie said obstinately. "Ethan's job is to do the producing, and my job is to do the on-air reporting. I *need* to be here. So get used to it."

Ethan was dumbstruck by Julie's reaction, her commitment to the story. So much different from Peter Sampson who'd want no part of a shoot as potentially dangerous as this one. The more he worked with her, the more he liked her.

Alvarez was about to protest when another call came in over the radio.

"Unit 14. Suspect just passed the United Nations. Over."

"Fall in behind him," Bowman said, "and use caution. Over."

"Will do."

"This is Nottingdale. I'm dispatching more units."

"Copy that," Detective Bowman said with authority. "All units continue to hold your position. Suspect still heading downtown."

Alvarez pressed ADA Highland. "Give me word, Patricia, and we grab motherfucker."

Highland hesitated. "Not yet." She tapped her fingers on her lap. "I hope we're not goin' down the path of no return, Ethan. But my instincts say you're right. Without you, we wouldn't have the killer in our crosshairs. So I'm gonna follow your lead." She slipped her gaze back to Detective Alvarez. "We wait until he gets to where he's goin'. Then we tighten the noose around his neck."

*****

The Butcher checked his rearview. Was that a cop car following him a quarter of a mile back? He picked up speed and glanced in his mirror once again. The cop was making no effort to match his speed and soon dropped out of sight behind a line of cars. *Not after me. No problem.* He hit his blinker and pulled into the right lane, making sure he was driving at the speed limit, then fantasized about Maria and how he was going to torture her mercilessly, before wrapping the rope around her neck and strangling her to death. He salivated as he envisioned her panicking, her eyes bulging, her tongue lolling from her mouth, her hands clutching at her throat as he pulled tighter and tighter, and she took her final breath, before passing away into nothingness.

Euphoria.

He licked his lips as he checked the time.

One thirty.

Right on schedule.

Grabbing his burner, he dialed Bingwen.

"Where are you?" he said, his voice hard.

"At the apartment," Bingwen said cautiously.

"And you have the girl?"

"She's waiting for you."

"Did you fuck her?"

"Ah—"

"Beat her?"

"Ah—"

"You know the rules, Bingwen. When the *Jiaofu* is finished with his whores, they belong to me, not you. You're just the delivery boy, the expeditor, the babysitter who takes care of the sweet, young delicacies until the Butcher is ready to get rid of them." He paused, listening to the fear pouring through the telephone. "I'll be there in a half hour, and so help me God, if my little Maria has one single hair out of place, I'll carve you a new asshole."

*****

Mindy was sitting a quarter of a mile behind the yellow van as it began to snow, her visibility deteriorating, her windshield wipers barely keeping up as the storm picked up steam. They drove past Bellevue Hospital, the sprawling complex of red brick buildings in Peter Cooper Village, and the exit to Twenty-Third Street. Mindy checked the van's taillights, making sure she hadn't lost him in the swirls of snowflakes, then checked her rearview.

"There's an army of police cars, maybe a third of a mile back. If I can see them, so can Quay. He's gonna figure out he's being tailed."

Lloyd lowered his Nikon and took a quick peek. "Get Ethan back on speaker."

Mindy dialed his cell phone.

"What's happening?" Ethan said.

"We got a problem," Lloyd said. "There are cop cars not too far behind us. You gotta call them off. If Quay spots them, we're fucked."

There was a short silence, then one by one, the patrol cars exited on Fourteenth Street.

"They're gone, Ethan," he said, raising his camera and snapping more pictures. Click. Click. Click. "What about the press? If they hear the radio chatter on their scanners, they'll show up wherever this guy takes us."

"We're on a special frequency they can't access. Where is he now?"

"You on speaker, Ethan?" Mindy said, pulling into the right lane.

"We're all listening—Julie, ADA Highland, and Detectives Alvarez and Bowman."

"What's Julie doing with you?" Mindy said, surprised. "Paul okayed you bringing her along?"

"I don't need Paul's permission," she said, snapping back.

"Enough. What's Quay doing, Mindy?"

"He's exiting the FDR at Houston Street," she said, flipping on her right blinker.

She could hear garbled arguing in the background as she exited the drive, then a voice blaring over the speaker, "All units, suspect is approaching Houston Street. Converge on the Lower East Side, and use extreme caution."

"Did you hear that, Mindy?" Ethan said.

"Loud and clear."

"You still following him?"

"A block behind."

"Lloyd still snapping pictures?"

"Haven't stopped," Lloyd said. Click. Click. Click. "We'll be there in fifteen minutes."

*****

The Butcher stopped for a red light on the corner of Houston and Avenue D, snowflakes now pounding his windshield, the wind whipping like a tornado. He peered into his rearview mirror and then at the traffic around him, confident nobody was following. He waited, steeling himself, until the light turned green, then made a quick right and drove north on Avenue D, his yellow van fishtailing as he hit the gas. Almost all the lights were turned off in the apartments lining both sides of the street, the usual hangouts were deserted, and the rows of parked cars were covered with a fresh layer of snow. He rechecked his rearview mirror. Still nobody behind him. Good. No nosy busybodies to get in the way. Then he glanced at the time, 2:00 a.m., and punched Bingwen's number into his burner.

"Five minutes. Bring her down to the street. And don't keep me waiting."

*****

"He's in Alphabet City, headed north on Avenue D," Mindy said evenly. "Where are you, Ethan?"

"Fourteenth Street. A block from Avenue D. We're running without headlights."

"Ditto," Mindy said.

Ethan spun around to Detective Bowman. "Where are your units?"

"Moving on Avenue D from different directions. We got him surrounded."

There was silence as Lloyd snapped another rapid series of pictures. "One block from the Dry Dock Playground, and there's a black Cadillac Escalade parked a little ways up and across the street from the park."

"Bingwen Ho?"

"Looks like it," Lloyd said, still taking pictures.

"Hold on, guys," Mindy said anxiously. "He just stopped in front of an apartment building—No. 148. That's where he's headed. The same building Randall Newton went the other night. I'm pulling over."

"I see him," Ethan said, tapping Alvarez on the shoulder. "Make the next left and park on the corner across from the fire hydrant."

Alvarez glided to a halt about a hundred feet from the yellow van. "Does he see us?"

"I don't think so," Ethan said. "He hasn't moved. He's sitting in the driver's seat and staring at the front door of the building."

Detective Bowman tapped her radio mic. "All units stand by and maintain radio silence. Suspect is at 148 Avenue D. Do not approach."

*****

The Butcher scanned the neighborhood. Nobody in sight. He got out of the van, oblivious to the cold and the snow, and walked around to the back, unlocking the door and climbing in. He scooted around his makeshift operating room, pulled the case of surgical tools from the storage space underneath the table, opened it, and placed it carefully on a built-in counter along the wall of the van. Then he ran his fingers lovingly over each instrument of torture, including a Karl Storz surgical knife, which he picked up and examined, and when he was sure he had everything he needed to maximize his pleasure, he hopped out of the van. Impatiently, he turned toward the front door of the apartment building.

What the fuck's taking him so long? he thought. *Two more minutes, and I'm outta here. Then Bingwen, the big fuck, can explain to the Jiaofu why the girl isn't dead. It'll be on him, not me.* He kicked the bumper in a fury, just before the door of the building swung open and Bingwen Ho walked through—a burlap bag slung over his shoulder.

The Butcher smiled.

Showtime.

*****

Ethan pulled his Canon out of his briefcase, never taking his eyes off Quay Chaoxiang, and touched Julie's shoulder.

"Hang low to the ground when we get outside and stay behind the car until after Quay is arrested. Then we'll move in and work you into the visuals. If the opportunity arises, ask him why he did it and who he's working for. This may be our only chance to talk to him."

"Got it."

"Sure you're up for this?"

"Bet your ass I am. Never been more excited in my life."

Ethan smiled wryly at her reaction, his eyes still glued to the small Chinese man standing alone in the snowstorm as still as a statue. "Somebody's coming out of the building," he said, pointing.

They all stared as a huge man descended the steps down to the sidewalk.

"Bingwen Ho," ADA Highland said calmly. "What's he got over his shoulder? Damn my eyes, can't make it out in the snow."

"A sack," Ethan said, raising the camera and starting to roll. "There's somebody inside." He quickly glanced down at the surveillance van. Mindy was crouched in the snow, getting video of Bingwen as he stopped and checked to make sure nobody was watching. *Mindy, be careful. Be careful. Please, be careful. I told you not to take any risks*, he thought, starting to panic as he desperately tried to keep his camera steady in his hands.

"Bowman, send an alert to all units and wait for my command," Highland said in a perfectly level voice. "I don't want to send in the troops until the two perps are together outside the van."

Bingwen Ho moved with great speed down the sidewalk as Quay reopened the back door, flooding an area ten feet square with a bright incandescent light. Not a word was exchanged as the huge man slipped the sack off his shoulder—two bare feet kicking, the person inside struggling to break free—and hurled it onto the floor of the van. A waif of a girl desperately slipped out of her shroud, dressed in nothing but a thin cotton shift, her hair mussed, her faced covered in dried blood. She screamed for help at the top of her lungs, then scampered away from Bingwen, whimpering.

Ethan pointed his camera at ADA Highland. "We shouldn't wait any longer."

"Damn straight we won't," she said, shouting at Detective Bowman. "Do it now. I want all the streets closed off immediately."

"All units, this is a go. Two suspects and a young girl in a yellow Ford Econoline Van. The men may be armed and dangerous. Move in with caution and do not, I repeat, do not fire your weapons unless fired upon."

Then Bowman and Alvarez drew their service revolvers, fully loaded Sig Sauer P226s, eased out of the car, and crouched behind the open doors. Pointing her weapon, Alvarez said through a bullhorn, "This is the New York City Police Department. We have you surrounded, *comprender*? Freeze and place hands on van where we can see them. You're under arrest."

Ethan was out the door in a flash and dashed around a parked car, his camera rolling on the two suspects. He finished an establishing shot and wheeled around, framing up Julie and motioning for her to slip out of the back seat.

"Get behind me and keep your head down," he screamed as police cars flooded the immediate area—lights flashing, sirens blazing—and surrounded the yellow van, armed officers in riot gear spilling out onto the street.

Alvarez raised her bullhorn. "Give yourselves up. You got nowhere to run." There was an eerie moment of silence as Quay and Bingwen hurried around the back of the yellow van, out of sight. "I repeat. Give yourselves up. You are surrounded, *criminales*."

There was another moment of silence.

The only sound the wind howling.

The snow pelting the ground.

Then Bingwen Ho emerged from the front of the van and Quay Chaoxiang from the back, both holding AK-47s. They opened fire all at once, the *rat-tat-tat* of machine guns ringing out, ricocheting off adjacent buildings, turning the quiet neighborhood into a war zone. *Rat-tat-tat-tat-tat-tat.* Two cops were immediately blown off their feet, blood spurting from their bullet-ridden bodies.

"Stay down, Julie, stay down," Ethan said, his camera shooting a medium shot of his anchorwoman with her hands covering her head. He jerked the camera wildly over to Detectives Alvarez and Bowman returning fire—flashes of bright yellow light streaming from the ends of their Sig Sauers. He stretched out on the ground, the snow wet and cold on his bare hands and swish-panned back to the yellow van, Quay and Bingwen now crouched in a shooter's stance, strafing bullets indiscriminately in a wide arc at the police.

Another cop went down ten feet from Ethan, bullets obliterating his face, blood and bone and brain matter splattering over everything in their path. Ethan framed up the camera on the cop's body lying facedown in the snow, his arms and legs crumpled at odd angles, his neck mangled and torn to shreds. Then he panned back to the two Chinese men, a stream of bullets ripping through the car window next to him, sending shards of glass all over him. Julie Piedmont, who had crawled under the car, slithered out and scampered over to him on her hands and knees.

"Are you hit, Ethan?"

"I'm fine. I'm fine," he said, shouting as he panned across the raging gun battle.

"There'*s* blood on your forehead."

He touched the gooey, warm liquid. "Must've been nicked by a piece of glass. It's nothing, really." He continued shooting. "Do you see Mindy and Lloyd?"

Rat-tat-tat-tat-tat.

"Mindy's shooting footage from behind a barrier in the playground. Lloyd's right next to her returning fire."

Rat-tat-tat-tat-tat.

Ethan kept rolling, zooming into the back of the van, hoping the image was clear through the snow, suddenly spotting the small girl crawling away from the open door. He zoomed in tight, ignoring the bullets whizzing around him, popping like firecrackers as they punctured parked cars, and focused on the girl as she climbed over the front passenger seat and disappeared onto the floor.

"The girl's alive," he said, screaming over the din, just as a bullet tore through Detective Alvarez's shoulder, blowing her off her feet and onto the ground. "Don't move, Julie," he said, duckwalking over to Alvarez, Detective Bowman already applying pressure to the wound, hoping to stem the flow of blood as it spread over Alvarez's clothes.

Rat-tat-tat-tat-tat.

"You okay?"

"Fuckers shot me," she said. "Stay down, Benson—before you get hit."

Ethan ignored the detective and panned back to the yellow van, just as a series of bullets ripped through the center of Bingwen Ho's body, the big man staring dubiously at his entrails spilling out of his stomach, his face screwed in a mask of pain and shock, before dropping his machine gun and falling flat on his back, his legs splayed, his arms spread to his sides, his chest heaving one last time before he died.

Suddenly, all the gunfire stopped.

Silence.

A cop in full battle gear holding another bullhorn said cautiously, "Drop your weapon and come out slowly. There's no place to run."

Everybody waited with baited breath.

As the seconds ticked by feeling more like hours.

Then Quay Chaoxiang tossed his AK-47 on the ground and walked out from behind the yellow van, his hands planted firmly on top of his head. He dropped to his knees and lay facedown then shouted to nobody in particular, "I guess you got me—the demon of death, the executioner of little girls, the infamous Child Sex Murderer." Then he laughed maniacally and said with a gleam in his eye, "Took you fuckers long enough."

CHAPTER 36

It was still two hours before sunrise, the air cold and biting. There were dozens of people staring out windows, huddled in doorways, shooting pictures on their cell phones, gawking at an army of cops and crime scene investigators and medical personnel as they poured over the carnage like an army of ants. Six cops had been wounded, three gunned down, their bodies now zipped into black body bags for transportation to the morgue at Bellevue Hospital. CSIs were hovering over Bingwen Ho's body collecting evidence as Quay Chaoxiang sat in the back of a police car, surrounded by cops, his hands and feet manacled in heavy chains. Ethan was rolling video as Patricia Highland read Quay his Miranda rights, Julie Piedmont right next to her holding a microphone.

"He won't talk," Julie said, her eyes moving from Quay to Highland.

Ethan framed his shot tighter.

"Not a word," the ADA said, "except to ask for a lawyer."

"You gonna take him in soon?"

"Not gonna get anything out of him here."

"Where you gonna book him?"

"One Centre Street, and then we'll throw his ass into Rikers where he'll await arraignment for the murders—all of them."

A CSI walked over to Highland holding a plastic evidence bag. "One Karl Storz No. 6 surgical knife."

"Evidence linking him to the other Child Sex Murders," said Highland. "Get it to forensics for fingerprints."

Ethan finished his shot, circled around the ADA, and pulled back to a wide shot as an EMS worker in the back of one of the ambulances motioned to Highland.

"The girl's in a bad way. You need to talk to her right now. It can't wait."

Ethan got in front of Julie and the ADA and continued rolling as they hurried over to the ambulance, still discussing the gun battle. He paused and let them walk out of the shot before framing the lens on the paramedic.

"The kid's got information you need to hear. Please, be quick. She took a hell of a beating, and I need to get her to the emergency room. Her nose is badly broken and maybe some of the bones in her cheeks and around her eyes. I gave her a small dose of morphine. She's beginning to get groggy."

They all climbed into the back of the ambulance, Ethan making a pan shot of the mini-emergency room, then focusing on Julie holding a microphone near the little girl's mouth. All but emaciated, she was lying on a stretcher, bundled in blankets, an IV dripping into her arm, wires hooked to monitors beeping and buzzing in the background.

Highland leaned over and said kindly, "What's your name, sweetheart?"

"Maria Fuente."

"And where are you from?"

"Humahuaca, Argentina," she said, licking her cracked lips. "Water. I need water."

"Give her a drink, please," Highland said.

The EMS worker brought her a cup with a straw.

"Where are your parents?" Highland asked.

Ethan zoomed into the girl's face. "Back home in my village."

They all looked at each other. "So how did you get here?" Julie said.

Maria burst into tears, her body racked by spasms. "I was abducted from my village and taken to a *basilica*, where a priest beat and raped me. I was tied in chains and put on a boat. More men raped me. And then I got here. I pretended to be out of it, so they wouldn't hurt me anymore. But an old man took me and raped me over and over and over and over."

"What old man, Maria?" Ethan said. "Honey, this is important."

"The Chinese man with the long hair."

"Who is he?" Ethan said, holding on a tight shot of Maria.

"The *Jiaofu*. The *Jiaofu!*" she screamed. "Please, the girls. Save the girls."

"What girls?" Ethan said, continuing to roll.

She began gasping for air, and her eyes rolled up into her head.

"No more!" the EMS worker yelled. "She's going into shock. We gotta get her to the hospital."

Ethan lowered his camera and jumped out of the ambulance then helped Julie and ADA Highland step down.

"What did she mean by 'the girls?'"

"No idea," ADA Highland said.

"And what the fuck is a *Jiaofu*?"

"That's the Chinese word for a gang boss," Highland said.

"Any idea who this *Jiaofu* is?" Julie asked.

"The man we're looking for," Ethan said coldly. "The mastermind behind all these murders." He turned from Julie to ADA Highland. "And he's holed up at the town house on Hester Street. That's where we'll find the girls and the answers to our remaining questions about the Child Sex Murders."

*****

Ethan and Julie were sitting in the back of the surveillance van with Mindy as Lloyd raced down Avenue D. They were following a line of police cruisers, lights flashing, heading to Hester Street in Chinatown. The snowstorm was beginning to taper off, a solid six inches blanketing the ground, snowplows moving like a convoy of tanks cleaning the streets ahead of them.

"Can we get around them?" Ethan said, pounding the side of the van in frustration. "This is taking too long. We gotta go faster."

"No way," Lloyd said, slowing down behind the ADA's Crown Victoria directly in front of them. "Too dangerous. That's why the cops called the Sanitation Department to give us an escort. We get there when we get there."

Ethan counted to ten, trying to calm himself, then turned to Mindy. "Did you call about the two camera crews?"

"Woke up the tech supervisor on call. He was pissed, but booked Glickstein and Raffalo. Should get there just ahead of us."

"And David?"

"Riding along with Herb."

"Good. We need the entire team to pull this off." Then Ethan's iPhone buzzed. He quickly checked the LCD screen. "Been waiting for him to call," he said before answering. "Morning, Paul."

"Don't morning me. It's the middle of the night," he said defiantly. "I just got a call from the president of Broadcast Engineering who was furious. Said you demanded two camera crews—Herb Glickstein and Bobby Raffalo. They just came off a shoot and are now on a continuous tour. Do you have any idea what that's gonna cost the show?"

"I need them," Ethan said calmly. "The cops just busted the Child Sex Murderer after a bloody shoot-out. I got the whole thing on two small cameras."

"So why do you need additional crews?"

Ethan glanced out the window. They were headed west on Houston Street, still plodding along behind the snowplows. *Shit. I hope we're not too late,* he thought before saying, "Because the cops are headed to the town house on Hester Street, hoping to take down the mastermind behind the murders. We need that to finish the story, and I need all the help I can get to capture it on camera."

Ethan waited as Paul hissed through the phone. "Does Julie know about all this?"

"She's here with me."

"Put her on."

Ethan handed her his iPhone and listened as Julie and Paul bantered back and forth for nearly five minutes.

"I'll tell him, Paul, and relax. This is a big story, biggest I've ever worked on, and it's about to get bigger."

She clicked off and handed Ethan his phone.

"Well?"

"He's bumping the first two stories on Thursday's show for us. We got three days to make air."

"We'll worry about the edit later," Ethan said, peering at the dozens of patrol cars lining up and down Hester Street. "Gotta finish shooting and figure out what the hell is going on in that town house."

Then his iPhone buzzed again.

Patricia Highland.

"Ethan, it's me. Just heard from the task force. Allied Shipping is an offshore company owned by a guy named Chang Kai Shu."

"He owns the town house?"

"Yes."

"And who the fuck is he?"

"The *Jaiofu*," she said, foreboding in her voice. "The head of the *Tong* in Chinatown, and if he's in that building, he's gonna be surrounded by an army of armed bodyguards."

*****

Lloyd pulled to a stop behind the ADA's Crown Victoria as a dozen cops carrying handguns and long guns spilled out of the patrol cars they'd been following. Ethan turned to his team.

"Julie, you stay with me. Lloyd, I want you to guard her. This could get ugly." He spun around to Mindy. "You direct the Glickstein crew as we head into the town house. We'll get David to work with the Raffalo crew as they go into the Chinese restaurant across the street."

They immediately exited the surveillance van one at a time, Lloyd drawing his Glock 9mm from a shoulder holster and punching a round into the chamber, Ethan and Julie crouching and making their way over to Detective Bowman who was leading a team of cops in tactical gear spread out in front of the town house.

"What's the plan?" Ethan said to Bowman diffidently.

"Waiting for ADA Highland to give us the order to go in." The detective pointed to a listening device in her ear. "She's directing all the teams from inside the car." She cupped her hand over her ear then turned to Ethan. "Highland wants to make sure you understand the risks."

"We're good."

"That's a ten four," she whispered into a microphone on the lapel of her overcoat. She whipped around to Ethan. "It's time."

*****

Mindy and Herb Glickstein stood to the right of the front door of the town house, sharpshooters positioned on top of the tenements, as Ethan and Julie crouched behind Detective Bowman. Two cops holding a steel battering ram waited for the signal, Bowman checking to make sure her SWAT team was in position, before yelling, "Break it down."

The two cops swung, and it crashed through the ornamental wooden door, the SWAT team storming into the lobby of the town house. Herb Glickstein was right there with them, his soundwomen, Zoe Whitfield, recording the yelling and screaming, the cops breaking down one door after another and searching each office. "Clear. Clear. Clear." The same scene was unfolding across the street as David and the Raffalo crew followed the second tactical team led by Detective Nottingdale as it poured into the empty Chinese restaurant.

"Nothing," Bowman said into her lapel mic.

"All clear in the restaurant," Nottingdale said, his voice coming through Bowman's earpiece.

They waited for instructions from ADA Highland. Then Bowman motioned her tactical team to split up, sending some up the stairwell to the upper floors as she continued to search the lobby with the rest of the heavily armed cops. Ethan and Julie followed as she moved stealthily, checking the concierge desk, a storeroom near the front door, and behind one expensive painting after another, the Glickstein crew recording their movements every step of the way. They reached an alcove adjacent to a bank of elevators and stopped.

"Kind of a strange place to hang an expensive piece of artwork," Ethan said as he ran his fingers along the edge of a Jasper Francis Cropsey landscape. He was about to move on and catch up to Bowman when his fingers brushed a small lever embedded between two darkly stained slats of wood on the wall. He stepped back and stared for a long moment.

"What is it, Ethan?" Julie said.

"Not really sure." He turned and looked for Bowman. "Detective, come and take a look."

She motioned to her SWAT team and joined Ethan, still probing the small lever. "What the fuck is it, Benson?"

"Not sure."

"Jiggle it."

Ethan pulled the lever, and a door hidden by the pattern of the wood paneling swung open. "Jesus, you getting this, Herb?"

"Got the whole sequence on a medium shot."

"Where the hell does it go?" Bowman said, peering through the door.

"Seems to lead down a short hallway," Julie said. "I see a couple of doors at the far end."

The detective spoke into the microphone on her coat. "Patricia, just found a concealed door in an alcove near the elevators leading to some kind of passageway. Send in backup. We're gonna take a look." She turned to Ethan. "You guys stay behind me."

She signaled her SWAT team, and they pushed through the door, Bowman and the cops sweeping the hallway from one wall to the next with their long guns, beams of light from high-powered LED scopes fastened to their weapons casting ominous shadows all around them.

"You okay, Julie," Ethan said quietly.

"Scared shitless. Never did anything like this before."

"Stay cool and behind Lloyd."

They got to the end of the hallway and found two locked doors.

"Break 'em down," Bowman ordered.

The SWAT team crashed through the door on the left, searching, strafing the room with their long guns. It led into an immaculately clean sitting room with a reception desk and expensive silk chairs and couches. Mindy and Herb followed as Bowman canvassed the room.

"What the fuck is a place like this doing at the end of a secret passageway?" she said as she rejoined Ethan, who was standing with Julie and Lloyd at the second door. "Open that one."

The cops smashed through the second door.

"Christ almighty," Ethan said, pointing. "Herb, you need to shoot this."

They followed Bowman into a lavishly decorated parlor with expensive red wallpaper, ornamental silk screens painted with Chinese landscapes, and a huge pile of pillows propped against the wall. Next to the pillows on a small side table sat a finely crafted wooden pipe, a wisp of white smoke curling from its bowl.

"Smells kinda sweet, like burning flowers," Julie said, furrowing her eyebrows. "What is it?"

"Opium," Bowman said, "and whoever was smoking it can't have gotten too far." She spoke into her lapel mic. "Patricia, we found a room at the end of the hidden passageway where an unknown number of perps just left in a hurry. Could be the *Tong* boss. Maybe some of his men." She turned to her tactical team. "Is there another way out of here?"

They searched the room cautiously then found a half door hidden behind a silk screen.

"Here, Detective," a cop said, gesturing.

She nodded, and the SWAT team broke down the door, kneeled, and peered down a steep staircase leading to an underground tunnel.

"I'm going with you, Detective," Ethan said, motioning to Herb Glickstein. "Julie, you stay here with Mindy and Lloyd."

"But, Ethan—"

"No argument. You're not going."

They descended the steps, the passageway dark, narrow, their footsteps creaking on the loose floorboards.

"This must lead to the Chinese restaurant across the street," Ethan said, ducking behind a cop, sweeping his Sig Sauer P226 from side to side, illuminating the narrow path in front of them.

Then a crackle of gunfire.

Bullets whizzing over Ethan's head.

Loud thumps as they embedded in the walls around him.

"Everybody down. Everybody down," Bowman screamed, Ethan and Herb Glickstein—still shooting video—hitting the ground as Bowman and her SWAT team returned fire, lights flashing out of the end of their handguns, illuminating four men up ahead spraying a barrage of bullets at them.

Bang. Bang. Bang. Bang. Bang. Bang.

Ethan's iPhone buzzed. David. "Where the fuck are you?"

"In the passageway." Bang. Bang. Bang. "Ran into an old Chinese guy and a couple of thugs as we were making our way over to the town house. I can see you on the other side of them."

Bang. Bang. Bang.

"We got them pinned between us."

Bang. Bang. Bang. Bang.

A cop next to Ethan was hit in the leg, spraying blood on the walls. Ethan crawled over to him.

"How bad?"

"Stay down, Benson, I'll live," he shouted as another cop shimmied over and began dragging him away from the shoot-out.

Bang. Bang. Bang. Bang. Bang. Bang. Bang.

"Ethan. Ethan," David said hysterically through the phone. "The old guy just went down. Shot through the head." Bang. Bang. Bang. Bang. "He's sprawled on his back. Looks dead."

"Stay out of the line of fire, David."

"I'm curled up in a ball on the ground."

Then another burst of gunfire.

"David?"

Silence.

"David."

"I'm okay. I'm okay."

More bullets whizzed over Ethan's head as he turned to Herb lying on the ground, camera pointed at the carnage. Then the gun battle suddenly stopped. Dead silence in the tunnel. Ethan raised his head slowly and peered at Detective Bowman who was cautiously making her way through the passageway followed by her SWAT team.

"They're all dead."

*****

A half hour later, Ethan was standing with Patricia Highland, Julie interviewing her on camera, David still down in the underground passageway with the Raffalo crew, as dozens of CSI poured through the crime scene collecting evidence.

"Have we ID'd the old man?" she said to the ADA, Herb Glickstein circling the two of them with his camera.

"He's the *Jaiofu,* Chang Kai Shu."

"So you got the ringleader?"

"Damn straight," she said, staring into the camera. "Once we collect evidence linking Chang to the four girls, the Child Sex Murders case will be officially closed." She turned to her CSIs. "I want every square inch of this place turned over—every fingerprint, fiber, hair, skin follicle, blood splatter, DNA—lifted and catalogued. I want to make sure we can prove that Bingwen Ho and Quay Chaoxiang have been down in this room so we can tie them to the *Jaiofu* and prove there was a conspiracy."

As Ethan watched the interview, he had a nagging suspicion he was still missing something, something important, something the little girl they'd rescued from Quay Chaoxiang had said to them in the ambulance. What was it? What was it? Then it hit him all at once.

Save the girls before it's too late?

What girls?

They hadn't found any girls.

"You guys gonna start processing the other room?" he said to Detective Bowman.

"I'm just heading in there."

"I'm going with you."

"Put these on," she said, handing him Latex gloves. "And don't get in the way."

Ethan followed her under a barrier of yellow police tape and into the sitting room, crime scene investigators already dusting for fingerprints and bagging evidence from the desk adjacent to the front door. Ethan wandered around the room, staring at the plush silk furniture, the thick carpeting, and the expensive artwork on the walls. Then he spotted a large book, opened in the middle, sitting on a small antique table, flanked by two high-back chairs.

"Detective, I found something."

Bowman barked an order to a CSI and slowly walked over to Ethan.

"It looks like some kind of guest book," Ethan said, pointing.

Bowman reached for a new pair of Latex gloves then flipped through the pages at the names.

"Jesus, Police Commissioner Langley signed this book just last week. What the fuck was he doing down here."

"And what the fuck is this place?" Ethan said, scanning the room until he spotted the outline of a door neatly concealed in the pattern of the wallpaper.

"Don't touch it," Bowman said, signaling to Patricia Highland now standing in the hallway with Julie Piedmont. "Ethan just found another door."

Highland hurried over, Herb Glickstein following Julie with his camera.

"Open it, Detective," she said commandingly.

Bowman turned the knob—it wasn't locked—and pushed through the door, revealing another large room with plush red carpeting and bright pink walls adorned with hand-painted pictures of dragons and serpents and naked young girls. A row of crystal chandeliers cast pools of yellow light on the floor, and a series of doors covered in more red silk was spaced every six feet or so around the room. Adjacent to the entryway were two seating areas with red leather sofas and lacquered wood coffee tables. Ethan circled the room then pushed open one of the doors and spotted a little girl lying on a mattress, totally naked, chained to the wall inside what appeared to be a dark bedroom.

"Light. I need light," he screamed frantically.

Detective Bowman dashed in, shining a flashlight crazily around the room, until she landed on Ethan, draping his coat over the girl, Julie and ADA Highland standing just outside the door watching from afar.

"This fucking place is a bordello for pedophiles," Ethan said, sitting and holding the child tightly—the little girl, shaking, sobbing, clinging to him for dear life.

"What's on her leg?" Julie said.

Ethan peered down at a small tattoo of a fire-breathing dragon. "She's been branded like cattle, marking her as property of the *Tong*. That's why the dead girls had that piece of skin removed from their ankles. To eliminate the evidence."

"Check each room," Highland said, "and see how many kids are down here."

Cops in ones and twos spilled into the chamber, flinging open doors and pushing into the darkness, each room containing a small naked girl sprawled on a bed, chained to a wall, and tattooed with a dragon.

"How many?" she said, now screaming.

"Thirty," Detective Bowman said, her eyes hollow. "All kids. All scared shitless."

Julie approached Ethan and knelt down next to the little girl. "What's your name, honey?"

She looked at them, frozen with fear.

"We're here to help. Please tell me your name."

The little girl sobbed, muttering.

"I can't understand her," Julie said.

Ethan leaned in, saying a few words in Spanish, and she looked up.

"Mi nombre es Elena. Buenos Aires."

Ethan and Julie exchanged a shocked look. "This kid was snatched from Argentina. Same as Maria," he said. "She's a sex slave, like all the kids down here, and that's why they were being murdered. To get rid of the kids who were getting too old for the sick clients who abused them, so the *Jiaofu* could hide evidence he was running a major international human trafficking operation."

"For the love of God," Julie said, a tear dripping down her cheek as she turned to the little girl cowering on the bed, before scooping her up in her arms and rocking her back and forth as she whispered in her ear and comforted her, telling her she'd be safe now.

His heart breaking, Ethan slowly backed out of the room, then hurried through the building and out to the street, ignoring the mob of reporters and television crews clamoring for a sound bite. Bending over, he breathed deeply, trying to calm his shattered nerves, then punched a number into his iPhone and waited as it rang half a dozen times before it was answered.

"Paul, it's me, Ethan. A two parter isn't going to do it. I need an hour to tell this story the right way."

EPILOGUE

Three weeks had passed since his story aired, and Ethan was perched at his desk surrounded by boxes. He was packing his office, getting ready to move to the tenth floor with the other producers on *The Weekly Reporter*. He had made peace with Peter Sampson, meeting with him in his over-the-top office, explaining in great detail why he'd never adjusted to being his senior producer, and apologizing for his behavior during the year they'd worked together. Sampson had been gracious, for Peter Sampson, saying there were no hard feelings and letting him stay in his office until the next senior producer was ready to take over as the anchorman's new whipping boy.

Ethan smiled as he thought about producing again, happy to get away from the headaches of management, happy to be back doing what he loved. Placing a stack of file folders in a cardboard box, he motioned for Mindy, holding two cups of coffee in the doorway, to come in and sit down.

"Any news?"

"Plenty," she said, handing him a cup before dropping onto the leather couch and putting her feet up on the coffee table.

"Make yourself at home, why don't you."

"Always do," she said with a toothy smile.

"So what's the latest?"

"Just got off the phone with ADA Highland, and she's finally traced all the girls. Twenty-one are from Argentina and the other nine from Thailand."

"And they're going home?"

"All except five whose parents she can't find."

"What happens to those kids?"

"Foster care while the authorities keep searching."

"That sucks."

"After everything these kids have been through, it's probably a blessing."

Ethan didn't respond as he sipped his coffee. *Too bad this isn't spiked with something a bit stronger,* he thought, craving a finger of Scotch. He placed the cup on the table.

"What about Maria?"

"Her parents arrive tomorrow to take her home."

"At least she has a happy ending."

"Touché."

"And the Child Sex Murderer?"

"No trial. He confessed to killing Detective Dinkus and at least sixteen girls who the *Jiaofu* no longer wanted as sex slaves. He was in charge of cleanup, the hit man whose only job was to dispose of what he called 'the garbage.'"

"Fuck. The guy's a monster," Ethan said, frowning.

He finished sealing a box with a strip of gaffer's tape and started filling another, Mindy shuffling her position on the couch as she finished her coffee.

"And how are you doing, Ethan?"

"Happy to be getting out of here and back where I belong."

"That's not what I mean," she said, heaving a sigh.

Ethan sat down on the couch beside her. "I've called a couple of times since we split up, but she still won't talk to me. I don't know what's going to happen to us. All I do know is Sarah's not coming home."

"And Luke?"

"She puts him on the phone when I call, but our relationship is more strained than ever. I'm worried he's drifting away too, that he's going to forget me."

"Jeez, Ethan, that ain't gonna happen."

"It already has."

Mindy hesitated, watching as Ethan slowly sank into the abyss. "You okay?"

"Not really."

"Are you seeing your shrink?"

"Yeah, a couple of times a week," he said, standing and turning away so she wouldn't see the tears welling in his eyes.

"Is it helping?"

"Not really," he said, shaking his head.

"And your drinking?"

"Better, don't you think?"

"Hardly."

"You're probably right," Ethan said. "Look, Mindy, I got a lot of packing to do before my move. Can we talk later?"

She stared into his eyes, seeing his loneliness, then headed for the door. "One more work update before I leave."

He waved his hand okay and resumed packing.

"ADA Highland said the Argentinean police moved in on the priest yesterday. Some guy named Pedro Juan Ignacio Rodriquez."

"They arrest him?"

"Nope. They found him stabbed and mutilated with a bullet in the back of his head. Contract killing."

"And what about the woman who murdered Randall Newton at Bellevue?"

"Cops are still looking, but she's somewhere in the wind. They may never find her." She walked a short way, turned once again, and said warmly, "You're a good man, Ethan Benson. Take care of yourself."

Then she scooted down the hallway and disappeared around a bend.

Ethan peered at the boxes scattered on the floor and checked the time. Four thirty. The rest of the packing could wait. He'd finish in the morning. Standing, he turned off his computer, grabbed his briefcase, and slipped into his overcoat. Waving good night to James, he made his way to the elevator bank.

Time to hit McGlades for a quick pop of Scotch.

Only one.

Well, maybe two.

No harm in a little hair of the dog to brighten the rest of his day.

ABOUT THE AUTHOR

Jeffrey L. Diamond is an award-winning journalist with forty years of experience in television news. He began his career in the early 1970s at ABC News where he worked at *Special Events*, *Weekend News*, and *World News Tonight*, before moving to the weekly newsmagazine, *20/20*. Producing hundreds of stories ranging from several minutes in length to a full hour of programming, his body of work includes breaking news specials, newsmaker interviews, investigative reports on consumer and political issues, entertainment profiles, and numerous crime stories. During his career, he collaborated with some of the biggest names in the business—anchors Barbara Walters, Charles Gibson, and Stone Phillips, and correspondents Tom Jarriel, Lynn Sherr, and Deborah Roberts. After taking a break from storytelling in 1991, Mr. Diamond embarked on a decadelong journey as an executive producer—managing broadcast, cable, and syndicated programming. He created *Dateline NBC* in the early 1990s, ran *Martha Stewart Living Television* in the mid-1990s, and launched *Judith Regan Television* in the late 1990s. As a show runner, he oversaw million-dollar budgets, supervised hundreds of producers, writers, directors, editors, and camera crews, and planned the creative content of programming.

Mr. Diamond returned to his roots the last decade of his career, devoting all his creative energies to producing stories, once again, for *20/20*. He's been nominated for dozens of journalism awards and has won six national Emmy Awards, two Dupont-Columbia Awards, one Peabody Award, one National Press Club Consumer Journalism Award, two CINE Golden Eagle Awards, and countless others. *Live to the Network* is Mr. Diamond's third novel in the Ethan Benson thriller series. His first, *Live to Air*, was published in 2015, his second, *Live to Tape*, in 2017, and he is currently writing his fourth novel, *All Cameras Live*. A graduate of Lehigh University, he lives in the Berkshire Mountains of Massachusetts, is married, has two sons, a daughter-in-law, two grandchildren, and a golden retriever named Bailey.

Other Heart Pounding Novels In The Ethan Benson Thriller Series

Live To Air

"Diamond has crafted a murder mystery that's an absolute page turner. His characters are charismatic, devious, and frightening—straight out of the annals of the best murder mysteries, except this one is set in the high-flying world of television news. He's captured the nuance of [television] production in a new and fresh way, using his vast experience as an award-winning writer and producer to take the reader on a wild ride. It's a thriller that will keep you reading, with a surprise ending that's more than just shocking."

Deborah Roberts, Correspondent, ABC News

Live To Tape

"Only those who have met evil up close and in person can understand how seemingly normal, successful people can sink to shocking levels of depravity. Author Jeffrey L. Diamond, in his decades of work as a journalist, has looked into evil's eyes in the real world, listened to calculated words, and used those memories to create one of the most terrifying killers in fiction, Dr. Rufus Wellington. *Live To Tape* is a rapid-fire thriller with...a behind-the-scenes look at the world of television news and its outsized egos coupled with a smart detective story that will keep you up many a night."

Don Dahler, Correspondent, CBS News

CPSIA information can be obtained
at www.ICGtesting.com
Printed in the USA
BVHW081419021219
565404BV00001B/51/P